LOVE STORM

Susan Johnson

BANTAM BOOKS
New York • Toronto • London • Sydney • Auckland

This edition contains the complete text
of the original hardcover edition.
NOT ONE WORD HAS BEEN OMITTED.

LOVE STORM

A Bantam Book / published by arrangement with the author

PUBLISHING HISTORY
Playboy Paperbacks edition 1981
Bantam edition / May 1995

ISBN 0-553-56328-9

Published simultaneously in the United States and Canada

Bantam Books are published by Bantam Books, a division of Bantam Doubleday Dell
Publishing Group, Inc. Its trademark, consisting of the words "Bantam Books" and the
portrayal of a rooster, is Registered in U.S. Patent and Trademark Office and in
other countries. Marca Registrada. Bantam Books, 1540 Broadway, New York, New
York 10036.

PRINTED IN THE UNITED STATES OF AMERICA

RAD   20 19 18 17 16 15 14 13 12 11 10 9

Kind jealous doubts, tormenting fears,
  And anxious cares, when past,
Prove our hearts' treasure fixed and dear,
  And makes us blest at last.

  John Wilmot, 2nd Earl of Rochester
              c. 1674–75

Dear Reader,

When I began writing LOVE STORM in 1979, I'd been seriously reading on Russia for several years. My own collection of research books had reached several hundred and I was steeped in the atmosphere of the Tzar's empire. The mysticism of Russian culture, its luxury and splendor, the autocratic, reactionary politics, the exotic influence of the East all were reflected in the literature, histories and memoirs I read. Thousands of details of nineteenth century daily life entered my consciousness. I even knew the streets of pre-revolutionary St. Petersburg as well as my local country roads.

Saturated by the mood and tenor of the time, fascinated by the Kuzans—who had become intriguingly real to me—I wrote LOVE STORM in an impassioned rush. Sitting at the kitchen table, the images of the nineteenth century vivid in my mind, I wrote furiously and drank Russian Caravan tea from glasses the way the Russians did.

LOVE STORM has a graphic intensity at times. But the story depicts a past world where male and female roles were quite different, where Russian culture was still deeply attached to its Eastern antecedents. Where an unrestrained intemperance existed in a world of powerful men and, in the far-flung reaches of the empire, women were a commodity to be bought and sold. It's a striking, raw, ostentatious world unrivaled in scale and degree.

I hope you enjoy your plunge into the life of Tzarist Russia.

Best wishes,

Susan Johnson

LOVE
STORM

PART I

The Meeting

1

"Damn it, Amalie!" Prince Alexander hissed into the soft pink ear so close to his lips as he twirled the tall, queenly, blonde beauty through the crowd of elegantly dressed, coiffed, and bejeweled nobles dancing in the gilt-and-white rococo ballroom of the Dolgorouky palace. "You said Beckendorff was leaving town three days ago!"

Amalie, eminently sure of her loveliness tonight, dressed in an exceedingly low-cut, figure-hugging violet velvet gown, the stylish train sweeping out around her as Alex faultlessly swung them among the dancing couples, lifted seductively lashed lavender eyes, coyly smiled up into the rather forbidding saturnine face regarding her, and softly placated, "But, Sasha darling, how was I to know Boris would win two nights running at the Yacht Club gaming tables? He stays yet another night to see if his luck holds."

"With him it has to be luck; a more heavy-handed player I have yet to see," the prince churlishly retorted, the hours of drinking at the Yacht Club that afternoon and evening not conductive to moderating his unbridled Kuzan temper.

"Now, sweet, not everyone can be as devilishly fortunate as you at cards," she said, and smiled winningly into the chill golden eyes glaring down at her. Amalie was a consummate flirt and seductress and had put her considerable skills to the ultimate test in retaining the fickle interest of Prince Alexander Nikolaevich Kuzan for five months. His liaisons rarely outlasted the new moon.

"It's not fortunate, my dear," the grim-faced man rebuked, "but practice and skill honed to a fine pitch through constant application. After gambling daily for ten years with a great variety of devout gamesters, one acquires a certain expertise. Your stupid husband's the exception to the rule," he discourteously concluded.

"Boris doesn't have to be clever, love; his father's estate in the Urals produces half the annual world output of platinum."

"The Kuzan gold mines in Siberia have long precluded a need to worry about money, my dove, but our family still expects a certain degree of intellectual proficiency in their offspring. To simply put wineglass or spoon to lips is not enough."

"Don't be so cruel, Sasha. Boris has always been a bit overweight, true; but then, see how much more I appreciate your lean virility." Countless Amalie Beckendorff delicately stirred her voluptuous body against the tall, muscular form of the prince and, her action having the desired effect, smiled complacently as she felt a rising hardness press into her belly.

"Damn you, Amalie," Alex groaned softly. He'd been anticipating a session in bed with the countess for three days. "To hell with Boris. If we can't go to your place, come to my town palace. My servants are scrupulously discreet. I'll have you home before Boris leaves the Yacht Club."

Clever and artful as Amalie was at dalliance, in the time-honored way of reigning beauties used to have men fawn over them, this time she miscalculated in assuming she had snared yet another admirer who could be teased and toyed with. She should have known better. Anyone acquainted with Prince Alexander Nikolaevich's amatory exploits—and many were, since discretion was not a Kuzan trait—should have exercised more prudence. Centuries of wealth, imperiousness, and arrogance had made the Kuzans impervious to the niceties of polite society; they did as they pleased, boldly and flagrantly, and if scandal dogged their heels, they never deigned to notice.

Despite the prince's notorious reputation for callous fickleness, the legions of pursuing women did not seem to be deterred; and he, for his part, delighted in their adulation, dispensing his favors with a democratic generosity. Beautiful, passionate women attracted him, and he was a most charming lover. Liberal with both himself and his wealth, he was unutterably irresistible. On one point alone the prince became intractable: He had a marked dislike for possessive women, and when the pretty faces attempted to cajole or coax him against his will, they very swiftly found themselves coolly and quickly displaced.

Countess Amalie was *not* prudent, and did exactly the wrong thing. In her monumental vanity, thinking to enthrall the prince more deeply, to draw him, in his need, more closely to her, she teasingly withheld her favors yet a third night. "I can't tonight, love, I'm sorry," she whispered.

Prince Alex was a practiced man about town—refined, sophisticated, supremely handsome, and incredibly wealthy. He had early on learned the rules of amatory courtship and was known, when the whim moved him, to genteelly court some striking belle for a fortnight or two; but no one in even the most optimistic state of mind would ever go so far as to declare that any of these capricious courtships were, even remotely, undertaken by an enamored man. He had never been enamored; the concept or feeling was totally foreign to his basically selfish, self-indulgent nature.

Alex had enjoyed the voluptuous charms of Amalie for an unheard-of five months precisely because those charms

were voluptuous. She was in bed the exact antithesis of the
cool, distant, golden-blonde goddess she portrayed in public. She was a wild, rapacious, adroit, and accomplished
wanton whose technical proficiency, in conjunction with
her natural inclinations, often boggled the imagination
and most certainly elicited the ultimate sensual pleasure in
the ageless dance of love.

"You can't or you won't, Countess Beckendorff?" Alex
spat coldly, never missing a step as he effortlessly glided
through the throng of dancers.

"I would if I could, Sasha," Amalie mendaciously cooed.

"Come to my palace, then. I'll have you home in two
hours," he curtly responded, his eyes cold as ice.

For the first time, a tinge of doubt appeared in Amalie's
mind. The proposal of two hours smacked very crudely of
a rendezvous with a prostitute or a gypsy girl rather than
with a woman by whose beauty and person the prince was
bewitched. "I'm sorry, Sasha, I really can't," Amalie murmured and, continuing in the style that had been so successful in the past, offered him a warm, alluring glance
from under heavy lashes.

"Bitch!" Alex exploded furiously. Disengaging himself,
he turned on his heel and stalked across the room, pushing
and shouldering his way rather rudely through the mass of
dancers.

The stately, gorgeous Countess Beckendorff was ignominiously left standing in the center of the ballroom floor,
while the heads of all the guests within twenty feet swiveled to stare as Alex's explicit denunciation resounded
through the room. Audible gasps escaped those near
enough to hear, and other dancers turned to watch.

Amalie's temper flared at the insult. Damn Sasha's black
soul! He'd pay for this evening's work, she swore heatedly
to herself. Mustering her dignity, she pressed her lips into
a semblance of a polite smile, raised her classic chin, and
walked slowly off the floor, trying to ignore the malicious,

spiteful titters of the gossips that broke out immediately after their momentary stunned silence.

Alex raced down the red-carpeted marble staircase to the ground-floor foyer, oblivious of the craning necks and speculative glances that followed his precipitous descent, Reaching the foyer, he imperiously snapped his fingers, summoning a footman to bring his sable topcoat, and seethed inwardly with a cold anger as he waited what seemed an interminably long time for the task to be accomplished.

Bitch, damnable bitch of a courtesan, using her contrived theatrics on him! *Two nights* he had waited for her! Good God, he didn't need any woman *that* badly. Females were a necessity to him, but never a compulsion. He could very nicely survive without Amalie, he reflected, while yet raging at her teasing artifice. Hell, there were gypsy women by the hundreds on the Islands, and plenty of soft, accommodating society girls and young wives, as far as that went, all equally willing. Still . . . Amalie *was* damnably pleasing to ride.

The apologetic footman finally arrived with the coat, and Alex shrugged his broad shoulders into the luxurious fur. A curt nod of dismissal; then he paused for a second, chastised himself for taking out his ill humor on the servant, and reached into his pocket and tossed the man two gold rubles, apologizing with a rueful grin. "Sorry, little brother; a cursed woman has put me out of temper."

The servant broke into a wide smile as he pocketed the money, and with an eloquent shrug, he replied, "No woman is worth a second thought. Find a gypsy, Your Excellency; she will warm your blood and soothe your temper."

Perhaps he's right, Alex mused briefly; a couple of gypsy wenches and a fortnight at his favorite retreat near Moscow would dispel his churlish mood. It would be relaxing to have a few weeks' respite from these feverish, enervating, ridiculous, disagreeable social activities. He and Ivan would do some wolf hunting. His mind, racing ahead, was already deep in contemplation, deciding which of his new guns he would bring along; and he mustn't forget two or three cases of the very fine old Tokay he had just purchased. And, with the perverse inconsistency and monumental optimism of youth, Amalie was quite forgotten.

By the time the footman swept the door open before him and the prince stepped out into a swirl of blowing snow, his black mood had already lifted, replaced by an exhilarating anticipation of the beauty, peace, and sybaritic pleasures a stay in the country offered. He had left orders with his driver, Ivan, to have his troika at the ready in front of the entrance, having expected to be leaving early with Amalie. Now, as he raced down the torchlit steps toward his waiting troika, he shouted jubilantly, "Ivan! Ivan! We're off to Podolsk—now, this instant!" and his heart soured with irrepressible exultation.

2

Another guest from the Dolgorouky ball was also out on the entrance steps in the lightly falling snow; but her mood was distinctly at variance with that of the man who was striding toward his beautifully accoutered red troika with such exuberance. This other guest was morose, partially frightened, and beginning to shiver as the wind blew cold gusts through the folds of her light cape.

Zena Turku had accompanied her aunt, Baroness Adelberg, to the ball with express orders to make herself accommodating to General Scobloff, who had asked for her hand in marriage. Zena had railed, cried, and cursed but had not moved one whit her aunt's resolve to marry her off to that hateful, fat, lecherous old general, who had already buried two wives during his sixty-one years. There was no love lost between Zena and her widowed aunt.

After Zena's beautiful Daghestani mother died in childbirth three years ago, her father had sunk into a lethargic despair from which he never recovered. He, Zena, and the infant had left their prosperous, picturesque country estate in Astrakhan one week after the funeral and come to St. Petersburg. Baron Turku had turned to drink and gambling in an unsuccessful attempt to exorcise his melancholy, only rarely appearing sober enough to notice that Zena needed him, at which times he would solemnly promise to go back home. But only painful memories awaited him there and he could not face them, any more

9

than he could face the sight of the boy child whose entry into the world had been the cause of his darling wife's death. One early dawn six months ago, Baron Turku, unable to endure another day of living, had put pistol to temple and blown the top of his head off.

Zena and her young brother, Bobby[1], were left alone with the baron's hateful half-sister, who took control of what was left of the Turku fortune, reminding Zena constantly and spitefully that she should be grateful for a roof over her head, as her father had gambled away practically every ruble.

Just three weeks ago, when Zena turned eighteen, Baroness Adelberg had informed her that she was to be married to General Scobloff, since the baroness no longer cared to support such an ungrateful niece. She hoped Zena realized how fortunate she was, for penniless maids were not resplendent catches on the marriage mart, while the further taint of a Circassian mother was practically insupportable.

Zena ignored the barbed jibes concerning her mother, having been as proud of her enchanting mother's heritage as of her father's more conventional nobility. Baroness Turku's father was a powerful mountain chieftain whose clan had ruled in the Caucasus for centuries.

The last three years since her mother's death had been sadly unhappy as Zena watched the slow, lingering disintegration of her once proud, vigorous father. He had hardly seemed the same man after his wife's death. Almost overnight the baron had changed into a remote, detached, perfunctorily polite figure of a man.

Baroness Adelberg had constantly and bitterly badgered the young girl, who was turning into a rare beauty in a gloomy and solitary environment. On infrequent occasions, when her father had still been alive, he would come out of his room in the afternoon and his eyes would mist over as he discerned in his growing daughter a startling resemblance to his beloved wife. The reminders were too poignantly wounding, and he had brutally avoided his young daughter more and more in the last few months of his life.

The week before the Dolgorouky ball had been a turmoil of vicious emotional altercations between Baroness Adelberg and Zena, the furious older woman finally threatening to throw her selfish ward out of the house if she did not agree to wed the general. Zena was still adamant; more stubbornly inclined than ever to do anything—anything, at all—rather than marry that hateful old man, with his florid face and tiny, evil repellent eyes that looked upon her so lecherously. He had been hovering near her every evening, whispering sweet phrases that were ludicrous coming from a man old enough to be her grandfather; touching her in a disgusting, familiar way when her aunt wasn't looking; leering at her undisguisedly as he informed the baroness that he wished the engagement to be short.

Having to dance with the general this evening had further hardened Zena's determination to resist marrying him at any price. He had held her too intimately, pressing his flabby paunch against her rib cage; and, shuddering with revulsion, she'd had to steel herself to keep from running from the dance floor. The minute the dance ended, she had begged to be excused for a moment to refresh her hairdo, and practically bolting from the room, she had rushed down the stairs and impulsively asked for her wrap, a driving need to get away from the contemptible old general outweighing all considerations of etiquette.

Zena had been standing on the steps of the palace now for several minutes, frantically searching her mind for any possible avenue of escape from the future her aunt had planned for her. Fleetingly, she'd even considered throwing herself into the Neva, but had rapidly discarded the idea when she realized that jumping from a bridge onto the frozen ice of the river would probably result in broken legs and a slow, freezing death. Zena was still youthfully optimistic enough to desire life rather than death; in any case, Bobby needed someone to care for him. With an energetic mind, a young, healthy body, and a resourceful personality, surely she could survive. She *would* survive! But first she must take herself as far away from St. Petersburg, and pursuit by a vengeful aunt and a lecherous suitor, as her wits would allow. After swiftly appraising the minimal options open to an eighteen-year-old woman with a three-year-old brother in tow, she came to a decision: She would go to her grandfather in the mountains. Somehow she would find him.

3

"Ivan! Ivan! Wake up!" The young noble was shaking his sleeping driver, who, muffled in fur carriage robes, had dozed off. "Ivan, wake up! We're off to Podolsk. *Vite, Vite!*" The tall, dark-haired prince chuckled indulgently as he vigorously shook the burly peasant.

Podolsk—*that* certainly was far enough away from St. Petersburg! Zena speculated tersely. A split second later, the decision made, she prepared herself to approach the stranger, then hesitated, all the training of a lifetime opposed to such shameless behavior. But, when she saw that the driver was now fully awake and the horses were prancing in their harness, in desperation she ran down to the sable-clad figure and tugged at his arm.

The prince swung around in surprise, and his heavy-lidded golden eyes swiftly appraised the slim young girl standing before him, wrapped in a much-worn gray cashmere cape with black lamb trim. The top of her head scarcely came to his shoulder, and lifted to his gaze was a beautiful, delicate face with large, deep-blue, imploring eyes.

"Well?" he said impassively.

Zena raised her hand, distractedly pushing aside a heavy tress of auburn waves that had fallen over her forehead, and shook the long cascades of hair back with a nervous shake of her dainty head. "Please, *monsieur* . . ." She spoke haltingly in French, paused, then took a deep breath and plunged on rapidly: "Please, sir, could . . . could you allow me to go with you to Podolsk?"

Her lashes fell before the prince's bold, deliberate scrutiny, and she held her breath in an agony of embarrassment and trepidation. Oh, God, how could she have sunk so low as to ask a perfect stranger for a ride? Humiliation overwhelmed her; then, with a vacillating seesaw of nervous anxiety, her mind swung full circle, desperation overcoming any wavering scruples. Holy Mother, what would she do if he said no? Sweet Jesus, let him say yes and she would be far from St. Petersburg and the repellent general by morning.

Alexander Nikolaevich coolly surveyed the young girl. She couldn't be more than sixteen, he decided, with her petite, innocent beauty. Not particularly young for a woman of the streets, however. Many of them commenced their trade at twelve or thirteen; at sixteen she was probably a practiced veteran, and in another three years her beauty would begin to fade. These fair flowers of the night withered rapidly.

"So you want a ride with me to Podolsk. Why?" he asked, as his eyes insolently raked her slim form from head to foot and slowly returned to the pale face.

"I . . . I can't say," Zena stammered, and her eyes fell again before the candid regard of the tall, handsome aristocrat towering above her. She involuntarily shivered as another gust of wind whirled the snow around her satin-slippered feet, and she tugged the cape closer for warmth.

The girl was obviously not dressed to survive very long in this below-zero winter night, the prince thought, measuring her with his cool, tawny eyes; and, if he took her with him (she was pretty enough—in fact, a rare, dainty little beauty), it would save him the trouble of driving to the Islands to find a gypsy girl to bring along.

Zena shrank back under that hard gaze. The gentleman's features had a vaguely predatory look about them—

like some fierce black panther, both beautiful and
terrifying in its cruelty: swarthy skin drawn tight over the
patrician bones of his face; feline eyes distinctly slanted
and framed by vivid black brows sweeping upward; a
haughty aquiline nose and a finely modeled mouth, now
pursed in reflection. It was a face without a trace of gentleness or pity but with a savage beauty that drew the eye.
Looking up timorously into those cold, calculating eyes,
Zena felt a sudden urge to turn and flee.

An imperceptible shrug of his muscular shoulders indicated the prince's decision. "Why not, *ma petite?*" he
drawled indifferently, offering his arm and courteously
handing her into the troika.

Zena, with immense relief but a heart still palpitating
wildly, sank into the cushion of soft furs Ivan arranged
around her. The prince lounged comfortably next to her in
the small sleigh, and within seconds they were galloping
at breakneck speed through the broad streets.

The prince spoke not a word to his passenger, his
thoughts concentrated on the few necessities he required
for the journey. Since his country estate at Podolsk was always kept at the ready for his erratic visits, very little had
to be conveyed there. However, he did want those guns
and the wine and maybe that new pastry assistant to his
chef who made such glorious *croissants*. Alex's mornings
had been infinitely improved, regardless of the state of his
pounding head, with the appearance of those new *croissants*
on his breakfast tray. To this day, he had a prodigious
fancy for sweets and often disgusted his fellow gamblers at
the Yacht Club by devouring bonbons and pastries with
his brandy in the wee hours of the morning when everyone
else's stomach was slightly queasy after ten or twelve hours
of drinking and smoking. This idiosyncrasy was the result,
plainly, of a spoiled and pampered childhood, which Alex's
certainly had been, but then, a Kuzan never questioned his

whims; he simply indulged them. Yes, the pastry cook would come along.

When they reached the imposing pink marble Kuzan palace on the Neva Quay, given long ago by Catherine the Great to her favorite Platon Kuzan, the prince issued a few abrupt instructions to Ivan, then helped Zena out of the troika and escorted her up the pretentious marble stairway rising gracefully from the street. Elaborate cast-bronze double doors were swept open before they reached the entrance, as though unseen eyes had been on the alert for their master's return.

Alex informed a very correct English butler that he was leaving forthwith for Podolsk and had only to change his evening clothes. "Rutledge, would you please show *Mademoiselle* . . . er . . ." He glanced at Zena inquiringly.

"Turku," she quickly responded, and then, fearful the name might be recognized, amended rapidly, "*Mademoiselle* Turkuaminen."

"Ah, of course, Rutledge, *Mademoiselle* Turkuaminen would no doubt like to freshen up a bit before the journey. Show her to the lapis guest room and send a lady's maid to her."

"Very good, my lord prince," the butler replied, assessing the inelegant appearance of the young woman with a cool dignity, immediately placing her precisely where she belonged in his very rigid hierarchy of rank. The Kuzan household was used to dealing with the sudden appearance of beautiful and colorful women in their master's company, and, as he had so often in the past, Rutledge rose nobly to the occasion.

Alex turned again to Zena and brusquely, in the manner of one accustomed to command, added, "Please, *mademoiselle,* no more than fifteen minutes. I detest waiting and I'm impatient to be off."

With the imperturbable calm of one long familiar with the gross idiosyncrasies of the entire Kuzan family menagerie, Rutledge conducted Zena to the lapis room, inquiring politely if she required anything in addition to a lady's maid.

"No . . . thank you," Zena softly declined, awed by both the opulent magnificence of the rococo palace and the restrained hauteur of the formidable butler. Her family's servants had always been Russian peasants, who, though childishly lovable and accommodating, never approached the noble, proud grace of this creature.

Minutes later, back downstairs, Rutledge permitted himself one raised eyebrow as he informed the housekeeper of the prince's "guest." "Mrs. Chase, we have seen a multitude of, ah, females come and go into the young master's bedroom, but usually he knows their names."

"No doubt he will know this one's name by morning," Mrs. Chase dryly retorted, as they both calmly waited at the bottom of the stairs in the event the prince had any final directions for them before taking his leave.

Within ten minutes Alex reappeared at the top landing, casually dressed in a cream-colored muzhik shirt belted with red suede over black cashmere trousers tucked into beautifully embroidered black kid boots, his overlong black hair tossed carelessly in disarray, for, in his haste to change, raking fingers had sufficed for a comb. He was slipping his arms into the sleeves of a greatcoat of pearl-gray lynx as he unhurriedly strolled down the ornate marble staircase flanked by Falconet marble nymphs of exquisite proportions. "Did Ivan send a messenger to hold the Moscow train?"

"Yes, my lord. It has been taken care of."

"Is the young cook up and dressed?"

"Yes, Prince, already on his way to the Moscow Vauxhall."[2]

"My guns and wines gone on as well?"

"Yes, my lord," Rutledge assured Alex confidently, for

he ran a well-ordered establishment. "Is there anything more you wish?"

"No, thank you, Rutledge. And thank you, Mrs. Chase; you are ever efficient."

The prince began to pace the immense entrance hall, while Rutledge and Mrs. Chase remained quietly at attention. On the third traverse of the inlaid-marble floor, he impatiently slapped his gloves against the palm of his hand and gruffly noted, "*Mademoiselle*'s toilette must have exceeded fifteen minutes by now. Please send someone to hurry her along."

Damnation, he thought, was there ever a woman who was on time? He'd give her five more minutes and then leave the impertinent female behind. She could fine someone else to convey her to Podolsk. Just as his ready temper was beginning to smolder, Zena came running down the stairs, breathlessly apologizing for the delay:

"I'm so sorry, my lord, but the fire was delightfully warm and my shoes were quite wet and—"

The prince rudely broke into this recital by grabbing her arm and propelling her briskly toward the door. "Yes, yes, well, never mind, we must hurry. They're holding the Moscow train for me. *Vite, vite*, my dear."

"Good-bye, Prince Alex," Rutledge and Mrs. Chase chorused in unison.

"*Au revoir*. I'll be gone a fortnight or so, in case my parents should inquire."

They were out the door, down the steps, and seated in the troika within a few swift moments.

"My Lord?" Zena timidly inquired as she looked up into a slightly fierce countenance.

"Yes?" he retorted brusquely. They were quite late, he noted with annoyance, and were going to keep the Moscow train waiting longer than usual.

"I must make one stop."

"*Must?*" the prince challenged, bridling at the demand.

Zena observed the flashing indignation in those steely eyes and avoided another direct confrontation with the scowling face. Keeping her lashes lowered, she said quietly, "I beg, sir, one small favor. It won't take me long."

Damn women! he thought. Always one more stop—one more piece of luggage; one more minute to adjust their coiffures. Sighing softly to himself, he reflected that the train *had* waited for him countless times before, and the little baggage *was* prettily contrite. "Very well, my dear, but do hurry. Where do you wish to go?"

Zena gave him the address, which Alex conveyed to his driver, and shortly they were in the narrow street that ran behind the mews of her aunt's town house.

"I'll be back directly, my lord. Thank you so much for stopping," Zena breathlessly declared, and quickly threw aside the fur robes and jumped out of the troika before either man could assist her.

Quietly opening the kitchen door, Zena stealthily trod the back stairway up to the third-floor nursery. The house was still; either her aunt and the general hadn't yet missed her, or, having noted her absence, were searching for her somewhere other than here—at least for now. She must rush! Bundling some of Bobby's clothes into a small blanket, she then wrapped the sleeping three-year-old in a warm down comforter, lifted him into her arms, stole silently past the room where the boy's nurse snored noisily, and retraced the rear staircase. The child slept on, undisturbed, and Zena breathed a great sigh of relief as she softly shut the kitchen door.

"Thank you for waiting, my lord," Zena said when she'd handed her burden to the waiting driver and climbed into the troika. Once she was settled, the impeccably trained Ivan impassively passed the young child back into her arms and covered them both with fur wraps.

The prince had been lightly dozing, his dark head resting against the quilted green velvet. He slowly opened his eyes and glanced down at the young girl. The golden eyes snapped open in alarm. *Good God—a child! She has a child!* Alex sat bolt upright and stared down in astonishment at the angelic face of the sleeping boy.

"I couldn't leave him behind, my lord," Zena whispered entreatingly, terror-stricken at the violent expression on the handsome face.

While a hundred alternative options, none of them pleasant, raced through the prince's stupefied mind, he quickly recovered himself and attempted to quell the young girl's obviously fearful apprehensions by mechanically replying, "No, of course not. Ah . . . well, now"—he hesitated, threw a distracted glance at the sleeping child, then continued gallantly—" *alors*, it seems we are ready. Ivan—the Moscow Vauxhall!"

The horses immediately broke into a dashing gallop.

"He's all I have in the world, my lord," Zena quietly explained to the silent, severe man beside her.

"I understand, *ma petite*," Alex politely assured her. But, *sacré bleu*, he observed to himself, this was decidedly *outre passé*. Most assuredly it was unique for a streetwalker to take her brat along on a "business trip."

4

The dash to the station was at furious speed, the horses' breath billowing frosty white in the crisp, cold air. Ivan crooned and encouraged the beautiful bays to ever greater speed, turning Zena's cheeks rosy pink as the cold wind rushed past.

When the horses finally came to a halt at the station entrance, a street boy ran forward to relieve Ivan of the reins.

"Ivan, carry the child," the prince commanded.

All the passengers had boarded fifty minutes before, and the station platform was empty. Alex presented his arm to Zena and they began the long trek down the deserted concourse to the waiting train. Several railroad officials were drawn up before a pale-gray coach with the Kuzan motif embellishing the center panel, and all snapped to attention as the prince drew near.

"Good evening—er, good morning (for it was now past two o'clock), Your Excellency. Everything is in readiness," one of them offered.

They all discreetly averted their gaze from the child the prince's servant was carrying; but the startling fact that the prince was traveling with a young woman and child would be common gossip throughout St. Petersburg by noon tomorrow.

"Thank you," Alex responded absently, thoroughly acquainted with traveling *en prince.* Hundreds of years of Kuzan privilege prompted this easy self-assurance.

Ivan transferred the sleeping boy to Zena.

"Have a pleasant journey, Excellency," the crowd en-joined as Alex helped Zena with the child up the stairs to the interior.

The prince smiled faintly in response, while Ivan pro-ceeded down the line of officials and distributed the usual gratuities that warranted, in part, this preferential defer-ence.

As the prince opened the door, Zena gasped in surprise at the magnificent decor of the railway coach. She cer-tainly was escaping from her aunt and the old general in fine style, she ruefully noted. Three manservants, the pas-try cook, and a maid stood at the ready. The room they en-tered was a drawing room paneled in lustrous rosewood with heavily silvered moldings and mirrored inserts. The drapes were a soft apple-green velvet, while a Persian *mil-lefleurs* carpet in tones of black, green, and gold covered the floor. Purest Louis Quinze furniture in embroidered cream satin was comfortably arranged throughout the car.

A barely perceptible nod from the prince brought the maid standing before them. "Put the child to bed in the small blue bedroom, Mariana, and stay with him to-night," he said.

"But, my lord . . ." Zena began.

"Yes?" he asked coolly. He was not accustomed to peo-ple querying his wishes. "Rest assured, my dear, Mariana is very good with children."

Mariana beamed happily and stretched out her arms for the child. One penetrating glance from the nobleman as-sured Zena that he disliked being crossed, and as she had no inclination to begin the journey with a scene, she qui-etly relinquished her young brother to the plump young maid, who walked from the room singing softly to the sleeping child.

"Now, please," Alex said affably, the issue having been resolved to his satisfaction, "*Mademoiselle* . . . er . . ."

"Turkuaminen—but please call me Zena, my lord."

"Ah yes, a delightful name and so much simpler than . . . Well, now, Zena, may I help you with your wrap and offer you a hot punch to warm yourself? Feodor, is the punch ready?"

"Yes, Your Excellency."

"Fine. Bring the bowl in and leave it on the table."

"Will you need anything more, Excellency?"

"No, that will be all. You may retire for the night."

A silver punch bowl was deposited on the table and the remaining servants dismissed. Alex poured two engraved-silver cups of the steaming punch and offered one to Zena.

"I don't think I should, my lord," she equivocated softly, slightly uncomfortable alone with the prince.

"Nonsense, *mademoiselle*, you're chilled. The hot drink is a restorative; it will warm you. I insist," he persisted.

"Very well, perhaps just a little," Zena consented, deciding to herself to drink a sip or so and then sit up until they reached Moscow. It was a nine-hour run from St. Petersburg, so they should arrive shortly before noon.

Alex sank into a down-cushioned *fauteuil* across from Zena and relaxed comfortably, holding the warm cup between his hands, his long legs sprawled before him. Through half-closed eyes, he studied the young woman who sat opposite him. She certainly didn't *look* like a streetwalker—at least not a successful one. Her light silk gown of aquamarine, enlivened with green and white beading, was two or three years out of style and a bit tight across the bosom, as though it might have been a hand-me-down or picked up from a used-clothes dealer. The slippers, too, had seen better days, while the narrow string of pearls around her slender neck was very modest indeed. Perhaps the finery had been presented to her by a protector a few seasons past and no one had yet taken his place. The winsomely beautiful face, framed with the heavy masses of dark auburn hair, was taking on color as the warm punch and the crackling fire in the small porcelain stove did their work.

Silently Alex drank the delicious brew, then refilled his cup. The punch was a favorite of his, the recipe purloined years before from a centuries-old recipe of the Berlin court and composed of several score ingredients in addition to the arrack and rum. As the girl appeared increasingly nervous in the quiet atmosphere broken only by the steady rhythm of the wheels, he attempted, in a somewhat desultory fashion, to arrest her discomfort with trivial social conversation. However, when she scarcely responded to his questions or answered in ambiguous phrases, he again lapsed into his comfortable lethargy. After all, he considered tranquilly, this was strictly a business proposition for her, and as far as he was concerned, she was merely a receptacle for future physical needs, so there really was no necessity for pretense or polite flirtation or any of the normal catering civilities. So very convenient, Alex reflected gratefully.

Strangely, he felt asexual, most unusual for him in the presence of a beautiful woman; perhaps it was the childlike appearance of the delicate beauty. She couldn't weigh much over a hundred pounds, and even in heeled slippers she scarcely came to his shoulder. Young girls had never been a particular caprice of his, his preferences decidedly in the direction of full-blown, voluptuous females, tall and fleshy enough so you knew you had a woman in your arms. This pretty little charmer reminded him very emphatically, in looks and timidity, of a dainty sparrow. How the devil had she survived on the streets with that utter lack of aggressiveness so typical of the world's oldest profession? The retiring little sparrow was hardly characteristic of those who practiced the vocation she'd chosen; nevertheless, the "vulnerable innocence" she projected was vaguely attractive.

In the hushed atmosphere of the private coach with those

cool golden eyes trained on her, Zena felt as though caught in a cat-and-mouse scenario. The prince's savagely handsome countenance, awesome size, arrogant composure—all served to unnerve her. She *must* stay awake until Moscow, and then she and Bobby could leave. Yet, when Alex pressed another cup of punch on her, she drank it, and though she valiantly tried to stay awake, her eyelids kept dropping shut. Two portions of the potent liquor on an all-but-empty stomach, plus the late hour, had combined to make her unable to hold them open.

After another ten minutes of surveying Zena's utter exhaustion, Alex suggested she go to bed. "*Mademoiselle*, you are all but asleep. The bedroom is the first door on the left. Please make yourself comfortable." He rose to refill his cup, then pulled Zena out of her chair and gave her a gentle shove in the direction of the bedroom.

She moved in a soporific daze born of the liquor, the late hour, and the emotional strain of the evening, vaguely recalling the way—first door on the left. Once inside the room, she hardly noticed the sumptuous appointments as she advanced directly to the carved mahogany bed and fell on it fully clothed, staying awake only long enough to pull a down counterpane over her.

The prince wasn't ready for bed yet, although it was late; he was used to later hours. He sat up for another two hours, slowly emptying the contents of the punch bowl and envisioning the myriad pleasant amusements his country estate offered. His library was amply stocked, as was his wine cellar, the hunting was superb, and, best of all, he was three hundred miles away from the brittle inanities of St. Petersburg society. The young girl he had taken along, in spite of the added baggage of her brat, for whom the servants could very easily be responsible, might prove to be a refreshing change from the hothouse variety of woman he felt surfeited with. All of her undeniable charms would no doubt help him forget the tedious bore-dom of fashionable society, at least for a few days.

As his thoughts wandered to contemplation of Zena's charms, his asexual mood was gradually altered. The soothing rhythm of the train, the warmth of the drawing room, the numerous cupfuls of potent liquor served to rouse his sybaritic nature, and his mind turned to more satisfying and obvious alternatives.

Alex pulled off his boots, rose languorously from his restful ease, and stretched lazily. Walking slowly to the bedroom, he shed his belt and silk shirt, carelessly drop-ping them on the floor as he continued his somewhat in-ebriated way to the pleasures awaiting him in the arms of the pretty streetwalker.

Good Lord, the woman had fallen asleep with all her clothes on! She must have been truly exhausted. Alex ex-perienced a momentary pang of conscience in waking her, but the stirring desire in his loins would not be damped. He wouldn't keep her awake long, and, after all, he cyni-cally rationalized, she would be well paid for the interrup-tion to her sleep.

Zena was sleeping on her back, one arm flung out above her head, her cheeks rose-colored from the warmth of the room, tousled auburn curls lying in a riot of waves on the lace pillow. The velvet coverlet had been partially cast aside, as the heat from the tile stove in the corner of the room made covers unnecessary; her breathing was slow and light.

Alex's eyes moved from the enchanting beauty of her face to the creamy flesh of her full breasts as they rose in splendor, forced above the tight décolletage with each gen-tle breath. A throbbing hardness pressed against his trou-sers, the insistent erection pulsing in anticipation. He stripped off the confining trousers, and his masculinity sprang free—taut, erect, quivering. He stood naked, a sun-bronzed giant of a man, wide shoulders and chest tapering in rippling muscles to taut stomach and narrow hips. Long, firmly sinewed legs were planted slightly apart as he paused for countless seconds and stared.

The bed sagged beneath Alex's weight as he sat gently on the edge, reached over, and smoothly began releasing the line of small, silk-covered buttons marching down the front of her bodice until Zena's magnificent breasts were freed from the confining pressure of her dress. Brushing aside the lace-trimmed chemise, he bent low and softly kissed one shell-pink nipple. Zena moaned small pleasure sounds in her sleep, like the purring of a contented cat, as Alex practiced the gentle arousal at which he was so expert. He had never viewed sex as a conquest, an achievement, or a performance but rather as a pleasure to be ripened, extended, taken to its limits before consummation. With saccharine fingertips, he stroked the warm, fragrant skin of her throat, her shoulders, the soft mounds of her breasts, lightly caressing each rosy crest until it stood pertly erect.

Zena's mind floated blissfully in this paradise of pleasure, in the deep exhaustion of her sleep, finding this dream exquisite; soft sighs of pure sensation escaped her lips in response to these new, powerful, luscious pulsings of her blood.

Alex deftly unhooked the flounces of her skirt, untied the ribbons of her petticoat and drawers, and facilely stripped them from her inert form, revealing the splendid beauty of her body to him. The momentary coolness of the air washing over her bared flesh caused Zena's eyelids to flutter, but when Alex bent to gently kiss her cheek, she smiled sweetly and dropped back to sleep. With a gossamer touch his fingers moved over her belly, twined soothingly in the silken mons, and tenderly slid into the warmth of her pliant flesh. Parting the soft folds, his finely tapered fingers searched and probed the lubricious crevices until they gained the minute, sensitive place he was looking for, and with a feather-light touch he delicately stroked until Zena's breathing altered, no longer slow and peaceful but ragged and agitated, and her hips rhythmically writhed, her body reaching for the source of that compelling sensation.

Lowering his body next to hers, Alex leaned over to kiss her trembling lips, gently at first and then more insistently, his tongue darting to probe the sweetness of her mouth as he rolled her underneath him, pressing himself intimately against her.

Zena's eyes snapped open. With genuine panic, she stared into smoldering golden eyes. This wasn't a dream! Aghast with horror, she realized that these exquisite sensations were *not* a dream! An urge to scream welled up in her throat, but Alex's demanding lips drew in the sound even as his practiced hands stroked, caressed, titillated; then his mouth released hers and moved slowly across her cheek to her ear, whispering love words that brought Zena's flesh to new heights of desire.

A silent cry pierced her pleasure-ridden senses: What was she doing? Determinedly she endeavored to struggle free of the sensual stimuli that were bombarding her pulsing body, but when Alex lowered his head to a swollen breast and touched it with a light, exploring kiss, new pleasures began exploding in her belly, sapping her resolution.

Weakly Zena attempted to protest. "Please, my lord," she whispered faintly, "this is a dreadful mistake. Please . . . stop. You must!"

Alex lifted his head briefly in mild astonishment. He exhaled softly as a slight shudder gripped him. "My sweet," he said gently, "it's too late to stop." He tenderly brushed her hair back from her forehead and bent to kiss her lips, and in that moment he felt in her the hesitation that presaged capitulation.

Violent tremors of fresh desire warmed Zena's melting

flesh as Alex's mouth touched a rosy nipple and his long, lean fingers insinuated themselves into her damp, moist inner warmth, stroking the tiny seat of pleasure until her hips arched involuntarily, stretching for more of that unutterable joy that was encompassing her. Her mind gave way as her body took over. Nothing seemed to matter at the moment; reality, conscience, anxiety receded. The only reality was his touch, his caress, his burning kisses tasting of the spicy punch he had consumed, and instinctively, instead of trying to pull away from this unscrupulous, dangerous man, she reached out for the strong, lean body poised above her, wrapping her arms around his broad, muscular shoulders and feverishly drew him closer, wanting to press her warm, soft flesh against his.

His responses rising to a throbbing urgency, Alex lowered his body, settling his weight upon her, his quivering penis probing her wetness as her hips moved in a dance as old as time. He met resistance, and his inebriated brain briefly registered perplexity, but his fevered, insistent passion ignored the minor hindrance; he desperately wanted to lose himself in her flesh, accommodate her breathless passion, gain relief for his engorged penis. He surged forward.

An anguished shriek of pain filled the small room, shocking Alex back to an unwonted sobriety.

Sweet Jesus—a virgin! his befuddled mind discerned.

Zena sobbed quietly as Alex's arrested, pulsating organ filled her. A moist warmth enclosed him, arousing an already volatile passion. God, she felt good: tight and enveloping, her nipples pressing into his chest, her silken skin beneath his fingertips. Almost instantly he shrugged away the momentary dismay. Virgins were not in his usual style; he preferred experience in bed, but it was too late now— too late for both of them.

His lips brushed her cheeks, kissing away the salty tears, as he moved, more slowly now, inside her sensuous warmth. Gently, deliberately, rhythmically he teased the interior places until her sobbing ceased, replaced by small gasps of pleasure, building each wave of sensation leisurely, lingering at the top of his stroke and then withdrawing so as to allow the piercing sweet tremor to reach fever pitch. He took his time, noting with a sensualist's expertise when Zena moved and squirmed and when she thrust herself at him, matching his rhythm to hers until he saw that she could no longer wait, and then, when he felt the climax break over her, he poured his warm seed into her.

Zena felt no guilt at that moment; the pleasure was so complete she only felt drained, content, unable to move, wishing never, never to leave the soft, warm bed.

Alex rolled over, pulling her into his arms; and, their bodies sated, they lay tranquil in each other's embrace.

All too soon, reality crowded in. What in the world had she done? How could she have allowed such freedoms? Was she truly depraved? Her aunt had constantly reminded her that her Circassian mother was little more than a savage, coming from a primitive mountain tribe. Was it true? Then Zena's sensible, practical nature overcame the mild hysteria. For heaven's sake, it wasn't the end of the world—and considerably better than having to bed that despicable fat old general! If that was chaste, respectable love, she would very gladly forgo the conventionalities. But Zena experienced a frightening feeling of vulnerability when this darkly handsome prince touched her; it was as though she no longer belonged to herself, as though he controlled her passion with his merest touch.

The prince must think her the most degraded wanton to allow him such liberties, to actually beg for release in his arms. A deep sense of humiliation swept over her as she tried to reconcile this astonishing, unprecedented sensuousness with the acceptable behavior required of young society debutantes. How could she have permitted these rapturous feelings of hers to overcome her genteel upbringing? Certainly the prince would never respect her now.

Zena's eyelashes fluttered up and she gazed surreptitiously from under their shield at the man who had so casually taken her virginity. He was disturbingly handsome: fine, aristocratic features; full, sensitive mouth; dark, long, wavy hair; smooth bronze skin. The brilliance of a huge emerald caught her eye as his hand rested possessively on her hip, making her acutely aware of the contrast between their circumstances. He was handsome, rich, charming, seductively expert, she ruefully noted. Plainly she had made a fool of herself, and her mortification was absolute. But then she reminded herself sharply that *anything* was superior to having to wed that odious toad of a general, and the prince *was* taking her away from St. Petersburg.

The emerald twinkled in the subdued light as Alex gently brushed the damp curls from Zena's cheek. "I'm sorry for hurting you, *ma petite*," he whispered softly. "I had no idea this was your first evening as a streetwalker. Had I known, I could have been more gentle."

At which point Prince Alexander was presented with some fascinating information, most of which he would have quite willingly remained in ignorance of.

"I'm not a streetwalker, my lord."

Alex's black brows snapped together in a sudden scowl. *Bloody hell, what have I got into?*

"I'm the daughter of Baron Turku from Astrakhan."

The scowl deepened noticeably.

"My father died six months ago, and my aunt began trying to marry me off to General Scobloff."

The frown lifted instantly, and Alex breathed a sigh of relief. At least, he mentally noted, there was no irate relatives to reckon with immediately. "Sweet Jesus! That old vulture must be close to seventy!" he exclaimed, horrified.

"Sixty-one, my lord, and he's managed to bury two wives already," Zena quietly murmured. "I didn't want to become his wife, but my aunt was insisting, so I simply had to get away. My little brother and I will—"

"Little brother?" Alex sputtered. "The young child isn't yours?" he asked in confusion, and then remembered. Of course he wasn't hers; Alex had just taken her virginity! A distinct feeling of apprehension and, on the whole, disagreeable sensations struck the young prince. *Merde!* This just wasn't his night! "You deliberately led me on," he accused uncharitably, choosing to ignore the fact that he had drunk so much in the past fifteen hours that his clarity of thought was not at peak performance.

"I did not lead you on!" Zena returned tartly, angry that the prince should think she had contrived this entire situation. "Modest young ladies of good breeding do not lead men on!" she snapped.

"Permit me to disagree, my pet, for I've known many modest young ladies of good breeding," Alex disputed coolly, "a number of whom have led me on to the same, ah, satisfactory conclusion we have just enjoyed. They're all quite willing once the tiresome conventional posturing has been observed."

The prince's obvious competence in an area of connoisseurship completely foreign to Zena's limited sphere served to squelch her ingenuous assertion.

Alex sighed disgruntedly. *Good God, for which of my sins am I paying penance?* "What am I to do with you—a damnable virgin? Of all the rotten luck! You try to be helpful and come to the aid of what appears to be a nice, ordinary streetwalker and look what happens. She turns out to be a cursed green virgin with a baby brother to boot, not to mention a respectable family."

"No, my lord, no family," Zena quietly reminded him.

A faintly pleased glint of relief momentarily shone in the depths of the golden eyes. "Thank God for small favors. Nevertheless, you, my dear, have become a vexatious problem," Alex censoriously intoned.

"You could take the honorable course of action and marry me, my lord," Zena timidly suggested.

The prince laughed harshly. "Ha! You don't know the Kuzans, my little dove," was the disdainful rejoinder. "Marrying deflowered virgins is unusual and extraordinary punishment for a rather ordinary occurrence, and not wishing to deny the excessive faults we philandering Kuzans possess in abundance, stupidity is not one of them."

The prince entertained the usual male practical assessment of such trifles as virginity. "Surely, my lord prince, you'll wish to marry someday," she persisted.

"What for?" he rudely queried.

"You'd give a wife some beautiful children," Zena softly murmured, as she swept a swift glance over the darkly handsome man lying beside her. "Don't you want children?"

"I have children," he replied.

"I mean children of your own."

"They *are* my own."

The quiet logic seemed unassailable; Zena did not pursue the topic.

Alex raised himself on one elbow and reproachfully scrutinized the naked beauty at his side. A multitude of conflicting speculations coursed through his inebriated mind. Did she intend to complain, perhaps to his father? It had been known to happen, and his sire could be damnably moral on occasion. (Alex still remembered with acute discomfort a reprimand he had received two months ago when some peasant girl had come to the palace with a baby she claimed Alex had fathered. It wasn't that he deliberately intended to ignore the wench; he simply hadn't known. One would think she'd have come to him first. Perhaps she was more shrewd than she appeared, since his *père* had been considerably more generous than Alex would have been.) Would this young woman's aunt try to force him into marriage? At least in that regard, Alex sighed gratefully, father and son were of one accord; his father saw no need for Alex to consider marriage when he was only twenty-four years old.

Damn it! Alex swore under his breath. He supposed it was his own fault for not asking any questions. But what respectable girl would have begged a strange man for a ride to Podolsk in the middle of the night, or agreed to go to sleep in an unknown man's bedroom, or been outfitted in a dress two seasons old *and* without corsets? Furthermore, could one expect any young girl with such a lush, opulent body to be some simpering debutante virgin? *Never*—and he'd seen scores—*never* had he seen a respectable society miss with such ripe, magnificent breasts or such sweetly swelling hips or—damn!—such an intoxicating, easily aroused passion.

As Alex's tawny eyes swept over the flawless womanly form, a warm tremor deep in his stomach signaled a nascent carnal urge. Disregarding any further troublesome speculations and forebodings about an uncertain future, symptomatic of the callous indifference with which he normally viewed all obstacles, he reached out to stroke the round firmness of one prime, delectable breast. There was a faint smile on his remarkable features as he effortlessly reverted to type: a libertine with a passion to do as he pleased.

Zena's uncomfortable, irresolute thoughts sank into the cocoon of sated sensuality that still embraced her. The room was warm, the down mattress and covers as substantial as gossamer, her newly awakened body still throbbing. She was aware of each flutter and subtle nuance of sensation. It felt as though her body positively glowed. All the romances secretly read could never hope to express these vivid, tremulous impressions. Then the nagging thoughts returned. She had been reared to believe that proper young women never enjoyed the mating act, only endured it. She must arise from this decadent luxury, put her clothes back on, and sit up in the drawing room for the rest of the journey. She must try to explain somehow to the prince that an irresistible impulse, a delicious madness, had come over her; it wouldn't happen again. This was all a terrible mistake. She had wanted only an opportunity to escape from her aunt and the disgusting old general. Surely the prince must think her nothing more than a disreputable tart. Oh dear, she *must* get up.

But then she felt the prince's sensuous fingers stroking her breast, and a palpable shock of pleasure gripped her senses. She opened her mouth to protest, but warm, tender lips covered hers and the words died in her throat. Arms that came up in remonstrance to push away the offending muscular chest ineffectually trembled and then, in capitulation, slid up around the powerful neck and clasped the hard male contours tightly.

Alex, by way of apology for hurting Zena last time, set out to please her, kissing and caressing each sensitive area—lips, throat, breasts—and Zena felt the world slip away. Only feeling mattered: the movement of his hands on her flesh, his lips worshiping each part of her body, lingering and tantalizing until her breath came in short gasps and her hips arched, seeking once again union with this man, seeking to fill the burning, pulsing emptiness. The ache in her loins brought each nerve screaming with the need for possession.

Alex reached up and gently unlocked her arms from around his neck, brushing her cheek with his lips. "Don't rusk, *dushka* ['little heart']," he whispered. "There's plenty of time."

Zena whimpered piteously as Alex moved away, and reached imploringly for him, seeking the elusive release. But he brushed away the imploring arms and languorously resumed the subtle stroking, running his hands over her belly, twining his fingers in the silken hair below, gradually forcing her thighs apart and caressing a delicate pattern along their inner contours. Soon again sensuous fever was provoked; Zena was dewy moist, running wet as convulsive waves of sweet passion built and built. Alex slipped down the bed between her thighs and rested his head on her belly. His face felt softly prickly to her tender skin. Moving downward, he kissed the downy hair, and his warm breath stirred her deliciously. Moving still lower, his lips nudged at the soft folds of her pulsing, turgid, fleshy gates of paradise.

What was he doing? Zena's eyes widened in alarm. He surely mustn't kiss her *there*. She reached down and frantically attempted to push the encroaching head away. Indifferent to her ineffectual efforts to dislodge him, Alex explored the outer lips, licking, kissing, softly biting until the horror of paralyzed shock in Zena's mind was overcome by a driving fever that pulsed in time to her frenzied heartbeat. Then Alex parted those lips with his long, cool fingers, and his tenacious tongue probed her innermost dew until he found the tiny lodestar of desire; and when he touched her there, Zena thought she would die. She was flooded with explosive waves of tumultuous passion as Alex tenderly sucked and tongued her rosy pearl. Her body writhed and twisted with the agony of her senses; her fingers curled into the black thickness of his hair and clung as shudders quaked her body.

When she thought she would explode from the building sensual hysteria, Alex moved the full weight of his body onto her, slid his muscled legs intimately between hers, forcing her soft thighs apart, raised himself, plunged his throbbing hardness into her with a low groan, and drove in hungrily. Zena's thighs closed savagely around him, fusing their bodies in primeval embrace. She felt the hard, flat muscles of his stomach pressing against her, the power of his arms, the broad muscles of his back flexing as each fierce thrust tore into her; the power and energy, the

gentleness and sensuous touch of this man filled her
senses.

Alex's hands reached down to grasp her hips, driving
home with all the frenzied power of his lower body; his
mouth closed over hers, and she moaned against the com-
pulsive lips as she was impaled on his exploding shaft of
love. Zena keened a wild cry of raw, primitive fulfillment
as her climax burst and rapture flooded every fiber of her
being.

They lay quiet for a long time. The prince felt heavy on
her, but she liked the feel of him. His breathing was still
harsh, his pulse racing wildly as he brushed her cheek with
his lips. Perspiration beaded his body, and Zena quivered
pleasurably as she remembered his hard, lean back arched
in ecstasy beneath her fingers as he'd released his passion.
Many moments later, he stirred against he as if to draw
away, and Zena realized with embarrassment that she was
still clutching him tightly. Her arms fell away, and the
prince immediately rolled off her and onto his back, expelling a long, low whistle of appreciative reverence.
Twisting back on his side, he planted a hasty kiss on
Zena's cheek.

"Never, sweet dove, never in my life have I encountered
such a hot-blooded virgin," he whispered. "What luck I
found you, *ma petite*. Our holiday from the boredom of
Petersburg will be *magnifique*." He chuckled deep in his
throat, contemplating the rich delight in tutoring such
untried passion.

Zena's heart plummeted in shame at the prince's smoldering look of satisfaction, at the lewd insinuation. He
wouldn't suggest such a thing to her unless he thought her
thoroughly sunk beneath contempt.

Since Zena had never participated in the conviviality of
St. Petersburg's aristocratic society, having only lately
come of age, she was not aware that liaisons and holidays
of passion were not the sole province of streetwalkers and

fallen women. If the arrangements could be cloaked with an acceptable discretion (and in some cases even that commodity was expendable), the upper classes were quite willing, if not daringly innovative, participants in the game of musical beds.[3]

"I couldn't go on holiday with you, my lord," she murmured uncomfortably. "I'm so ashamed of myself."

"Ashamed?" Alex questioned, mildly shocked at such a curious revelation. "It's not *your* fault I mistook you for a woman of the streets."

"Ashamed of succumbing to your advances, my lord. It isn't right," she sadly replied.

"Your flesh just responded to its natural desires; it was bound to happen eventually. Look, my sweet," he said soothingly, reaching out with a fingertip to turn Zena's face toward him, "let me reassure you, from vast experience in the boudoirs of Petersburg, virginity in the brittle, impious society in which I move is as rare and elusive as the unicorn of fable."

In order to salve the poor girl's conscience, Alex might have been stretching the truth somewhat, but not a great deal, he mused. There was a certain amount of virginity, of course, but generally it was closely allied to squinty eyes, grossly ugly features, or avoirdupois that even flowing silk and tightly laced corsets couldn't conceal. The only reason a lush beauty like the *mademoiselle*'s hadn't been ravished yet was apparently that she had been in seclusion—although, from the sound of it, the old general had been doing his damnedest to remedy that circumstance even before the engagement.

Could he pride himself on having introduced her more subtly, with considerably more expertise and gentleness, to the congress between a man and a woman than ever the aged general would have been able to? Could he assuage his brief twinge of guilt over taking her virginity by assuming that his tutoring in the art of love would be infinitely more enjoyable than that of a fat, corrupt, and practically senile lecher? The answer to both questions was yes, if rationalization was required, but it wasn't, since Alexander Nikolaevich had always done more or less as he liked, taking a page from the behavior of a long line of wealthy, arrogant, charming Kuzan rogues who'd never seriously curtailed any of their desires.

Alex acknowledged the basic inequity in the matter of female conquest, but he acknowledged it impartially—that is to say, he recognized the necessity in life of female submission to male domination. With a true aristocratic disdain for the prescribed conventions of society, he felt no compunction to resist ruining a virgin. All women were fair game, regardless of age, rank, or condition. The prince would deflower a virgin as casually as he would mount the bawdiest wench. It was simply a need, sometimes a scintillating pleasure, sometimes a vivacious game, sometimes no more than a compelling physical desire that required quenching. It was as natural as breathing and eating, and only his mood determined the direction of his libertine eye. He would never consider forcing a virgin—or any other woman, for that matter. His sexual appetite did not require the erotic stimulation that resistance offered, and his sexual proficiency precluded the necessity. His females were always exceedingly compliant.

"Don't cry, my dear," Alex comforted as he brushed away the tears tracing a path down Zena's glowing cheeks. "Sleep," he soothed, drawing her into his warm embrace. He stroked her hair gently as he clasped the frail shoulders. "Don't worry—there's nothing to be ashamed of. You'll feel much better in the morning."

Zena allowed the consoling words to erase her dreadful fears and guilts and uncertainties, for she was very young and very tired and no one had comforted her in three long years. She had almost alone had to care for her brother, ease her father's despair, and, unaided, bear the brunt of her aunt's constant carping hostility. She would worry to-morrow; at least the repulsive general was far behind, she reflected with relief. Within seconds, Zena was fast asleep in the prince's arms.

It seemed like minutes later, but several hours had passed, when a loud rapping woke Alex.

"Yes, what is it?" he inquired groggily, his head still beclouded from the bowl of punch.

"The young child is sick, Your Excellency," a worried woman's voice answered through the door.

"We'll be right there," Alex answered promptly, fully awake now. He gently shook Zena's shoulder, for she was still sleeping soundly. "Wake up, *ma petite*," he murmured in her ear.

Zena's eyes opened languorously at the touch of his breath. Drowsy yet, she lazily wrapped her arms around his neck, seeking the delicious warmth of his body.

For a virgin, his mind noted rapidly, she had an instinct that was decidedly pleasing. He carefully released her arms from around his neck and said softly, "My dear, I'm afraid your brother is ill."

Zena sat up in panic, her blue eyes now fully alert.

"Allow me to find you a robe," Alex stated, and went to a built-in wardrobe next to the bed and began pawing through it. Tossing aside numerous garments, he emerged with a brilliant magenta silk wrapper. In an apologetic manner, he showed the dressing gown to Zena. "Sorry, the rest are mine—quite unsuitable. This color is garish, but at least it's female in gender."

He wrapped the ruffled and beribboned froth around Zena's shoulders, then quickly slipped into his robe. When she'd tied the sash and run her fingers quickly through her tousled curls, he opened the door and gestured down the narrow hallway. "Second door down. I hope it's nothing too serious," he added, with conventional sympathy.

Bobby was cradled in the maid's lap, his breath coming in labored, rasping gasps.

"Good Lord!" Alex exclaimed in alarm. "He's having trouble breathing. We'll stop the train and find a doctor." He was several yards down the hallway before Zena could stop him.

"Please, my lord, that won't be necessary. Bobby's often like this in the winter; his chest is so susceptible. If we could just have some kind of steamer brought into his room, he'll soon be quite comfortable."

Alex had servants scurrying about in a thrice, and within five minutes a large silver samovar was bubbling furiously in the center of the room, steam drifting from it in wispy trails up to the ceiling. The mist soon saturated the small room. Zena held her young brother in her lap, crooning and soothing the feverish child as the water droplets in the air eased the horrible rasping breath. When the boy at last fell into an untroubled rest, Alex lifted him into his bed and admonished the maid to call them should the wheezing begin again.

When they'd returned to Alex's room, Alex propelled Zena toward the bed and gently tucked her in. She looked quite exhausted. Sinking down on the edge of the bed, he said gravely, "Bobby needs a doctor. We must find one as soon as we reach Moscow."

Zena nodded in agreement, dispiritedly, for she was all too aware that a doctor's services were definitely beyond her means at the present.

The prince, studying one quilted cuff of his robe, obviously choosing his words with care, suggested with formality, "If you would reconsider granting me the pleasure of your company on my holiday, I should be happy to render service to Bobby in any way whatsoever."

Zena dropped her eyes before the bold invitation.

With the ruthless male practicality that selfishly overlooked the subtle nuances of respectability or decorum or sentiment, Alex coaxed softly, "Come now, *ma petite*. Think how Bobby's health would improve. Don't let considerations of virtue intervene, for you can't lose twice that which is already irrevocably lost." His golden eyes caught her and held them. "You can't bring back yesterday, little dove," he said gently, and a mild discomfort gripped him as he saw the confusion in her eyes. Casting aside the momentary pang, he briskly continued, "And, as an alternative to bedding with General Scobloff, surely I'm more . . . er . . . satisfactory." A brief smile touched his mouth.

He encountered a stony silence. Zena had half turned her back on him and was staring at the wall.

"My *dacha* will be secluded and remote," he whispered into the auburn ringlets curling softly against her neck. "I'll make love to you in the sunlight and by firelight, *dushka*," Alex murmured persuasively.

Zena hesitated, unwilling to admit to herself that even on this short acquaintance (but *acquaintance* was hardly the word for such base sensuality! she snorted to herself) she was decidedly inclined to go with the charming prince anywhere, anywhere at all.

"Think of Bobby," Alex repeated as he turned her toward him. "His cough will disappear. He'll have the finest of care, anything money can buy." Knowing how deep was Zena's love for her young brother, how concerned she was for his well-being, he struck where she was most vulnerable. "Just be my guest for a few days until Bobby is better. Look . . . on my honor, I promise not to touch you." (At least, not until you want me to, he thought confidently.) He spread his hands wide in an open gesture of conciliation and smiled winningly.

Zena looked up, startled at his sudden capitulation to integrity, not understanding the smug self-assurance that motivated his promise. "Very well," she said quietly, telling herself she was doing this so Bobby could get well, but knowing deep in her heart there were other, more

complex, bewildering, indefensible reasons for her acquiescence.

The prince allowed himself only the smallest smile of
triumph. "Excellent decision, my sweet." He bent to caress her cheek. "We reach the Moscow station in forty
minutes."

5

Alex cradled Bobby, who was securely wrapped in a sable robe, while Zena, despite her shabby appearance, in deference to the fact that she was apparently the mother of this child Prince Alexander was personally carrying, was offered the arm of the stationmaster as escort. A veritable phalanx of porters and railway officials, with the consummate efficiency produced only by immense wealth, once again conducted the prince's small party down the length of the train shed. A certain arrogance and pride of bearing, both utterly unconscious and unfeigned, characterized the prince as he strolled unhurriedly toward the street. Two elegant troikas were waiting, cordoned off by a row of black-uniformed security police. All this obsequious homage was casually accepted with perfect equanimity by Alex, who'd had a lifetime of such deferential treatment.

Ivan distributed the prince's generous acknowledgment in the form of hundreds of rubles, and beaming faces and ready hands helpfully assisted the prince, Bobby, and Zena into the cherry-red troika, while servants and baggage were stowed, equally respectfully, into the second, teal-blue, sleigh.

Zena was seated pressed close to the prince in the small velvet-upholstered seat, holding Bobby in her lap. Her baby brother was still drowsy, resting comfortably against her shoulder. All three occupants had been securely covered with numerous fur robes. Despite the unorthodox situation and the gross irregularities of the previous turbulent night, she couldn't help but feel a cheerful elation. She briefly, ever so briefly, chastised herself for not feeling the requisite remorse and humiliation that society would have prescribed, given the circumstances that had befallen her, but her youthful *joi de vivre* kept her from responding in this suitably contrite form.

As the prince had pointed out with such blunt practicality, there was no sense in bemoaning the loss of her virtue, for no amount of self-reproach, not the most punctilious future conduct, would ever restore it. And, she *was* far removed from the ugly general, who would have robbed her of that virtue soon enough in any event. If one was obliged to be ruthlessly pragmatic—and for the past three years, ever since her mother's death, Zena had been forced to embrace the unvarnished reality of the adult world—the loss of her virginity was simply a relative issue; it had happened last night instead of next week, that's all, and she was *not* tied for life to a sixty-one-year-old loathsome toad. She and Bobby would soon be with her grandfather and he would take care of them. With the exception of one minor drawback—if one could consider lost virtue minor, she thought wryly—everything had worked out quite well.

The three matched horses were restless in anticipation, held in check by a young street boy. Prince Alexander, leaning forward and speaking rapidly in a subdued voice, was imparting some last-minute instructions to Ivan. This was the first time Zena had seen him in the light of day and she regarded him with admiration, noting the finely chiseled profile against the thin, gray, wintry light, the crinkling round his eyes as he chuckled softly over some rejoinder from Ivan. When he suddenly leaned back in the seat and smiled lazily at her, she was a little disconcerted to be caught staring and looked away, quickly focusing her eyes on the beautiful horses, which were tossing their heads with impatience.

"The horses are absolutely exquisite," she exclaimed appreciatively, feeling a need to make conversation with this virtual stranger.

"Yes," the prince answered absently as he relayed one last order to the sleigh behind, then turned back to face Zena. At sight of that fair cameo face framed by a soft cascade of auburn curls, those wide, bewitching blue eyes, that captivating soft pink mouth, his breath caught and he repeated quietly, apropos female rather than horse flesh, "Exquisite. Very exquisite indeed."

Zena blushed crimson at the intensity of his gaze and lowered her eyes.

Alex reached out to caress her cheek, but arrested his gesture in midair when she shrank from him in alarm. Throwing his head back, he laughed boyishly. "Forgive me, *dushka*. I did promise not to touch you, didn't I? A momentary lapse. Please don't cringe; it's extremely lowering to my reputation as a *bon vivant*. Come, we can be friends. I'm really quite harmless." He turned his most prepossessing smile upon her, profoundly confident of the devastating effectiveness of the Kuzan charm.

Zena found herself impetuously returning the smile, as she was meant to do, no more immune to the irresistible Kuzan magnetism than scores of females before her.

The prince winked conspiratorially, "Capital! Friends, then?" When Zena nodded, his grin widened appreciably— an unguarded, natural grin far more effective and dangerous than the most seductive smile. "Ivan, we're off!" he called, and in an instant the horses were sprung and the troika was flying through the bustling streets of midday Moscow.

Zena, allowing herself the blissful extravagance of having someone take care of her, sank deeper into the luxurious warmth of the fur robes. She and the prince were veritable strangers, she knew, despite the incredible events of the previous night; yet she had an uncommon feeling of closeness to him. (The intimacy of bedfellows did expedite the usual protracted maturation of an acquaintanceship, she mused drolly.) She knew she had no right to be so happy, considering the "unacceptable" situation she found herself in, but she was. Flashing a sidelong glance at Alex out of dancing eyes, she said gaily, "Isn't the morning just marvelous?"

Having drunk a prodigious quantity of liquor over the past twenty-four hours, Alex could not view the morning with quite the same degree of exuberance as the *mademoiselle*; but, discrediting the slight headache that pounded in his temple, he did have to essentially agree. "Perfectly marvelous, my pet." (When I have talked you into my bed once again, perfection indeed, he thought smugly.) Not wishing to alter this childishly bright mood the young chit was in, but deeming it as good a time as any, Alex entreated her politely to please tell him her name once again.

Zena's eyes opened wide in surprise, she being still naïve and romantic enough to presume that one should at least remember the name of the individual with whom one has just shared such extraordinary intimacies.

Alex immediately dissembled, presenting the most outrageously woeful countenance. "Now, Bobby's name I know," he said, having heard it spoken several times that morning, "but I fear I was greatly in my cups last evening when you introduced yourself and hesitate to admit I've forgotten what you said. You see, I'm quite neglectfully poor with names. I've a memory like a sieve. Forgive me."

"Oh! Of . . . of course, lord. My name's Zena—Zena Turku."

" 'Zena'? Lovely and rare—extremely appropriate." Alex turned his eyes too quickly as he glanced toward his companion, and winced in pain. Damnable head was getting worse. He leaned back against the velvet squabs, shutting his eyes against the too-brilliant rays of the harsh winter sun. Sweet Jesus, he was tired. The peaceful country *dacha* would be welcoming indeed.

"The headache, my lord?" Zena questioned, having the past three years seen her father similarly distressed mornings without number. "Lemonade with honey used to work prodigious well for my father," she offered solicitously.

Alex mumbled something unintelligible in reply, speculating that lemonade may have relieved her father, but *his* cure tended toward a somewhat more potent remedy with alcohol as the base. Damn chit was amazing, though, he considered indulgently: no hysteria, no simpering. He was somewhat surprised. How many young *mademoiselles* would be so amiable to the rogue who had seduced them the night before? She was remarkable to have adjusted so complacently. Then an uneasy feeling stole into his brain. Was she three steps ahead of him, having planned this encounter? She *had* appeared at an extremely unlikely place at a damnably convenient time. He raised one eyelid fractionally and shot a suspicious peek at the fetching young thing next to him. Her charmingly naïve appearance immediately cast aside these misgivings. She *had* been a virgin, after all—at least that much he remembered quite vividly in the somewhat hazy recollections of last night. And good God, at the very worst what could she demand? Money? They *all* cost money. She couldn't be any more expensive than the rest. All in all, the next few weeks should be most entertaining. A young virgin to tutor in the intricacies of love was quite a change of pace from the usual style of female sharing his leisure.

Since the mumbled reply from the prince did not seem to encourage conversation, Zena lapsed into silence as the horses flew over the snow-covered road winding through quiet birch forests. Her thoughts were equally of her companion, but somewhat more confused and disarrayed then the practical considerations of the prince, who disregarded the finer delicacies of emotion and sentiment in favor of the tangible considerations of how best to have this young woman serve his purposes.

Zena knew she should be feeling very wicked and contrite for being seduced in such a cavalier manner. No apologies or polite disclaimers had passed the prince's lips. He was shockingly casual about the entire episode (Zena wished he'd been sober enough to remember her name), and she suspected she should be cold, abrupt, and frightfully offended by his arrogant treatment of her. The canons of social usage demanded it. But illogically Zena remembered only his burning touch on her flesh, the passion of her response, and the unutterable delight Alex had roused in her, rendering it quite difficult to simulate the required fervor of hateful, raging contempt. It was her first experience of joy in passion, and memories of last night swept a warmth and sweetness over her.

Could she be so immature and gullible that the prince's arrestingly handsome face and tall, muscular physique could turn her head? Was she so depraved to all the finer sensibilities that the tumultuous climax to their lovemaking could temper her opinion of the man? Was it dreadfully wrong to feel happiness at being in company with this charming, elegant prince instead of fending off the crude obscenities of General Scobloff? Somehow she was unable the summon the smallest shred of sobriety, and Zena's mouth curved into a sunny smile despite every mindful stricture of society.

Zena was free from the cruel treatment of her aunt, her young brother safely with her, and her first taste of passion pleasantly savored. Could there be any other conceivable response except the youthful exuberance she was now experiencing?

The remainder of the journey passed in silence; the prince dozed despite the swaying of the sleigh, Bobby slept comfortably, but Zena was much too ebullient to think of rest. After an hour of swift passage through pine and birch forests, Ivan halted the troika on the crest of a hill overlooking a large valley intersected by a meandering river.

As Alex's eyes opened slowly, he surveyed the familiar scene. "Ah, here at last. It's a good feeling, eh, Ivan?"

All time spent in the city was wasted, in Ivan's opinion. The froth of society had no attraction for him, and he had been waiting weeks with an iron patience for the word that would send them south. "The best place on earth, Sasha," Ivan replied familiarly, for he was more than a servant, having been a devoted friend from childhood. The ritual never changed. This was Ivan's home, and he knew it was his master's favorite retreat. They always paused at the top of the hill and exchanged the identical phrases—a cherished secular rubric upon returning home.

A tranquillity lay over the vast estate buried deep in the forests, removed from the bustle of Moscow by a two-hour drive. Every time he returned, he wondered why he had been such a fool to leave. This was the only place in the world where he really felt at peace.

While the ceremonial exchange passed between Alex and Ivan, Zena could only stare in open-eyed wonder. A magnificent estate lay beneath her gaze. An imposing neo-baroque palace sprawled majestically across acres of cleared land, surrounded by parterres, now only visible as geometric areas beneath the covering of snow. A complicated evergreen maze looked like a child's toy from this distance, and a fairy tale village of painted cottages decorated in peasant carving was set around a wooden church. "My God," breathed Zena quietly. "It's splendid! I can see why you love it here. The heroic proportions! It's colossal!" she exclaimed.

"Great-grandfather never quite understood the notion of intimacy. Great-grandpapa's conception of rustic charm approximated the royal. His idea of bucolic repose, you see, was a staff of two hundred servants and a occasional wolf hunt or stag chase to break the monotony. Except when the entire family's down, I prefer to set up housekeeping in a small *dacha* a few miles down the river road. If you'd prefer, of course," and he swept his hand toward the arresting display before them.

"Oh, no—no," Zena stammered, "your choice is entirely suitable—by all means, the *dacha*."

Zena's family home had been sufficiently grand, so a country estate of the ordinary type would not have rendered her so completely speechless. But arrayed beneath them in the shallow valley was a rather faithful rendition of Stupinigi with all its attendant garden landscaping. The regal panorama elicited visions of vast, extravagant royal hunt parties of an era long past and suggested a worldly existence of princely proportions.

"Well, Ivan, in that case, on to the *dacha*," Alex murmured.

Shortly they were driving up to an exquisite jewel of craftsman expertise. A large wooden mansion, intricately decorated in the baroque exuberance of peasant wood carving, greeted them at the end of a long driveway lined with towering pines. The windows alight, the front door thrown open, a multitude of servant muzhiks poured out to help with the arrival. Zena, somewhat overwhelmed, watched quietly as Alex jumped out to hug and kiss several of the beaming and chattering servants. He returned to help Zena and Bobby out of the troika and, holding the slightly awake young child in his arms, introduced Zena to all the cordial, amicable servants.

"This is Bobby," he then explained with a warm smile, "who was extremely ill last night and needs some rest and care." A sympathetic murmur of concern rose from the crowd.

A tall, dignified butler detached himself from the crush, stepped forward, and his sober face broke into a smile as he solemnly stated, "May I express our pleasure, my lord, at having you back."

"It's good to be back, Trevor, I assure you," Alex exhaled happily in return. The prodigal son, Zena thought, feeling very much alone amid the happy crowd, but then Alex turned his warm smile on her and washed away the loneliness. "Come, Zena, I'll show you around."

Alex proudly exhibited the rustic charms of his twenty-room *dacha*, each room aglow with polished wood, hand-crafted furniture, embroidered lace, and tapestries. Hothouse flowers from the greenhouses at the main estate adorned every room so that one forgot for a moment that it was January, their pungent perfumes sweetly wafting through the warm firelit rooms. Fur rugs scattered atop and beside museum-quality oriental rugs on the highly polished wooden floors vied in opulence with jeweled and enamaled icons twinkling in the subdued winter light. To further add to the powerful sense of phenomenal, luxurious affluence, Zena beheld servants at every turn; each whim was anticipated, every desire fulfilled. One need never open a door nor pull aside a curtain; if one dropped one's handkerchief, three devoted, beaming muzhiks jumped to retrieve it.

The short tour sufficed, allowing Zena a general understanding of the direction of most rooms. She and Bobby would be installed in adjoining rooms on the second floor. The prince's suite was situated next to hers with a connecting door. The prince offered no explanation concerning this arrangement and Zena demurred comment, not wishing to appear difficult and ungrateful. She could always lock the door between the rooms, she thought, if Prince Alex was inclined to disregard his promise to honor her reputation.

"Now, first we must eat, and by then the doctor should be here. I left word in Moscow to have Dr. Anechev drive out immediately to examine Bobby. He should be here within the hour."

"Thank you very much," Zena responded gratefully.

"Think nothing of it, my dear," Alex shrugged off the thanks with a cheerful smile.

Bobby had been surveying Alex with quiet, wide-eyed attention during the house tour. The three-year-old still in his arms, Alex inquired, "What's your favorite food? Tell me and we'll have cook make it."

"Ice cream," the little voice piped up without hesitation.

"Ice cream—very good choice. It's one of my favorites as well. Since that might take a bit of time to prepare, let's have a second choice. What else do you like?"

"Black cake," with the high-pitched, emphatic reply.

"He means chocolate cake," Zena interpreted.

"That's available, I'm sure. Come, Bobby, I'll find you a chair and we'll eat black cake."

As Alex settled Bobby at the table in a chair piled high with cushions, a maid was given the command to produce some chocolate cake as soon as possible. "And tell Valentina we'd like a light luncheon, too. Maybe we could squeeze some more nourishing food into Bobby between bites of ice cream and black cake, if we're lucky," Alex teased Zena softly. Then, in a more serious tone, he added, "You look tired. Please sit down." Alex offered Zena a chair and patted her shoulder avuncularly as she sank into the softness of the down cushions.

"Thank you so very much," Zena expressed once again. She was so appreciative of his taking responsibility, however briefly. For several years now she had had to be strong, responsible, and sensible, both mother and father to Bobby. She hadn't realized how strenuous and demanding the task was until the present, when this short respite from duty was offered, and the taxing strain was lightened by the kind solicitude of Prince Alex. It was dangerous, no doubt, to become indebted to this charming prince, she thought, but she was so weary and young to have shouldered so many obligations for so long. She'd cast pragmatic considerations aside just for the moment and allow herself the luxury of being taken care of.

"Please don't keep saying thank you. It unnerves the hell out of me." Alex smiled with disarming grace. "It's the simplest thing to offer you the hospitality of my *dacha* until Bobby is well," he assured Zena smoothly.

The most dishonorable intentions underlay his easy hospitality, but he had plenty of time to move into the young chit's bed. The prince contented himself with putting Zena at ease for the moment. For a green virgin she had been a damnable hot piece. Before long he'd be enjoying her again, he told himself. Alex's self-assurance had been amply reinforced over the years by a plentitude of amorous females in hot pursuit. The unlimited Kuzan fortune alone would have been enough to insure a steady stream of eager women. When combined with the devastating Kuzan looks and charm, his lean, powerful physique, and— perhaps most indispensible and democratically revered by all females—a reputation for stamina in bed, Alex had always enjoyed a profligate's pick from the beauties of his day. Surely one could understand how Alex had acquired a taste for having things his own way.

The black cake arrived promptly, followed by a sumptuous luncheon that everyone enjoyed, including Bobby. The ice cream appeared within the hour, piled in a silver bowl cushioned with crushed ice. The food eased Alex's painfully drumming temples slightly, but what he really needed was some sleep.

"Could I suggest a short nap? I'm hellishly tired. Didn't get much sleep last night." Too late he caught his tongue as Zena's face flushed a rosy hue. Further commentary would only serve to exacerbate the embarrassing slip, so he continued unabashed, "Please feel free to ask the servants for anything you wish. If you'll excuse me, I'm going to rest."

The flush had diminished somewhat on Zena's fair complexion as she determinedly adapted to Alex's casual attitude, and she resolved with ingenuous pluck to present a mien equally nonchalant.

"I think Bobby and I'll nap soon. We'll wait for the doctor first."

"I'd forgotten about him. Sounds sensible. Until this evening, then." Alex wearily pushed his chair from the table, offered Zena a brief smile, rose and grabbed a bottle of brandy from the sideboard as he passed from the dining room He reflected whimsically on the possibility that *if mademoiselle* would care to keep him company during his nap; he *might* be able to muster the necessary energy to . . .

6

The doctor soon appeared and prescribed rest, warm broths, and steaming for Bobby's chest. Having nursed this same malady numerous times in the past two years since Bobby had been diagnosed as having "weak lungs," Zena was familiar with the regimen for the convalescence, and considerably relieved to be assured that the inflammation had not progressed to the stage of pneumonia.

Bobby and Zena both fell asleep after the doctor left, waking in late afternoon. Several hours later when Alex rose from his rest, he found Zena and Bobby in the young boy's room. Zena was relaxing in a comfortable chair and smiling delightfully at the chubby, dark-haired, rosy-cheeked three-year-old. Bobby was seated in the middle of the floor, happily surrounded by a vast number and variety of toys that Mariana had fetched from the nursery.

"I see Mariana has found the toys," Alex remarked as he entered the doorway. Zena turned to see her host leaning casually against the doorjamb, arms crossed on his chest. He was attired in elegantly tailored, pearl gray slacks and an immaculately white, open-neck shirt that partially displayed a muscular, dark-haired chest. The prince was undeniably virile, Zena noted with a small leap of her heart. It was impossible to remain impartial to his good looks.

"Yes, Mariana's been very helpful. Bobby hasn't ever seen so many toys," Zena replied quickly, attempting to assume a civil equanimity in the presence of her boldly handsome seducer.

Whose toys were these? Zena pondered uneasily, recalling the prince's remark in which he acknowledged having children. Could his offspring be here at the *dacha*, Zena speculated uncomfortably, or perhaps he brought them out on visits? For some unexplicable reason, these musings evoked a sharp twinge of jealousy. Shaking herself mentally, Zena reminded herself pointedly that their acquaintance was of less than twenty-four hours. She was a silly fool to react in any way to Prince Alex's mode of life.

"I see my little sister's toys are once more of some use. Bobby seems to be enjoying himself," Alex said amiably. He pushed away from the doorjamb, moved into the room, sank down on the floor next to Bobby, and began assembling an intricate ferris wheel.

Inexplicably and despite her sober attempt to maintain an unruffled mental calm, Zena's disposition altered irresistibly to a most piquant cheerfulness. "You have a young sister?" she inquired with incisive interest.

"Yes, a younger sister and also two brothers and an older sister," the prince replied without looking up. Alex had captured Bobby's interest with the sizable ferris wheel and was guiding two chubby hands in manipulation of a small, wooden cross brace. "Perfect, Bobby," he encouraged as the brace finally slipped into place.

" 'Nother one, Papa. Bobby do 'nother one!" the excited young boy crowed in delight.

Zena turned crimson in embarrassment and rushed to explain, "Please excuse him, Prince Alex. Since our father died, he indiscriminately calls anyone in pants *Papa*. It's quite awkward."

"It's perfectly all right," Alex soothed politely, reassuring Zena, who was so obviously distressed by the faux pas. God, it's an age since I've seen a woman blush, he thought. And it was devilishly pretty on her. The women he'd been entertaining himself with lately were too jaded, world-wise, and too beyond embarrassment to blush. It was a refreshing change from the scenes he was all too familiar with between a man with seduction on his mind and a woman prepared to be seduced. "When one has been raised," he continued, "with four brothers and sisters, all given to outrageous behavior, one finds nothing the least bit startling—least of all a three-year-old child. I'm sure he sorely misses his father," Alex added gravely, fully conscious of how fortunate he had been to have the warmth and affection of a loving family.

Zena's expression had become inexpressibly pensive as profound impressions of loneliness engulfed her. Both her parents were gone forever and, although he was precious to her, Bobby couldn't fill the void of companionship sometimes so achingly real.

Alex saw the bleakness of her face and, in a considerate attempt to divert the morose direction of Zena's mood, coaxed gently, "Come, help us. We need another pair of hands to construct this God-awful, complicated apparatus. Move over, Bobby; make room for your sister."

Bobby obliged obediently, patting the carpet next to him. "Here, Zena, here, by me. We make giant wheel," and he threw his arms wide to emphasize his statement.

Zena flashed a warm smile at her young brother's enthusiasm, forcibly set aside her melancholy, and rose to join the assembly crew on the floor. Ten minutes later the entire wheel was complete, and small wooden passengers were enjoying a wildly reckless ride as Bobby twirled the wheel with vigor.

Mariana interrupted this cozy scene *en famille* when she appeared with Bobby's supper. After laying the invalid's fare out on a low table, she cajoled Bobby into a small chair and attempted to help him with his meal.

"Papa help, Papa help!" Bobby insisted loudly and closed his lips tightly as Mariana tried to put a spoon of

porridge into his mouth. Zena winced in embarrassment
again as Bobby screamed for his "Papa," but the little
maid was the model of decorum as she looked hesitantly at
the prince.

"Here, give me the spoon. I'll feed Bobby, Mariana.
Would you tell Trevor to bring up some champagne when
you leave?" Alex seated himself on a very small chair designed to accommodate children, forcing his long legs to
one side to avoid upsetting the table. "Open wide, now,
Bobby," Alex enticed, a spoon of porridge poised high in
the air, and the game commenced.

Trevor brought chilled champagne, poured two glasses,
and withdrew. Zena lounged on the floor, enjoying the
sport at the small supper table. She chuckled silently at
the incongruous sight of the enormous prince balanced on
the fragile chair. Bobby giggled while Alex zoomed food
into the baby mouth. The young child occasionally insisted that Alex eat some porridge, too. With infinite good
nature the prince consumed several spoonfuls of porridge
until the food on the tray was disposed of. Bobby returned
to his toys on the floor while Alex unraveled his long legs
to lounge on the floor next to Zena.

"Porridge and champagne isn't exactly my idea of *haute
cuisine*," he grimaced jestingly. "I must request your utter
secrecy in regard to this gourmet blend, for if any of my
friends get wind of it, I can envision hundreds of bowls of
porridge appearing at the most awkward moments in the
future. Practical joking assumes monumental proportions in
my bizarre coterie of friends, as boredom plagues them so."

"Never fear, sir, you can trust my discretion completely.
Although," Zena giggled softly, "your stoic look of resig-
nation was marvelously funny as you manfully swallowed
all those spoons of porridge." The memory forced her to
giggle again. Had she drunk too much champagne already,
she wondered briefly, or was it just pleasurable to laugh
again after so long?

"Over the years I have quite regularly found myself in ridiculous situations, so laugh all you like, my dear; I'm absolutely immune." Alex chided in cheerful, high spirits as he refilled their glasses. In this delightfully warm proximity, Zena and Alex drank three bottles of champagne, although the prince accounted for more than two bottles himself, while Bobby entertained himself with the huge assortment of toys.

As the third bottle was emptied, Zena tucked Bobby into bed, and she and Alex proceeded downstairs to the dining room, where a bounteous table was laid out for their meal. Alex continued drinking as he ate. Zena noted with some alarm that he was starting on his second bottle of wine since the meal began.

Observing the anxious glance as he broached the second bottle, Alex blandly explained, "It's common gossip that I'm very reliable until my sixth bottle. Rest assured, my pet, I never become difficult," and he smiled warmly to dispense the lie, for, as any of a score of close friends would attest, Alex could become difficult on the slightest provocation, with or without alcohol. Perverse intractability had bred true through generations of Kuzans.

As the meal progressed, Alex, in one of his most expansive moods (not necessarily the result of several bottles of wine but more pertinently related to the fact that a most ravishing, delectable young woman was seated opposite him at the small table in front of the fireplace), regaled Zena with engaging anecdotes and gossip about the St. Petersburg *ton*. He was witty, clever, unutterably *dégagé*, charming the young woman as easily as all the other women in his life. His enchanting gallantry wasn't contrived; on the contrary, Alex had from a very early age adored women, and, this frank, genuine admiration of the female species was his most effective and irresistible asset. Every woman melted before this unabashed flattery, and Alex, in turn, enjoyed women with unalloyed delight.

This sweet young thing would be his very soon, he calculated, but he saw no need to rush her. His promise to not touch her had been offered honorably, but his intent was the reverse. If (and to his mind, the *if* was merely a question of time) the *mademoiselle* should make the first move, it behooved him as a gentleman to respond to her initiative.

In this delicious little game of seduction Alex was simply laying the groundwork: warm proximity; amiable conversation; soothing comfort when problems such as Bobby's health arose; dazzling charm; and that most potent of weapons, the undercurrent of desire that flamed repeatedly in his tawny eyes and wrapped Zena like encroaching wisps of warm mist.

The memories of passion shared evoked potent forces within Zena's mind, which she deliberately thrust aside, finding the images too disquieting to contemplate. In an attempt to gain some control over these dangerous, insidious impulses and the ambience of the conversation that was becoming too ardently perilous, Zena abruptly inquired "Tell me, my lord, do you agree or disagree with the notion of a *duma* with peasant representation."

Alex hid a satisfied smile behind his raised wine glass, all too aware of the reason for Zena's sudden shift in conversation. With the address of a consummate stalker, unhurried and confident of the outcome, Alex eased smoothly into disinterested avuncularity, which obviously calmed the young *mademoiselle*. He answered seriously, "It's only a matter of time before a *duma*, a working *duma*, must become a reality. Absolute autocracy is fast becoming an untenable anachronism as we approach the twentieth century. Since the peasantry comprise a vast majority of this country, yes, it's essential that they have representation in the *duma*."

The prince cheerfully pandered to the desire of the young chit to bring the topics of conversation back onto safe, respectable ground, and a vivacious discussion of the relative merits of representative monarchy occupied the time as the prince continued to drink himself into a well-mannered, affable intoxication.

"The emperor isn't exactly the quick-witted paragon of intellectualism one could wish for in . . ." Alex was saying in explanation of the reactionary tendencies that were hindering the formation of even a diluted form of representative government when an emphatic, slightly strident female voice was heard very clearly from the hallway through the closed double doors of the dining room.

"I insist on seeing him, I tell you! I insist!" the woman's voice demanded, rising dangerously near a scream.

With only the slightest pause to indicate that he had heard the high-pitched demand, Alex continued urbanely, ". . . a monarch. The tsar is also, unfortunately, under the influence of Von Plehve, who has exceedingly reactionary notions. I could but wish that Witte had not fallen from favor. He was always a mitigating instrument against the harsh repression so prevalent at court. Do you care for Witte, my dear, or do you find him too much of a merchant?"

Zena found the disturbance in the hall a bit difficult to ignore, but was attempting an answer to Alex's question, when the doors quickly slid open and shut and Trevor slipped into the room and hastily approached Alex. Bending low, he whispered rapidly in Alex's ear, while Zena, a mere two feet away, couldn't help but catch snatches of his brisk sentences.

"A certain female," he said with a sniff of disdain, "wouldn't take no, my lord," and Trevor's haughty face pursued in annoyance, "very angry, I'm afraid," he explained anxiously.

The prince acknowledged the information with the barest of nods, uttered one crisp sentence in which Zena heard the words *my suite*, thanked Trevor curtly, and ordered some brandy and coffee.

As Trevor left to carry out his directions, Alex smiled apologetically. "Excuse me, my dear, a minor misunderstanding. All is reconciled. Now, where were we? Oh, yes—do tell me your opinion of Witte."

Zena was engulfed in a violent emotional mosaic composed equally of curiosity, chagrin, and malice, but she smothered these sensations to muster a response to the prince, who obviously wasn't going to confide in her about the noisy events in the hall.

Over brandy and coffee Alex continued the conviviality of the perfect host, explaining in detail his family's interest in the peasant villages adjacent to their estates and the function and usefulness of the peasant councils.

Unaccountably, Zena was irritated at the thought of some woman waiting for Alex in his suite. She acknowledged purposefully that it was none of her concern how Alex spent his evenings; nevertheless, she derived an unwonted degree of pleasure from the fact that Alex evidently was in no rush to appear upstairs.

Feminine instinct took over, producing an illusive transmutation in Zena's behavior, fostering the faintest aura of enticement. This subtle change did not go unnoticed by the prince, who was long familiar with the full gamut of feminine competitiveness. It was enchanting to see the hesitant, unsophisticated allure so tentatively offered. Alex stayed quite some time enjoying Zena's captivating company. He was, after all, fully apprised of who was upstairs in his suite, and he knew that Mrs. Askov would wait.

Zena sipped on her coffee; after Alex consumed several glasses of brandy, he suggested they retire for the night. "Let's check on Bobby and then I'll see you to your room," Alex offered. After seeing that Bobby was peacefully sleeping. Alex walked Zena to her bedroom door, stepped close, and lifted her face, as though he might kiss her good night. He was so close she could see the pulse beating evenly against the smooth, bronzed throat. He gave her a rather searching look, but his hand fell away, and he laughed softly, "Such a temptation, my pet, but I promised not to touch. Good night, Zena," and bowing briefly he turned and walked down the hall to his room next door. It had taken all the self-control he possessed not to bend down and kiss those beautiful, trembling lips.

Zena was left standing susceptible and bewildered, having wanted Alex to kiss her while simultaneously feeling it wasn't really right for her to feel that way. Alex reached his door and opened it; a yellow beam of light spread into the hallway, and Zena winced as she heard a breathy, inviting feminine voice cry out, "Sasha, my love!"

"Tamara, *mon ange,*" Alex intoned warmly, "what a pleasant surprise."

The door closed with a tiny click, and Zena stood alone in the dimly lit hall, burning with an unspeakably black rage. Flouncing into her room, she tossed off her clothes and tumbled into the huge feather bed, but sleep eluded her; for quite some time she lay there wakeful, staring into the dark as the muted sounds from the adjacent room bombarded her reluctant ears. *Mon ange* was decidedly vocal in her passion, and the moans of pleasure and cries of delight assailed the senses of the furious woman lying next door. Damn slut, Zena cursed rancorously, couldn't she shut up, and, as if on cue, no sound could be heard but the rhythmic creaking of the bed. The persistent cadence hammered at her eardrums. Would it never end! she disgruntledly raged. Moans of ecstasy from female lips rose above the sound. Silence. All was quiet fractionally, then all too soon the feminine cries of rapture began again.

Zena indignantly covered her head with two pillows, burrowing into the soft mattress, cried quiet tears of frustration, and presently worn out from the long day and manifold extremes of emotion, fell into a restless sleep.

7

Bobby woke her up at a respectable nine o'clock after Mariana could restrain him no longer. Zena dressed quickly in her only dress, smoothing out the wrinkles on the skirt as best she could. Then she and Bobby proceeded downstairs for breakfast.

The morning meal was being served in a sunny little parlor at the back of the *dacha*. It was a gloriously beautiful January day with a brilliant sun sparkling on the snow.

About an hour later Zena and Bobby were finishing breakfast, when a wan, slow-moving Prince Alex, dressed in buckskins and a muzhik shirt, entered the room and dropped wearily into a chair, disposing his long legs and bare feet into an extended sprawl. Trevor hovered over the prince solicitously, offering the great variety of dishes available, but Alex waved them all away and gruffly ordered hot coffee with lots of cream and a small tot of brandy. Bobby had crawled down from his chair when the prince appeared and now stood in front of Alex solemnly surveying the half-slumped form. Zena eyed the prince balefully. He was an unutterable picture of exhaustion this morning; his long, raven hair was disarranged, his face was pale though shaved, and the dark circles under his eyes were painfully obvious.

"Papa play with Bobby!" the little boy demanded and began pulling on Alex's hand, which draped limply over one arm of the chair.

"Leave the prince alone, Bobby," Zena snapped irritably. "He's obviously tired," she peevishly continued, unable to hide the resentment in her voice.

Alex lifted one eyebrow quizzically in response to the patent ill humor of his guest but let the cutting remark pass, too fatigued before his coffee and brandy to enter into any verbal sparring. Little bitch, he thought with a mild testiness, if you would have tumbled for me, I would have gladly sent Tamara on her way.

"Papa, Papa, play!" Bobby persisted, heedless of Zena's remonstrances.

Alex pulled the little boy up into his lap and whispered in his ear. Bobby's eyes widened in excitement. Immediately the young child tumbled off Alex's lap and scurried out of the room as fast as his sturdy little legs permitted, calling for Mariana at the top of his lungs.

"What was that all about?" Zena inquired coolly.

"Come, sit in my lap, and I'll whisper in your ear," Alex teased provocatively, relishing the sparkling flash of anger spilling from Zena's vivid eyes.

"I most certainly will not!" Zena tartly replied. "Don't think we're all like *mon ange*," she finished acerbically.

Alex narrowed his eyes consideringly and softly murmured, "No, my pet, not like *mon ange* at all—you're much, much better," and his mouth lifted into a mocking smile.

"Oh!" Zena exhaled indignantly, speechlessly infuriated at the bold crudeness, but seconds later she dropped her lashes sheepishly before the knowing leer Alex bestowed on her. The memory of her ready responses on the train from St. Petersburg made argument awkward.

Trevor interrupted with the brandy, which he poured into coffee au lait and handed to his master. Zena bit her tongue on the angry retort she would have liked to make, while Alex seemed oblivious to her as he sipped the warm drink, eyes closed, his head resting heavily against the chair cushion.

Within minutes of drinking the hot liquid, he knew his heart had begun pumping again, and Alex conceded optimistically that perhaps he wouldn't collapse this morning. Mrs. Askov was too damn demanding. He'd have to either see her more often so that she wouldn't be so ravenously insatiable, or he'd have to give up seeing her at all. In the ambivalent position she now occupied in his life, Mrs. Askov would exhaust a regiment of rapacious recruits. Lord, he was tired!

A beaming Bobby preceded Mariana and two footmen into the room. The men carried an enormous wooden rocking horse accoutered with a diminutive saddle and silver-embellished bridle. Real horsehair flowed from the mane and tail, while the trompe l'oeil painting of the hide was meticulously accurate to the smallest vein.

The hubbub of the small cavalcade served to lever the prince's eyelids open a scant quarter inch, but the squeals of elation from Bobby as he was lifted into place induced the eyes to open fully. A smile of unalloyed delight appeared on Alex's face as he viewed the toddler riding the horse with utterly reckless abandon. It enhances the melancholy of the world, Alex thought, smiling, to see it occasionally through the enchanted eyes of a child; he wondered whimsically whether old Pasha enjoyed being brought out of retirement.

Zena's heart warmed to the prince for his thoughtfulness and attention to her young brother, and she forgave him marginally for having kept her awake half the night with his paramour's squeals. Sh experienced a desire to reach out and brush back the soft dark curls from Alex's forehead or to touch her fingers lightly to his ashen, fatigued face. She felt peculiarly undone by his pale vulnerability. It was really very kind of him to even appear downstairs this early after the long night he had endured. Immediately the direction of her thoughts created a strange yearning in her fledgling emotions that flustered and confounded.

Alex played "tired Papa" with Bobby after the novelty of the rocking horse had paled. The game very simply consisted of Bobby crawling all over Alex while he lay on the floor recuperating his strength. More toys were brought downstairs, and each new addition was consideringly discussed and demonstrated by the lounging prince.

By lunchtime Alex's youthful reserves of energy were rejuvenating his powerful body. Zena's sensual beauty, so close he could almost touch her as she participated in the games with Bobby, necessitated a change of position, as his buckskins became extremely uncomfortable. Alex rolled on his stomach to hide the erection. In deference to modesty he passed the greater part of the afternoon in this prone position, although he wondered vaguely why he was restraining himself when he would have much preferred tossing up Zena's skirts and plunging into her right there on the floor. Alex was astonished, libertine that he was, to discover he apparently was harboring some dubious scruples. He was surprised at his generosity of spirit.

The enigmatic incredulity of uncovering previously unknown reserves of principle was too much to contemplate with the God-awful hangover he had, so the remainder of the afternoon passed restfully and uncomplicated by additional reflection.

Alex would frequently offer advice to Zena and Bobby in assembling some of the toys, sometimes reaching out a long arm to help find a difficult puzzle piece, sometimes resting his head on his arms and dozing occasionally. He also quite regularly studied Zena through dark downcast lashes, which affected his erection even more urgently as he took in the details of her fair, porcelain face, the charming intonations of her soft, mellifluous voice, and the innocent impudence of her bounteous, saucy breasts, which fit into her aquamarine dress no better today than yesterday. He'd have to buy her some clothes, he thought, deeming it perfectly permissible for his gaze to admire those fine breasts, but with an uncustomary male possessiveness unique to his former unreserved habits.

Zena, too, in guarded glances viewed the incredibly attractive man sprawled so near her. Every nerve in her body was conscious of his presence, and if she had dared, she would have reached out and touched him. When he dozed fitfully, she drank in the lithe lines of the lean form encased in buckskin straining against leg muscles. She admired the rippling power beneath the fine linen shirt stretched across brawny shoulders, and she was enchanted by the soft black waves of hair that fell over his fine cheekbones. And those heavy black lashes—my lord, they were indecently long for a man!

As the day wore on, the prince, being driven to a torturous state of affairs by the casual proximity of a gorgeous female he had promised not to touch, was racking his mind for an escape from this dilemma. His erection was under him, pressed between the floor and his stomach, engorged, strained, crazy for relief. Your cock is throbbing and hard, and you're doing nothing about it, you fool, he thought.

He had given his word on the train in a casual but not altogether benevolent fashion, and honor demanded that as a gentleman he was obliged to keep his word, but damn it all, he couldn't walk around with a constant erection. Much as he would be enchanted to regard the *mademoiselle* with benign friendship and observe his word, he was only human. This was the first time in his life he had ever denied himself a woman. And he was denying himself now because manners decried the necessity, honor must be served. Damn! He wasn't capable of this brotherly coexistence.

Fortunately the indelible streak of ruthlessness that had served the reprobate Kuzans so faithfully for more than a thousand years obligingly reminded him that he was an aristocrat and a prince. When one had the good fortune to possess power in the world, reasonableness, decorum, and propriety were as expendable and irrelevant as yesterday's brioche. He was a nobleman, for Christ's sake, one thousand years of arrogant breeding insisted. He didn't need manners!

His dilemma mercilessly disposed of, all scruples be damned, the prince smiled faintly as he dozed on the floor and set his mind on contriving exactly when and where he would empty this insistent throbbing erection into the delicate young miss seated opposite him. No guilt. The world, like a fine wine or a fine woman, was meant for his pleasure. It was his for the taking. Regardless of the mixed blood and diverse passions evident in the lineage of Kuzan males through the centuries, in one characteristic, in one particular attribute of their ancestry, all were in firm accord—their moral scruples were rudimentary.

8

Glancing up quickly, a small, pleased smile playing across his handsome features, Alex startled Zena, who was scrutinizing him in a most ill-bred fashion. A gleam appeared in his eyes, and his smile broadened into a warm, appealing grin as color surged into the young lady's cheeks before she hastily looked away. Eminently experienced in the pursuit of females, the prince swiftly and correctly assessed the maiden's state of mind. It appeared, he was disposed to think pleasantly, that the attraction was mutual.

Zena felt a frisson of alarm and pleasure and, with a determined effort, attempted to resist looking at the prince for the remainder of the afternoon, but occasionally her eyes would slip in his direction and be captured by his distracting, tawny gaze. When Alex suggested a sleigh ride to entertain Bobby, Zena grasped eagerly at the invitation, hoping to divert the very uncomfortable, disquieting focus of her thoughts.

It was impossible to ignore the sensuous masculinity of Prince Alex, and Zena's agitated reason leaped at the opportunity to cast off the spell of his vital sensuality. The cold, brisk winter air and a variety of interesting sights to show Bobby would shatter this awesome enchantment Alex's powerful presence was spinning around her.

"A sleigh ride sounds marvelous!" Zena exclaimed, somewhat too brittlely, as she jumped up in a restless flurry.

The little filly was jibbing at the sight of the bridle, Alex ruminated metaphorically. It had been easier to mount her the first time, he thought drolly. She was damnably frightened now of where her feelings would take her, it appeared. Never rush a temperamental filly, he cautioned himself. He preferred a willing partner, but his aching testicles reminded him—willing or unwilling—it better be damned soon.

Presently they were all snugly settled in the sleigh. Ivan drove them to the village that had been visible from the hill yesterday. When they stopped in the tiny village square, the sleigh was surrounded by smiling, chattering peasants. Prince Alex was obviously as fondly adored by the village peasants as he was by the household servants.

The prince had a cheerful word for everyone, calling each by name, and gossip flew furiously for twenty minutes as Alex inquired and was assessed of the happenings since his last visit two months previously. Bobby sat alertly intent, taking in the wildly jabbering crowd and the roaring guffaws as a joke was bandied about, and he noticed the small children who pushed up to the sleigh and stared at him in return.

"I'll be staying for a while," Alex assured the pleased throng of peasants. "Before the *baryshna* ['young miss'] and baby become chilled, we're on our way." He waved to the parting crowd, and soon the silent forest once again surrounded them as the road wound through dark pines.

"You're obviously well thought of by the villagers," Zena remarked as they sped through the deepening shadows of the evening twilight.

"I've spent a lot of time here as I grew up, and since my parents gave the estate to me on my sixteenth birthday I've lived here many months every year, enjoying the peace and tranquility." Glancing down at Bobby, Alex smiled. "See the tranquility. He's almost sleeping again."

"A carriage or a sleigh ride always produces the same

results. Bobby's still almost a baby," said Zena. "Although," she sighed blissfully, "the quiet, snow-covered forest is indeed restful."

"By the way," Alex remarked, apropos a subject very much on his mind, "I left instructions to have the sauna heated while we were gone. In my youth whenever I had a croupy cold the sauna was kept heated around the clock, and I was whisked in periodically to relieve the congestion. My colds always succumbed to the sauna treatment. If you care to take Bobby in before he goes to sleep, I guarantee he'll spend a peaceful night."

"That's a good idea. Thank you again for thinking of Bobby," Zena remarked gratefully. She was always somewhat surprised at the polite concern the prince showed for her young brother.

As if in answer to her unspoken speculation, Alex retorted affably, "I've always had younger brothers and sisters, so I am quite familiar with children underfoot. *Your* childhood must have been quiet with no screaming, yelling crowds of siblings constantly in attendance, unlike mine. Was it lonely?" Alex inquired sincerely.

"I never thought of myself as lonely when I was a child," Zena replied reflectively. "My parents spent a great deal of time with me. Don't laugh now," she said lightly, "but my father called us The Three Musketeers. I really had a very happy childhood."

"The Three Musketeers? No!"

"Yes, I'm afraid so." Zena smiled. "He was quite incorrigibly romantic at times. In fact, my father fell in love with my mother in a thoroughly unconventional way. Papa first saw *Maman* on one of his trips into the mountains when researching the migration routes of the Finno-Ugrian tribes. My parents fell in love at first sight, and Papa simply carried her away."

"Carried your *Maman* away? Just like that?" The prince flashed a critical look upon the *mademoiselle*.

"It's very acceptable," Zena explained, "in the traditions of the mountain tribes. You capture your bride but ultimately pay the family for her. So *Maman* was all paid for right and proper, and *Maman* and Papa never needed anyone but each other. They hardly socialized at all, preferring their own company to that of relatives and neighbors. I think that's why Papa collapsed so completely when *Maman* died giving birth to Bobby. He quite literally couldn't exist without her. In the years after her death he was rarely sober. Reality without *Maman* was too much for him to face. He blamed himself for her pregnancy. If it weren't for him, he'd say over and over, she'd still be alive."

As the poignant memories of those difficult years were revived, Zena's beautiful blue eyes filled with tears. At the time, she had simply reacted, doing what was necessary to raise Bobby and to comfort her father, but it had been a dreadful, melancholy time. She sadly missed her parents. Zena was still only eighteen.

When Alex noted the trembling lips, he reached over and drew her into his arms. "The memories are too painful, *dushka*. Cry and you'll feel better," he murmured gently. He felt old and protective looking down on the unhappy girl. Maybe he should send her on to the grandfather in the mountains. Perhaps it would be the decent thing to do. She'd had a difficult life the past few years. He glanced down again, taking in the flawless beauty and feeling her warm body beneath his hands. The attack of conscience fled before a wave of healthy lust. Hell! He didn't feel that old and protective.

At the comforting words and strong arms holding her close, Zena's reserve broke, and the tears she had refused to succumb to in the past spilled over; she quietly cried for all the miseries and gloom endured in the past three years. Today for the first time she allowed herself to relax the de-

termined steadfastness that had given her the fortitude to
resist utter despair in her situation.

Turning Zena gently in his embrace, Alex pressed her
cheek against his chest as the tears soaked into his jacket.
After several minutes the sobs subsided, and he raised her
face from his shoulder and wiped away the wetness with
his handkerchief.

"Better now, right? I did my share of crying when I was
a child, and it always helped."

Mutely Zena looked up and attempted a smile of gratitude. "You're very kind," she whispered.

"At the risk of extreme impertinence," he murmured
softly, "it seems to me, my little dove, that you really need
someone to take care of you." Zena's eyes opened in startled alarm. "Now, now, don't get excited," Alex admonished conciliatorily, as he flashed her a smile, "it's just a
passing thought. Your responsibilities have been considerable the past years; that's all I was thinking."

Zena relaxed and returned the smile. "I'll be fine, really.
Forgive me, I usually don't give in to emotional outbursts
like that. I'm feeling much better now. Don't worry, I'm
so used to coping with responsibility, I'll manage very
well. When Bobby's chest cold is better we'll find my
grandfather, and he'll help us, I know." Realizing with
some embarrassment that she was still in the prince's arms,
Zena drew back awkwardly, and Alex tactfully withdrew
his arms.

In some ways, Alex thought, she was still a child with
a naïveté in facing the world that bespoke a sheltered existence. In other ways she had been forced into a painful
maturity beyond her years in coping with a small baby, an
inaccessible father, and a malevolent aunt. You may think
you can manage, my sweet, Alex continued to reflect, but
unfortunately the world is full of repacious vultures waiting to pounce on such a succulent morsel as yourself. And
with a cold, practiced rationality, he decided Zena would

be treated more gently under his protection. There was a soft vulnerability about her that touched even his cynical soul. Better me than them, he thought with practical candor. "Of course, my dear, whatever you think," he affably conceded. The agreeable mendacity caused him not the least qualm of conscience. Little chit was appallingly innocent; to be perfectly, bluntly honest about it, the role of protector to this guileless and beautiful maid was a function he was looking forward to with undeniable pleasure. He'd tenderly teach her the game of love and indulge her every whim. What pleasure she'd bring to him—such maidenly virtues, such artless innocence, was the ultimate eroticism—a decidedly refreshing change from the bizarre, decadent dissipation so symptomatic of his life-style.

"Now tell me," he said briskly, "what did your nanny feed you when things weren't going right? What childhood food comforts you most? Hot chocolate and toast? Rice pudding with cinnamon and milk? Strawberry tarts with cream? Name it and Valentina will make it for your supper. I'm a firm believer in indulging oneself when life becomes gloomy. I suppose it's black cake again for Bobby. After supper you take Bobby into the sauna, and his cold will be much improved in the morning. I assure you. Come, *dushka*, lean back, we're almost home." Alex carefully placed his arm around Zena's shoulders and snuggled her close. She didn't pull away. He exhaled softly in relief. "Warm enough?" he leaned over to inquire, his smile indulgent.

"Oh, yes," Zena sighed contentedly. "Just perfect." She sank back against his shoulder. "Warm blueberry muffins with lots of butter," she breathed serenely.

"Pardon, my dear?" Alex bent low to catch the soft murmur.

"Warm blueberry muffins with melting butter, *that's* what I want," she dreamily replied.

"Blueberry muffins it is, then! This evening's meal is

going to be a gourmand's nightmare, because I've a craving for biscuits de Reims and champagne, and you can be damned sure black cake will be required by the youngest member of this group."

Zena gurgled, her tears forgotten.

"Luckily my cook and pastry chef aren't temperamental. Home quickly, Ivan! We're getting hungry!"

Zena rested in the satisfying warmth of Alex's embrace and reflected pleasantly but with an underlying trepidation that he was like a friend, a mother, a father, and a lover, all comfort and kindness and security. She sighed wistfully. It was very hard to resist his charming ways. Simultaneously, Alex was calculating pragmatically, *All I have to do is be a friend, a mother, a father, and a gentle lover.* With practiced confidence he knew she would soon succumb to his charming ways. He'd wait no longer. Tonight she would be his.

Alex had always gone to any lengths to get what he wanted, and the prize was so tantalizing near. Making love in the sauna *was*, after all, one of his favorite and most gratifying forms of amusement, the most notorious rake in St. Petersburg mused.

9

After their meal Zena brought Bobby into the sauna, and they took steam until Bobby's breathing was clear and relaxed. An hour later Zena emerged from the sauna with a drowsy Bobby, and later he had been toweled dry, dressed, and had fallen half asleep on a long wooden bench, Mariana appeared.

"I'll take Bobby, my lady, and put him to bed."

"That's not necessary, Mariana; as soon as I dress I'll bring him in myself. You may go."

Mariana giggled and exchanged an uncomfortable glance with a maidservant who had just carried in an armload of fresh towels. Mariana shifted awkwardly from foot to foot but didn't leave.

Zena glanced up from toweling her damp hair. "What's amiss, Mariana?"

"Your pardon, my lady, but I'm to bring Bobby in— His Excellency's orders."

"It's so silly, really, one can hardly lift a finger for oneself around here. Oh, very well. I'm sure Prince Alex's motives are kindly."

Mariana's impish face presented an expressionless mask.

"Yes, ma'am." She bobbed and turned to pick up Bobby. Wrapping him warmly in a fur robe, she, Bobby, and the other maidservant disappeared into the cold, brisk night. A gust of sub-zero air swirled into the sultry warmth of the outer dressing room as the door shut behind them.

Zena wrapped herself in a large, soft towel and lay down on one of the wide benches. Saunas always made her lethargic, and she resolved to rest just a minute before dressing. The heated room was so comfortable that Zena relaxed indolently for quite some time before rallying her energy to return to the *dacha*. Wiping the steam from a large mirror, Zena began brushing her tousled curls in an attempt to arrange her long auburn tresses into some order. The moist, hot air caused her hair to curl riotously, and the brush kept snagging in the wavy tendrils.

"Damn!" she swore softly as the brush caught again, wrenching her hair painfully.

"Could I help, *mademoiselle*?" a familiar husky voice inquired. Zena swirled around to find Prince Alex in the dim shadows of the far wall, leaning casually against the closed door. Gasping in surprise, she quickly reached for her dress. "Allow me," the prince murmured and advanced into the small, snowbound room lit only by the rosy glow of a small stove and one lamp on a wall bracket near the mirror. He proffered a soft, azure blue woolen robe and with studious politeness held it as Zena slipped her arms in. His hand lightly brushed against the softness of her breast as he dropped his arms. Zena jumped as if burned.

Nervously tying the belt around her waist, Zena turned to face the prince and choked back a small breath as she looked up into the dark, handsome face looming above her. In the silent room only the sound of their breathing was heard.

The prince stood motionless as his pale eyes, predatory now, roamed Zena's opulent contours so startlingly revealed by the soft, clinging blue fabric. He hadn't intentionally chosen the color, having selected the first warm robe he saw from the closet reserved for his "overnight" guests, but the light shade of blue was a perfect foil for the *mademoiselle*'s shimmering, midnight blue eyes.

"Your eyes are beautiful," the prince murmured faintly.

"Quite beautiful," he amended thoughtfully. The compliment was without design—simply a spontaneous reaction, involuntarily uttered. In the dim, lamplit room, the *mademoiselle*'s luminous deep blue eyes radiated a glowing, seductive allure.

Lord, what eyes! he thought, enticing, intriguing, tantalizing, breathless. The prince knew he would not long be proof against those melting dark blue eyes that were gazing up at him, but he made a herculean effort of restraint and said urbanely, keeping his voice carefully neutral. "I was worried about you, *mademoiselle*. You hadn't returned and Bobby's been sleeping for somewhat more than twenty minutes. Nothing's wrong, is it?" he inquired pleasantly, and it took all his elf-control to keep from touching her.

"No, no, my lord," Zena stammered. "It's just so comfortably warm, and saunas always make me drowsy. I . . . I . . . just lay down to rest and the time slipped by. You needn't have worried. Really, my lord, you've been more than kind to Bobby and me." Zena lifted her gaze once again to the warm, golden eyes so firmly fixed on her, and she flushed at the message she read in their heated depths.

"As your host it's my duty to be helpful, *mademoiselle*," he replied with a frank and unaffected simplicity designed to calm the young woman's obvious trepidation, but his composed disclaimer belied the transparent sensual message in his eyes. "A duty, let me assure you, *mademoiselle*," he added with a warm smile, "I find exceedingly agreeable."

The close proximity of the prince, the ardent message in his eyes, and the sense of lithe, coiled tensile strength emanating from him caused Zena's floundering senses to flutter desperately. He casually held his hand out. Zena nervously moved back a step. An amused smile played across his fine features as he pointed languidly and said, "The brush, *mademoiselle*. I'll help with the tangles in your hair."

"Oh!" Zena squeaked skittishly. "The . . . the . . . brush," she quavered.

"Yes, *mademoiselle*, the brush if you please," Alex soothingly replied. "I promise not to hurt." The double entendre further stiffened his erection. He lost a little of his sangfroid and shifted unobtrusively.

Why had he ever been so rash as to promise not to touch her? Given her desperate circumstance, he could have struck any bargain he pleased with her. What a fool he'd been to be so charitable; such careless impetuosity was the result of being exceedingly drunk. Had he been sober, he would have been considerably more hardhearted. Christ, she was penniless and homeless, prey to any adventurer and blackguard, and what did he do?—made some goddamn noble gesture that necessitated this charade. Devil take it! Five minutes, he fulminated silently. I'll give her five minutes more, and if she hasn't fallen into my arms, integrity be damned! I'll rape her. He was amazed and disconcerted with the attendant consequences of his careless generosity on the train. Normally it wasn't his way to disturb himself over anything. His principles had always been lax, and now he was envisioning rape. Whimsically he considered the absurdity of noble gestures.

Zena handed the hairbrush over compliantly. Grasping her gently by the shoulders, Alex turned the young woman around so that her back was presented to him. He lightly brushed the long waves, stopping occasionally to undo some knotted curls.

Zena was quite sure it wasn't altogether appropriate that the prince be here brushing her hair when she was in such a state of dishabille, but he seemed to have come out of concern for her long absence. Maybe St. Petersburg's country manners were more relaxed, allowing casual encounters like this without the censure of impropriety. In any event his fingers were very gentle, and the long, slow brush strokes were soothingly pleasurable. She shut her eyes contendedly and smiled happily.

The prince noted the long, dark lashes lower with felicitous gratification. "Pardon, *mademoiselle*," Alex murmured. "This may pull a bit; a very stubborn tangle." Bending near, his warm breath touched her cheek, sending shocks down her spine as he pushed her long curls aside. His brown fingers lightly touched the back of her neck to untangle the snarl. At his touch Zena shivered as a hot glow began to spread. The prince's smile deepened. The tension of the long day in his presence, the soothing warmth of the sauna, and the delicate feel of those long, lean fingers served to kindle Zena's desire. Her slowly awakening senses made her want to touch the powerful, masculine body as she had wished to do a hundred times that day. Every quivering sensation in her body yearned for the seductively magnetic nobleman while he blandly and coolly, with a civil cordiality, resumed brushing her hair. This piqued and provoked her. With a woman's perversity she wanted him to desire her. Did he feel no attraction to her? Was she less appealing then *mon ange* of the previous evening? Had he found her wanting in their encounter on the train to Moscow? His eyes minutes ago had seemed to speak an ardent message, or in her own confusion was she misreading the expression.

Taking exception to the prince's disinterest with a deep-seated womanly umbrage, Zena in a thoroughly feminine *volte-face* lifted limpid, deep blue eyes and, staring straight at the prince's face in the mirror before her, said in a lightly teasing way, "Is it only a host's duty, my lord, that prompts your kindness?"

Bestowing an extremely penetrating stare on the young damsel, the prince murmured, "Would you have it otherwise?"

"A soft blush followed by a delightful confusion struck the flustered *mademoiselle*, telling him quite clearly they understood each other. He expelled a soft sigh of relief. Zena had made the first move. Thank God, for his composure had been near to cracking. Standing a hairbreadth away from an all but nude beauty in the privacy of a dimly lit sauna without grasping the ripe, opulent fruit was as near to torture as he had ever come.

The prince dropped the hairbrush and followed through with consummate skill; reaching out to hold Zena gently by both shoulders, he turned her slowly around, took her unresisting hands in his, lifted them around his neck, and locked his mouth on hers. Burying his fingers in her silky hair, he delicately kissed the warm parted lips. His voice dropped to a dulcet whisper as he caressed her rosy mouth.

"Would you have it otherwise, sweet *dushka?*" he repealed as his hands slipped down her slender back, molding her pliant, thinly raped body to his hard frame. He groaned as his manhood swelled. His mouth traced a path down Zena's silken throat, lightly caressing the slender column. Practiced fingers untied the robe. His hands moved up her arms until they reached her shoulders, pushing the fabric back and down her arms until the garment fell to the floor; his warm, broad hands set her blood burning. He parted the folds of draped towel, and it too fell unheeded to the carpet. Alex's hand cupped her bare breast, lifting the firm flesh lightly until his lips tasted a rosebud pink nipple. Zena's eyes closed as a frisson of pleasure coursed through her heated, tingling body.

The prince's dark head remained bent as he nibbled and softly sucked both rosy peaks now hardened under his lips. Zena caught her breath and melted back against the strong arm that held her firmly, luxuriating in each new wave of sensuous warmth racing through her veins. She looked down at the black, wavy hair and lifted her hands hesitantly to caress the dark head. The poised hands fluttered.

Then Alex's hand, previously employed stroking her

breasts as he nibbled at their tips, glided down her belly and slipped between her thighs. Zena moaned in soft surrender and clasped his beautiful head to her breasts. Slender, bronzed fingers toyed with the moist and dewy entrance to her inner warmth, caressing the silken tissue, pulsating and damp with desire.

The prince lifted his head slowly and looked into blue eyes hot with passion. "Tell me you want me." His voice was low.

Zena's lips parted. She could hear her own labored breathing. A pink, rosy blush suffused her ivory skin. Uttering small soft sounds of building rapture, she clung to Alex with breathless urgency.

"Tell me," he repeated firmly, needing the sop to his honor.

Zena hesitated, her emotions in turmoil, passion overwhelming every rational thought.

Alex's lips closed over hers; his tongue licked tantalizingly, then plunged into the velvety depths of her tremulous mouth. Zena's fingers convulsively tightened their grip, digging her nails into his powerful shoulders. He shifted his body to hold her closer, pulling her against them. The prince's warm, demanding lips forced an ardent moan. Lifting his head, Alex waited for her reply. Zena searched for his mouth, but he drew back. *"Tell me!"*

Her mouth inches from his, Zena breathed softly, "Love me."

Ah—the needed words! Since when did he have so much principle?

"My pleasure to oblige, *mademoiselle*." The hushed whisper tickled her ear, and his mouth met hers in pleasurable response. He pulled her down on the fur-carpeted floor of the dressing room. He was smiling again as he commenced to oblige the sweet young miss. He kissed her throat, her breasts, her belly, and the insides of her thighs. He stroked her leisurely, delighting in each nuance of emotion he provoked. Under his sensitive, skillful mouth and hands waves of spreading desire inundated Zena's senses. Dextrous fingers brought her to a feverish pitch, his hands slid under her hips, and his mouth followed where his adroit fingers had toyed. Zena felt warm breath and a lightly teasing tongue on the very seat of her desire, and she shuddered convulsively, writhing slowly under the soft, flicking tongue as searing waves washed her to the very edges of ecstasy.

Zena pressed greedily against him, pleading with rapturous eyes, "Please, please don't make me wait."

Lifting his head, Alex chuckled indulgently. "Patience, my pet," he said as he covered her with his body but withheld his prize. Moving off her, he commanded, "Undress me."

Zena's eyes snapped open at the terse request. She shuddered slightly, shivering in exquisite torment, bringing herself back to full consciousness from the depths of her hot, flaming ardor. Sitting up slowly, she obediently reached out, still only half aware, to unbutton the prince's silk shirt and slip it from his muscular shoulders. She ran her fingertips over his broad chest, sliding delicately over the muscles of his torso.

An ache spread over Alex's body, and he caught his breath.

"Very dutiful, my little puss," he murmured huskily. Alex ran his fingers over her honeyed wet lips. Zena shuddered in ecstasy.

"Now my boots," and he stretched out his long legs.

Zena submissively knelt to remove Alex's brown riding boots. She was hungry for him. Just to touch him caused heated, pulsing waves to throb through her body. The sight of her full, swollen breasts bobbing and bouncing as she tugged and pulled on the tight-fitting footwear stirred Alex's penis to new dimensions. Finally the task was accomplished.

"My buckskins now, but first a reward for your efforts." Alex reached out and inserted two long fingers deep into her sweet passage. Zena groaned as small explosions began building, and the exquisite sensations ran through every screaming nerve.

"Almost there, my hot little piece?" Alex murmured triumphantly. "The buckskins now, love, and I'll be happy, as a dutiful host, to soon satisfy that yearning of yours."

Zena hastened to unfasten the buttons of his leather breeches and after some difficulty managed to slide the formfitting trousers off. Her heart was pounding against her ribs, and the fever in his veins seemed to be closing her throat. Alex's maleness sprang free, large, pulsing, and rigid, the erect phallus lying thick, arched, and hot-looking against his stomach.

Trembling in anticipation, Zena ran her hands lightly over Alex's hard body. "Love me, please, my lord, please."

"So bold now?" he teased.

Her hand slipped down and closed around his swollen manhood. He groaned. The teasing light was gone from his eyes, and twin flames glowed in their golden depths. Rolling Zena under him, his knee quickly spread her thighs, and in one economical gesture he plunged in boldly. The first powerful thrust sank in to its utmost length, and Zena screamed a piercing cry deep in her throat as Alex held himself firmly against her womb while her climax broke in crashing waves of blazing-hot passion from his inflamed, rigid shaft. When he could feel the convulsions subside, he shifted lightly inside her.

"Greedy little puss, haven't you ever heard of the delights of anticipation?" he whispered. "Hold me," he ordered as Zena's clinging grip had slackened on his back. "Hold me, little one, and you'll soon be screaming again." He smiled mildly as he slowly deepened his penetration. The prince was proud of his proficiency at pleasing women.

Slowly and with extreme care he restrained himself, driving in with long, slow movements, for he had learned at a very young age that the surest way to excite a woman's passion was with long, gentle thrusts and slow withdrawals. Zena's breath began to shorten, and she held Alex in a fierce embrace. She panted against his shoulder as every nerve thrilled and quivered. She melted against him, small and delicate in his arms, and his desire grew, grew in a different, more tender way—intense still, but gentle—and he moved inside her like a penetrating caress. His penis rose larger still as she became infinitely desirable to him. She felt the urgent force like a burning fire, and Zena opened herself to him, helpless before his powerful, assertive passion. He plunged deeper and deeper, touching the very center of her, and she clung to him, meeting his hunger. She clung with a terrible, consuming love for this unknown man until suddenly in a shuddering consummation they both blindly felt the blazing potency of bliss.

He didn't withdraw but lay still above her, kissing her gently. Her hands strayed lightly over him, still half-shy and sensitive to the wonder of his body and the tender power he held over her. He felt beautiful, and her heart cried out at the fragile loveliness he had given her. She fluttered her hands timorously down his back, feeling the play of hard muscle and the firmness of rib and flesh. He held her close and was silent as she softly explored him. She moved gently under him, pressing nearer to his incomprehensible sensual mystery. And then she felt it, the slow, surging stirring of his sexual desire, and all her newly felt passion reached out to him.

He was very patient; he had never been so patient, wanting to give the sweet miss the fullest pleasure as she learned the exquisite possibilities of her sexuality. Each slow stroke slid into her honeyed depth, and he rested against her arched pearl while her tumultuous passion grew. He was aching now and watched her as she drew near the edge. She hung on to him as if she were drowning. He felt a tremor in her belly, and she moaned a sound of helplessness against the coming storm. She was almost there. Her moan gave way to a soft cry of rapture, and he felt all his passion rushing down, rushing down as the throb of his groin pumped and poured the hot fluid into her.

Warm and sated with his exertion, he dropped a kiss on her lips, murmured softly, "Sweet, sweet, lovely puss."

Twenty minutes later he carried a very subdued beauty into the *dacha* and up the stairway to the bedroom.

10

Unobtrusive servants, their features politely composed, efficiently cleared their master's progress, silently opening and shutting doors as Alex strode through the *dacha* carrying his houseguest.

Minutes later Alex reclined against the carved and painted headboard of his canopied bed, curving Zena into his arms. She snuggled her head against his shoulder, and he idly caressed her tumbled auburn curls. He lightly kissed the top of her head as he reflected that the Kuzan luck had indeed not deserted him, for how remote were the chances of finding such a delightful innocent flower of passion on the steps of the Dolgorouky palace in a snowstorm. Odds even he would decline to wager on, and he was notorious for betting on the most unfavorable percentages.

Stretching out his left arm, he groped in the darkened room for his August Hollming gold and enamel cigarette case on the bedside table. Finding it he flicked up the lid, extracting one of his custom-made blue silk cigarettes of harsh Turkish tobacco.

As he held it in his mouth while his fingers renewed the blind questing for matches, Alex muttered the obligatory courtesy, "Do you mind if I smoke?" Without waiting for an answer, a match flared in the dark, and Zena looked up to see his handsome dark features illuminated brilliantly in the flare of the phosphorus glow. He bent slightly to touch cigarette to flame; looking down he noticed Zena's curious scrutiny and winked wickedly before waving out the match. As Alex drew a deep draught into his lungs, the burning tip glowed brilliant orange, the only light in the darkened room. He exhaled lazily, his fingers stroking Zena's arm as he held her against his chest. "Forgive my animal ways, little one. I hope I didn't hurt you," Alex apologized quietly.

"No, of course you didn't hurt me," Zena replied. "But you see, that is . . . ah . . ."

"Come, child," Alex interrupted with easygoing tranquillity, "don't worry about being tactful. Just tell me. But what?"

"Well, I will own to a certain apprehension that you'll think me too ready to respond. It's not considered ladylike."

Alex threw back his head and chuckled deeply. "It's quite acceptable, *dushka*, to leave ladylike ways at the bedroom door. Let me assure you, my pet, your eager responses are of unalloyed delight to me. In fact, I'm sure there isn't a single male on the face of the earth who would disagree. There's nothing you could do that would shock me, child."

Zena didn't know her seducer very well, or she wouldn't have been uneasy with apprehensions of unladylike behavior.

Since adolescence Prince Alexander Kuzan had done exactly as he pleased, looking down his insolent, well-bred nose with contempt at any who would dare cry scandal. After initiating or being involved in the most perverse and wicked excesses of the past eight years as the leader of St. Petersburg's fast set, one could understand the merry chuckle and raised black brows at the *mademoiselle*'s shy consideration of propriety.

"If I didn't know better," he said speculatively, "but there's no doubt I took your maidenhead, I'd be inclined to think you were not an innocent at all. Do women's romances instruct so explicitly?" he teased. "I was under the impression they were all of sighs and languishing looks and unrequited, passionless love."

"Oh, you're quite right about romances," Zena agreed. "I tried to read a few of them, but the silly airs of the heroines are really too idiotic to stomach. My reading instead followed the classics and the histories so adored by my father."

"Hmm," said Alex in faint surprise, "I detect a different side to you—not all beautiful, charmingly female, it seems," Alex mocked softly. "A bit blue, I think."

The *mademoiselle*'s want of sophistication caused her to miss the cynical overtones, and she continued quite earnestly, "I've always been fascinated by history, my lord, a taste my father encouraged."

"My father and a long line of dissolute Kuzans, as you see, encouraged rather different tastes in me. You're the first woman I've known who admits to reading."

Alex had always found learned women an awful bore, invariably too determined to exhibit their erudition. He heartily embraced the masculine notion that women as a sex were meant to be feminine, dainty, exquisite creatures.

A startled pair of eyes looked up at him. "That seems odd, my lord," Zena said. "I find reading one of my favorite pleasures."

"Please, *mademoiselle*, I beg of you," said the prince lazily, "no more *my lords*."

"Very well, My l . . ." She hesitated. "Prince Kuzan?"

"Good God, no! My name is Alexander Nikolaevich Kuzan. My family calls me Sasha. My friends call me Archer. My acquaintances call me Alexander Nikolaevich."

"Why do your friends call you Archer? What an odd name. Do you like archery?"

There was the hint of a smile in his voice. "Not particularly, but on occasion it's amusing. Better call me Sasha. Archer won't do."

"Why not, if your friends call you that?"

"It's a long story, and one that would not interest you." Again she heard the smile in the dark. "Now, no more *my lord*s. Puts me in mind of a servant girl. Sasha, all right?"

"Yes, my l . . . yes, Sasha," Zena demurely replied.

His cigarette had been rushed out, and now both hands were languidly stroking Zena as she lay in his arms.

"Very pretty, *mademoiselle*." The prince's long finger traced the outline of a dainty flower-shaped scar on the rise of Zena's hip.

The young woman blushed at his tantalizing finger on her flesh. "A childhood accident," she explained.

His fingers wandered lightly over waist and hip, traced a silky drifting pattern on the inside of her thighs, softly roved upward to caress the lush female breasts, stopping a moment to rub his thumb against a soft nipple. Zena's body was slowly warming to his touch, and his stiffness quivered as the tumescence grew.

"Bluestocking or no, little one," he murmured idly, "there are other roles set aside for a woman in this world of ours. You'll surely want children someday."

"No!" Zena's emphatic response resounded in the hushed room. "I intend to finish my father's research and haven't time for children." Her determined reaction momentarily stilled Alex's roving hands.

He delicately lifted his eyebrows in mild astonishment. Is this young chit so naïve that she's unaware of the correlation of their lovemaking and the possibility of children? Does she innocently believe a passionate nature like hers housed in a voluptuous, exquisite, womanly body, even now beginning to stir passionately, can ignore the ofttimes consequences of that pleasure?

Then with an almost immediate indifference, the prince shrugged off her naïveté and its attendant difficulties. It wasn't his problem. Light fingers delicately squeezed a peaked pink nipple. Zena shuddered and made a little helpless sound.

He bent to kiss the soft yielding lips so close to his and guided her hand to the arched instrument of pleasure pulsing in anticipation.

They stayed awake all night making love, drinking champagne, and talking about every imaginable subject. Breathless and warm from love he would pull her atop his body and she'd lie on the heated, muscular bed of his torso, inches from his face; he poured her chilled champagne and, in altering moods of teasing and seriousness, they talked of their lives. Reaching up occasionally or drawing her down to kiss her lips, Alex would attempt to recover the train of thought but, often as not the kiss set off a passionate embrace that in a leisurely manner ultimately resulted in a renewed exploration of their mutual paradise. He brought her up countless times that night to shuddering, clutching peaks of enchantment while he melted quivering in numerous sweet deaths within her lush warmth.

At times positions would be reversed, and he would ride lightly above her, feeding her champagne with his kisses.

"Only half a mouthful, my sweet," he teased, "for my selfish instincts prevail—the other half is mine." Thusly in a bantering, joyful fashion another bottle of champagne was consumed. As the bubbly effervescent liquor inundated Zena's senses, her last inhibitions vanished; she opened her heart to this charming rogue, opened her mind to the warmth and security he genially offered, and opened her body to the overwhelming rush of passionate desire roused by the experienced proficiency of a consummate, skillful, courtly libertine, reaffirming his noted reputation as the Archer.

It was dangerous to want anyone as she wanted Sasha, Zena warned herself, and after such a whirlwind short acquaintance, but to a young woman who felt very much alone in the world and had known only cold tolerance the past few years, Sasha's comforting arms, softly murmured phrases of love, and sensuous pleasure were intoxicating.

As dawn approached, the exhausted young maid fell asleep. The prince watched her briefly from the vintage point of one elbow—long, dark lashes falling on flushed pink cheeks. What very long eyelashes the *mademoiselle* had, thought Alex, apropos of nothing. They made great shadows on her cheeks. The heavy mane of red-brown hair was disarrayed in wild waves around her dainty face, one arm flung in exhaustion above her head while the delicate petite body, of proportions Venus would have envied, glowed white against the shadows of the morning light.

The faint color of dawn seeped into the quiet room. Zena's soft breathing stirred the silent air as she lay warm and replete at his side. He gazed at the young *mademoiselle* with an uncommon tenderness. Alex was neither so dissolute nor so blasé as to be untouched by the quiet magic of the moment. He was aware of what she had given of herself, of the frank adoration and melting acquiescence presented gratuitously with an open heart.

He reminded himself that she wasn't one of his usual companions. The attendant implications confounded him, and he brusquely dismissed the uncomfortable thoughts with a slight frown.

He rose then and drew a blanket over her in a friendly, protective way, as if she were somehow in his charge. He wrapped himself in his squirrel-lined gray silk dressing gown and retired to a chair by the fire to await the early entrance he anticipated from Bobby.

He'd let the young chit sleep until afternoon. She was unfamiliar with sleepless nights. His normal careless, dissipated life routinely experienced periods without sleep, and three continuous days of drinking and carousing was not in the least unusual.

The eminently satisfied prince spent the morning entertaining a talkative, engaging three-year-old, and only when the dressmaker he had sent for arrival did he wake Zena.

"It's two o'clock, little one," he whispered in her ear, "and duty calls. Are you ready to have pins stuck into you?"

Zena's eyes snapped open in apprehension. Had the considerate, unutterably charming prince of the previous night turned into a perverted sadist?

The warm look in his eyes and the smile flashing his even white teeth belied the startling, alarming inquiry.

"Pins?" Zena squeaked and struggled to a sitting position.

Reacting to the panic in Zena's eyes, Alex chuckled genially and hastened to reassure her. "A dressmaker's here—that kind of pin, my pet. Really, child, sadism isn't my style. I feel deeply offended," he mocked, teasing still, but his soothing reassurances didn't have the desired effect.

"Dress . . . dressmaker?" she now quavered in renewed horror. "Oh no, my lo—(he scowled) er, Sasha. I couldn't. I'd be too embarrassed."

"Good God. Embarrassed about what? There's no need to feel embarrassment before a tradesperson. Come now, I'm wearied of that green dress."

He drew her forcefully from the bed, wrapped her in the silk comforter, and with the curt injunction to do as he said, forced her, still weakly protesting, through the bedroom door into the adjacent sitting room.

"Sasha, really this isn't necessary. I'm sure I could . . ." Zena was objecting as he propelled her into the center of the room, "just redo that green . . ." The sentence died abruptly at Zena noticed an elegantly dressed woman standing the window. Clutching the sapphire silk comforter with redoubled intensity, Zena threw a distracted, frightened look over her shoulder at the impassive prince.

Alex ignored the pleading in her eyes, determined, as

was his custom, to brook no interference with his wishes. Gripping Zena's shoulders, his long fingers digging painfully through the silken coverlet, he held her firmly imprisoned before him.

"May I introduce Mrs. Mvaky, my dear. She has kindly consented to put your wardrobe to rights."

No explanation was given the dressmaker as to either the name or the relationship of this young woman. Curiosity consumed Moscow's finest modiste, but the prince's lucrative patronage commissioned so often over the past years sealed the haughty woman's lips. Prince Alex's generosity often indulged a lady love's whim for new gowns, which in turn filled Mrs. Mvaky's pockets with gold rubles. The prince's openhanded liberality stifled the dressmaker's native curiosity. The prince never quibbled over prices, his bills were paid promptly by his man of business, and his taste in female attire was richly articulate. Indeed, he was one of a handful of her male customers who understood what looked best on a woman and who never asked the price.

It appeared Prince Alex had yet another light o'love to embellish. Not in his usual style, this one, Mrs. Mvaky observed rapidly through shrewdly assessing eyes.

No customary Junoesque female here; instead almost a child. Certainly unprepossessing, frightened almost (hers not to question the fear nonetheless; none of her business the bizarre proclivities of this gilded youth), certainly a decided change from the haughty pretentions of some of the aristocratic sluts he usually preferred.

An aura of innocence about the young thing? Certainly the look of it, but in the company of one of Russia's most thoroughly disreputable rakes, clearly impossible, and from the looks of it stark naked underneath, with bare feet peeking out from the blue silk.

These swift musings were cut short and her speculations put to rest as the prince swept the silken comforter from the nervous girl and, much as a proud Pygmalion might show off his masterpiece, left the young woman uncomfortably nude in the center of the antique carpet. The most prominent modiste in Moscow heroically concealed her inadvertent gasp. She had been right: not a stitch on. Alex's eyes gleamed in appreciation. His lordship's attention seemed to have wandered, but at a discreet cough from the modiste he brought his gaze from contemplation of Zena's ripe beauty and, looking directly at the dressmaker, said urbanely, "A complete wardrobe, Mrs. Mvaky, everything. I trust you brought some dresses out as my man requested."

Gathering her composure, for naked women were not even in the prince's usual unorthodox repertoire, Mrs. Mvaky quickly brought out a navy silk morning costume. Without so much as a blink of the eye to indicate her consternation, she avoided the embarrassed gaze of the young auburn-tressed female and threw the full skirt over the head of the girl. Some seconds later, securing the buttons and hooks down the back while the prince stood critically assessing the fitting, she conversed in businesslike accents, "With the exception of the bodice the entire frock is too large. Everything will have to be taken in."

"Navy is much too severe for the lady. (The word "lady" increased the dressmaker's curiosity.) But we'll have this altered until more suitable gowns can be made," the prince broke in curtly.

"What else did you bring with you?" Alex was oblivious to Zena's embarrassment and strictly enjoined himself to remember that this time he was outfitting a respectable female. He studied the suitability of all the dresses Mrs. Mvaky had with her and, ignoring the pointed looks and pained glances of the young *mademoiselle*, further ordered a magnificent wardrobe with a practiced expertise that did not go unnoticed by Zena.

Short of making a scene in front of this intimidating

woman, Zena had no choice but to submit to the ordeal, while Alex promised himself that once Mrs. Mvaky left he would bend his every effort to cajole and coax Zena into accepting both his gift of a wardrobe and, more significantly, the incontrovertibility of her future position with him.

Having women to bear him company at his *dacha*, buying gowns for them, living life with a bohemian disregard for conventions, dealing pleasurably in the lighthearted game of amour, all were eminently natural in the elegant, aristocratic class to which he belonged. He couldn't expect the girl to understand the careless, pleasant world he lived in, but he must do his captivating best to give her delight in this unfamiliar milieu into which she was thrust. She was obviously startled after the quite different world from which she had come—one, no doubt, in which a man must live with one wife to whom he is lawfully wed—a world in which a girl should be innocent, a woman virtuous, a man stalwart and steady; in short, all the foolishness he chose to ignore and ridicule as his youthful, pleasure-loving instincts flitted delightfully from amusement to amusement.

With an abrupt flick of his wrist he dismissed the dressmaker.

Then taking both of Zena's little hands in his, he raised them to his lips and pressed a light kiss into the palms as he glanced down at her from under his lashes. "You look delightfully beautiful in this cream lace tea gown, little one," Alex said with his brightest smile. "Relax, child. I promise Mrs. Mvaky is discretion personified. She won't breathe a word about you," he dissembled to set the chit at ease. He knew before the day was out all the polite world of Moscow would know of Zena's arrival, as if it mattered. No one dared censure his liaisons. In any case, he didn't give a damn for the opinion of any member of the *haut monde* from the tsar down.

"If it bothers you to take clothes from me, consider it

a loan that can be repaid at a later date." He kissed the tips of her fingers as he still held her hands in his, and gazing at her over her clasped hands with just the suitable degree of penitent apology, begged forgiveness with his devastating eyes.

"My grandfather could pay you back," Zena hesitatingly suggested.

"Of course, if you wish," the prince readily acceded.

Zena broke into a relaxed, merry smile, for once the dilemma of payment was reconciled in her confused mind, what woman could resist the magnificent wardrobe the prince had ordered. She had to own it would be pleasant to see Sasha's admiration when she was clothed in her new gowns.

Alex, heartened by the warm smile of the pretty woman, tranquilly noted that another minor crisis had been averted.

Crushing her in a bear hug, he nibbled one soft pink ear. Zena melted against his body, the confounded, warring jumble of perplexing emotions overwhelmed by the dominating presence of this bewitching man.

She knew what she was doing wasn't right. She knew modesty and virtue were respected qualities in a woman, but when Sasha (she warmed her heart with the intimate name) held her and kissed her, all staid resolutions flew away, and all she wanted was to be near him. Luckily, for the peace of her already uneasy mind, she didn't know that Prince Alex had this same devastating effect on all the women in his vast acquaintance.

"Let's turn on the Gramophone in my study and dance to the new waltz records sent from Vienna. That lace gown makes you look so good I may have to take it off soon."

As Zena blushed, Alex burst into gay laughter, kissed her on both cheeks, and twirled her out the door and down the hall to his study.

Prince Alex's very pleasant holiday had begun.

PART II

Love's Idyll

1

In the ensuing weeks the young chit was just where Alex wanted her, near him or in his arms or under him. She was more enchanting and diverting and sensuous than his most vivid imagination could have depicted or expected. The pretty maid learned the game of love with a facility and captivating celerity that piqued the jaded appetites of this surfeited young rake. She was sensitive, sensuous, responsive, tender, spirited, and impassioned; the full gamut of her vivacious personality never ceased to amaze him. He even listened politely to her vehement monologues on women's rights, feeling it only courteous *quid pro quo* for all the delectable, incomparable sensuality she offered him.

A charming domestic routine was established at Podolsk. The days were spent in joyful companionship together and in company with Bobby: skating, skiing, going for sleigh rides, building snowmen, playing indoor games in the nursery; in short, amusing themselves in childish youthful pleasures. Zena had sorely missed such youthful pleasures in the cold atmosphere of her aunt's establishment. For Alex these pleasures were simply his usual indulgence to sybaritic whims. It pleased him to please her. Her childlike joy was intoxicating to watch, and at night she intoxicated him in countless other ways, offering him Venus's delights in earthly form. The weeks flew by as in some blissful Elysium. The prince never thought beyond gratifying his fancies; only rarely had the need arisen in his pampered existence. Zena dared not think at all. The prince was satisfied with the course of events. Zena repressed the uncomfortable manifestations of right and wrong, duty, and virtue. When they surfaced, she surrendered to the exquisite joy and affection Alex offered her and did not think of the future or even of tomorrow. The past three years of her life had been a living hell and she now had, by the merest snatch at fate, avoided a forced, hateful marriage to a dreadful old man and had entered a paradise on earth. She chastised herself occasionally for having no moral strength to resist the audaciously charming prince. But was there a woman born who would have been able to resist once the elegant, notorious Archer set his mind on conquest?

No matter that Alex had intended to keep her for his normal eight or ten days. It was quite impossible for him to forego her company at the moment. Never mind that it was wholly unprecedented behavior on his part. Well, damn it, he thought mutinously, must one become rigid in one's actions? She was just too damn good in bed to give up so soon, he told himself with what he considered grave practically.

Six halcyon weeks blissfully passed at the *dacha* near Podolsk. It seemed a magic world to Zena. Alex catered to her every caprice, remembering each like and dislike. He listened to her intently as she talked in her soft, indolent voice of the confusing threads of her life. He was devoted, tender, and perfect in his lovemaking. Zena was captivated, indeed as she was intended to be. Her subconscious would surface occasionally, eliciting nagging doubts that she was losing her hold on the strong, level-headed pragmatism that had always served her so well. She was becoming enslaved by this irresistible man who fulfilled her every desire and longing. Heaven help me, she thought; like a green, lovesick girl she was head over heels in love with this cavalier libertine.

One bright, sunny morning in early March Alex announced at the breakfast table that business obliged him to ride into Moscow that morning.

"I won't invite you along, *ma petite*, since this damnable meeting could take some time." He had, in fact, received a curt summons from his father, who requested his presence at their apartments in Moscow that afternoon.

Zena's face reflected her desolation.

"I really dislike going at all, my dear." The brusque tone of the note from Nikki boded ill. Alex had been racking his brain for hours trying to fathom which of his numerous scandals had surfaced to once again offend his parents.

He rose from his chair, walked over to Zena, and dropped a light kiss on her cheek, "I'll be back late this afternoon. Smile, child, I won't be long."

Zena looked up at the tall, handsome man dressed in morning tweeds and buckskins and forced a smile she was far from feeling. Much as she tried to deny her enslavement to this elegant youth, the truth was that she was happy only when he was with her. Compelling herself to act with some degree of rationality, she politely wished Sasha a pleasant journey.

"I hope your business meeting isn't too tedious," she continued in deference to the required social amenities.

"Tedium I can live with," Alex cryptically remarked. Zena cast him a puzzled glance. Alex, however, chose not to explain his retort. Reaching for a decanter of brandy on the sideboard, he poured himself a healthy bumper and drained it in one swallow.

Yes, he heartily hoped tedium would be the worst of his problems. Unfortunately, he thought, as the brandy burned a warm path down his throat, the coldly civil summons presaged a grim inquisition. Damn it, though, try as he could he wasn't able to come up with a single excess or debauch he'd been a party to lately. It was disconcerting.

Usually he knew vaguely what disreputable peccadillo he was being upbraided for. But this time he was at a loss. What the hell were his parents doing in Moscow?

"*Au revoir*, love. I'll bring you back some bauble. What do you prefer? Rubies, pearls, emeralds, diamonds?" He paused as he reached the door to the hallway and turned inquiring eyes on Zena. My heavens! He was serious, Zena thought. Asking about jewels worth a fortune as carelessly as requesting whether she preferred caramels or fondant creams.

"Don't be silly. I don't need any jewels," Zena remonstrated quickly.

"Don't need jewels?" Alex repeated with amiable perplexity. "Of course you need jewels. Every woman needs jewels," he said flatly. "Maybe pearls for you, my dove, to enhance that irresistible innocence of yours."

He waved casually and left. "Maybe pearls and emeralds," he was muttering to himself as he strode down the hall. She would look exquisite with emeralds in her hair, he mused as he shrugged into his sable topcoat. It had materialized silently in the hands of a footman as if by magic when he entered the entrance hall. Then again, black pearls and diamonds would be an exotic combination resting on those luscious, creamy breasts of hers, he contemplated as he settled himself comfortably in the troika. He was oblivious to the numerous servants hovering around him adjusting the fur robes and warm bricks. Something perhaps by Fabergés Kostrioukoff. Maybe lapis and gold.

With the characteristic facility of youth Alex was capable of banishing the worrisome thoughts of his ensuing interview, and the ride into Moscow passed quite pleasantly while he envisioned various types of jewelry displayed on various parts of Zena's exquisitely proportioned body.

2

Arriving in Moscow, Alex decided to first fortify himself at the Nobles Club with a bottle of brandy to brace himself for the coming ordeal. After being greeted cheerfully by the doorman and steward, who enjoyed the democratic friendship of the Kuzans' eldest sprig, Alex proceeded up the grand mahogany staircase to the gaming rooms. Alex ordered a bottle of brandy, began to empty it without benefit of a glass, and sauntered into the smaller adjacent rooms in search of a comfortable chair.

"Sasha!"

Alex turned toward the sound and saw his friend Yuri walking over from the roulette table.

"Where the hell have you been? I heard you were in the neighborhood, but no one's seen you for weeks. Unlike you, Sasha." Yuri eyed him suspiciously, "to miss the gambling here at the Club."

"I've been busy," Alex said shortly.

"Rumor has it you had a female with you on the train. It's amazing how accurate gossip can be. Is she what's keeping you busy?"

"Maybe," the vague reply equivocated. It was obvious the prince was not to be drawn.

"Christ, she can't be a whore, or we'd have been invited out to sample the goods. Can't be Amalie, as I saw her at Golitzin's last night." Yuri's eyes opened wide as the process of elimination left him to speculate on the only kind of female Alex would care to keep in seclusion. "A respectable girl?" he whispered.

"Not anymore."

"'Not anymore? A virgin?"

"Formerly," Alex retorted dryly.

"I don't believe it! You've always railed against them, said they were useless in bed."

"Well, actually, it was a bit of a mistake, and then it was . . . er . . . too late to stop."

"You raped the poor thing?" Yuri exclaimed.

"Of course not," Alex answered, deeply offended. "Pray consider my reputation," he entreated.

"Are we going to hear wedding bells?"

Alex laughed.

"Does she have an irate family?" asked Yuri.

"No, thank God. But it doesn't signify. There isn't a man born who could force me into marriage."

"Is she blonde or brunette?"

"None of your damn business." A vague chivalry stirred, prompting Alex to shield the *mademoiselle*'s reputation.

"Christ, you're guarding her jealousy. She must be damnably good in bed. Is she a hot piece?"

Alex's eyebrows went up a fraction. "Leave off, Yuri." The prince smiled amiably as he strolled toward a row of leather chairs near the windows.

"Come on, details, details," Yuri coaxed playfully, following his unusually reticent friend.

"Go to hell," Alex murmured pleasantly.

Alex apparently wished to avoid the subject. Sasha was showing a new and very dull regard for the proprieties, Yuri thought. His refinement in protecting the *mademoiselle*'s respectability was quite out of character. Undeterred by such uncustomary gentility, Yuri called out across the thronged clubroom, "Kiril! You know who Archer has . . ."

"Auburn," Alex interjected hastily in a low voice, "and yes, damn hot."

"Forget it, Kiril," Yuri waved cheerily. "Tall or short?"

Alex sighed resignedly. "Up to here." He indicated his shoulder.

"Plump or thin?"

"Thin."

"You've never liked then thin."

"She's not exactly thin everywhere."

"Where and how isn't she thin?" Yuri leered.

"Christ Almighty!" Alex gave up good-naturedly. His virtuous attempt at concealing the *mademoiselle*'s identity and reputation was dismissed when pitted against such friendly persistence. "You might as well come out and see for yourself."

"My good fellow," expostulated Yuri, grinning, "I thought you'd never ask!"

As a renowned womanizer himself, Yuri had a healthy regard for Alex's notorious reputation and suspected only the finest prime piece could elicit such a protection response. Curiosity and connoisseurship demanded he view this extraordinary female for himself.

As the two friends sprawled comfortable in black leather chairs, Alex said morosely, "Have an interview with *mon père* this afternoon."

Yuri whistled softly. "That don't sound good. What's up?'"

"Damned if I know. Can you think of anything I've done out of the ordinary lately? Been exceedingly quiet and well behaved, if you ask me."

"I really hate to sound so absurdly conventional, Sasha," Yuri sighed sardonically, "but perhaps the respectable virgin you seduced and spirited away to your *dacha* could, just could, mind you, have something to do with it."

"Good Lord! Do you think so?" Alex sat upright. "She said that first night she hadn't any family, so I didn't give the possibility of vengeful relatives another thought. Do you suppose she was lying?"

Yuri snorted derisively. "Don't all females lie, you damn fool! From anyone else I could excuse such naïveté, but really, Sasha, naïveté ain't your usual style."

"*Merde!*" Alex exploded. "If some son of a bitch thinks he can put a gun to my head, he's going to be unpleasantly surprised."

"You could marry her and ease your troubled conscience," Yuri teased.

"Like hell!" Alex exclaimed indignantly. Marriage had never occurred to him as a possibility. A wife and family were, in his eyes, alien and repugnant and the most witless folly. Alex's love affairs had always been outside society, where *danseuses* and actresses knew the boundaries of intimacy, or within society with acceptable, adulterous ladies of rank, who also knew how to play the game by the rules. For the first time in his life he was intimate with a sweet, innocent girl of his class, and he felt the charm of innocence juxtaposing inescapably with the coarse opulence and decadence of his previous amours. Although he never said anything to Zena that he wouldn't have said to any other woman, he felt she was becoming more and more dependent on him, and inexplicably, for a man who had always cursed clinging women, he found the more attached she became, the more he liked it. This particular role of seducing an innocent miss and then courting her tenderly with no intention of marriage was not unique in the annals of magnificent young men such as he. But it was new to him, this innocence. It seemed he had found an unusual and tantalizing pleasure, and he was enjoying his discovery.

It never occurred to Alex that there was any harm in his relationship with Zena. After all, she was free to leave if she wished, he reasoned heedlessly, disregarding the circumstances which left her without funds or friends in a

thoughtless, indifferent world. If someone had told him
that he was making her unhappy, he would have been bewildered and wouldn't have believed it. How could the exquisite and enchanting pleasure they enjoyed be wrong?
He was in no doubt that Zena enjoyed it too.

"Like hell!" he repeated. "We're getting along marvelously. Why ruin a good thing?" he mocked playfully.

Checking his watch, Alex took a last swig from the bottle and rose from the chair. "Off to the parental rebuke,"
he drawled. "I just have to remember to be properly contrite and say *yes sir* and *no Maman* at suitable intervals."

"Good luck, Sasha. Wouldn't be in your shoes for a million," his friend sympathized. "I'll be out to see your hot
piece soon, thought." Yuri leered roguishly.

"Just so long as you only look, my friend," Alex said,
"don't touch. This little puss is exclusively mine."

Alex was shown to the drawing room, determined as he
leisurely mounted the shallow stairs to remain polite and
courteous. But, it rankled, damned if it didn't, both the
tone of the summons and the speculation concerning the
probable topic of discussion. Damn it, he was twenty-four
years old, and he'd bed whomever he pleased. It was
scarcely a subject that required a family conference, he
thought crossly.

Breathing deeply to control his rising ire as he entered
the room, Alex greeted his *maman* with a kiss on the cheek
and acknowledged his father with a polite bow. Alisa
smiled up at her son fondly as she sat on a brocaded settee,
presiding over a tea service. Nikki, as was his custom, preferred his tea time to take a more alcoholic form. He was
doing justice to a large brandy.

Swiftly appraising Alex with a stern scowl and glittering, tawny eyes, Nikki snapped, "I trust you're still in
good health."

Taken aback by the brusque greeting, Alex's well-intentioned considerations of conciliation evaporated abruptly.

"Of course. Is there some reason I shouldn't be?" he inquired rudely. Over his mother's head Sasha met his father's cold eyes.

"Taking up with streetwalkers has been known to be detrimental to one's health," Nikki sardonically drawled.

Alex's thin lips curled. "Sermon, father?" he said testily.

Alisa looked anxiously from the face of her incensed husband to the equally annoyed visage of her oldest son. The explosive Kuzan temper was going to cause trouble again. If she could calm them down, maybe this problem could be dealt with quietly and rationally. She loved them both and didn't want this meeting to deteriorate into a bitter brawl.

"Nikki, dear," she began placatingly, "I'm sure Sasha has a reasonable explanation, if you'll only give him the chance. Sasha, sweetheart, would you like a brandy or tea?"

Alex looked at his mother distractedly, wrath forcing an ominous glint in his golden eyes and a distinctly tense atmosphere about her person. Compelling himself to respond to the civilities, he abstractedly answered, "Ah, brandy wuld be find, *Maman*."

Alisa poured several inches into a glass and handed it to her handsome son. "Now, Nikki, really, love, give the boy an opportunity to catch his breath," she interceded tranquilly, reaching up to pat Alex's hand affectionately.

Nikki took a long draught from his glass and continued scowling at his son but refrained from immediate comment.

Alex looked down at his mother's concerned expression and gently said, "Really, *Maman*, my health is excellent."

"For how long?" Nikki interjected caustically.

At this juncture Alex could have repudiated the error of their assumptions about Zena, but the incorrigible Kuzan stubborn irascibility was part of his character as well, and his father's goading perversely affected it. Flushing under the rebuke, Alex peevishly said, "Since when have you begun monitoring my liaisons?"

"Since we've heard news of this street woman, you young cub," Nikki retorted heatedly.

"Forgive me, sir, if I wonder at your duplicity," Alex drawled sarcastically, and one black eyebrow rose in incredulity as derisive as his father's scorn. "Not wishing to seem indelicate before *Maman*," he continued languidly, "but you're hardly one to chastise such conduct."

"Watch your tongue, my boy. I'm still capable of thrashing you," Nikki barked. "And, as you well know, my amorous escapades ended when I met your *maman*."

"Very laudable," commended his unrepentant son. "However, I'm not married yet, so my amorous escapades should be of no concern to anyone," Alex challenged.

"Your *maman* is worried," Nikki responded stiffly.

Alex glanced swiftly at the beseeching eyes of his beautiful mother, and the brittle anger drained from his eyes.

Before Alex could reply, Nikki glanced reflectively at his eldest son, his distaste only thinly disguised. "And I'm worried about your bringing a common street slut into our family. I had no longer thought it possible for any of your profligacies to astonish me, but let me congratulate you," Nikki's nettled voice informed. "I have been persuaded to change my opinion. You have eclipsed all previous excesses. This unsavory female has outlasted your usual liaisons. A fortnight was your previous record, if I'm not mistaken," he murmured acidly. "I think we are now approaching the seventh week, if my calculations are correct," the chill tone continued. "I confess, Alexander (only in moments of the most severe censure did "Alexander" replace the familiar "Sasha"), I do not care for the thought of a common prostitute as a member of the family. You can hardly suppose I relish hearing a streetwalker's name seriously coupled with yours."

The red light reappeared in Alex's eyes. "Such parental vigilance unnerves me. Seven weeks, you say," Alex insolently mused. "Very edifying. I hadn't been keeping count," he smiled grimly. "Rest assured, there's no need to concern yourself. Gossip may be rife apropos my affairs, but not, I think, regarding my imminent nuptials."

"I should hope not," Nikki drawled, distinctly comforted to find his major worry was baseless.

"I am not inspired to marry, sir," came the careless reply.

"I stand relieved," Nikki politely said. "It's never been my custom," he continued smoothly, favoring his son with a cool smile, "to inquire into your outrageous affairs, despite your mother's occasional protests. I've always allowed you to indulge in almost any intemperance, but on one point I stand firm. You will not be allowed to commit that one indiscretion. You are, after all, a Kuzan. Amuse yourself, with my blessing, so long as it's only an amusement."

A provocative light gleamed in Alex's pale eyes. He shot his father a roguish glance. "I have your blessing, then?" he queried cheerfully.

By all means, enjoy yourself," Nikki was so far mollified as to inquire indulgently, "Do you need any money?"

"No, thank you, sir. I have plenty."

"I'm sure you're the first Kuzan to admit to such prudence. Alisa, my dear," said Nikki with a twinkle in his eye, "can we take credit for raising such a paragon of monetary circumspection?" He turned fond parental eyes on Alex and interrogated sportively, "Is there one vice, after all, that has eluded you?"

"At the risk of incurring your censure once again, Papa," Sasha grinned, "it's not a matter of abstaining from extravagance so much as it is the rather heavy winning at the gaming tables that supports my spendthrift tendencies."

"Can't fault your skill with cards," Nikki generously conceded, his humor once more charitably disposed toward his firstborn. Finishing his glass of brandy Nikki announced convivially, "I'm off. Promised Cernov a few hours of baccarat today. I'll be home in time to dine with you and the children, dear." He always disliked the punitive role as parent and was pleased the controversy had been resolved in a way exactly suited to the interests of them both. He left.

Patting the brocade cushion next to her, Alisa gently said, "Sit with me a moment, dear, and finish your drink."

As Alex sprawled next to his mother and leaned his head back she remarked quietly, "Tell me now, just who is this young woman?"

Alex sighed resignedly. "*Maman*, don't worry. It's nothing, just another woman."

"Are you sure, dear? I don't want to pry, but she's been at the *dacha* a long time."

"Rest easy, *Maman*, I can handle my own affairs."

"Your father was very worried. You're sure you're not serious about this female?"

Alex's eyebrows quirked sardonically. "Serious?" he said, then stood up and placed his empty glass on the table. "I'm not serious about anything," he laughed, "I'm only twenty-four. *Au revoir, Maman*." He bent to kiss her goodbye.

After the interview that had concluded so reassuringly for all parties, Alex strolled down the avenue to Alexandre's with a light step and an exuberant spirit. He was in the grandest mood; the ordeal with his parents had been pleasantly consummated with his father's benediction on his amusements. Evidently no vengeful relatives had surfaced to accuse him of trifling with Zena. His mother had been soothed, and the most delectable bedwarmer awaited him at home.

Entering the ornate plate-glass doors to buy Zena the promised bauble, Alex was disposed to purchase every imaginable luxury for his pert and saucy plaything. As long as she was amusing him so masterfully, it would be miserly of him to not return the favor. At Alexandre's no price tags could be seen, but one could feast one's eyes on displays of malachite, jade, ivory, tooled leather, umbrellas, walking sticks, purses, scarves, silver, jewelry, and china. Young Prince Alex walked the aisles swiftly, pointing and nodding affirmatively. When he left the exclusive establishment twenty minutes later, a laden shop clerk followed him to his sleigh carrying numerous boxes. From Alexandre's he walked to Druce's, the famous *magasin anglais* where they sold Harris tweeds, English soap, gloves, and hose. More packages were added to those in the troika. Beyond was Cabassue's, small and select, where Alex purchased two dozen pairs of French gloves for Zena. Fragrance poured from the doors of Brocard's, and now the *mademoiselle* had enough French scent to last a lifetime. And last he entered the jeweled splendor of Fabergé. When he left a short time later, the prince carried several white holly wood boxes lined in white velvet, the hallmark of a Fabergé purchase.

Carelessly tossing the boxes into the sleigh, Alex jumped in, dropped into the soft upholstered velvet, and said in the most jovial good humor, "Don't spare the horses, Ivan, I long for the comforts of the *dacha*."

Alex dozed on the way back as the early winter twilight fell across the peaceful woodlands of dark pines and starkly white birch. The windows glowed warmly golden as two hours later the sweat-streaked horses pulled up to the *dacha* entrance. Alex directed the servants to carry the packages into the study.

As Alex walked into the foyer, a small body hurtled toward him and wrapped chubby arms around his legs.

"Papa! Papa! Where been? Where *been*?" Bobby

screamed. Sweeping the excited child up into his arms, Alex grinned cheerfully and said, "I went to buy you some toys."

"Toys? See! See! Bobby see!" the young boy squealed. Zena stood back in the shadows of the stairway, irrepressibly happy to have Alex back. The day had been endless without him. Against her will, against all her plans, this careless rake had won her heart. She missed him terribly. He had only to enter a room and her spirits soared dizzily.

Scanning the entrance hall with a searching glance, Alex spied Zena and, moving toward the study, encompassed her within the circle of his free arm and bent to bid her hello with a kiss.

Her world was complete once again. Alex was back.

"Come see Bobby's toys and the trinkets I brought you. Missed you, *ma petite*," he said as he squeezed her gently.

The packages were spilled on the leather couch and on the carpet near the fireplace. Alex deposited Bobby on the rug and laid a package at his feet. Little hands ripped and tore the paper while Alex helped with the ribbon. A miniature golden train emerged from the silver tissue, and Zena's eyes opened in disbelief.

"Sasha!" she expostulated in wonder. "It's gold! My Lord, it's gold!"

"Don't worry, love, it still works," he indulgently affirmed, a small smile playing across his face. "See, here's the track; you wind the train with this key. Can you turn this key, Bobby?" he kindly asked. "Look, I'll show you how."

The track was quickly assembled, and soon the little solid gold train was gliding around the track, glistening in the flickering firelight. Some of Bobby's other toys were soon strewn in disarray on the floor while the young boy concentrated on the silver reproduction of a Volga paddle steamer by Henrik Wigstrom and a circus set with animals, acrobats, and clowns sculpted in enamel, gold, and semi-precious stones. A large pan of water had been carried in so that the paddle steamer could function, and the toddler was now very seriously teaching the circus performers and animals to swim. He subscribed to the "sink or swim" method of instruction.

Zena was awestruck by the extravagance.

"Here are a few things for you, too, child. I hope you like them," said Alex as he tossed several small wooden boxes in Zena's lap. With undiluted pleasure he watched her eyes sparkle in astonishment at the magnificent array of jewelry that spilled out of the velvet-lined boxes: a three-strand necklace of enormous pearls; a diamond brooch in the form of a Catherine's wheel; emerald earclips with glittering diamond teardrops; a ruby pendant worth an emir's ransom; and the *pièce de résistance*, an Art Nouveau necklace composed of sinewy golden links embellished with sapphires and emeralds that supported an elegant dragonfly fashioned from an enormous baroque pearl, its wings crafted from translucent mother-of-pearl and sapphires, the eyes gleaming emeralds, the whole poised between infinitely delicate water droplets fashioned from hundreds of diamonds.

"Do you like them?" Alex asked tranquilly.

"Do I *like* them!" Zena breathed in a whisper, tears streaming down her face as she sat near the fire, her lap filled with sparkling jewels. "Of course, I *love* them!" she said. "But Sasha, I couldn't accept them. They're much too expensive," she softly cried.

"Nonsense!" Alex uttered flatly. "Absolute nonsense. I'm tolerably rich (which avowal took honors as the understatement of the century). I assure you, my man of business won't raise an eyebrow at the bill. Now, enough said. You'll keep them or I'll hold my breath until I turn blue," he teased, and a smile lit his dark, handsome face.

Zena couldn't help but laugh at his ridiculous threat,

which was exactly what he wanted her to do. Tears always made him uncomfortable.

"If you want to please the hell out of me," he said as he leaned over to gently brush away the tears under her eyes, "you might consider wearing the dragonfly necklace when you dress for dinner tomorrow. Tonight we're going to *pique-nique* here in front of the fire and listen to the unrestrained squeals of that brat of a brother you have, who seems to be gleefully set on drowning each of his toys." His smile belied the gruff words, and the evening progressed precisely as he wished. No more talk of "can" or "can't accept your gifts," no more tears, and much later, no more chatter as a sleepy Bobby was bundled off to bed by Mariana. The evening ended on the pleasantly sensual note envisioned by the young prince. The delicate, voluptuous beauty in his arms cried softly that night in sated release as she warmed him again and again.

3

At ten-thirty the following morning, just as Zena, Bobby, and Alex were finishing breakfast in the sunny east parlor, voices were heard in the entrance hall.

Very soon Yuri appeared in the doorway, flushed and emanating healthy fresh air.

One winged eyebrow rose slightly as Alex drawled with friendly sarcasm, "Don't waste any time, do you, Yuri?"

Turning to Zena he smoothly commenced introductions. "Zena, I'd like you to meet one of my oldest friends, Yuri Petrovich Bolotnikov."

"A most exquisite pleasure to make your acquaintance." Yuri smiled winningly into Zena's eyes as he bowed elegantly over her hand. Yuri was a tall, handsome, blue-eyed, blond of Slavic splendor. His warm manner was redolent with friendliness and boundless cheer. Zena couldn't help but respond to the warmth of his personality.

"Good morning, Yuri Petrovitch," she said, bestowing a glowing, half-shy smile upon the towering blond man. "Alex talks about you with the highest regard."

"What a perfectly lovely *intime* domestic," a sultry feminine voice cooed archly from the open doorway. Amalie stood dramatically poised, the epitome of elegance and womanly loveliness in a lavender velvet traveling gown bordered with ermine. There was no missing the dazzling effect of the countess's entrance: the lavender gown set off her magnificent body to perfection as well as reflecting the sparkle in her luminous, lavender eyes; her ivory skin was flushed delicately from the cold; the glorious face and golden hair were framed becomingly by her fur hood.

The vision immediately induced an apprehensive twinge of discomfort in Zena, while Alex repressed the start her appearance caused him and damned Yuri inwardly for his crudeness. Alex quickly recovered himself; he was seldom disconcerted and never for long. Amalie glided toward Alex with feline grace. Fobbing off her attempt to embrace him by taking both kid-gloved hands in his, he gazed at her with a cool arrogance.

"What are you doing here, Amalie?" the prince said with a conspicuous lack of gallantry.

The countess opened her exquisite lavender eyes very wide. "Why, I've missed you, darling," she murmured soulfully.

Alex was unmoved. "Come off it, Amalie," he calmly replied, and then proceeded to make the necessary introductions with a careless politeness.

As the women were greeting each other, Amalie sweetly malicious and Zena uncertain and uncomfortable, Alex cast a scowling, questioning glance over their heads to Yuri, who shrugged his shoulders apologetically in response.

"Brandy, Yuri?" Alex inquired and jerked his head in the direction of the window where a cellarette of decanters stood on a small table. Crossing to the mahogany table, scarcely out of hearing distance from the women, Alex snarled, "What the fuck do you think you're doing?"

As Alex poured two generous measures, Yuri quickly explained *sotto voce*, "Lord, don't think I planned this. Last night at the Demidoffs' I inadvertently mentioned I was dropping by here this morning, and Amalie insisted on coming along. You know how demanding Amalie can be."

"Don't I know," Alex replied with disgust and lifted his eyes heavenward.

"Sorry," Yuri apologized.

Alex exhaled slowly, releasing his frustration, then drained his glass of brandy. "It's not your fault," Alex said gently. "Forget it." Amalie's brittle, spiteful laugh resounded from across the room. Alex sighed resignedly, "We'd better go and save Zena from Amalie's gilded claws. The young chit's no match for the bitch. She'll be verbally savaged within minutes. Come, Yuri, a little help to hold the tigress Benckendorff from my lamb's jugular."

The men sauntered back just as Amalie was tweaking a retreating, abashed Bobby under the chin and sweetly cooing, "And whose little boy are you?" Bobby stared at this strange, intense face that was much too close, pressed himself timidly into the back of his chair, and clung to the padded arms with an anxious intensity.

"You're frightening the poor boy, Amalie. Desist," Alex said softly, bent down, and swept Bobby up into his arms.

"Papa!" Bobby cried in relief and buried his head in Alex's shoulder.

Yuri's eyebrows rose into his hairline while Amalie audibly gasped. Zena raised panic-stricken eyes to Alex. Alex grinned benignly at her, disclaiming mildly to Yuri and Amalie, "Merely an affectionate childish expression, I assure you."

Amalie turned on Zena immediately, even spurious polite courtesy discarded. "The child is *yours* then, *mademoiselle?*"

"No, madame," Zena stammered somewhat faintly. "Bobby is . . . he's . . ."

"He's her young brother, my dear, curious Amalie." Alex smoothly finished Zena's faltering sentence. Still holding Bobby snugly in his arm, Alex placed his free hand on Zena's shoulder, a gesture both protective and possessive. Looking coolly into Amalie's dubious eyes, Alex drawled gently, "Zena and Bobby are old friends of the family merely resting here briefly on their journey south. Now, Amalie, does that sufficiently satisfy your avid inquisitiveness?" Considering the explanation more than Amalie deserved, he turned abruptly. "How about a game of billiards, Yuri? We were finished with breakfast."

Zena's head swiveled up toward Alex, her large blue eyes filled with stark appeal.

Interpreting the plea accurately, Alex amended smoothly, "Ladies, do join us. Amalie, you've played often enough with us." The double entendre was not intended, and Alex was immediately sorry it had occurred, for Amalie preened glowingly.

Yuri stepped in to bridge the faux pas diplomatically, explaining to Zena that Amalie was quite an expert billiards player. "Alex and I have a devil of a time winning," he attested.

Bobby went off with Mariana while the two couples retired to the billiard room. As Alex broke to begin the game, Amalie seated herself next to Zena on the high-backed, cane-seated billiard chairs.

"Now my dear," Amalie simpered with artificial amiability. "Tell me where you come from." Gossip had insinuated that Alex's houseguest this time was not the usual ballet dancer or young matron but a woman from the streets. One glance at Zena's delicate, refined features and one sentence uttered in her mellifluous, perfectly accented French disclaimed the gossip. The question was, Whose daughter was she? Obviously she was an innocent of the first rank, judging from the uncertainty and blushes.

Zena blanched at the direct inquiry, unused to dissembling with ease. An inarticulate murmur and tightly clenched hands were Amalie's only response.

Overhearing the bluntly worded question, Alex looked up from the three-cushion double rail shot he had just scored and decided this was no time for finesse. It would be wasted on the feline countess. Alex gave the countess a most quelling look, his drawl very pronounced. "You talk too much, Amalie. Enough of the prying questions, my dear. Is anyone asking you where your husband is or where he thinks you are? Now, we all could put inquiries to you which you wouldn't care to discuss, such as: What in the world did you tell Boris when he found you on the terrace late one night last fall with only a velvet cloak to cover your nakedness, hmm? Or perhaps you'd care to answer how you can stand to be married to the fat pig in the first place. You will, I'm sure, understand what I'm saying." Smiling faintly, Alex serenely accomplished a difficult two-corner billiard, oblivious to the cold-eyed countess who flashed him a seething glare of anger.

The prince looked up. "Agreed, then Amalie?" he asked blandly, a marked degree of sarcasm evident in the drawling voice. "You don't ask any questions and we won't ask any questions." The words fell into a small pool of silence, and for a long moment there was a complete and unnerving hush. Yuri was staring into the distance, his eyes cool and remote.

Alex stood there for a full thirty seconds, holding the countess's blazing eyes in a mild glance as he lazily chalked his cue, a glance nevertheless that held more than a hint of steel. Quickly Amalie realized it would serve no good purpose to further antagonize Alex. She'd find out about the little bit of fluff in other ways.

Amalie's eyes flashed a warm compliance. An amused laugh broke from between flawless white teeth and full rose lips. "Touché, Sasha. No more questions."

The prince sighed gently and set down the chalk. "Very astute, my dear," he murmured.

At which point Amalie abandoned any further pretense of friendship with Zena and spent the next hour doing what she did best. She flirted and enticed with both face and figure. She brushed against Alex as she moved to her next shot. She touched him familiarly as she bantered and reminisced about old times and mutual acquaintances.

Yuri, between turns, gallantly attempted to explain to Zena that this was Amalie's usual behavior and not singular to these circumstances. He could see Zena was uncomfortable, struggling bravely to ignore the honeyed coquetry enacted before her. Yuri's attempts to allay Zena's intense discomfort were deeply appreciated by the young woman.

This was a rare charmer Alex had found, Yuri thought, uncommonly pretty with fine, dark blue eyes that had a disconcertingly direct gaze. It was a pleasant change from the usual limpid blue. Her eyes could twinkle, though in a most disturbing manner. This little *mademoiselle* was a singular combination of the most matter-of-fact common sense and the most winsome, delicious folly. It was readily apparent why Alex's interest had persisted beyond his usual fortnight, as it was equally apparent that the little *mademoiselle* adored her seducer. Like a moth to the flame, Yuri mused uneasily, and he couldn't help pitying her. He banished the thought as disloyal, for both he and Alex had always freely sought their pleasure without undo concern for the consequences. But this fragile beauty was too obviously vulnerable, and the thought of her hopeless future with Alex kept returning. Sasha was not the person to bring happiness and requited love to the young miss.

Alex was casually indifferent to Amalie's posturing. He had never cared for her personality in any case. Only her bedroom activities had interested him, for she was beyond the common in her amorous proclivities and knew just how to drive a man to desperation. But now he had found in Zena a rare combination of sweet tenderness and sensuous delights that fascinated him beyond the abilities of Amalie's technical proficiency.

As the game progressed, Alex began to notice Yuri was spending altogether too much time amusing Zena as she sat on the sidelines watching the play. Rapidly concluding the contest by running out the game, finishing with a very difficult *force-masse* that he executed effortlessly, Alex racked up his cue and shrugging depreciatingly, rather discourteously said, "I'm afraid you'll have to excuse us now. Zena and I've made plans for this afternoon."

Striding over to Zena, Alex offered his hand to help her from the chair. Startled but grateful for the lie (they never made plans to do anything, but rather let their whims decide their activities), Zena placed her small hand in his and smiled appreciatively into the dark, handsome face.

Alex bowed briefly to Yuri. "Thank you for driving out. I trust you will have a pleasant journey back. Good afternoon, Amalie." With an abrupt nod in her direction, Alex escorted Zena out of the room.

"Well," Amalie exploded. "Discourteous boor! What's come over Alex?"

"I fear we're intruding on an idyllic love nest, my sweet. Sasha doesn't want company at the moment, and you know as well as I do that polite civilities aren't in Sasha's repertoire.

"Come, we'll drink a couple of bottles of champagne on the way back. Then I'll be better able to face the boredom and insipidity of the evening round of soirées, and you'll be better able to face the boredom and insipidity of your husband's company."

"He wants her now," Amalie jibed, "but it won't last. They never do for Sasha."

"I'm sure you're right." Yuri had to agree, having observed Alex's pattern of amorous sport these many years.

The two proceeded to their covered sledge, a perfectly matched couple, like a pair of bookends—both tall, classically proportioned, their heavy, golden hair the color of cornsilk in the sun, their eyes as blue as the sky on a clear summer day, their Ukrainian heritage evident in every feature.

As they adjusted the fur rugs, Yuri mocked playfully, "We could pass the time under the fur rugs, Amalie, in-

stead of drinking. Think what our child would look like—
another pure, classic Slav."

Amalie hurled Yuri a contemptuous glance and exclaimed, "Good Lord, Yuri, are you insane? What would
I do with a child?"

Yuri reflected briefly as he wrenched the cork from a
bottle of champagne. "True, Amalie," he observed facilely,
"what would you do indeed?"

"Really, Yuri," the countess sighed. "Sometimes I don't
know why I put up with you."

"You put up with me, Amalie darling, because we grew
up together. Don't forget all that adolescent groping and
lovemaking," he laughed, "and also because," he paused to
direct a quelling look at her, "you can get close to Alex
through me."

The countess stared him straight in the eye and, because
of their old friendship, made no attempt to dissemble or
evade. "Oh, Yuri," she sniffed, tossing her pale, silken
mane. "Sometimes you're impossible."

He grinned complaisantly, altogether familiar with the
golden goddess and the young girl underneath who had
come from the Ukraine six years ago and taken St.
Petersburg by storm. "Have a swig, your ladyship. If we're
too old to grope together anymore, at least we can get
drunk together. To Boris, the fat pig." He toasted, wink-
ing at her, and raised the bottle to his lips.

"Oh, Yuri, really, you shouldn't say things like . . ."
Then the countess burst into giggles and mirthfully snick-
ered, "I'll drink to that."

4

"I'm sorry, *ma petite*," Alex was saying as they walked upstairs to their suite. "I saw Yuri in town yesterday and, since he's an old and close friend, I invited him to come out sometime. But Lord, who'd ever think he'd bring Amalie, although he said she had forced her company on him. She's a bitch of the first order. Accept my apologies for her discourtesy to you."

"It's all right, Sasha. I'm just not used to such blunt questions. I'll prepare some answers for the future, and the mendacity will come easier."

Entering the sitting room, Zena glanced up shyly and said, "Is Amalie an old friend, too? She seemed very familiar with you."

"Not a friend," Alex replied curtly, "an acquaintance, my dear, merely an acquaintance. Let's have a drink and then find Bobby and go for a walk."

Yuri stopped by quite often in the following days. He and Alex had been friends since adolescence. In fact, the past weeks of Alex's seclusion with Zena had been the longest separation their friendship had undergone. Normally if Alex retired to his *dacha*, Yuri and assorted females were invited as well.

Yuri had quietly formed his own opinion about Alex's newest paramour. Unlike the amusements in Alex's past, she was more than an idle receptacle for Alex's erotic lecheries. Apparently this observation had not touched Alex as yet, for he treated her with his usual casualness toward women, albeit with considerably more concern for her wishes than normal.

Yuri hoped he was right in his conclusions. If he wasn't, and Zena was just another of Alex's frivolous fancies, God help her. Alex was carrying on a long family tradition of dalliance. His father's affairs had been legion, although he was virtuous enough today. Yuri was well aware of the broken hearts left in Alex's wake over the past six years. If Alex was just toying with her, Yuri pitied Zena, who was so obviously in love with her seducer. The little *mademoiselle* was no match for the notorious Archer. If Alex really didn't care, he'd break her like a china doll.

One sunny afternoon in March the three were sitting at a table in the small back parlor. Yuri and Alex had been sampling the virtues of several bottles of wine from a recent French shipment. Zena tasted sips of each vintage but had fallen far behind the enthusiastic testing of Yuri and Alex.

The warm sun streamed into the room through Venetian bow windows facing south and west. Both men were lounging in their chairs, restfully content with the peaceful afternoon.

"Quite idyllic here, Sasha. Dammed if it ain't. Beats the hectic pace of St. Petersburg or Moscow."

"Amen," Alex answered and lifted his wine glass in salute before emptying it. He poured out two more glasses.

"Don't have to offer any polite civilities or evade the snares of designing mamas. Oh, by the way, speaking of designing mamas, Malekov bit the dust last week. Lydia finally caught him. He'll be a papa before long, or I miss my guess," Yuri signed deeply. "It'll happen to all of us someday, I fear."

"Not to me," Alex retorted tartly. "I don't want a wife and children."

Yuri winced at the blunt disclaimer. This was Alex at

his worst. Yuri glanced at Zena's flushed face in dismay. In a kindly attempt to mitigate Zena's obvious embarrassment at Alex's insensitive remark, Yuri tactfully changed the subject, allowing her time to recover her composure.

"Say, Sasha, do I still have first option on Pasha's latest offspring?"

"Certainly. Want to see the colt? He's magnificent. Excuse us, dear," Alex said to Zena. "I'm going to show Yuri Pasha's latest effort."

Alex went out to the stables with Yuri, totally unaware of the distress he had caused. His remark had been incidental to the occasion and uttered with his customary casual disregard for sensibility. Accustomed to treating women negligently, he was unfortunately immune to the delicate emotions of those recipients of his dégagé manners. This quintessential distance he cultivated was a technique honed to perfection through necessity; at a very early age he had been made cognizant of the distinction his name, rank, and wealth signalized in the hopeful eyes of society's maids and mamas. He had been warned by his father to beware of making offers he had no intention of honoring.

"I make these suggestions," Nikki had said many years ago, "for your personal edification and also for purely selfish motives. It will save me from having to confront irate friends who accuse me of having raised a roguish scapegrace son who seduces their young daughters' affections. Stay away from virginal young misses of good families," he advised, "if you can. I'm not fool enough to say it's always possible. Many of those sweetly pure maidens are damn anxious to hop into bed too, as we both know. If I didn't love your mother, my boy," Nikki had sighed, "sometimes it's damned trying on one's fidelity, let me tell you. I can understand them running after young bucks like you, but why they continue to be interested in tossing their virtue in my direction is hard to fathom." Nikki's deprecating modesty was ingenuous, for he was, with the exception of gray waves of hair streaking his temples, as fit, splendidly muscled, and unconscionably handsome as ever.

"In the long run," Nikki had cautioned, "you're safer with married women and females of a certain class. They're both in no position to demand marriage. They know as well as you that the game don't end with a wedding."

In Nikki's and Sasha's milieu the game *d'amour* was played by a strict code, and the ladies who participated knew the rules—rules devised by men and operating in a man's world.

At the time, the young boy was of an age to accept advice gracelessly and had heatedly and crudely commented, "I'll fuck whom I please."

To which remark Nikki replied smoothly and calmly, "In that case, I must sharpen my diplomatic skills, which I envision will soon to put to the test." And they were on numerous occasions.

While growing up, Alex came to realize the perspicuity of his father's admonitions and had, by the age of twenty-four, fallen quite easily into society's accepted standards of dalliance, acutely aware by now of the sterling advice his father had imparted. He had attained an exceeding proficiency, indeed an effortless and guarded circumspection. He never promised a woman anything at all.

Zena went upstairs nursing a splitting headache, chilled by Alex's vehement assertion against a wife and children. She lay on the bed paralyzed by the awful fear that Alex might very well soon become a father. She had suppressed acknowledging the obvious signs for several weeks now. Alex's blunt pronouncement had quite thoroughly squashed any girlish dreams of marriage. Consciously she knew better, of course, having accepted his favors as unreservedly as they had been offered. She knew how youthful rakes like Alex felt. He meant no good toward her. Good God, she knew his type and the reputation he must have. She was under no illusions about Alex's companionship. He had promised her nothing more than the comfort of his home and person until such time as she chose to continue her journey. She was the romantic fool, the childish woman who hoped for miracles, who dreamed idiotic dreams, and who wove silly fantasies around a relationship that was for Alex nothing more than a convenience. If he hadn't taken her that night, he would have found someone else to accompany him from St. Petersburg. From Yuri's conversations she had become aware that Alexander Nikalaevich Kuzan was never without a female on his arm. A warm, feminine body in close proximity for his use and comfort was as natural as breathing for him. She was simply the latest of the frivolous sorority.

Zena threw herself down on the bed and indulged in hysterical, uncontrolled sobs. Good Lord! *What* was she going to do?

The tearful emotional storm soon passed, but the headache wouldn't go away as her heinous subconscious apprehensions browbeat her pragmatic restraints. She wanted to stay with Sasha. She wanted him to make love to her. She wanted to wake in the morning feeling the warmth of his body. Those wishes, however impractical, defeated momentarily the assaulting fears. Some residue of sense told her it was madness to care for such an unprincipled rogue, but what chance had reason when she was held in Sasha's embrace.

Strolling into the room an hour later, Alex informed her that Yuri had left. "Some ball at the Strindbergs' tonight. Thank God I don't have to go. This hermitage is quite to my taste. Don't you feel well?" he asked solicitously as he approached the bed.

"Just a little headache, Sasha," Zena admitted. "Nothing serious," she dissimulated valiantly when, in effect, her whole future was in the balance.

"Poor child," he soothed as he sat on the edge of the bed. "Too much wine, *ma petite*?" he probed gently.

"No, I don't think so."

"Just relax, little one," and his long, slim fingers massaged her temples with a gossamer fluidity, moving like whispers to lightly brush her eyelids shut, gently stroking the translucent lids.

He soothed her temples, forehead, and eyes in a tranquilizing rhythm. For a man who stood inches above most men, his powerful hands were capable of the most unbelievably delicate touch. What capricious qualities, she reflected, coexisted in the essence of this vital man she loved: cold indifference and tender solicitude; absolute kindness and genuine selfishness; base sensuality and striking self-denial.

"Feeling better?" Alex asked after several minutes.

"Oh, yes, thank you, Sasha. Where did you learn to do that?"

"My nanny was proficient at soothing the most horrendous temper tantrums. I, as you may have noted," he grinned disarmingly, "am used to having my own way."

"It has come to my attention once or twice, my lord," Zena acknowledged demurely.

"I don't suppose you'd care for a drink," Alex said, apparently undeterred by the several bottles of wine consumed that afternoon. He reached for the bedside decanter of brandy, poured himself a glass, and lay down next to Zena, his boots carelessly sprawled on the velvet coverlet.

"Not right now. Sasha, do you always drink so much?"

"Most of the time. It depends. Out here in the country I'm modestly temperate, my dear. You should see us during the war games in August. Don't draw a sober breath for three weeks. It's a miracle some can sit their horses. You, sweet child, intoxicate me with your beauty. I don't need as much liquor," he teased, turning to touch her cheek briefly with the back of his fingers.

"Other than during my retreats to the country Yuri and I are more drunk than sober most of the time. Makes the round of necessary socializing more bearable. Jesus, do I hate those accursed balls. For your ears alone, pet, I confess I have never gone sober to one. Yuri and I usually arrive late and very inebriated. I've found dancing with simpering belles requires a minimum of two bottles of brandy to tolerate the ridiculous flow of chatter. Although," he mused tolerantly, as he raised the glass to his lips, "Yuri and I have had our share of good times." He chuckled. "I guess Yuri knows just about anything there is to know about me."

"Tell me now why he calls you Archer. He does sometimes. Do you really like archery?" Zena asked.

"On occasion," and Alex smiled wickedly at the memory.

"On occasion. You're not overly fond of archery then," she persisted.

"No, dear. But it's nothing you'd be interested in." The iniquitous grin reappeared and whetted Zena's curiosity.

"I want to know," she pouted prettily.

"You'd rather not know. Let me assure you."

Zena sat up in bed and fixed the smiling face with a steely, determined glance.

Alex shrugged resignedly and deprecatingly said, "Oh, very well, I won a contest once."

"What kind of contest?"

"Nothing special. Just sort of a test of competence," he equivocated, looking into the liquor he was slowly swirling in his glass.

"What test of competence? Explain, I'm piqued."

"No, really. It was just a youthful lark," he answered vaguely, still trying to evade.

"Damn you, tell me, you've roused my interest."

"Modesty forbids me . . ." the prince smirked.

"As if you know what modesty means, you arrogant egotistical rogue."

"Leave it to a woman to be persistent," he grumbled.

"No doubt you are intent upon knowing." Unintimidated, Zena sat there sternly eyeing Alex.

"Very well," he sighed resignedly, "if you must know, There was a costume party. I came as an archer, one of Robin Hood's band," the succinct recital went on impassively. "The party got out of hand, as was often the case, and a fucking contest ensued."

"A what?" Zena's blue eyes widened in shock.

"It happened a long time ago. I was young and reckless." he commented by way of explanation.

"How long ago?" she asked with suspicious sweetness.

"A year ago," he admitted ruefully.

"A year ago! That's youthful?"

"Well, I was damn drunk, too. Hadn't drawn a sober breath in four days."

"How *exactly* did you win this contest?" Zena inquired with acid saccharinity.

"I fucked steadily for twenty-six hours," he grinned. "Beat Yuri by an hour and a half. He's never forgiven me."

"What in the world did the woman look like after twenty-six hours?" Zena's expression mirrored her shock.

"Oh, we had to change women several times. They're too damned tender. I kept track of the women by the number of arrows in my quiver, hence the allusion to my costume and the nickname. It's all very childish."

"Did everyone watch?" Zena asked horrified.

"Of course."

"That's disgusting," Zena spat indignantly.

"Now you're mad, *ma petite*. I told you not to ask. I knew you'd rather not hear. Wish I would have known you then," he murmured playfully. "We could have set the record single-handedly." Alex quirked his eyebrows at Zena and his languid smile broadened.

Hot color flooded Zena's face. "You despicable cad! How dare you suggest such a thing," she exploded resentfully.

"Really, love, don't take offense," Alex replied soothingly. "I meant it as the sincerest compliment."

Anger boiled up so violently it practically choked her. "If that's the way you consider me . . . like . . . like . . . a whore!" Zena sputtered.

"Good Lord," Alex protested. "I didn't mean that at all. Forget what I said, Zena, you misunderstood. Look I just meant . . ." he broke off lamely, recognizing his inability to vindicate the sportive statement in light of her flashing eyes. But then, unfortunately, his mind flew to a fleeting vision of he and Zena in that beguiling embrace, and his mouth twitched into an irrepressible grin.

"Misunderstood!" Zena cried, and the unfortunate grin fanned her already volatile rage. "*You're* obviously the one who misunderstands!" Then with an imprudent artifice, fully intended to provoke, she altered her voice to a sensuous purr and asserted archly, "If I've become as accomplished a lover as you suggest, perhaps I shouldn't conceal such glowing virtues. With my adroit versatility it would be foolish to limit myself to only one man. I, too, might discover additional delights with other men. You say Yuri was only one and a half hours short of you in this, ah, competency contest. I could begin with him," she declared with reckless audacity. Zena had the satisfaction of seeing a muscle begin to twitch near Alex's mouth. He towered above her, his fingers biting white-knuckled into the brandy glass in a hard-fought effort to control his rising ire.

"No one touches you but me," he grimly uttered.

Zena tossed her head airily. "*You* are no longer going to touch me! I don't particularly care to be considered in terms of the receiving half of a twenty-six-hour fucking contest. *If* you don't mind!" she disdainfully derided.

Zena'a direct and obdurate rebuff was a grave mistake, as any number of Alex's friends would confirm. Alexander

Kuzan, to everyone's certain knowledge, had never backed down from a confrontation.

"I'll touch you whenever I please," the stern-faced prince ground out between his teeth.

"You will not!" the foolhardy girl continued, indignant affront goading her impetuosity and Alex's detestable, overbearing insolence further aggravating her bold defiance.

"You think not? I assure you, pet, you're quite wrong." The purred words and look accompanying them held a distinct menace. "If it's rape you're looking for," he said in a voice silky with venom as he glanced down at her impatiently, "I'm in a temper to oblige you."

"You wouldn't," Zena gasped.

"In a minute."

The angry woman pugnaciously retorted, "I don't believe you!"

Alex tossed aside his glass, which shattered into splinters on the floor. His hand lashed out, grasped the collar of Zena's dress firmly, and ripped the soft georgette bodice from the neck to waist.

Zena froze in shocked silence.

"Don't look so pained," Alex laughed unpleasantly. "I'll buy you another."

Irrepressible fury welled up through the frozen shock. Midnight blue eyes grew stormy with wrath.

As rapidly as Zena's ire escalated, Alex's exasperation mollified. The grimness contorting his features disappeared. "Sweetheart, relax! You're overwrought," he conciliated, his peremptory act of tyranny having purged his fury. "I'll buy you three, four, five frocks to replace it," he grinned, triumphantly in command, delighting now as victor, relishing the endearing beauty of Zena's rage.

He was enjoying himself, toying delicately not only with the silken remnants of her bodice, but toying as well with the woman's fierce ideals, playing with Zena on a light-hearted, boyish level. He was enjoying the game between a man and a woman. He relished the saucy vivacity of the *mademoiselle* and her ability to taunt him with her show of independence. Complaisant women bored him. Zena was a fiery citadel when she was in one of these moods, and his senses stirred with desire as he contemplated the storming.

"*No, thank you.*" Each word of Zena's refusal was bitten off frigidly. "Keep your damn new gowns!" she witheringly retorted.

"Oh, ho! You won't take any clothes from me?" Alex's tawny eyes glittered brilliantly as he drawled the question languorously.

"Absolutely not!" she snapped.

"In that case, I'll rip all your clothes off you this week and soon have you exactly how I most prefer you," he paused and dropped the word softly into the heated atmosphere, "naked."

"I'll take two," Zena retorted hastily.

"Smart girl," Alex murmured. "Flexibility, my puss, you've flexibility. You'll go far. Come here now and wrap those flexible legs around me, and I'll apologize contritely for my insufferable conduct and rudeness."

Zena hesitated, trying to reconcile her turbulent emotions as Alex's mocking eyes played over her half-nude form.

"Do we start this rape all over again?" asked Alex, lowering his soft voice to the nearly inaudible. "You must learn that frank and willful females are not widely tolerated in the world. Submission, my pet, is the answer. Come here, darling," he whispered and slid his hand around her waist.

She went then.

He pulled her down on the bed. Viewing the quietly distraught woman compassionately, he could understand her distress. He felt a twinge of guilt at the woebegone,

humbled look on her face. He knew he had beaten her un-
fairly; the contest was uneven, and he had all the advantages. But damn it, she'd better become disposed to a
woman's role. She couldn't fight it forever. And he wanted
her, wanted her for himself. An inexplicable urge to keep
her welled up in him.

"Remember, I share you with no one. You're mine," he
said with a quiet stiffness. He lay over her. "Are you
mine? Answer, woman," he said gruffly.

Zena turned her head away.

Alex shook her gently. "Answer. Are you mine?" he ordered, his voice as cutting as a lash.

"Yes, Sasha," agreed a small whispered voice. Looking
up at him she asked sadly, "Am I simply another of your
possessions?"

"Not just *another* possession, *ma petite*," Alex reasoned.
"But in truth my finest acquisition to date."

"You'd keep me here against my will?" she asked incredulously as Alex played with the ribbons of her chemise.

"Why not?" he answered blandly, thinking to himself
pragmatically that she wasn't really suffering unduly, and
she'd be considerably richer when she finally left. She had
no money. He could keep her here indefinitely through
lack of funds until such time as he chose to pay her and
let her go. What the hell, that little technique—that little
form of coercion—in one form or another had been around
for three thousand years.

"I won't allow it," Zena responded, hotly jerking away.
The long, lean fingers carelessly grasping the ruffled chemise neckline tightened automatically, and the sheer fabric
tore under the strain.

"Come, come, my sweet. So many harsh words. I'm not
entirely used to such disobliging treatment from females.
Rest content now, my pet. Is the captivity so vile?" And
his fingers lightly caressed her exposed breast.

Alex's golden eyes began to glow with a sensual, predatory gleam. His arms closed around her, and his mouth came down on hers. She felt the warm desire begin to stir, and she was sick with shame. She fought against him faintly, turning her head from side to side, trying to evade the burning lips while her traitorous body was heating with yearning passion.

Zena tried to recall the antipathy, anger, and humiliation he had roused. But he was all contrite apology now, petting and comforting her, murmuring softly affectionate words of atonement as he brushed his lips down the alabaster column of her throat.

When confronted by those sensual eyes, warmly whispered regrets, and heated, stroking fingers, Zena began to melt. She knew if he continued, all was lost.

But at the moment, as his arms pulled her close, her heart prevailed. She wanted him. She loved him with every fiber of her being. When Sasha held her in his arms, his smoldering eyes searching hers, she knew she would be anything he wanted as long as he kept her near. Her struggles ceased, her lips acquiesced, and she responded to the flame burning in her lover's eyes. Her body arched to him, and her thighs fell apart. And he pleased her then in all the ways he knew best.

5

The next week brought restored content. Alex was utterly charming and quietly accommodating to her abrupt mood changes, which swung dangerously with her love of Alex and her fear of the future for her child, which appeared more of a certainty with each passing day. Alex pampered her in little ways, being accessible not only physically but offering small anecdotes about his youthful holidays spent at the *dacha*, occasionally opening up enough to respond warmly to Zena's affectionate nuzzles and kisses. He no longer asked, "Why did you do that?" when she would impulsively stand on tiptoe to touch her lips to his cheek. He only smiled impassively now at these sudden, spontaneous kisses. She loved him, she knew that, and after last week her spirits soared. It seemed that perhaps his cool, impersonal reserve was indeed vulnerable. Could he care a little about her, too? Was it possible? Zena felt a joyful exuberance that would reappear despite momentarily depressing moods. She hopefully considered—indeed, felt almost a surety—that Sasha cherished her as a person and not simply for the comfort of her body in bed.

The pattern of their days lapsed into a familiar, restful routine. Zena was slightly on edge, perhaps quicker to take offense. She was certain she was carrying Alex's child now and terrified of telling him. If Alex had had any experience with pregnant females, he might have recognized the unstable emotional signs of gestation, but since these phenomena were auguries with which he was unacquainted, he unwittingly regarded these quirks of pique as simply female temperament.

Alex's muzhiks had immediately upon their arrival taken to addressing Bobby affectionately as "the little prince." Assuming their master would not bother himself over a young child without paternal considerations and noting the dark hair and light eyes of both, they reached their own conclusions.

Zena had carefully explained initially that the boy was her brother. Blankly polite stares had accepted her explanation, and in her presence they were careful to refrain from referring to Bobby as "the little prince." But away from her vicinity they continued addressing the young boy with the deference due their master's son. Alex was quietly amused at the subtle battle operating between Zena and the servants and allowed them to continue addressing the boy as his. He was altogether familiar with the dogged stubbornness and intractability of the Russian peasant mind. Even if he had forbade them to regard Bobby as his, they would devotedly accede to the *batiushka*'s orders, but their hearts wouldn't change.

In addition, the title bestowed on Bobby served as a subtle means of provoking Zena when he was in a humor to tease her or revenge himself mildly for one of her frequent fits of temper.

He had retaliated at dinner that night, when Zena flashed furiously at him during a trifling disagreement that perhaps she and Bobby should leave. Alex knew her threat was simply offended pride. He took on a suitably distressed and hurt expression. The prince, quite aware of the breathless interest of his household, gratified his pique by woefully lamenting, "I'm devastated, *mademoiselle*. Would you deprive me of Bobby's company?" The numerous servants attendant to the meal were shocked at the *baryshna*'s unfeeling attitude to the father of her child and expressed their disapproval in their scandalized expressions.

Alex bit his lip to hide his smile and chuckled to himself while Zena fumed helplessly. She expressed her displeasure by a cold silence through the brandy and excused herself with a headache shortly after.

Alex drank his way leisurely through the rest of the bottle while pondering these frequent and volatile outbursts of Zena's. Although he was well content with her, such a combination of sensuality and spirit had, to date, eluded him in his previous congress with women, and she pleased him mightily; yet the tantrums were more numerous. The quiet, gently complacent child was being displaced. As well, he thought, with a wry understanding; ennui would be arrested that much longer. The tedium of cloying women was all too familiar.

Midway through the second bottle Alex decided he missed the warmth of his companion. Doors opened noiselessly as he progressed from study to bedchamber. Hovering servants shadowed his passage upstairs, although it was well past midnight. Upon entering the bedchamber he turned the latch on the door. With the silent click the crowd of muzhiks melted away. Several lamps were burning low in the large room. Pouring himself another brandy from the bedside decanter, he sauntered slowly around the room and extinguished most of the lamps. Seated by the porcelain stove, he drained several more glasses and undressed leisurely in the quiet room. Zena was sleeping restlessly, moving from side to side on the large bed.

Alex decided she wasn't sleeping so deeply that it would matter if he woke her. He slipped into bed and bent to kiss her lips. All he received for his gentle caress was a kick in the shins and a hissed. "Don't touch me."

"Ouch," he exclaimed, querulously rubbing his leg. "Good Lord, woman. What's come over you?" he inquired in slightly inebriated astonishment. He searched the furious face of the woman beside him. "You're all claws and fangs and threatening abuse lately."

"That's how much I care what you think," Zena hissed unforgivably and snapped her fingers under his nose.

Alex stiffened. His eyes narrowed contemplatively at the affront, and he baited her then for her audacity. "You would do well," he said smoothly, "to cultivate some womanly wiles."

He was retaliating in frustration, for in truth, her utter candor was a delightful and pleasant change from years of viewing all the womanly wiles regularly paraded for his benefit.

"I've never felt the least desire to stoop to such disgusting measures, as you very well know. I'm here precisely because I chose not to debase myself with that pig Scobloff," the cold, haughty, belligerent woman shot back, her chin jutting, her blue-black eyes blazing.

"I see. A man beds you, it appears, at his own risk," Alex drawled ominously.

"If you want a soft and yielding woman," Zena snapped, "there's always that hussy Amalie."

Alex signed. Zena was right, of course. But he didn't want Amalie. He wanted her. "Give me a few minutes, *mademoiselle*, and I can make you soft and yielding as well," his voice came out assured and arrogant.

"Oh!" choked Zena. "You odious, overbearing . . . Never!"

"Never?" His black brows shot up. "Care to place a small wager on the duration of 'never,' my pet?" drawled his husky voice as he studied her thoughtfully. Zena's eyes were like agates. His golden eyes swept the beautiful, raging figure from head to foot. Zena lay exquisite, defiant, her long auburn hair tumbling in waves about her soft, white shoulders. Her heaving bosom was half exposed above the appliquéd lace, low-cut décolletage of the ivory satin nightgown.

Alex's eyes diminished to glittering slits as the scowl on his fine brow deepened, and he braced his body against the expected onslaught. Rolling over the infuriated woman, he looked down at the flashing eyes and softly breathed through his teeth, "Make ready, my dear. 'Never' has arrived."

Mademoiselle Turku slapped his face. Alex laughed and caught her more firmly in his arms. His mouth found hers in a bruising, ruthless kiss that lasted until all rational considerations were driven from her head. When he finished, Alex stayed scarce a moment in her, rolled over, and soon after was asleep, content, and sated, sleeping off the two bottles of brandy he had consumed.

Zena lay wide awake and troubled, having regained her disordered senses, angry with herself for succumbing once again so easily.

The next morning Alex was all apology and cheerful bantering, holding her close, calling her his own *dushka*, teasing an answering smile from her. "I'll be a paragon of civility. Just watch. No more raging masculine ego. Friends?" he asked contritely as he kissed her palm.

"Friends," she whispered softly and forgave him all.

She could never describe exactly why she was so drawn to him. He was a mixture of impressions like cynical, mocking, moody, or quizzical and yet teasing, laughing, tender, insouciantly gay. He never posed. He was always himself, quite simple but uncommon in his style. He was learned, too, although he laughed away pretense of any kind. What would he be like if he ever cared about anything intensely, if anything in life really mattered to him?

6

Two days later in the early afternoon they were interrupted while relaxing in Alex's study.

"Guests, Your Excellency," Trevor announced.

Zena gave a start.

Alex cast her a stern look as she opened her mouth to protest. "My turn this time. You stay, no pouting upstairs."

Zena was about to retort heatedly when Alex broke into his winning smile. "It's only fair, isn't it?" he demanded. "I sent them away for you last time." And he had only a week ago given in to Zena's pouting tantrum and turned Amalie and Princess Baskirseff away when they came to visit. "You be pleasant to them for me this time?"

It was only fair and Zena knew it. "Of course, Sasha," she smiled back ruefully, "you're right." She had every good intention of being pleasant and friendly, but as the afternoon wore on into evening, even her best efforts couldn't withstand Amalie's persistent sweet malice as the hours stretched tediously one into another. No one, thought Zena while viciously studying Amalie's fair face, has the right to be so flawlessly perfect.

Yuri and Amalie had come this time in company with two other friends, Captains Loris Grudtsyn and Peotr Diebitsch. The drinking was deep and heavy. Zena declined spirits since they upset her lately, while Amalie sipped delicately on champagne. The visitors had all been

Alex's friends since childhood, and Zena listened bleakly as
the conversation fell into reminiscing.

"Remember, Sasha," said Amalie at her sweetest, "when
we all used to swim on those hot summer days in the river.
For fourteen-year-old boys you were all quite childishly
silly, swinging from ropes and pretending to be Viking pi-
rates."

"Speaking of childish," Loris Grudtsyn interpolated,
"who was the one who slipped frogs into everyone's bed at
night?" and he cast an amused glance at Amalie.

She blushed prettily. "We were all young then."

"Yuri had one of the chambermaids in bed with him,"
Sasha explained to Zena, grinning boyishly, "and she let
out a shriek heard halfway to Moscow when her foot
touched that slimy little creature. Did you ever calm her
down, Yuri?" Alex asked innocently.

"I managed to think of a way," Yuri smirked, his pale
blue eyes narrowed in pensive memory.

"What about the time the dancers you had brought
down from St. Petersburg were dancing nude in your private theater with all of us drunkenly enjoying the spectacle,
when your mother and her friend stopped by unexpectedly?" Peotr Diebitsch asked facetiously. "You got hell for
that embarrassment, I'll bet."

"Oh, *Maman* can always be talked around," Alex
drawled languidly. "She's always been a most indulgent
parent. After having put up with Papa, I think nothing
shocks her any longer."

Moving to the drawing room after dinner, Amalie insinuated herself with casual familiarity between Alex and
Yuri on the embroidered settee. Brushing Alex's cheek
with her fingertips, she breathed intimately, "Sasha, dear,
could I have more champagne?"

He rose to do her bidding, remarking cheerfully,
"Amalie, you did always have a hollow leg when it comes

to champagne. Let's put a bottle here," and he slapped it on a nearby table, "so I don't have to keep getting up."

"Thank you, Sasha," Amalie murmured softly as she kissed him in gratitude for his courtesy.

Good God, Yuri thought. What was Alex doing? Here he had Zena, as entrancing woman as anyone could wish, and he was openly flirting with Amalie. Vividly he recalled Zena's stricken look of a moment ago when Alex had so ardently kissed Amalie. Yuri had half a mind to importune Zena for himself and teach the callous bastard a lesson. She was astonishingly lovely and had an unmitigated mischievous sparkle in her eye at times that spoke of a spirited, irreverent nature. Zena would make any man a splendid, vivacious companion, and if Alex so rudely disregarded her feelings, Yuri would be more than happy to offer her solace.

Alex was half drunk by now, and the intimate presence of Amalie seemed familiar and natural.

"Sasha, play for us," Peotr interjected, humming a few bars of a mournful gypsy air.

"Oh, do, Sasha," Amalie pleaded, standing up to pull Alex to his feet. "Play 'Islamey,' please, Sasha, please," she cajoled.

Zena saw Amalie give Alex a long, lingering look of such naked sensuality that she looked away in embarrassment. Alex returned her smoldering glance with a faint smile of understanding.

Giving in to his friends' demands, Alex sat before the keyboard of the huge grand piano, Amalie seated at his side, her arm thrown over his shoulder.

"Remember 'Selim's Song,' Sasha. Play 'Selim' first."

Despite the hours of drinking, Alex's fingers glided surely over the keys, eliciting a compelling melody, redolent of tragic love and melancholy surrender. Everyone sang the poignant lyrics in voices raw with liquor and emotion.

Zena could no longer stand the sight of Amalie draped over Alex. It was obvious they had been lovers; even their acerbic remarks indicated intimacy. They had past memories to share, common bonds of friendship and family, and Zena felt isolated and saw how tenuous and fragile her hold on Alex was. And now they were laughing, the beautiful couple, two superb creatures, ideal foils for each other, blond head against raven tresses.

She had a sudden savage longing to kill Amalie. Zena quietly slipped from the room as the five voices rose once again in swelling harmony on the last chorus. She had tried; she had really tried to be courteous and friendly, but Alex asked too much if he wanted her to stay and watch him playfully wooing Amalie. Zena began to cry, giving in to the misery she had been holding in check for hours.

As the chorus ended in a crashing chord, Alex looked around for Zena. "Where's Zena?" he inquired offhand.

"She just left," Yuri replied. "She's tired, I think."

"Damn it. I want her here," Alex insisted arrogantly.

"Let her go," Amalie petulently declared. "Really, Sasha, she looks barely out of the schoolroom."

With a drunken brutality Alex replied, "As you should well know, my dear lady, age is of little consequence when it comes to passion. How old were you, my sweet, when you first spread your legs?"

A flush illuminated Amalie's face.

"Sasha, that's enough," Yuri interposed hurriedly. "Play us another song—a gay one this time."

Alex allowed himself to be persuaded, and soon everyone was raucously singing the rollicking chorus to "The Shepherd Lol." As the group broke into the second chorus, Yuri quietly slipped out of the room.

He strode upstairs and down the long hall to Alex's apartment. Knocking on the door he called out softly, "It's Yuri."

After a lengthy interval during which he was unsure his

voice had been heard, the door opened and Zena's tear-stained face greeted him.

Gathering the woebegone woman in his arms, Yuri kicked the door shut with his boot and gently guided her over to the settee in front of the fire, where they both sat down. Passing a practiced arm around her drooping shoulders, he drew her to him.

"I'm sorry, Zena. Sasha can be a brute when he's drinking." Yuri had been watching Alex's casual treatment of Zena for weeks and felt a genuine concern for her wounded feelings. She had a poignant vulnerability noticeably lacking in the society hussies with whom he associated. If she would have accepted his affection as consolation, he would have offered it gladly, but her adoration of Sasha was too patently obvious for him to engage her feelings. He could be a friend to her, at least, but when she turned those deep blue eyes on him, he was a lost man.

"It's all right," Zena gulped convulsively as she tried to stifle the tears. "I'll just stay upstairs until everyone's gone."

"Is there anything I can do?" Yuri asked compassionately.

"No, not really. I shouldn't carry on so anyway. I tell myself it's ridiculous, but. . . ." her voice trailed off wearily.

"Do you want me to say something to Sasha? He can be damn disagreeable when he wishes, but when he's sober he can be quite obliging and kind," Yuri allowed.

"Don't I know," Zena laughed bitterly. "So *very* obliging. Oh, Yuri," she wailed, as fresh tears fell. "God forgive me, I love him so."

Holding her close, Yuri rocked her softly, administering an awkward pat now and then to her tousled hair. He let her weep her fill, and when the sobs and flood of tears abated, he carefully wiped her face dry.

"Everything will be fine, just see," he promised rashly. "I know Alex cares about you."

Zena's beautiful face lit up pitifully, "Do you really think so?"

"Of course," Yuri pronounced with a certainty he was far from feeling, but Alex had kept Zena for weeks longer than anyone else. Surely that's a hopeful indication, he thought.

"I hope you're right," Zena signed happily, and in a few minutes Yuri had cajoled the tears away with one of his outrageous anecdotes.

Time passed swiftly as Yuri engaged to dispel the unhappiness from Zena's eyes.

As they were both gayly laughing, Yuri's arm comfortably on the back of the settee behind Zena, a sardonic voice broke into the cheerful mirth. "What a perfectly charming scene," rasped Alex, his eyes full of wrath and astonishment. Then his voice chilled ominously. "Our usual custom of friendly sharing, Yuri, doesn't include Baroness Turku. I trust we understand each other on that score. I've warned the *mademoiselle* and, if I'm not mistaken, you were also apprised of my feelings on the lady's availability. She is not, you may recall, available."

"Sasha, please," Zena pleaded. "Yuri's just being nice."

"Pray do not insult my intelligence, *mademoiselle*. Allow me to know just how *nice* Yuri can be to a beautiful woman. I have always admired Yuri's utter lack of scruples when it comes to satisfying his physical urges. Am I too late and reduced to seconds tonight, my pet?" Alex murmured silkily.

Zena blanched at the insult.

"You're a fool to treat Zena this way, Sasha," Yuri exclaimed angrily. "You're blind drunk!"

With a chill politeness that required stern restraint on his boiling temper, Alex said, "I'll thank you to mind your own business, Yuri, and kindly take your lecherous hands off my mistress. Now if you'll excuse us," Alex informed with resentment, "I'd like some private conversation with the *mademoiselle*."

Ignoring Alex's cold indignation, Yuri spoke quietly to Zena. "If you need me," he said soberly, looking directly into her tremulous blue eyes, "just call."

"Very touching, I'm sure," drawled Alex, looking straight through him.

"Sasha, for God's sake! Sober up!" And then, disregarding Alex's jaundiced retort, Yuri reiterated as he left the room, "I mean it, Zena. Just call me."

"Well, *mademoiselle*," Alex stood rocking a little on his heels, his eyes bright with drink, "is this how you entertain my guests? Well, one guest anyway," he sneered, slurring his words together. "Come back with me now," he ordered.

"You'll manage without me," Zena retorted.

"But I don't care to manage without you," he said icily. "Come downstairs at once. You're insulting my guests."

"Insult a brazen hussy like Amalie? Impossible," Zena gave a short laugh. "I'm not coming back until that bitch stops hanging all over you," she snapped angrily.

"Christ, is that your problem? We're just old friends. It's nothing," he brushed her remonstrances aside.

"It may be nothing to you, but it's humiliating to me. How do you think I feel watching you kiss her in front of everyone?"

"I've been kissing her for years. I tell you it means nothing," he repeated.

"It means something to me," Zena whispered painfully.

"*Mademoiselle*, you would do well to remember that I live my life as I choose. I answer to no one for my actions. Do you understand, *mademoiselle*, to no one," he snarled. Alex's face was set, and his eyes blazed furiously.

"Don't you care even a little how I feel?" Zena asked

quietly. "Don't you care?" She had to have an answer, no matter how painful.

His golden eyes met hers unblinkingly. "I don't know," he said bluntly. It had crept up on him, this general indifference to women. Love simply had never affected him. Women were a convenience, nothing more.

"I don't want a wife and children," Alex continued coldly. Zena was terrified and appalled by the indifference in Alex's tone.

"Why not?" she faintly asked, wondering why she tortured herself with wanting to know.

"I don't. I don't, that's all. What more can I say? Isn't that plain enough?" he cruelly asked.

"Yes, very plain," she whispered softly and cast a glance at the fierce expression on the cold, handsome face. His brows were drawn together in a hard scowl, and his mouth compressed into a tight-lipped, unrelenting sneer. "Then maybe it would be best if I left and didn't bother you anymore," Zena quietly said, her pride forcing her to repeat the statement while her heart cried out a silent prayer that Alex would say no.

"Yes, maybe that would be best," he said with a deadly politeness.

"You can't mean it." cried Zena, stepping back with stricken eyes.

"I never say anything I don't mean," he drawled. That drawl meant he was drunk—the only discernible signal, but one not to be ignored, as any of his close friends or household staff would attest. That softly blurred speech indicated he was dangerously drunk and quite capable of anything his devilish temper prompted. The *mademoiselle*, not familiar enough with the prince, was not of course attuned to the warning.

The silence in the room was absolute. A sudden cold, sick chill struck through Zena. At that moment her world fell apart. He didn't want her. He could ask her to leave without a qualm. Damn him! Damn him for making her love him and never, never returning the affection! Had he no heart? Was he incapable of feeling love or affection? He could sleep with her, make love to her, live in the same house with her, and father her child, but he could not and did not care one scrap for her. She had been a convenience, a delightful diversion, his latest whim, but never his love, never ever remotely his love.

She hated him at that moment, hated him passionately for sapping her independence with his exquisite touch and delightful smile. She hated him for his ability to caress her to insensibility. She hated him for the warmth of his body as he drew her close when he woke each morning. And she hated him for the hundred small ways he had insinuated himself into her heart without giving a shred of his heart to her. The fury at her dependence on this man reached crisis point, and in an uncharacteristic action she drew back her arm and slapped him across his arrogant face with all her strength. The blow was delivered with such force it jarred her momentarily, but before Alex's steely golden eyes could recover from the shock of the blow, she had whirled around and with a small cry fled sobbing from the room.

In the bedroom Zena attempted to recover her composure as each word that had been said swirled repeatedly through her mind. No matter how many times she went over the dialogue or rearranged the statements, the meaning was unmistakably and depressingly clear. She must go. She who now was carrying Alex's child in her womb would never see him welcome a son or daughter into the world. He didn't want her, and he certainly wouldn't want her child. That fact had been made patently clear. "I do not want a wife and children" echoed dreadfully over and over in her brain.

Hastily throwing a few clothes into a small leather satchel, Zena contemplated her future.

Forcing her mind to practicalities, she swiftly assessed her options. She didn't have much money. Bobby'd had a relapse of fever and couldn't travel. She would go to her grandfather's village alone, and some of his warriors could return for Bobby.

Composing herself into a reasonable semblance of normality, she washed the tears from her cheeks, smoothed her hair, drew a deep breath, and walked to the nursery to explain to her young brother that she was going to visit their grandfather and would return for him in two weeks.

Alex was nowhere in sight, but the noisy sounds of the revelry downstairs indicated his return to the festivities.

Bobby was bright and cheerful despite his fever and babbled in his normal fashion as Zena tried to explain where she was going. "Alex will be here to keep you company until I come back for you."

"Papa play. Me like Papa," he cooed in his baby talk.

"Yes, Papa will play with you sweetheart. Give me a kiss, and I'll see you in two weeks."

The chubby arms wrapped around Zena's neck, and she fiercely hugged her dear, young brother until he began to squirm uncomfortably in her arms. Thank God, he was too young to be seriously disturbed by most of the events transpiring around him, she gratefully noted. Bobby was again absorbed in the mechanics of a new toy wagon Alex had given him that morning.

Zena called a servant to summon the coachman, went back to her room, threw a warm cloak around her shoulders, and had a maid carry her small satchel downstairs.

Alex had returned downstairs after their confrontation and was now recklessly drinking himself into oblivion. He just wanted to forget Zena. It was for the best. He was beginning to feel on occasion vague, indefinite emotions in regard to her, and he was in no mood to change his lifestyle. He was still young and had much living to do. He didn't want to be tied down with a wife and children.

That fucking, sweet little piece was beginning to get under his skin; she was becoming necessary to him in ways he thought a woman could never be. She made him want her near day and night.

It was best to break the relationship before it became unwieldy. She was becoming a nuisance, always wanting reassurances and soft words of affection; she made subtle demands on his independence. A nuisance, that's what she had become, and he was exceedingly relieved to be rid of her.

All his angry musing, which seemed decidedly logical at the time, scarcely penetrated his alcohol-dazed understanding. But no amount of brandy could blur his ability to comprehend a perpetual constant in his life—a beautiful woman who desired him.

"Amalie, my love, come turn the pages for me. And bring another bottle of champagne."

The coachman drove Zena to Moscow. The drive brought her to the center of town at eight o'clock. She had traveled the miles spiritless and unseeing, sitting in dumb, silent, hideous agony that crushed belief and hope. In Zena's brain jostled a morass of endless recriminations and pointless, fruitless speculations. If I hadn't insisted on pressing the issue, if I had had enough sense to simply resist the temptation of having to know if he cared. . . . You must be a masochist to insist on forcing such an idiotic question. Why, oh, why couldn't you have held your tongue and your temper, and even if he didn't care, you at least would have gone to sleep tonight in his arms. What difference if the arms are unloving arms, as long as Alex is holding you close to him? You ask too much. You ask for what he can't give, and in your insistence you lose all.

She was numb from the loss of the man she loved. The carriage came to a stop. She was helped down, her luggage was deposited on the ground, and she assured the coach-man she was perfectly fine.

He drove away reluctantly, for the vague, distant eyes of the beautiful young mistress did not appear fine to him at all.

After several minutes Zena noticed she was attracting attention and quickly picked up her leather bag and slowly moved in the direction of the Southern Rail depot. Nothing mattered anymore. A feeling of desolation swept over Zena. She could have turned to Yuri for help but shrank from the thought of passing from man to man. That sort of future was appalling.

Anesthetized by the incredible depression that engulfed her, she moved dazedly through a world that couldn't touch her. If spoken to, she didn't answer; if accidentally brushed against, she didn't notice; she was to absorbed in her own grief.

Part III

Flight and Pursuit

1

Once in the dim light of dawn Alex stretched luxuriously, murmured "darling" to no one in particular, and slept on.

The sun was high in the brilliant sky of a balmy March afternoon when Alex lazily rolled over and flung one arm around the soft body next to him. His hand swept slowly upward caressing one plump, warm breast. An uneasy presentiment nudged at his tired, dulled perception. The sensation beneath his fingertips was puzzlingly incorrect. No delicate, lean, taut body here. He dubiously levered open one eye, and the undefined confusion in his dazed brain was irrefutably clarified.

Amalie's bounteous, opulent form greeted his bewildered eyes. For a few horrible seconds he didn't know exactly where he was. Memory quickly returned. He groaned softly to himself and quietly swung up to a seated position, cradling his pounding head carefully between both palms. Resting his elbows on his knees, he remained for several minutes supporting his head while chastising himself mentally for drinking too much.

As well as he could remember, which was frankly damn near nothing, there had been another fight with Zena. She had been angry because of Amalie. What the hell had he said? Zena had become increasingly stubborn and querulous lately. He probably had told her to go to hell. Unfortunately, after several bottles of brandy he very commonly told most anyone to go to hell.

Sweet Jesus, what a mess! First, how to get Amalie out of his bed and out of the house quietly. Then he must find Zena and offer some kind of plausible, conciliatory explanation, no matter now deceitful.

The servants could show Amalie out. He'd better find Zena. She had obviously slept somewhere else last night.

Goddamn women could be a bitch of a problem. But he did prefer Zena's company. He'd cajole and appease her somehow. He was quite confident of her affection. Years of enamored women in his wake had disclosed the obvious signs, and Zena was manifesting the usual symptoms. He wasn't presumptuously vain regarding his attraction to woman, simply conscious of well-established, orthodox patterns of female behavior.

What the hell had he said last night? It would help if he could remember. Oh, well, he'd bring Zena around. It might take some persuasion.

Alex silently slipped into a navy shantung dressing gown, eased quietly out the door, and immediately questioned the servants stationed in the hall. "Which room is Mistress Zena in?"

Neither of the footmen would meet his glance. Both nervously eyed each other, the floor, or some distant object over Alex's left shoulder.

"Well?" Alex demanded irritably as the nervous silence lengthened.

"Er . . . she isn't here," the youngest one finally blurted out heroically.

"Is she outside with Bobby?" the prince inquired hastily.

"No sir," they both replied, fidgeting.

"Well, where the blazes is she?" Alex challenged.

"Don't know, Your Excellency," they murmured in unison.

"You don't know!" Alex thundered. "Who the hell does know?"

"No ... no ... no one, my prince," a faltering voice quavered. "The coachman drove her to Moscow last evening and left her."

"Moscow!" Alex roared.

"She left a note, Excellency, in your study," and they both melted into the wall as Alex brushed past them and dashed down the stairs.

Two servants rushed to open the study doors as Alex suddenly appeared. The servants stood stiffly outside against the wall waiting for the storm to break.

The sealed letter was in the center of his desk. He put his hand out and remained for a moment motionless. Then with a violent movement he grasped the envelope and ripped it open.

The note was brief, dry, and to the point with no unnecessary words of explanation:

Bobby is too ill to travel. I will have someone fetch him in two weeks.

Baroness Z. Turku

Zena had left! She had really left! No empty threats, a *fait accompli*.

Unpenitent anger mounted dangerously. Just because he had kissed Amalie once or twice. ... He chose to overlook the fact that he had found her in his bed that morning. *Mademoiselle* Turku was too impertinent for her own good. He'd bring he back and lock her up this time. Damnable pert miss, walking out. He wasn't tired of her yet. Goddamn it, how dare she leave!

A resounding crash echoed out in the hall, and the servants eyed each other apprehensively. "The Ming vase, I think," the elder of the two said. "Better get Ivan."

Two more shattering explosions occurred before Ivan appeared. "He found the note," Alex's steward declared dryly.

"The Ming collection is dwindling, sir," the old retainer said expressionlessly.

"Send for three maids to clean up the mess," Ivan ordered.

An incredible blast of splintering wood and glass reverberated. "And the carpenter. . . ."

Opening the door to the now silent room, Ivan proceeded in. Alex sat behind his desk, a glass of brandy at hand, cooling his angered brow. A frigid breeze blew through the opening once graced by French doors.

He looked up absently as Ivan entered. "She left, Ivan," he said simply.

"I'm sorry, Sasha."

"No need to feel sorry." Alex's eyes narrowed dangerously as he tossed down the brandy. "I'm bringing her back."

The prince had spent a brief moment wrestling with his conscience (after all, he couldn't keep her here against her will) and his common sense (damn, she was just another female). But neither prevailed against his ungovernable temper and his craving to have Zena again. He'd be damned if he was going to let the hottest little piece west of the China Sea escape *that* easily. He'd have her back by tomorrow, he resolved ominously. The enraged prince vowed with a regal finality, she wouldn't leave again until he was damn good and ready to let her go.

After rapidly dressing in a random manner that horrified his meticulous valet, Feodor, then visiting briefly with Bobby, who was cheerfully ensconced in the nursery, Alex was on the road to Moscow in fifteen minutes. He left Trevor orders to clear his house of the evening's guests as soon as they woke. Trevor impassively accepted the prince's instructions, which were actually worded more colloquially.

"Get the goddamn fucking bastards out of my house,"

were the precise words to which Trevor murmured masterfully, "Very good, sir."

Ivan and two grooms accompanied Alex as he whipped and spurred his mount mercilessly during the reckless afternoon ride to Moscow.

Alex's thoughts raced ahead. Briefly he considered Zena's route, assuming she would head south to her grandfather. But questioning of the railway porters and ticket clerks seemed to indicate a woman of Zena's description had taken the night train to St. Petersburg. Unreasonable as it appeared, evidently she was headed back to her aunt's. Maybe the distance to the Caucasus had intimidated and deterred her.

Actually St. Petersburg was more convenient for him, only a few hours' journey and a known destination. Her aunt wouldn't be hard to locate. Young Prince Alex had no scruples about seeking Zena out at Baroness Adelberg's.

If the baroness was willing to callously deliver Zena up to the old beast of a general without a single qualm, Alex felt sure she was the kind of woman he could deal with felicitously. He was confident some mutually profitable bargain could be reached for Zena's return to his protection. When one was heir to the larger portion of the gold mines in Siberia and the Urals, not to mention a comfortable percentage of the oil fields in Baku, negotiating in terms of money was merely an exercise in rhetoric.

Alex arrived at the pink palace on the Neva Quay early the next morning in a surly mood. The train ride had been tedious; it seemed like the hours dragged. He would change clothes and immediately present himself at Zena's aunt's house. Damnable chit, putting him to all this trouble! But first, he reminded himself reasonably, he would attempt a more courteous approach.

The double doors were thrown open by two of the army of servants, and Alex stepped through and tossed his gloves at a footman. He shrugged out of his coat as Rutledge greeted him with his usual composed serenity.

"Good morning, my lord," he said, as if Alex hadn't been gone two months but was only returning from his usual evening activities. "Would you care for breakfast?"

"No, thank you, Rutledge," Alex muttered. "I'm in a damnable hurry. Have a bath drawn for me and bring up a bottle of brandy."

Rutledge noted the black scowl and set lips. There was trouble ahead for someone, he surmised. Alex wore one of those glowering determined looks that boded ill for the recipient of his displeasure.

"As you wish, my lord." As Rutledge turned to carry out Alex's directives, he narrowly missed colliding with a scooter moving at breakneck speed into the vast marble entrance hall.

A young child with a cap of close-cut red curls, eyes shining in excitement at her burst of speed, sailed across the black and white parquet floor, balancing precariously on the two-wheeled vehicle. Midway across the foyer she spied Alex, squealed with delight, hopped off the scooter which bounced on the marble floor, and ran across the huge foyer toward her brother.

The sight of Natalie erased Alex's churlishness, and his countenance broke into a broad smile. He threw his arms open as the little girl careened into him. Holding her in a tight hug, he swung her around as she giggled in delight.

"Sasha, Sasha, you're back," she cried as he set her down once again.

"As you see, my little pigeon," Alex replied with a grin, his ill humor forgotten momentarily as Natalie warmed his spirits. "Tata, you're growing so fast. Every time I see you you're at least two inches taller. How old are you now?"

"I'm six," Natalie replied proudly, standing stiffly erect to show her added height.

"Six already?" Alex teased. "Soon I'll have to start chasing your boyfriends away. When did you get into town? I haven't seen you in months."

"We came into town three weeks ago, and boys are ever so stupid, so I shall never have boyfriends," Natalie answered both questions promptly.

"Oh, ho! Talk to me in ten years, little sister," Alex laughed. "Then you'll think that maybe one or two aren't so stupid anymore when they start fawning all over you."

"Do you fawn over your new mistress, Sasha?" Natalie brightly questioned.

Alex choked on his last chuckle and replied shortly, "You're too young, moppet, to know of such things."

"But I do know, Sasha," she solemnly retorted, gazing up at the towering height of her oldest brother, "and I know something else, too. You're in trouble, because Mama and Papa have been scrapping about your new mistress."

Alex lifted one eyebrow ever so slightly and cautiously inquired, "How do you know?"

"Papa was hollering ever so loud, and I couldn't help but hear one morning when I was playing in the breakfast room and Mama and Papa were discussing," Natalie's six-year-old tongue carefully articulated, "discussing you and your new mistress in the morning parlor. Papa was raising his voice, and Mama was saying he needn't shout and tell the whole house of his feelings, but I don't think he heard her, because his voice stayed really loud. Mama said your reputation was even worse than Papa's ever had been, and you were into one of your scandals again, but Papa said you were only young and high-spirited."

Alex breathed a little easier hearing that his father at least understood.

"What's a reputation, Sasha?" Natalie inquired uncertainly.

"It's something men can afford to have and women can't, little sister," Alex explained with a sardonic smile. "What else did *Maman* and Papa say?"

"Well," the little girl earnestly related, "then Mama said that it was different this time, because there was a child involved and the woman was a streetwalker. It must be ever so tiring to walk the streets, Sasha," she commiserated.

Alex choked.

"Is that what streetwalkers do, Sasha?"

Alex cowardly ignored the childish inquiry and prompted her instead, "What did Papa say then?"

"Then Papa said he would find out what was going on if it would make Mama happy, and he would send some money for the child. Then Mama raised her voice too and said you Kuzans always think your gold is a pana . . . pana . . ."

"Panacea," Alex helpfully interposed.

"That's the word, panacea," she carefully pronounced, "a panacea for everything. Then Mama said," and the young girl parroted the words exactly, "it isn't that simple this time. A *streetwalker*, Nikki, do you *comprehend*? A *streetwalker*. Mama was pretty mad I think, but then Papa said don't be angry like he always does when Mama gets upset, and then Mama cried and Papa kissed her and held her until she stopped crying. Papa doesn't like Mama to cry, you know, so I think you're in *big* trouble," Natalie gravely concluded.

"Where *are* Mama and Papa?" Alex asked warily, not particularly in the mood to face either a distraught mother or a purposeful father.

"Lucky for you Papa is at the barracks, and Mama is with Georgi at the tailor's. He goes to Paris next month. He's almost eighteen now."

Alex reflected that he would have time to take care of Zena at her aunt's before anyone came home. He could face his parents after the problem with Zena was reconciled. One crisis at a time. And for Christ's sake, he was twenty-four years old and had had control of his own fortune for years.

He'd just have to soothe his mother's temper later. She always came around in the end, he reminded himself confidently.

Striding up the stairway to his apartments, Alex vaguely responded to Natalie's steady stream of chatter. His mind wrestled with the problem of convincing Zena to return with him. She was bound to be horrendously angry, and utmost diplomacy would be required.

He was in and out of a bath and into a change of clothes in record time as servants diligently scurried about their tasks.

Natalie perched on the edge of the tub and then on the bed, jabbering steadily as Alex swiftly bathed and changed. She was a cheerful distraction from the confusion of his thoughts, which ranged from anger to frustration to conciliatory musings and back again to resentment as he considered the trouble he was being put to for one saucy minx of a *mademoiselle*.

Bending to see in the dressing table mirror, Alex quickly brushed his long, unruly hair back with twin silver-backed brushes, then threw the brushes down and turned to Natalie, who was seated on the enormous gilded bed. "Be a dear, my little heart, and tell *Maman* or Papa when they arrive home that I may be late for supper. I've some business to attend to. Can you remember that?"

"Of course I can," she retorted, keenly wounded.

"I guess you can at that," Alex replied with a chuckle as he recalled her detailed report to him. "*Au revoir*, Tata." He bent and dropped a kiss on the curly mop of hair.

"*Au revoir*, Sasha. Bring me back some candy," she demanded as he walked out of the room.

"I'm not going near a candy store," Alex replied as he walked down the hallway.

Skipping behind him, she leaned over the railing and, with childish optimism undeterred by his negative response, shouted as he descended the stairs three at a time, "I want coconut bonbons!"

Ivan in the meantime had discovered the location of Zena's aunt, and ten minutes later Alex was being ushered into the drawing room of a house on the Fontanka Canal.

A short, plump, tightly corseted figure with dyed red hair and the vacuous, painted face of a faded belle greeted him. "To what do we owe the pleasure, Prince Alex?" Baroness Adelberg simpered, fluttering her ring-bedecked, fat, little hands.

Since Alex was aware of the misery this woman had caused Zena for three years or more, he found himself unable to completely conceal his loathing. The usual sycophant, he thought angrily. "Where's Zena?" he churlishly demanded, choosing to ignore the deferential greeting.

"Zena?" the aunt questioned with amiable perplexity. She was puzzled and slightly alarmed but cautious still in the presence of such an illustrious visitor.

"Yes, Zena, your niece," he demanded, glaring at the toadying woman. "Did she come back here?"

In an instant the entire situation cleared as with a vision from above.

The baroness's eyes narrowed, and the cordial demeanor vanished as rapidly as a pebble in a pond. "So, that's where the little slut went," she sneered. "And now you've misplaced your doxy. Well, she isn't here, Prince Alex. She's smart enough, that one is, to know she's not welcome. After all I did for her, too, the ungrateful tart. Put up with her, that brat of a brother, and her drunken father for three years. Couldn't marry General Scobloff to please me, could she, the obstinate snit. No, had to embarrass me and run off. Well, if you find her, you're welcome to her. Don't send her back here!"

Alex drew himself up to his full, formidable height, looked down his well-bred nose at her, and said contemptuously, "Madame, rest assured there is nowhere on earth I would be less likely to send her."

Oblivious to the censure in Alex's retort as her mind dealt only with the affront to her own self-interest, the baroness irefully continued, "I knew she'd be a slut just like her mother. Blood tells," she said tartly. "Those Circassians are nothing but promiscuous savages. They have harems—*harems!*" she shrilled. "I knew Zena would be the same. All those savages have loose morals. So I tried to see her properly married off in order to nip that salacious tendency in the bud, nip it in the bud, I say," she righteously declared.

"To a seventy-year-old doddering fool?" Alex inquired sarcastically.

"She needed the firm hand of an older man," the baroness mulishly replied. "As the twig is bent, so grows the tree, you know. She had a mind of her own, the wicked girl, and was hard to control. It comes from being educated. It just isn't womanly. I told her father he was making a mistake instructing her like a man—imagine, Latin, geometry, pistol shooting!" she sniffed disdainfully. "Made her shockingly intractable, that's what it did. I told him it was a mistake. Never saw such a self-willed, stubborn girl. The little hussy had the nerve to argue with me for a month about her marriage to General Scobloff, refusing . . . refusing!" the outraged woman venomously cried. "The nerve when I had arranged such a suitable match!"

"Suitable!" snorted Alex witheringly.

Ignoring the snorted comment, she said primly, "I wash my hands of her, I tell you. I did my duty for the sake of my poor, departed brother (and his money, Alex thought cynically). But she's sunk beneath contempt now—nothing more than a harlot. I hope God punishes her for her sins," the plump woman zealously asserted.

Or perhaps God may punish you for yours, Alex reflected, which he would find infinitely more suitable on the scales of justice.

"Good afternoon, madame," Alex said curtly. "You have set my mind at ease in regard to the concern and interest of Zena's relatives."

"I hope to say I did my duty," the baroness pettishly bristled.

"Zena is very young, after all, and faced with responsibilities of a brother," Alex reminded her coldly.

"Humph! The general would have taken care of her most satisfactorily."

I'll bet he would, Alex raged with silent contempt.

"She's made her bed. Let her lie in it!" The baroness's obstinately narrow-minded venality remained unmoved by Zena's plight.

Good God, Alex thought exasperatedly, the old bat was a veritable lexicon of trite clichés. "As you say, madame," Alex said sardonically, "time waits for no man. There's no rest for the wicked," and bowing infinitesimally, he turned and walked out.

"What very curious things to say," the baroness muttered huffily. She knew the Kuzans were unconventional, but really, this young man was quite odd. No rest for the wicked? Indeed! If even half the stories circulating about Alexander Kuzan were true, he and Zena could go most conveniently to the Devil together. Luckily the little tramp was unaware of her father's quite comfortable fortune, which in the absence of his children rested very satisfactorily in the baroness's charge.

"Damnation!" Alex swore as he ran down the steps to the waiting troika. Vexed at not finding Zena, he was now compelled to retrace his steps to Moscow and start inquiries all over again. The trail would be two days old by then. Jumping into the sleigh, he gave directions for the Moscow Vauxhall and settled back, relieved to know Zena had not come back to the baroness, since her welcome there would have been scathingly callous.

For the first time since Alex had discovered Zena's disappearance, selfish irritation at her flight gave way to compassionate regard for the young woman thrown so mercilessly out into the world by her unfeeling aunt. Uncomfortable pangs of conscience smote Alex momentarily as he attempted to recall the events of their last evening.

He could be damnably rude and difficult after hours of drinking. He functioned well physically, but his attitude became dangerously and easily provoked, and Zena wasn't the kind to remain demurely silent. He supposed it was his fault, her running off; he upbraided himself mildly, but *merde*, who would think anyone would be silly enough to run away on a cold winter night, when the nearest town was two hours distant.

Zena's aunt was right on that count, anyway. The *mademoiselle* was the most rebellious, stubborn female he'd ever dealt with. Fool shouldn't go traipsing off by herself. It just wasn't done. A woman traveling alone could find herself in hazardous circumstances. Why, any number of men would just love to offer their assistance to a beautiful young lady alone.

Alex sat bolt upright and swore afresh. What if Zena accepted some stranger's assistance? She had been ready enough to assent to his advances. A fierce and overwhelming anger kindled precipitously. He'd kill any man that touched her.

Alex chose not to examine his motives for this unprecedented possessiveness. If he had scrupulously questioned this unusual behavior on his part, the results may have been disquieting to a libertine of his reputation. But since self-examination was uncustomary to the ancient Kuzan family, where self-indulgence had become both a family tradition and a fine art, Alex didn't question his reasons for going after Zena. He wanted the chit back, and he must have her back, and that was that. The principle now established, it was simply a matter of accomplishing the task efficiently and speedily, for in addition to their other charming, unrestrained qualities, the Kuzans were notoriously impatient.

"*Vite, vite*, Ivan. We're back to Moscow." Learning forward, Alex rapidly filled Ivan in on his interview with the baroness. "The *mademoiselle* must have gone south to find her grandfather. She said she'd send someone in two weeks for Bobby. Evidently she expected help from someone. The only one left is the grandfather."

"Sounds reasonable," Ivan replied with his usual cool taciturnity. "We'll pick up the scent back in Moscow."

"I want a special train arranged. We'll be traveling with the stable car as well as my private car and another car for the trackers. That should do. I'll wire ahead, so we'll be met in Moscow with the horses, men, and supplies. It'll save us half a day."

"How far south?" Ivan asked, his blue-gray eyes staring ahead, his placid face quite imperturbable.

"Into Daghestan. The grandfather's village is somewhere near Gumuk."

"Nice country," was the laconic reply.

Before they left St. Petersburg Alex had a box of coconut bonbons dispatched to Natalie with a note of regret for missing supper.

Trevor was waiting at the Moscow station when they arrived.

Alex immediately commenced his catechism. "Twenty horses?"

"Yes, my lord."

"Grooms?"

"Yes, my lord."

"How many trackers?"

"Four, sir."

"Food, supplies, clothes?"

"All arranged, my lord."

"Bobby and the nursemaids?"

"Having supper in your car, sir."

"Excellent, Trevor. Damn efficient of you on such short notice. Take a couple of cases of my Tokay for your private moments while I'm away."

"Very good, sir," was the placid reply, but both Alex and his majordomo knew the fine wine would be appreciated.

"Well, lead the way. Where's my train?"

"This way, sir."

As they were striding through the train sheds, Alex exclaimed abruptly, "Hell! I forgot about money. Oh well, I can write a draft at Kharkov or Stavropol tomorrow. My credit will stand, I'm sure."

"Sir, I took the liberty of authorizing the removal of several bags of rubles from your desk. They're in your bedroom in the black leather *nécessaire de voyage*."

"You are a marvel, Trevor, a veritable marvel," Alex beamed.

"We try, sir." A faint smile shone briefly on the dignified face.

Bobby was overjoyed to see Alex, and the first hundred miles of their journey south was spent rearranging toy soldiers on imaginary battlefields spread out on the bed.

When Alex tucked him in for the night, Bobby said, "Papa, Zena gone. Where Zena?"

"She went to visit your grandfather. We're going to go see her."

The explanation seemed to satisfy the little boy, for he asked no more.

Alex sat up late that night making plans with Ivan.

They brought out maps and searched for possible routes Zena might take at Vladikavkaz, where the railroad ended.

"We'll check at each stop to see if she's been sighted, but at least this time I think we're going in the right direction. She'll have to hire a carriage to post from Vladikavkaz to Gumuk. It shouldn't be difficult finding her trail at Vladikavkaz. How many exquisite, auburn-haired beauties are hiring hacks to Gumuk? Christ, I hope she's all right. Damn foolish of her to attempt a trip like this alone."

Ivan smoked on immovably, only raising one brow ironically.

"All right," Alex admitted as he noted the skeptical brow, "so it's all my fault, And you don't have to say 'as usual'," Alex grinned.

Thirty-four hours later they arrived at the end of the railway line, Vladikavkaz. The Caucasus range lay to their south. There it stood, a snow-streaked rugged wall of pale, misty, violet gray, like a thin veil between Europe and Asia. Beautiful, majestic, gloriously grand, and in its rocky defiles and remote, isolated valleys and byways, awesome and dangerous.

2

Zena's flight south had been uneventful, devoid of all the possible dire perfidies envisioned by Alex, since directly from Moscow Zena had made the acquaintance of a hearty, old peasant woman who was traveling to visit her son garrisoned in Grozny. This bluff, vigilant duenna had effectively rebuffed any improper overtures by men daring enough to attempt conversation with Zena.

Vladikavkaz was reached safely and securely. The old woman bargained frugally for the cleanest, sturdiest telega, horrified at Zena's suggestion for hiring an expensive carriage. Zena, in a hot-tempered pique over Alex's wooing of Amalie, had helped herself to the gold in his study, so she was quite amply supplied with funds. Call it compensation for your child I carry in my belly, she had brooded resentfully when she left. She hadn't told Alex about the child because it wouldn't have mattered to him. Illegitimate heirs meant nothing to a man like him. He had many. His feelings for her wouldn't have changed for the sake of an infant, an infant after all illegitimate. There was Alex's damn family honor, regardless that he mockingly scoffed at the notion.

The hot blaze of indignation at her treatment had sustained her at first, curbing the helpless, hollow desolation that threatened to engulf her. But the anger and resentment had abated as the days progressed, and try as she might, Zena couldn't conjure up the old rankling spleen.

Despite courageous resolutions to dismiss thoughts of Alex from her mind, the anguish and pain of loving him and missing him remained. Would she ever be able to forget him?

The old woman made them both quite comfortable in the rope seat slung between the bare, wooden sides of the primitive vehicle. She traveled with the usual bundles of supplies to ward off the discomforts of a long journey: food, comforters, a small samovar, and cooking pots. She even had a brightly colored canary in a cage, which she intended as a present for her son.

They were now bouncing and jolting at a rapid pace over the rough post road to Grozny. The day was warm and beautiful. March in the south meant blossoming spring.

The son certainly didn't take after his plump, dumpy mother, and Zena immediately understood the reason for the mother's adoration. At Grozny Lieutenant Vlastov met them in undress uniform but managed nevertheless to suggest a *gentilhomme trés comme il faut*. If the mother's tales were to be trusted, this brilliant, handsome young blade was thoroughly spoiled, but he turned out to be warm and natural, not a bit arrogant or overbearing. He hugged and kissed his plump little mama, then turned to bow to Zena with extremely well-bred style. Neither Lt. Vlastov nor his mother wished to hear of Zena continuing south that same afternoon, but she insisted, so the lieutenant courteously procured a carriage and a guide for Zena. "You're sure you won't stay?" he asked wistfully as he helped her into the caléche.

"Yes, I'm certain. Thank you for your kind invitation, but I must make all speed to my grandfather's village."

Madame Vlastov bustled up and offered a well-meaning but lengthy list of advice, after which Zena began her long journey to Gumuk, where the post road ended.

Each mile took her farther away from Alex, and she

mourned her loss; she huddled in a corner of the carriage and was oblivious to the beauty of the passing scenery.

Late evening of the second day she reached Gumuk, where they stayed the night.

In the morning her Lezghian guide, Ma'amed, greeted her as she exited the small house in which she had slept. He was a tall, hook-nosed, very thin old man of perhaps sixty with a kindly expression despite his harsh features. He knew some Russian, so he and Zena were able to communicate in phrases and short sentences. Yesterday, with a Lezghian interpreter, Lt. Vlastov had given complete instructions. He was to guide Zena to her grandfather, Iskender-Khan. Ma'amed was familiar with the location of Iskender-Khan's aul and equally familiar with the formidable influence of this powerful mountain chieftain. Although Russia nominally ruled in the Caucasus, once removed from the garrison towns on the main post roads, the law of Russia ceased to command. Mountain law, the adat, prevailed in the highlands, and wealthy, noble chieftains like Iskender-Khan in their strongholds ruled as absolutely as any feudal king.[4] Patriarchal law and the power of the princes and elders stood for more than the countless orders issuing from the great palace in Tiflis, where the Russian viceroy of the Caucasus dwelt.

Zena was dressed in a buff twill riding habit, which wasn't too practical on the mountain pony that carried the usual high-pommeled and cantled, padded Caucasian saddle. Undeterred by etiquette in this remote village, she hoisted up her skirts, placed her left foot in the high stirrup, and sprang into the saddle. Arranging her voluminous skirts sedately to cover her legs, she was ready to start out.

The small party left the main road to strike off westward. Their path lay directly toward the double-peaked rocky ridge at the base of which the town of Gumuk was situated. The narrow road was by no means bad, and it meandered up one narrow, grassy valley after another for about an hour. Villages were generally in view for that first hour, built on a site more or less inaccessible on one side, generally on the brink of a precipice.

By degrees the valley grew narrow until it formed a regular defile through which a stream rushed, with perpendicular cliffs on both sides, forming a grand and imposing scene—a spectacular combination of rock, wood, and water in stern and wild splendor.

Although it was the year 1899, the slave trade of the Caucasus that had been carried on for a thousand years still flourished.

As Russia had subdued the Caucasus, the commerce in human lives had been declared illegal. Under Russian dominion the yearly payment of human tribute to the Sultan of Turkey and the Shah of Persia ceased, but the demand for women and boys from the Caucasus persisted in the harems of the East.

Outwardly the slave trade no longer existed, but actually it thrived more than ever. The entrepreneurs in this extremely lucrative business were simply more cautious now, since exile to Siberia for life was the penalty if caught. Needless to say, the new hazards meant the prices went up accordingly. The actual trade didn't suffer at all, as it was a serious undertaking, organized and conscientiously cultivated; only the buyers suffered, for the prices soared higher and higher.

As Zena and her guide struck off from Gumuk onto the mountain trail, their direction was noted carefully by the leader of a band of brigands (Abreks) as he sipped his sweet tea slowly on the veranda of a small lodging.

3

When Alex and his party reached Vladikavkaz it was ten
o'clock at night. One tired droshky driver dozed at the station. He was hired to drive Bobby and the nursemaids to
the hotel.

Alex would have preferred starting out immediately after arranging for Bobby's care at the hotel, but Ivan had
reminded him sensibly that the people they must question
in regard to Zena were all sleeping and to set off pell-mell
in an unknown direction was witless.

Alex agreed. Of course, Ivan was right. One couldn't
drag every hired driver out of bed that night and question
whether a beautiful, auburn-haired woman had engaged
their telega. For one brief, arrogant moment Alex thought,
Why not? He could indeed do exactly that; he could wake
up the local police inspector or hie him from some party
and have his men question every driver in town. It took
the utmost of stern self-control to withstand the temptation to carry out that plan. *Merde!* He hated wasting any
more time. Zena already had a two-day start on him, and
now he was wasting another night. He wasn't going to be
able to sleep tonight anyway, as he missed Zena by his
side.

He was right. The night was spent tossing and turning.
Before the first streaks of dawn appeared, he was dressed
and pacing the floor. As soon as decency allowed, he woke
Ivan. While Ivan roused the trackers, Alex bid his adieus

to Mariana, placing a kiss on the sleeping brow of her young charge.

"Whatever you need, ask the manager. I've left instructions for your wishes to be observed. If there's any trouble at all, send telegrams to all the garrisons between here and Akhti, and they'll see that I receive the message."

After the men had eaten breakfast, the little town began to stir. Everyone spread out to begin the search for the driver who had carried Zena south.

When the men returned with their results, Alex was relieved to hear Zena was apparently traveling with an old woman. Their destination had been Grozny.

The telega driver had mentioned their being met by an army officer. He was unfamiliar with the officer's name or rank. The old woman had called him Grisko, that's all he knew. The information relayed to Alex made the driver several hundred rubles richer.

Alex and his men were in Grozny by two o'clock. Immediately Alex presented himself to the commander of the garrison. Colonel Chiev was all civility and cordial aid when he heard the Kuzan name. Three officers with the Christian name Grisko were under his command, but only one had a recent visitor from Moscow.

Alex was given directions to Lt. Vlastov's villa on the outskirts of town.

When Alex rode up to the villa, dusty, hungry, and fatigued, he took in the splendid palace at a glance and strode up the steps with mixed feelings. He was of a mind to beat Zena if she was friendly with this lieutenant, while alternately, he would be relieved if this were the end of his search.

Alex was ushered into the drawing room and had no more than a two-minute wait before the elegant lieutenant made his entrance. Alex glowered as his eyes swept the brilliantly arrayed officer from the tips of his polished, handmade riding boots to the top of his sparkling epaulets and well-coiffed head.

Approaching the frowning visitor, Lt. Vlastov politely bowed and inquired affably, "What can I do for you, Prince Alexander?"

"I came for Zena," Alex answered shortly.

"Ah!" the fair-haired man exclaimed softly. This jealous-eyed aristocrat was the answer to the *mademoiselle's* firm desire to leave immediately. "I'm sorry, she's no longer here," he answered.

"She *was* here?" Alex growled menacingly.

"Zena accompanied my mother south but continued on to her grandfather, I believe," the lieutenant replied calmly.

"When did she leave?" Alex harshly inquired.

"Two days ago. I assure you, she was most anxious to resume her journey. I was able to recommend a very reputable guide for her."

"Two days ago," the prince snapped.

"Yes, I'm afraid so."

"Thank you. Good day." Alex turned unceremoniously and strode out of the room. His precipitous departure may have appeared rude, but it would have been far ruder to have smashed the handsome lieutenant in the jaw, which was precisely what his Kuzan temper was recommending. Only his mother's past admonitions on approved behavior had in this instance saved the lieutenant from a thrashing. "Count to ten, Sasha darling," she had counseled, "and your temper will cool." Luckily for the lieutenant, when Alex reached the number *ten* he was halfway down the entrance hall.

The *mademoiselle* had seemed vaguely melancholy, Lt. Vlastov mused after his visitor left. Would she be pleased or displeased by the illustrious prince's pursuit?

Alex's party was on the road to Gumuk in a few minutes. The band of trackers, grooms, and magnificent blood stock turned heads as they thundered down the post road. Alex led the troop, traveling at a suicidal speed.

Ivan and the trackers grimly pressed their mounts to match the galloping stride; he understood the need that impelled the prince's wicked, reckless pace.

Brief rest stops for the horses were combined with questions for the inhabitants concerning a carriage with a lone woman, followed by a guide known as Ma'amed. They were on the right trail. She had indeed passed this way. The first night they spent camped out in the open; they slept in their clothes, wrapped in fur-lined greatcoats to ward off the chill of the mountain night. At dawn Alex impatiently woke everyone, and they breakfasted at the first posthouse, where the inevitable questions were asked.

The band pounded into Gumuk at noon of the second day. Alex had picked up nine hours on his quarry. If it was three more days to the mountain aul, he might overtake Zena before she reached it.

He wasn't particularly concerned with Zena's grandfather's authority, since the absolute verity of the Kuzan influence had long ago been established. Little did Alex realize how important gold was in the civilized world for establishing this prerogative, and little did he realize that with the wild mountain men of Daghestan money had no power.

Inquiries at the lodgings in town acquainted the party with both the date of Zena's departure and the direction she had taken.

On the evening of their second day out of Grozny, the party slept with shepherds above the region of trees at the top of a mountain pass.

It was too cold for Alex to sleep well, although the shepherds seemed inured to the frigid temperatures. He endured the discomfort in commendable silence with only an occasional silent grimace.

The ground was covered with hoarfrost when Alex rose

at 3:30 A.M., unable to sleep for the cold. One of the trackers blew up the fire with great alacrity, put a saucepan on it, and soon had some hot mutton broth that helped thaw everyone a bit. The horses were given a feed or barley, and by then the mist began to fade away.

Looking east and west, part of a main mountain chain became visible. For one brief moment the mountains were tinged with the flush of dawn and glowed a vivid golden magenta, then relapsed into their normal frost-bound appearance. To the north the view was bounded by a rugged chain of mountains with large patches of snow here and there. At their feet lay a steep precipice, the bottom of which was invisible.

Taking leave of the shepherds, the group regained the path and immediately began ascending a bare mountainside by steep zigzags. After a climb of about 1,000 feet, they reached the summit of the pass, which according to the map was 9,283 feet above sea level. In about two and three-quarters hours' time the path turned sharply to the right and descended to the bottom of the valley, then gradually ascended again. The trail progressed up and down the mountain peaks and valleys. By late afternoon the horses were extremely exhausted. The afternoon had been spent over bad ground under a broiling sun.

"We'd better stop soon and rest the horses. They're pretty nearly exhausted. You'll lame some of them soon if we don't stop. They're starting to stumble."

Alex nodded agreement, Ivan was correct. They needed the horses. "How about that next valley, then? The pasture looks good," Alex said.

The descent to the bottom was very steep and had to be made by a series of zigzags down the grassy mountain slope.

"We'll spend the night here," Alex muttered, his thoughts far ahead. He worried about Zena and a single guide in these treacherous mountain paths. There were

186   *Susan Johnson*

trails that permitted only one horse to cling to the side of the rocky cliff with thousands of feet of empty air below. And the country was absolutely desolate. They hadn't met a single soul since leaving the shepherds that morning.

Alex lay morosely on the ground with his saddle as a pillow and prayed they would overtake Zena and her guide soon.

4

Zena and Ma'amed had spent the first night in a caravansary in the form of a subterranean stone house.

"Only last January," Ma'amed said, "ten men died here from the cold." In the winter months there were men in charge of the caravansary who lived there, but as it was spring and the danger was past, Zena and Ma'amed had the house to themselves.

Early the next morning their trek continued. Zena and her guide were making good progress on their rough mountain ponies; the animals knew how to amble steadily along at the rate of five miles an hour. In midafternoon they approached another of the numerous defiles that cut through the rugged, craggy mountain landscape. Ma'amed rode ahead, and they entered the cleft single file, for the path would not permit two abreast.

A volley of shots rang out int he silent valley, and suddenly all was turmoil as Ma'amed's horse reared squealing in agony as it was struck in the neck. Then another burst came, and the guide slid slowly out of his saddle to the ground, spreading stains of crimson appearing on his brow and chest. Zena screamed in horror as her eyes focused on the crumpled, bloody body of Ma'amed lying awkwardly on the jagged schist, one leg unnaturally disposed beneath him. Terrified at the attack from where and by whom she knew not, bereft of her guide now dead at her feet, Zena pulled her horse around so sharply that it went back on its haunches and wheeling took flight.

Her mount was unhurt, and at her urging raced powerfully over the rough ground at breakneck speed. Discharges of rifle fire followed Zena's panic-stricken flight, bullets whining past her as she rode. Bending low over the pony's neck, she gave it its head. Glancing once behind, Zena shuddered to see four fierce mountain warriors brandishing rifles and shashkas and racing after her, laughing and shouting to each other as they rode effortlessly on their fine Kabardinian horses.

Within minutes they had overtaken her and glancing sideways she could see their horses' heads level with her. A large chestnut surged ahead, swerved close, and a man rising in his stirrups with apparent ease, despite the mad gallop, plucked her out of her saddle, and she was swung into the arms of a laughing hawk-faced warrior. Another grasped the bridle of her stalwart pony and hauled it to a standstill.

The galloping horses were pulled in with a suddenness that amazed her, and all four riders began to shout raucous, wild cries. Zena was clasped in the powerful arms of their leader, terrified by their savage appearance heightened by faces blackened with gunpowder. With a whoop of triumph Zena's captor leaped to the ground, pulling her with him. The other three wild men jumped down also, crowding around their prize. One of them seized her only to have her wrenched from his grasp by yet another warrior. She was passed from hand to hand, sick with terror, for who could hear her or help her in these bleak, wild mountains.

Her clothes were torn from her, leaving her in chemise, petticoats, and a pair of kid boots from Moscow's finest bootery. Zena screamed and tried to break away, but her attempt to escape brought her a cut across the shoulders with a heavy whip. The bandit leader grinned sardonically, and the shocking torment of the whiplash served to convulse Zena into a maddened fury. Fear was dismissed momentarily.

Zena's face was scarlet with blind rage and humiliation. She drew herself up haughtily, her blue eyes flashing sparks of anger, and broke into a torrent of abuse, crying finally, "Iskender-Khan will have your heads. I am his granddaughter."

The arrogant leader's whip hand lowered slowly to his side. He stood staring at her, his face incredulous. "You Giaour woman[5]? Iskender-Khan's granddaughter?" he said in awed tones.

"I am, you . . . you assassin," she raged, her eyes glittering dangerously as she thought of her mortally wounded guide.

The leader abruptly turned on his heel, and a whispered conference among the four bandits ensued. Heads nodded in agreement as dark eyes flicked over Zena briefly.

The leader returned in minutes, threw a large burka over Zena's nakedness, and said expressionlessly. "So be it. We go to Mingrelia, then. Iskender-Khan's kanly ["blood feud"] may not reach us there."

For the next few days their pace was forced as they drove themselves through the wild, almost impassable, back country, avoiding traveled trails and mountain paths as much as possible. They struggled up tracks so steep that they often had to dismount to save the horses. The little band pressed on mercilessly, the specter of Iskender-Khan's vengeance spurring them on.

Progress was difficult as they drove themselves rigorously for several days, struggling hand over hand up sheer ravines before descending again to torrid, almost impenetrable brush that had to be hacked through with their shashkas. This nightmare journey was punctuated by a series of river crossings each more alarming than the last. Sometimes they had to swim the raging, icy torrents be-

side their horses, sometimes they had to cross a chasm
bridged by a single felled tree.

Zena's chemise and petticoats were ripped to shreds, her
body torn by brambles, bruised and scorched by the burning sun, and frostbitten by the snows through which they
foundered crossing the high passes. The heavy burka protected her from much of the abuse, but the loose cape was
often pushed aside as she crawled and climbed up and
down steep mountainsides.

Their food consisted of a few pieces of dried meat or
Koumeli, a mixture of rough millet flour that the moun-
taineers moistened with water and kneaded into a sort of
dough. Occasionally they supplemented this meager fare
with a handful of rhododendron leaves they regarded as
particularly sustaining.

Zena's captors deliberately took the most circuitous
routes, wishing to avoid other travelers. None of the men
molested her now, for the threat of Iskender-Khan's revenge was fearfully real. She must not be harmed. If she
died kanly demanded compensation. But over the days of
the torturous journey Zena gradually gave way to exhaustion and suffering. Each day, each painful step took her farther away from her grandfather's aul, from hope or help. It
was a timeless, fearful journey into the unknown, and
Zena was so starved and weary she could hardly distinguish day from night and didn't care if she lived or died.

Taking pity on his captive, the leader offered her a
handful of apricots and an apple one day. "I know you
Giaour are used to eating every day," he said with a kindly
curiosity.

Within the code of the mountains these brigands were
not outlaws. The only acceptable roles for the mountain
men were warrior or brigand. Abreks were an honored
caste in the Caucasus. They were proud of their profession
and hated all authority. They were a knighthood, even if
robber knights, seeking danger for danger's sake, stealing

to give to their lovers and wives. Fighting was a way of life.

Slave trading too was accepted within the traditions of mountain law, and so these captors of Zena's weren't anxious over the moral issues of abduction and slave selling. These independent brigands were fearful only of being recognized by Iskender-Khan as the captors of his granddaughter.

It was dusk when they descended the steep approaches to Suram. They had been on the move for four days, and the tattered, exhausted, pale woman was scarcely recognizable as the finely dressed young baroness who had left Gumuk less than a week ago.

Riding slowly through the village streets, the party reached heavy iron-studded gates that creaked open, and Zena's horse was led into a large courtyard hedged by rough masonry walls with a wooden gallery running around three sides. There was a great bustle of men and horses, and some veiled trousered women ducked into low doorways beneath the galleries. Torchlight flickered, glinting off the silver mounted pistols and shashkas of her captors.

Into the circle of light strode a tall, gray-bearded figure dressed in a long white cloak. He regarded Zena intently. "Khazi," he softly admonished the band's leader, "You've misused the poor thing."

"Haste was imperative," the hawk-faced warrior answered shortly.

"Of course, I understand. A prize such as this is much sought after. Never fear, the bruises and cuts will heal. Quite an exquisite beauty, although I shouldn't tell you that, or your price will escalate." He laughed softly. "My indiscretion is of no consequence. A pearl of such refinement will sell readily. Will you stay the night?" he asked politely.

"No."

"Very well. Name your price, it's yours. You can be on your way. Come inside and I'll have your money fetched."

As the leader dismounted, the white-robed figure snapped his fingers and two servants appeared. "Carry the woman upstairs. Have her bathed and fed."

As the brigands were riding out of the courtyard, their payment in gold comfortably weighing down their saddle bags, Zena was carried into a tapestry-draped room and deposited on silken cushions piled on the carpeted floor. She was in the home of Mulloh Shouaib, the most prominent slave trader in Mingrelia.

5

An outraged oath was torn from Alex's throat, while curses and the vilest abuse were heaped on the heads of Zena's captors when Alex's party arrived at the scene of the attack. The horse tracks, blood stains, and bullet trajectories etched on the granite walls of the defile all told a grim tale of ambuscade. The traces of Zena's flight were revealed at the site of her capture—torn remnants of her riding habit and blouse. Alex flew into a rage, breathing maddened revenge. If the brigands had been within a range at that moment, he would have torn them limb from limb. Since that option wasn't available, the inexorable journey continued. Alex's mind dwelt on various and sundry forms of slow torture the culprits would endure once captured. It would be an agonizing death, and he would relish gloatingly each anguished groan and scream of pain.

The intricate, labyrinthine, almost trackless path the fugitives had taken was laboriously followed. One whole day was lost, as all vestiges of their passing were obliterated by a violent mountain rainstorm that moderated into a day of heavy, gray skies with murky, impenetrable mists reaching the leaden heavens. All footprints had been washed away on the steep, rocky mountainsides.

The men fanned out across the desolate terrain, looking for a clue of Zena's passage. It wasn't until late afternoon that double rifle shots signaled success by one of the trackers. The party they were following were experienced mountain men and trackers skillful in eluding pursuit in their flight; but the prince's hunters were indefatigable. A grim smile graced Alex's harsh, lean face as they once more stalked the trail.

Late the next day a clear path of footprints was visible, as Zena and her captors had evidently led their horses across a mountain valley covered entirely with a thick bed of bluish mud. Disintegrating slaty rock from the mountainsides had decomposed into what at first appearance was a hard surface. The effect was deceiving, for underneath the exterior it was quite soft, and even without riders it was obvious that the heavy horses had sunk in at each step. Ordinarily nothing would induce the mountain ponies to go near these quagmires, but the valley was the shortest route at this point, and the bandit leader had coaxed and led his horses across.

Zena's petite form was light enough so that her boots had not settled very deeply into the soft bed.

After leading their horses through the treacherous valley, the prince's party remounted and continued on their way. Alex was unusually quiet, a pensive scowl and pursed lips accenting his sun-bronzed face. He and Ivan were in the lead, riding side by side, looking very much like mountain men themselves in buckskins and sheepskin coats. For perhaps twenty minutes they rode in silence, Alex's reflective expression altering only occasionally as a muscle high on his cheekbone would tighten convulsively.

Ivan observed all with his usual silent reserve. After another two miles or so, he turned to Alex at last and said gently, "You saw her footprints?"

Alex nodded his head but didn't speak.

"It was obvious, of course."[6]

"Of course," Alex answered softly.

"You didn't know?" Ivan inquired.

"No," the curt voice answered.

"For God's sake, why didn't she tell you?" Ivan asked in a tense murmur.

"Why do women *do* or *not* do anything in their lives? Lord, how should I know," Alex retorted bitterly.

"She may lose the child with the pace these mountain men are setting. The trail is appalling." Ivan paused delicately. "You were the first, weren't you?"

For once, the prince's famous poise deserted him. "The first," he faltered and shut his eyes briefly. "Yes, the first," Alex finished gruffly.

"No more than a couple of months at the most, then," Ivan calculated meditatively.

"At the most," Alex murmured soberly. "We'll stay on the trail until it's impossible to see anymore tonight," the prince declared harshly.

His thoughts turned inward. He should have suspected. That explained all the tears and recriminations and erratic melancholies that had risen suddenly. Alex's experience with pregnant women was scanty at best. The brevity of his liaisons had curtailed any prolonged contact with *enceinte* females. He had normally received the news of impending fatherhood in tearful *billets doux*, which were answered with impersonal bank drafts and instructions to apprise him of his offspring's financial requirements upon their entrance into the world. He assuaged his conscience, on the extremely rare occasions when it was necessary, by reminding himself that the Kuzan partrimony entailed not only golden eyes (which had incredibly bred true for hundreds of years) but also the gift of an extremely comfortable, if not extravagant, lifetime honorarium.

Shortly after the departure of Khazi and his troops Mulloh Shouaib and two lieutenants went upstairs to inspect the new bit of merchandise with a view to perhaps sampling her delights as well. Clean clothes and food had restored

Zena's sinking spirits dramatically, and Mulloh Shouaib was in for an unpleasant surprise.

"If you lay one hand on me," their new purchase spat as she crouched in a corner lined with silken cushions, "my grandfather, Iskender-Khan, will lay kanly on you and yours unto the third generation, you son of a pig."

Now Mulloh Shouaib hadn't survived and become rich in the hazardous trade of slave dealing without possessing an acute and agile intellect.

Immediately the name of Iskender-Khan was uttered, it was tangibly apparent his purchase must be negated. "Go after Khazi at once and bring him back," he ordered his two minions, and they sprang from the room to obey his orders.

He boldly assessed the woman confronting him ferociously from across the room, clad immodestly in the harem raiment of silk trousers and scanty bolero, her heaving breasts displayed conspicuously, as the sheer material of the vest was inadequate to cover the bounteous curves.

"A pity," he sighed without reserve, "to think I must forgo the enchantments of such a luscious tidbit."

Iskender-Khan's vengeance held a palpable threat, however. Survival far outweighed transitory gratification in Mulloh Shouaib's hierarchy of values, and he wished to avoid a crude sordid death at the hands of Iskender-Khan.

Briskly dismissing pleasant images of Zena's opulent form impaled on his engorged instrument, he sensibly said, "Prepare for a further journey, *mademoiselle*. I fear I must forgo the pleasure of your company."

A short time later Khazi wrenched open the door and stalked into the room. Tossing a burka at Zena, he acrimoniously growled, "Women are always a trial, and you're no exception. Mulloh won't keep you, so we head farther south. Bah! I've half a mind to slit your throat and be done with a bad bargain. Come," he ordered, grabbed her by her arm, and dragged her out on the veranda and down the stairs.

When they were all mounted again, Khazi informed his cohorts that they were heading south to Ibrahim Bey's camp. Mulloh Shouaib had suggested Khazi take Zena there. In the event they were unsuccessful in locating Ibrahim Bey, for he was moving daily on his yearly excursion north to acquire new women for his seraglio, they could return to Gori, where Mulloh would give instructions to his agent to attempt to sell the girl to the Persian emissaries. For this gesture he expected a fee, of course, he had added with a bland smile, the enticement of profit too strong to relinquish entirely. He sent the message to Gori at once. There was a beautiful woman for sale, and Mulloh's risk in this capacity as intermediary would be minimal.

Coming out of the mountains onto the rolling hills of the highlands, Alex's party entered the village of Simonethi. Each tracker went in a separate direction, scouring the small municipality for information about Zena.

Alex tied his magnificent stallion Pasha outside a café and sank tiredly onto a bench near the door. He ordered tea and brandy and leaned his elbows on the table in front of him, cradling his weary head between his hands. They were still on the trail, but as each seemingly endless day passed into another, his anxieties concerning Zena's ability to survive such hardships mounted. She was the merest slip of a woman, too fragile and delicate to be put to this punishing adversity. He forced himself not to even consider the child she carried. That train of thought was insupportable, giving rise to an amorphous ferment of torment, guilt, and censure.

When his brandy and tea arrived, he threw the brandy down straightaway but sipped on the sweet tea, allowing himself five minutes to rest before he resumed his search.

Mulloh's agent had seen the magnificent animal tied outside, accoutered with gold-bedecked Russian saddle and bridle, and had concluded that the Giaour inside the café must be rich. Perhaps *he* would be interested in buying the captive woman of Khazi. They were all lechers anyway, the Giaour savages.

Alex raised a disinterested eyebrow in inquiry when the short little man sat down. "Would you be interested in buying a young girl?"

"No."

"She's very young." (Alex frowned.) "But not too young, Your Excellency, perhaps sixteen or seventeen," Abudullah hurriedly amended. (One never knew the specific tastes of one's customers.)

"Sorry, I'm not interested."

"You could teach this young filly to please your inclinations, sire. The young ones are more amenable."

"No doubt you're right. Perhaps another time," the prince replied indifferently.

The seller persisted.

"She could warm your bed tonight, Your Excellency. When was the last time you rode a beautiful, young girl?" he crooned suggestively.

Ten days ago, Alex thought pensively, and a multitude of delightful memories raced through his consciousness.

"No," the prince repeated firmly, "I'm not interested."

"You'll be sorry, Excellency—a dazzling, luscious, young, auburn-haired beauty with such magnificent, deep blue eyes, such white, delicious flesh." He kissed the tips of his fingers and closed his eyes briefly. Leaning conspiratorially across the small mosaic table, he added, "And a tiny rosebud scar in the most enticing spot, my lord."

"Sold," the prince softly murmured. Alex lifted his heavy-lidded pale gold eyes and fixed Abudullah with a chilling, basilisk glare that froze the smile appearing on the dark Mingrelian face. "Where is she?" Alex demanded.

"At Gori."

"Take me there." Alex rose, his pulse beating wildly. There couldn't be two women with a rosebud scar. It must be Zena. She was still all right, then. Relief flooded through him.

They reached the small village in record time, and the little agent ushered the troop into his spacious courtyard. "If you'll wait one moment, Excellency," and he bowed even lower than previously, since he had heard one of the trackers address Alex as "Prince." "Please sit for a moment, and I'll have a servant bring you refreshments. I must check on the whereabouts of the woman. You understand, I'm only a poor deputy acting for another."

He scurried into the house.

Alex refused to be seated, pacing impatiently back and forth in the tiled courtyard, clenching and unclenching his fingers on the braided riding whip he carried.

"Do you think it's true?" he asked as he stopped momentarily in front of a dusty, fatigued Ivan, who lounged against the wall. "Do you think it's Zena?" His tawny eyes were flinty and looked tired.

"I don't know, Sasha. You can't trust these scurvy Mingrelians. They'd sell their own mother for thirty kopecks. Don't get your hopes up."

Alex twisted around sharply as the plump agent returned, wringing his hands distressfully. His distress was sincere, for the course of events had robbed him of a substantial commission. He had intended to raise the price considerably for a Giaour prince. "It grieves me painfully, Your Excellency Prince, to inform you that the woman you desire was sold three days ago. I have many other delicious morsels you may like to peruse, Your Honor," he avowed sycophantically.

Alex lunged for the little commis, a growl issuing from his throat. He was constrained from doing him harm by Ivan's strong and sober admonitions. "Let be, Sasha!" Ivan urged as he held Alex back forcefully. "He can't help you dead! He knows who bought her!"

Still surging with suppressed rage, Alex paused trembling to withhold his terrible frustration and considered Ivan's words. Lashing out with his riding whip, Alex shattered a delicately filigreed ivory lattice window, then wheeled away from the terrified agent and strode out of the courtyard. "Find out the buyer's name!"

Minutes later Ivan issued from the house with the information. "A sheikh by the name of Ibrahim Bey. Very important, very influential. A personal friend of the Sultan at Stauboul."

"I don't care who he knows," Alex snapped. Ivan was consequently treated to the full benefit of Alex's pithy and Rabelaisian pronouncements on the entire race of Turks, to which he comprehensively consigned everyone south of Stavropol. "So then," he finished curtly, "where is this exalted sheikh? Let's get going."

"Consider now, Sasha. Don't be a fool. There are only six of us, and according to the terror-stricken little man in there, Ibrahim Bey's camp numbers two hundred or more. He travels with a princely entourage and a harem."

"A seraglio overcomes all inconveniences, didn't someone once say," Alex sneered embitteredly. Then bristling with spleen he added provocatively, "But I intend to deprive him of one of its members."

"Let's find lodging, Sasha, clean up, and decide how best to approach this sheikh and remove Zena from his harem. That's in the event that rascal agent is telling the truth in the first place and she's even there."

As they were cleaning up from the dirt and grime of days on the trail, Alex and Ivan haggled over the details of their undertaking. "Wear your uniform; it projects the might of the Russian Empire. No small advantage sometimes in dealing with these perfidious border tribes who are constantly changing their allegiance to suit the circumstances."

So it was resolved Captain Prince Alexander Nikolaevich Kuzan would request an audience with Ibrahim Bey as a diplomatic envoy from St. Petersburg. Alex could not be convinced to wait until morning. "Damn it, Ivan, I'm acceding to all your counsels of prudence and civility now, when I'd much prefer hiring three hundred warriors and leveling the sheikh's camp. If I weren't afraid Zena would be harmed in the melee—if she is in fact there—I'd be damned tempted to do just that. So enough expedient caution," he said with a grim smile. "We're going tonight."

What Alex didn't say was that he couldn't stand the thought of Zena staying another night in Ibrahim Bey's harem. An ungovernable fury raged through his mind when he envisioned her in a harem assaulted by another man.

"Any more objections?" said Alex.

"Not the least." Ivan's tone was absolutely noncommittal. Whatever Ivan's private opinion, once Alex had made up his mind Ivan paid him the homage of absolute acquiescence, and he and the trackers would follow Alex without question.

"Come, my dear, another small sip of wine and perhaps one more bonbon."

Zena's eyes stared in the direction of the coaxing voice and although registering on the speaker correctly, looked opaquely through the dark, lean Turkish face. Obediently she lifted her lips, and a goblet of wine was pressed to her lips. She drank the fragrant, heavy wine[7] and opened her mouth for the almond-apricot sweet poised before her full red lips. Long, thin fingers held the honeyed treat, and honeyed words offered terms of praise as she dutifully surrendered to the mellifluous voice and accepted the confection.

"Ah, my fair, winsome flower, you will feel even better soon. One must eat and drink to sustain one's health," and the thin brown hand reached out and caressed Zena's soft cheek. "You're so docile, my love; soon, very soon, you will feel a warmth in your veins that will strike urgently at that passivity and eagerly move you to yearn for more ardorous activities."

The cantharides in the wine would take no more than forty minutes to wash through her bloodstream, Ibrahim Bey observed pragmatically.

He glanced up from the arrestingly beautiful, white-skinned woman he had bought and spoke sharply to the two servant girls.

"She has been eating well?" he snapped.

'Yes, venerated lord, most assuredly. The hashish in the bonbons does much to restore one's appetite."

As well as inducing a suitably amiable lethargy, he reflected as he smiled thinly. When he had purchased the woman from the small troop of hill bandits, she had been far from agreeable—a screaming, cursing, scathingly vocal virago, more aptly. He had never seen such a wildcat, and while he appreciated a certain amount of spirit in a woman, he disliked a recalcitrant, shrewish bitch in bed with him.

Khazi had warned Zena that if she mentioned Iskender-Khan he would slit her throat, Zena saw in his ferocious glance the sincerity of his words, and so she refrained from mentioning her grandfather that first night, although she hadn't refrained from abusing Khazi and the sheikh in various other verbal attacks. Almost immediately she had been fed, for Ibrahim Bey fancied the woman but not her critical tongue. Hashish had been mixed into the food, and within the hour the acrimonious diatribe had ceased. For three days now she had been fed hashish with her food in small amounts, but the quantity was suitable to encourage her appetite and to promote the gentle, tractable quality Ibrahim Bey preferred in the bedchamber.

The woman had been a shade too thin for his refined, aesthetic sensibilities when she was hauled in by the leader of the bandits. The young Abrek explained that they had been eluding trackers searching for her and had scarce time to water their horses let alone dine properly. Three days of gentle, persistent feeding had rounded out the shapely curves to a lush opulence.

"Dress her now and bring her to my tent in one hour," issued the curt command, and he left.

Tonight she would be his, Ibrahim Bey mused as he walked back to his headquarters tent. She held promise of vast sensual delights. He had waited patiently for three days, and this night after entertaining the visiting chieftains with the piquant, delicious sight of her at his side, he would make use of that voluptuous female for whom he had paid so extravagant a price.

With a certain lazy detachment Zena allowed the two dark servant girls to administer to her. She was bathed in a large copper tub; her hair was washed, toweled dry, perfumed with an aromatic floral scent reminiscent of lilac, and brushed into a shiny, rippling mane that hung down her back. They shaved her body, her legs, and under her arms. When they began to shave between her legs she forced herself briefly from her soft, golden haze of contentment to protest feebly. Her weak objections were ignored as the girls continued shaving with short, sure strokes. Zena sank pliantly once more into the warm, enveloping lassitude, a soft cloud bank of the mind. She decided rather giddily that the entire issue was highly inconsequential.

Next Zena was laid on a low linen couch and massaged with a wonderfully warm perfumed oil. She squirmed restlessly, moaning softly as the dark hands caressed her skin, sending frissons of pleasure coursing through her.

The black eyes of the servant girls met over the supine form, and they nodded their heads in agreement. The cantharides were beginning to inundate the woman's body. Soon the least touch would cause a sensual response.

They pulled Zena into a standing position and slipped her arms through a delicate harness of sea-green kidskin embellished with gold bangles and silk embroidery. Under her breasts two wider straps of the colored leather sewn with hundreds of small golden beads were adjusted. The leather of the harness over her shoulders was tugged gently, tightened slowly, and Zena's large, voluptuous breasts were pulled inexorably higher until they perched like two luscious melons on the wide shelf of bangled leather. Her breasts were delectably full, her nipples saucily pert, and the cleavage pressed forcibly together by the pressure of the fine leather; the whole a picture of bursting ripeness ready for the plucking.

Taking out an ivory cosmetic case, the two attendants proceeded to paint the soft, pink nipples a lush, vivid carmine, and Zena giggled as the sable brushes tickled her tender, thrusting nipples. A last dab of carmine, a shiver and a soft moan from Zena, and the two silent girls slipped a heavy golden mesh belt low around Zena's hips. Attached to either side of the golden belt was diaphanous silken gauze that hung down to the ground and was gathered into a circlet of material. Zena's bare feet were slipped through each small aperture of tucked gauze, and both legs were transparently sheathed in brilliant green vaporous cloth. Since the material was affixed to the belt solely at the verge of her hips, it covered only her legs, leaving the silken skin of her belly, groin, and buttocks exposed. Even the legs were covered with no more than a filmy suggestion of fabric.

The costume was never intended as more than an exquisite, elaborate embellishment to accentuate the female pride of snowy, swollen breasts and delectable mons; filigreed leather thrust plump breasts up and out for the touching, while green gauze served as a foil to accent the satiny smooth cleft of pleasure. The costume manifested a primitive female fertility figure ornamented, festooned, and spangled.

Zena was led through the cool evening air to the tent of Ibrahim Bey. The breeze felt refreshing on her skin, which was beginning to warm and pulsate. An incipient, insistent throbbing was starting to surface in her groin and occasionally penetrate the torpor of her soft, comfortable nirvana of lethargy.

A heavy tapestry was lifted aside, and Zena was shoved through an opening into a large chamber brilliantly lit by hundreds of small lamps. Her pupils instantly constricted in reflex to the startling radiance.

"Come here, my little pigeon," that familiar cajoling voice intoned, and Zena lifted her eyes to follow the sound. Focusing somewhat unsteadily on the tall, lean, robed figure coming toward her down the steps of a shallow dais, she began to move forward with a slow, graceful rhythm to meet the outstretched hand. Her breasts bounced and trembled gently, held high in their leather harness, as she walked across the center of the tent, the golden bangles ornamenting the leather, swaying and jingling lightly with her movement. It seemed an eternity to reach that dark, outstretched hand.

She touched him at last, and his fingers felt cool, so cool to the touch—ah, so pleasantly cool; her body was racing with heat. Zena looked up into dark, black-browed, fierce eyes and stared pleasantly, impersonally back as he lustfully pierced her gaze.

Ibrahim Bey twirled Zena once before him, exhibiting her bursting, rosy-cheeked charms to his dozen guests.

"See, my friends, what a delicious bonbon I shall nibble on tonight. Later she shall dance for our pleasure."

A dozen pairs of black eyes admired the flawless beauty

of the female poised before them: washed, oiled, perfumed, and packaged as delectably as the fairest jewel in a sultan's tribute.

"Ibrahim Bey, when you tire of her, perhaps you could be persuaded to favor a nephew. I'll pay well for her, and you can realize a profit even after you've pillaged the fruit. I'm a patient man."

"Perhaps, Abdulhamit, I will consider," his uncle laughed. "In my declining years boredom strikes more readily. You may have her sooner than you think."

Other lustful eyes coveted the woman as well but knew better than to assert a claim if Abdul desired the wench. Not only was he rich and his uncle's most influential advisor but his reckless temperament, foolhardy sword arm, and unbridled temper forestalled any other claimants to the lady's favor.

"Come, my sweet, and sit at my side." Ibrahim Bey led Zena up the carpeted dais and eased her onto a satin cushion. Seating himself beside her, he clapped his hands, and the meal commenced. They ate leisurely, Ibrahim Bey feeding Zena morsels from each dish as they listened to the soft, quiet music played by a small group of musicians.

"One more sugarplum, my love. We must keep a fine balance of sensation," and as Zena's mouth opened, he popped in another sweetmeat laced with hashish. The heavy doses of cantharides in the wine she had drunk would last all night, while the effects of the hashish would wane after two or three hours.[7] When the violently salacious effects of the wine commenced, he wanted her well lubricated both in mind and body, and hashish very effectively accomplished both.

This restful, languorous repast was interrupted by a nervous servant who bowed and scraped and stammered apologies.

"Ibrahim Bey, most illustrious lord, a thousand humble

pardons, but a Russian visitor is here requesting admittance."

Now Ibrahim Bey was an astute and careful man who at the moment had not chosen sides in the continuing conflict between Russia and the Turks, preferring to straddle the sidelines for as long as possible before throwing in his support to, hopefully, the victorious side. An archpragmatist, he had lately been seriously reviewing the combatants and was ruefully forced to admit to himself, although it sat none too well with his ancestors' memories, that the industrial energy and endless recruits the vast Russian Empire was able to marshall could eventually overrun the many fierce, independent Turkish border tribes. Although the tottering Turkish Empire was bolstered by mighty England, a few minor frontier tribes could be conceded and compromised conciliatorily to a bellicose Russia in the interests of good public relations without affecting Britain's long-range goals in the Middle East. Ibrahim Bey chose not to spend his last hours swinging from a gibbet at the gates of some dusty, godforsaken garrison town. With these shrewd, sagacious motives in mind the guest was welcomed with full honors.

The Russian officer strode majestically into the chamber and began crossing the distance between door and dais; then he caught sight of Zena and froze in his tracks.

Ibrahim Bey had risen and advanced toward the tall rangy man.

"Ah, I see, Captain, you, too, are struck by her beauty. A veritable masterpiece of female pulchritude, don't you agree?"

Alex wrenched his eyes from the all but naked woman seated languorously on the satin cushions, her eyes distant and vague, and forced his gaze back to the Turk. He remarked in an apparently calm, composed drawl, "Certainly, a diamond of the first water."

He drew himself up to his full, magnificent height,

bowed gracefully, and said, "Captain Prince Alexander Nikolaevich Kuzan, sir. Forgive me for intruding on your festivities."

"Not at all, not at all, Captain Prince. Please be so kind as to join us."

Alex's eyes slid once more toward the sight of Zena unclothed in this room of men, and with an effort he controlled his mounting rage.

A quick inclination of his head.

"I would be honored, Ibrahim Bey."

"My friends, meet Captain Prince Kuzan," and introductions went around, Alex acknowledging each man's name with a courteous greeting. "Now, Captain, please meet my precious confection just lately become a member of my household and tonight, I confess with a young man's enthusiasm, to be at last the fount of my passion. I purchased her but three days ago, and she required a certain amount of . . . should we say 'gentle persuasion.' My little pigeon, lift those beautiful, midnight blue eyes and meet our guest. Captain Prince Alexander Kuzan, meet Delilah. I have named her that for all the obvious reasons," he murmured deprecatingly.

Prince Alexander Kuzan—the words faintly pierced the veil of haze surrounding Zena. Prince Alexander Kuzan, such a familiar name. Her eyes lifted. She attempted to focus, to draw that huge, fuzzy bulk of a figure into some clarity, to force her mind to register what her eyes were very clearly seeing. Zena's pupils opened wide, and her mouth formed the stupified accents—Alex—but no sound was audible. Then her disjointed mind flitted off once again into a new channel of thought, discarding the present moment with the careless abandon of a frivolous child. The eyes became distant once again, and she dwelt on images, infinitely personal and utterly detached from the events of the evening.

"My apologies, Captain Prince. As you see, she slips off

from time to time into her own world, but she can be swiftly recalled. Delilah, my love!" He snapped his fingers. before Zena's face, and she intently surveyed the fingers. "Here, love, look at me!" Dutifully the dark blue eyes followed the voice. "You see, Captain, she is most obedient. Please be seated, Prince Alexander. Delilah will dance for our pleasure."

Ibrahim Bey led Zena down to the floor directly in front of the dais, no more than six feet from where Alex sat. A handclap and the music altered, gently transmuted into a modified tempo, the soft chords and monotonous melody remaining unvaried.

The drugged wine was singing through Zena's veins, her body glowing with a kindling heat of passion. Carnal urges were surging and undulating in her loins, and the music stimulated and excited these swelling, agitated sensations.

Zena stirred to the tempo, reaching out for the vibrating, lilting sounds as she twirled and swayed to the wicked beat, each note almost tangible, something she could feel. The soft resonance enveloped her body, caressed it, soothed it, and sensitized it to deeper awareness of the torrid fever that twisted and curled down her belly into her loins.

The shapely, graceful legs glided and turned; her beautiful, soft arms rose and fell in time to the music; the full, delicious breasts held fast in their leather harness quivered and trembled as she undulated provocatively; the carmine-red nipples thrust hard and taut as passion swept through her. White drops of sweet liquid ran down her inner thighs, and her body was roused to unbridled sensuality.

"Ah, the love juices begin to flow, I see. The pretty little piece is suitably primed."

And indeed a steady stream of pearly white fluid oozed out between the pouting pink lips of the shaved vulva and ran in white rivulets down Zena's legs.

"What a copious flow, do you not agree, my prince? Perhaps I'll have her couple with all my guests this night. Surely with that profuse abundance of lubricating essence the fourteenth cock will glide in as easily as the first. Is she not a hot little jade, my captain, and, ah, such marvelous breasts."

"Prodigiously warm, it appears," the prince murmured in reply.

A sharp clap and the frenzied music stopped.

"Come here, Delilah," Ibrahim Bey commanded and Zena obeyed. She stood before him, and he reached out with his napkin and slowly wiped the drops of fluid from her thighs, moving upward and caressing the exposed shaved seat of pleasure; at his touch Zena shuddered in ecstasy.

A cry of rage caught in Alex's throat, and his nails dug into his palms. Restraint, you fool, he thought to himself. If he could retain some control over his feelings, he might get her out of here. But he was no match for thirteen men. He had left the four trackers and Ivan outside, but they were outnumbered.

"Sit between my guest and me, sweet Delilah," and Ibrahim Bey gently lowered Zena onto the cushion between the two men. He delicately arranged her legs, thighs spread wide and ankles crossed so Zena's shaved vulva was licentiously exposed, pink lips pouting and glistening wet.

"Umm," he murmured, viewing his handiwork, "the gates of paradise and so very near." Ibrahim Bey ran a finger up the juicy slit, and Zena moaned sensually. Drawing his wet finger up her belly and over her breasts, Ibrahim Bey passed it over her ruby lips and pressed it into her mouth.

"Your love juices, my sweet, soon to be flowing around my cock and balls." He slowly eased his finger out and moved down her buxom breasts, caressing each soft, white

globe, squeezing the carmine nipples between his thumb
and index finger.

A low wail escaped Zena's lips as tremulous, agitated,
sensuous waves washed over and over her, moving down to
her burning-hot cunt.

Gesturing to a servant, he beckoned toward a bowl of
plums, and the menial presented the bowl with a bow
of obeisance. Ibrahim Bey subjected the dish of plums to
close inspection, finally selecting the largest and plumpest
fruit. Delicately lifting it in thin, lean fingers, he proceeded to direct it toward Zena's delightfully revealed bottom, pink and soft and denuded of hair.

Her eyes were half closed, her skin flushed a glowing
rose, and her flesh was warm and blooming to the touch.
She existed in a misty world of sensation and carnal urges.

"See, my dear," and Ibrahim Bey held up the dark crimson fruit before the vague gaze that floated off into space,
"an embellishment to garnish the gates of paradise."

He reached down and spread Zena's distended, wet, ooz-
ing pink lips and forced the large plum into the crevice
between them. The pouting tissue covered no more than
half the round plum, while the remainder of the deep red
sphere protruded from those moist, succulent lips. Ibrahim
Bey caressed each side of the taut skin stretched over the
crimson fruit, and Zena shivered in pleasure. A rush of
pearly fluid ran over and around the wine-red plum and
glossed the color with a white opaqueness.

A glimmer of passion flamed in Ibrahim Bey's dark
eyes. "Is that not a delectable dish just crying to be nibbled at, eh, my captain?"

"Fairly crying," the prince replied dryly, but his prick
stood stiff at the sight. The bulge in Alex's buckskins did
not go unnoticed by Ibrahim Bey. "You like the little trol-
lop, I see," he grinned wickedly. "Here, see how hot she
is." Carefully so as not to dislodge the purple plum,
Ibrahim Bey with skillful fingers stretched wide the upper

portion of the pouting cunt lips to display Zena's clitoris. "Look at that distended little organ," and Ibrahim Bey flicked the engorged bit of tissue with a soft, gentle nudge. Zena jerked in response and shuddered at the feeling coursing from that turgid, vital area. "See how she craves the revelry, my prince. All is in readiness. Each organ, each tissue swollen and engorged, hungering for satiation, yearning for surcease. Soon, my love, very soon," he whispered softly.

With the courtesy of a polite host Ibrahim Bey inquired, "Would you care to examine my newest prize, Prince? As you can see, she is ripe for the taking. Aren't you, my sweet?" and the black-eyed Turk reached over and tweaked one painted nipple, sending a rapturous throb pulsating through her veins. Zena emitted a quiet groan.

"Please," he insisted hospitably, "be my guest."

Alex leaned over and slid a finger over the wet, pink lips, dislodged the plum, slipped in two long fingers, and probed the soft warmth beyond. The feverish thrill of the probing, tingling touch snapped open Zena's eyes, and she gazed for a fraction of a second into the smoldering anger in Alex's tawny eyes.

"Alex," she breathed, "Alex," but then her mind drifted away once again, and all she could feel and think of and understand was the raging passion that beat at her brain. Her body was on fire, and she craved surfeit. Her flesh tingled, quivered, and pulsated, wanting nothing more than satisfaction—gorged, replete satisfaction.

"She seems to like you, my prince," Ibrahim Bey observed tranquilly.

"It's no more than the open familiarity so common to whores, sir, but I warrant she'll like me well enough if I sheath my cock in that dripping slit of hers. Perhaps we can bargain, for I have a lech for that warm cunt. I'll offer you fifteen horses and five thousand rubles," Alex said.

"Impossible. I paid much more for her."

Alex knew better, for he had been offered two beautiful
young virgins yesterday for less than that, but granted,
this skin was very white.

The bey wanted her very badly himself, but avarice far
outweighed sexual desire in his hierarchy of values.

"Very well," Alex went on, "twenty horses and seven
thousand rubles."

"Uncle," Abdul interrupted vigorously, "if she is on the
block, allow me to bid. The sight of her makes my blood
run hot."

"Now, Abdul, we don't want to insult a guest."

"Uncle," Abdul snarled menacingly, "I want my turn."

Ibrahim Bey had not survived the internecine affrays so
common to harem families by being dull-witted or insensitive.

"Of course, Abdul," he placatingly soothed, "enter the
bidding if you wish."

The Turkish bey was not unfamiliar with the Kuzan
name and knew if the prince chose, he could buy this entire section of the country, let alone one dancing girl. He
could mollify Abdul and at the same time not jeopardize
the prince's purchase if he truly wished to have the
woman. And naturally, it went without saying, Ibrahim
Bey was not adverse to advancing the price by some active
bidding.

"While the bidding goes on, my friends, we must entertain our little hot, juicy sugarplum."

Ibrahim Bey produced a beautiful red leather dildo.
"These are much in demand in the harem, as you can no
doubt realize. I can service only so many women at a
time." The device was gigantic. "A formidable machine,
would you not say, gentlemen?" It was about seven inches
in length and three inches in diameter; even the heart-
shaped mushroom protuberance had been skillfully repro-
duced in red leather. At the base of the object hung two
enormous red leather testicles, soft to the touch, filled

with down, and in gentle contrast to the rigid, stiff, monstrous dildo.

"Abdul, would you care to provide this service for Delilah? It will suitably bring her to fever pitch for the lucky bidder. Several preliminary orgasms will stretch her sensations to a peak of enchantment, and she will be primed for a night of love."

Abdul moved to a position in front of the cross-legged woman. Her breasts were displayed swollen and bobbing above the leather harness.

Abdul reached over with a napkin, dipped it in a perfumed finger bowl, and proceeded to wash the carmine paint from Zena's nipples. Each stroke of the cloth provoked a moan from Zena's lips. Satisfied that the paint was removed, Abdul bent his head to the luscious nipples and sucked both full, delectable breasts. Zena squirmed in her seated position at the pleasure the pressure of his mouth induced. The heat of urgent desire warmed her entire body, raced up from between her legs, and filled her mind.

Abdul lifted his head and fondled the heavy, plump breasts. "Uncle, are those not the most luscious white globes? So large and firm for such a slender woman. I dream of seeing them full and heavy with milk as she nurses my child. Each ripe melon would weigh ten pounds, I'm sure. Tonight, my love," he whispered to the unhearing woman, "I plant my seed in you, but until such time you must content yourself with this machine."

Bending forward he parted the wet lips and inserted the red leather dildo slowly, easing into the willing passageway.

"What do you think, my captain, can the small, delicate female accept such a monstrous organ?"

Thinking to himself that he knew she could, Alex only shrugged his shoulders and lifted his brows. "We'll no doubt soon see."

Abdul had introduced half of the rigid leather device

and bent to kiss Zena's mouth, which was so temptingly
near. He forced her lips open and ran his tongue deliciously around her mouth. As Zena moaned with desire,
he drove the last three inches up her cunt and held her
steady with one arm as she swooned from the ecstasy.

"My uncle," he said, "a very pliant, dutiful cunt. It has
engulfed the entire organ." Taking both of Zena's hands,
he moved them down to the base of the dildo and placed
the enormous testicles in her hands, exerting pressure on
her fingers so that she squeezed the leather bags.

"And see, my pigeon, a gentle push upward on these
marvelous bags, and you'll feel an added thrill." Abdul
pressed the leather appendages toward her cunt, and Zena
swayed in rapture. All her senses were concentrated in her
hot, vital interior. No thoughts but yearning carnal passion, no feeling but that ravenous craving between her
legs. Her body throbbed and pulsated as wave after wave
of sensual urges coursed through her.

Zena played dreamily with the large leather testicles,
now running wet with her love fluid. The leather felt
warm and slippery and soft as she caressed the object that
was holding her in thrall. Abdul turned toward her,
reached out, and ground the dildo up with a fierce thrust.
The world exploded in a screaming orgasm, and Zena
panted in short gasps as the hashish maintained the climax
for second after second.

"Ah, the first of many this night," Ibrahim Bey said.
"Once more, Abdul, to show her what lies in store," and
Abdul reached over to thrust the point home again. Zena
shivered uncontrollably as another orgasm stretched
through her body, lasting and lasting, curling through her
pulsing vagina.

"Give her a few minutes to rest, and you, Captain, will
bring her up once again. As you can see, it takes but the
merest touch."

The bidding was rapid and fierce.

Abdul sullenly dropped out at fifty horses and sixty-five thousand rubles.

The object of this auction was unresisting and submissive, unaware that the very vital question of her future was at stake.

"I've only twenty horses with me at present. I can pay you the money immediately and will give you written guarantee of the other thirty horses. I'll telegraph tomorrow and have them sent down from the Kuzan stud."

Ibrahim Bey, ever prudent, said, "In what condition will I receive these horses? The Kuzan stud is thousands of miles away. It could be a bad bargain."

"Rest assured, Ibrahim Bey, they'll arrive in perfect condition. I've a railroad car that stables twenty horses. Each horse travels with his own groom. In two trips you'll have your horses. A month, no more, will complete the transfer. Now, if you'd be so kind as to supply me with a cloak for the female, I'll take my purchase and be off."

"Very good, my prince, and you will put in a gracious word for my tribe if the occasion arises."

"That I shall."

Alex wrapped the cape around the drugged woman and lifted her effortlessly into his arms, inclined his head in departure, nodded to the assembled guests, and strode out into the night. Torches burned at the entrance of the tent where his trackers had been left waiting. As he carried Zena out to the waiting horses, Ivan gasped in agitation. "Mistress Zena!"

Alex swung up into the saddle and settled Zena before him.

The sentries at the entrance to the tent whispered, "Mistress Zena?"

Ivan and the trackers hauled themselves into the saddle.

The guards inside the entrance to the tent whispered, "Mistress Zena!"

The six horses wheeled and galloped through the village of tents.

The whisper passed like a whirlwind from servant to servant inside the main chamber of the tent.

"Mistress Zena?" Ibrahim Bey cried and then threw back his head and laughed uproariously. "By all that's holy, Abdul," he smiled benignly. "Mistress Zena! She was no stranger to him, then. That's old Iskender-Khan's granddaughter everyone's looking for, and if I don't miss my guess, young Prince Alexander's paramour." He chuckled irrepressibly. "By the beard of Allah, Abdul, we could have beggared the man!"

As they rode out into the desert, Alex issued a curt command to his cohorts. "Keep your distance, no closer than five hundred yards."

Le coït de cheval was going to serve him this night. Lifting the warm, soft woman in his arms, he pushed her cape aside and turned her toward him. She automatically wrapped her arms tightly around his neck and began pressing her soft breasts into the medals and buttons on his tunic.

"Soon, love, soon." Unbuttoning his riding pants, Alex pulled out his engorged penis, raised Zena slightly, and impaled her on his erect stiffness. Wrapping Zena's legs around his waist, he gave a gentle nudge to Pasha, and the black stallion broke into a slow gallop.

Rocked by the gentle motion of the horse, Zena came to orgasm after orgasm, clinging to Alex and sobbing with pleasure. Alex restrained himself, wanting to offer her as complete satisfaction as her burning, passionate body demanded. Soon she began to quiet, the shudders of ecstasy less pronounced, her agitated movements stilled. Kicking Pasha into a mad gallop Alex had his way with Zena, and when morning came, he carried a much subdued, peacefully sleeping woman in his arms.

6

When Zena awoke, she found herself lying on a padded carriage seat. Glancing around in fright, the terror died in her eyes as she saw Alex lounging on the opposite seat.

"You finally woke up, *dushka*," he said as he leaned across the aisle and gathered her into his arms.

Zena burst into tears as all the horror, fear, and humiliation of the past week overwhelmed her. Rocking her gently, Alex patted her soothingly. "It's all over, my sweet. That terrible nightmare is past. You're safe with me." He kissed her wet cheeks and then softly caressed her lips. "Bobby and I have missed you damnably," he breathed. "Don't run away again. The world is too dangerous for innocents like you."

Zena just sobbed harder, clinging to the man she loved, lying heavily against him in a kind of disbelieving dream, afraid it might end and she'd be back with the bandits. She wanted this moment to last forever, just feeling his arms around her while she clung to him, breathing in his familiar, lovely masculine scent. Alex reached up and pulled one of her hands from around his neck, turned the palm to his lips, and ran his mouth over the soft surface. Still grasping her hand, he looked at Zena over her fingertips.

"Why didn't you tell me about the child?" Alex asked softly.

"I thought . . . I thought you wouldn't care."

"Of course, I care," Alex remonstrated gently. Zena's

eyes brightened with hope. Maybe he did love her after all. "As soon as we get back, I'll buy you a house in St. Petersburg or Moscow." He paused. "Why not in both cities? Ask for whatever you want, child, it's yours."

Renewed tears streamed slowly down Zena's pale cheeks.

"Did I say something wrong?" Alex inquired, genuinely perplexed at the fresh outpouring of tears. He had offered what he thought was a generous settlement. Women could be strangely puzzling, and he had the uncomfortable feeling that he had just made some mistake. No doubt her pregnancy was contributing to these peculiar, changeable exhibitions of emotion. Wasn't erratic behavior, as well as bizarre food tastes, a characteristic of *enceinte* females?

Zena sighed softly, wiping away the wet paths on her cheeks. "No, Sasha," she said sadly, "you didn't say anything wrong."

Relieved, Alex hugged her tenderly. "Don't cry anymore, *dushka*. I'll take care of you and the baby."

There was no mention of marriage. It hadn't even entered his mind.

She loved him with all her heart, and she overlooked the omission. Maybe someday her pride would return and she could reject the warmth of his arms, the tender passion he offered her. But now, right now, all she wanted was to be with him on any terms at all. It was as if she had been dead and now her lifeblood came flooding back.

"We'll have a nursery decorated at the *dacha*, too," he said, presuming all women relished the decorating and redecorating of rooms. He was seeking to offer suggestions Zena would like, trying in a vague, imperfect way to indulge her wishes. His masculine expertise in matters of feminine pleasures outside the bedroom was rudimentary. He wanted to please and gladden her. He wanted her happy because he was happy. Alex didn't realize (his notion of the concepts of love and marriage inchoate) that what Zena wanted, money couldn't buy.

They traveled back to Vladikavkaz by carriage. Alex was solicitous and charming, taking great care to avoid topics either controversial or melancholy. The reunion with Bobby and the nursemaids was joyful, and soon they all boarded Alex's private car to make the trip to Kislovodsk. Ivan stayed behind a few days to organize the first shipment of horses to Ibrahim Bey.

Alex had insisted they proceed to Kislovodsk, one of the four towns built at Besh-Tau, where the famous Caucasian health springs were. His family had a villa there, and he wanted Zena to recuperate fully from her ordeal before continuing the journey north.

Kislovodsk, the most beautiful of the four towns built in the neighborhood of Besh-Tau, was far superior to the most worldly European spa in luxury and magnificence. Villas and palaces formed a municipality that boasted some of the finest gardens in the East. The whole town was a unique delight of nature created by the nobility and bankers of St. Petersburg for their leisure pleasure.

It was a fairy-tale city: tropical plants and forests, rushing mountain torrents, craggy cliffs, and picturesque people. There was never such a mixture in the world between the romance of the East and the refined culture of the West as evidenced in the luxurious spa of Besh-Tau.

Alex, Zena, Bobby, and the servants settled into the Kuzan villa that evening. The next two weeks were nonpareil. Alex pampered Zena extravagantly, exerting himself in unprecedented style to divert and amuse her as she regained her strength after the fearful trek over the mountains.

He personally served her breakfast and lunch, insisting she stay in bed to rest until noon. In the afternoon they rode abroad or took the mineral water at one of the baths or just lay on the veranda in the sun. Bobby gamboled in

the extensive park surrounding the villa and thrived in the
warm, salubrious climate. All traces of chest congestion
that had plagued him disappeared.

It would have been the most absurd folly to despise the
luxury, the gentle tenderness, the solicitous concern Alex
showered on Zena, and she derived comfort from Alex's
care and basked in the delicious gratification of her senses.
He soothed and flattered her emotionally until she felt like
a purring cat whose fur had been stroked the right way.
Alex had always been disposed to render her a helpless ad-
dict to his enchanting sensuality. Their pleasures in bed
reached hitherto unknown heights.

One evening Zena and Alex lay in each other's arms
sated from lovemaking; gentle spring breezes wafted
through the open doors of the veranda, and a portion of
the dark, twinkling sky was visible through the door. After several hours of unrestrained and uncommon lovemaking, Zena was disturbed again with one of her awkward
flutters. Having been bred to conform to society's etiquette of decorum, yet witness to the withering humiliation of her aunt's contemptuous, vile allegations that all
Circassian women were sluts, she pondered unsurely over
Alex's reaction to her venturesome audacity in the rapturous throes of passion. She had never discussed the propriety of eager, unconstrained activity in the bedchamber.
Would he truly classify her as a harlot for her perhaps
overzealous ardor? Did he think less of her for her enthusiasm?

With a certain degree of faint heart she decided to risk
finding out. "Sasha?" she murmured, lying with her head
on his chest.

"Ummm?" Alex responded languidly as he rested comfortably in the huge bed, one arm holding Zena, the other
propped behind his head.

"Do you find me too aggressive sometimes?" she asked
bashfully.

"What do you mean?" he placidly replied.

"Oh, I don't know, maybe too crude or vulgar or presumptuous in bed."

Alex smiled lazily in the darkened room. "Still worried about ladylike behavior, child? Just so long as you don't throw up on me, that's all I ask. I have never been accused of squeamishness, but at that vulgarity I draw the line. It quite cools my ardor. Satisfied, *ma petite*?" he laughed. "Let me assure you," he continued seriously, "the notion that well-bred ladies don't debase themselves by succumbing to animal passion is the invention of glacial, unresponsive prigs. It's all the most deceptive humbug, and I speak from experience with a great variety of aristocratic, well-bred ladies.

"Ouch!" Alex exclaimed as Zena's teeth bit into the flesh of his arm. "What the hell was that for?"

"*That* was for the *great variety* of aristocratic ladies."

"*Tiens!* Darling, you can't suppose you were the first," he said with brutal candor. Then his eyes twinkled. "If you're disposed to nibble, though, love," Alex teased mockingly, "my aristocratic ladies preferred other areas on which to nibble. Should I show you, child?" At which point, he expeditiously warded off a violent blow directed toward his face, and a tussle ensued, punctuated with much laughter and chuckles of delight.

Having effortlessly pinned Zena to the bed, after what he considered a reasonable indulgence of her desire to pummel him, he now rode above her, a wicked smile lifting the corners of his mouth.

"You lose, pet. Now you must pay."

"No!" Zena cried gaily, struggling to gain her freedom.

"No?" Alex exclaimed in mock indignation. "You dare to say no? I'll tickle you into submission," which course of action he immediately pursued.

"Stop, stop," Zena squeaked and giggled. "Stop. I'll pay. I'll pay."

I knew you'd eventually see the error of your ways," Alex grinned engagingly. "For your forfeit, my prisoner," he mocked regally, "you must name your baby after me."

"Sasha," Zena wailed. "Not Alexander Alexandraevich. It's too long."

"No, not Alexander, Apollo—for my great beauty." He gave her an innocent smile.

"Such modesty," Zena chided.

"Don't blame me," Alex abjured laughingly, "blame my mother. She always told me I was beautiful."

"And you believed her," Zena jibed.

"Well, a few other ladies have, on occasion, agreed with my mother's assessment," he drawled, a warm golden glow flashing in his mocking eyes. "The selfsame aristocratic ladies, alas." His eyelids drooped in feigned apology.

Blue eyes deepened into turbulent violet sparks of vexation. Only lightning-fast reflexes saved Alex as he snapped back out of range of one very dangerous knee.

Leaning back on his haunches at the end of the bed, he laughed joyfully. "It's a frightful cliché, but has anyone ever told you you're beautiful when you're angry? Seriously, dear, I surrender," he offered gallantly. "Forgive the teasing. Name the child anything you wish, of course. You are, sweet pet, the joy of my life."

Zena capitulated to the blissful delight of such a charming avowal. She gave a quiet sigh as she looked at him. He was so sweet, so beautiful, so intensely alive. "I love you, Sasha," she whispered, holding out her arms.

He had never been subjected to such an overwhelming look of adoring love, and it made him uncomfortable. "And I am going to keep you always," Alex replied lightly and evasively as he swept her into his arms.

7

One morning several days later Alex, Zena, and Bobby were enjoying breakfast on the terrace. The view of the mountains was spectacular from their vantage point, and another beautiful day seemed promised as their second week at the villa drew to a close.

Zena was applying plum jam to Bobby's toast when her eyes caught a flash of motion over the blade of the poised knife.

The dark speck that had arrested her eye at the extreme end of the vista of garden before them was soon followed by another flicker of movement.

Zena nervously clutched at Alex's arm as he lounged in the chair beside her, reading the paper.

He looked up mildly.

"Sasha! Look!" she whispered, frightened.

The two initial dark flashes had now increased to several more while the first two objects had come sufficiently within the range of vision to be plainly identified as two mountain men on horseback.

They cantered slowly up the straight, smoothly raked gravel path that lay in a direct line with the terrace.

The cavalcade behind the two leaders swelled into a swarm of horsemen as interminable numbers of warriors sailed over the high wrought-iron fence surrounding the park and then followed the passage of their leaders.

Alex rose quickly, indignant at the trespassers, walked to the edge of the marble parquet, and waited impatiently.

Upon reaching the marble pavement of the terrace, the two horses came to a halt. With a brief nod—the mountain men doffed their hats and bowed to no one—one dark, swarthy warrior said, "Prince Alexander Kuzan." It was a statement rather than a question. They knew exactly where they were.

"Yes?" Alexander glowered.

"Iskender-Khan requests the honor of your presence at his home. We are to invite his granddaughter and grandson as well.

"Invite?" Alex inquired sarcastically, his temper rising by the second.

"The escort is merely to assure your safety in the mountains, Prince Alexander," the leader smoothly dissembled, his face impassive before the glaring, golden fury in Alex's eyes.

Alex quickly raked his glance over the assemblage of warriors in his park and, calculating swiftly, remarked curtly, "Over one hundred men for escort?"

Iskender-Khan had but recently learned of his granddaughter's tribulations with the Mingrelian slave traders. Ma'amed had been found and succored by some shepherds who saved his life. When his message was relayed to Iskender-Khan, a party was sent south to find her, and the trail eventually led to Kislovodsk.

"Our chief is most anxious to make your acquaintance and also to meet his granddaughter and grandson. The bodyguard is to see to your safe arrival."

"If I refuse?" The question was sharp.

"We are to renew the invitation," the warrior said firmly.

Zena had come to listen to the exchange while Bobby stood awed by the magnificent troop of mountain knights armed with kinjals and long-barreled, silver mounted pistols thrust into silver belts, their rifles slung on their backs.

"Sasha, he's my grandfather. It can't hurt to accept his hospitality."

"I don't like the coercion," Alex muttered.

"Maybe an escort troop like this is normal," Zena temporized.

"Like hell," Alex snarled. "Not that there's a great deal of choice, it appears." The old man had seen to it that his "invitation" would be accepted. Alex was reckless, but not a fool. He'd go. "I'll be bringing some of my men along," Alex informed the leader.

"Of course, Prince Alexander, bring as many of your household as you wish. We have a litter for Iskender-Khan's granddaughter."

"I'd rather ride," Zena protested mildly.

"Iskender-Khan prefers you travel in the litter, *mademoiselle*," the leader stated resolutely. They too had seen the tracks etched in the blue-gray clay of the distant mountain valley.

"Very well." She turned to Alex and shrugged her shoulders.

Two hours later the cavalcade proceeded slowly through Kislovodsk, and soon the gradual ascent into the mountains began. Even accounting for shortcuts unknown to Europeans, the passage through the mountains to Iskender-Khan's aul required seven days.

8

The fortress aul of Iskender-Khan overlooked a large valley through which a mountain torrent ran. The floor of the vale was planted in fields of maize and prosperous orchards of apricot and pear, while the shallow basin was bounded by a range of low hills covered with a profusion of lush, verdant grass, on which herds of horses, cattle, and sheep were grazing.

At the far end of the wide gorge atop a severe climb lay the aul, a formidable fortress village dominated by a great square tower.

Beyond the village the snowy peak of the Shalbuz Dagh could be seen towering up grandly to the south. The horizon wherever one turned was bounded by an unbroken chain of pale, whitish mountains that looked very imposing, presenting a barrier to the world outside.

After slowly ascending the sheer path, the cavalcade rode through the village streets bustling with people who quietly viewed the visitors. Arriving at last before a large villa, the chief Iskender-Khan made his appearance. There was no doubt as to his identity. He was a tall, elegantly dressed, imposing man flanked by two lieutenants equally richly attired in gold, lace-trimmed tcherknesses and beautiful embroidered boots. Although past his middle years, as evidenced by his neatly trimmed gray beard, he was a well-built, vigorous-looking man.

As head of his clan he made the party welcome with

proud courtesy. He warmly embraced Zena and Bobby, bidding everyone enter his humble dwelling for refreshments. Personally escorting Zena and Bobby to their rooms, he spent some time in conversation with them, while Alex was shown to his own room and given time to bathe and rest from the journey.

The villa was magnificent, the rooms carpeted with exquisite, colorful rugs and lined with dazzling cascades of brilliantly patterned silk.

After a sumptuous supper washed down with excellent Kakheti wine, Iskender-Khan showed Zena and Alex some of his curiosities. He was a connoisseur and collector of antiquities unearthed in the numerous kurgans or tumuli on the great plain north of the Terek. The objects were chiefly of bronze or green glazed earthenware. Zena listened courteously as her grandfather expounded articulately on his favorite topic, the recital punctuated every now and then by a lazy "Very interesting, sir," from Alex. The collection was extremely valuable, and one could see it was a consuming pleasure for Iskender-Khan.

He was a warm and congenial host conversing easily with Bobby as well as Zena and Alex. As the evening became late, he apologized for the long journey to his village and wished Zena and Bobby a pleasant rest as his two grandchildren were escorted to their bedrooms.

"If you can spare a moment, Prince Alexander, before you retire," he inquired gently as Bobby and Zena disappeared down a long passageway.

"Certainly," Alex replied crisply. Only the obligations of good breeding had rendered him agreeable during supper and the evening following. The long forced journey to this remote village was still grating on his nerves despite the pleasant civilities of their host.

Alex was unfamiliar with the quality of submission and totally inured to the need to answer to anyone but himself. His temper, held in check for seven days through the mountains and then throughout the civilized formalities of social intercourse this evening, was now rather close to tinder point.

As Iskender-Khan carefully closed the door into the room and turned to face his guest, Alex's impetuous, hotblooded temperament overwhelmed the constraints with which he had disciplined it for so many days.

"What the *hell* is going on?" Alex demanded with typical Kuzan disregard for anyone else's authority.

The imperious, hawk-faced old man faced him, staring haughtily at him, ignoring his challenge. He coldly assessed the angry, dark-haired young man. He looked his visitor through and through with his black piercing eyes. So this was the young pup who had seduced his granddaughter. He certainly didn't have the pale look of a Giaour. There must be mountain blood somewhere in his veins.

The gray-bearded chieftain appeared undaunted by the remark. No affability or deference to a Russian aristocrat here, Alex thought, undeniably an autocratic overlord of thousands of tribesmen. But at the moment prudent considerations of civility were low in Alex's priorities. He was incensed at having been coerced into this village and kept here against his will.

"I am not exactly cheered being forced one hundred fifty miles into this camp. What the hell is going on!" he repeated wrathfully.

"Forgive the impetuous invitation, please," the chieftain spoke softly in a chill murmur. "A whim of mine, alas, to meet the companion of my granddaughter." The words were politely courteous, but his keen, dark eyes were cold as ice.

"Perhaps I wasn't in the mood to meet anyone, damn you. What's the idea of dragging us here without so much as a by-your-leave!"

"We are anxious to talk to you." The old chieftain used

the regal pronoun comfortably. The heavy-lidded eyes un-emotionally swept Alex from head to foot. "I think it would all go more smoothly if you were less insolent. You will force me into a position where we will have to relinquish our doubtful grip on civility and rather insist."

Alex studied him carefully. "Insist? You intend to insist?"

"We do indeed," came the gelid reply. "But, of course, since you're a guest in my home, we would rather not."

Alex was an experienced, skilled gambler. He knew when a bluff was a bluff and . . . when it wasn't. "What do you want to talk about?" he said.

"It has come to our attention that you and my grand-daughter have had, ah . . . a significant relationship. It has also come to our notice that she is with child and, alas, despite the fact that you are a Giaour, she has an abiding affection for you. I tried to talk her out of this foolish infatuation, but I fear she is too far from our tribal ways and as independent and headstrong as her mother. May her soul be blessed." His mind went back to the beauty who had been his favorite daughter. A fleeting moment of sorrow distracted him briefly. Then in a tone heavy with regret he continued.

"Since she won't give you up, the only solution is marriage. I promised her the pick of my warriors, but she would have none of them."

"Marriage?" Alex stiffened, the ominous word hanging in the air as threatening as vultures circling overhead.

Iskender-Khan paused, reluctant to continue but obliged to see honor served. "I give my granddaughter to you in marriage," he announced flatly.

"Sorry, I'm not the marrying kind," Prince Alex said through clenched teeth, politely declining the frigid offer from old Iskender-Khan. Damned wild barbarians anyway, Alex fulminated. Good God, he was only twenty-four. Marriage now was out of the question.

"If you'll excuse me," Alex snapped curtly, "I'll see to my people." He turned rudely and strode toward the doorway.

The prince experienced a fleeting premonition, an acute animal instinct of danger, and then something unbelievably painful crashed into his back. He buckled to his knees, momentarily stunned by the excruciating agony tearing through his senses.

He couldn't understand the rude, barbarous tongue, but the denunciatory voice of Iskender-Khan, raw with fury, was definitely hurling curses and thunderous maledictions at him.

The incensed old tartar continued to wreak his vengeance upon his granddaughter's seducer. Alex tried to ward off the blows of the punishing cudgel, but his stupefied brain refused to function rapidly, and much damage was wrought as over and over again the heavy, oaken club met human flesh and bone.

"Think to use my granddaughter and cast her aside, you young whelp!" The Russian was very loud and clear now. Alex marveled dimly at the vigor of the old man. He was scarcely breathing hard. "You'll marry her, hear me, you Giaour cur!" Iskender-Khan stormed. "You'll marry her or die!"

As another vicious stroke lashed downward, an agonized paroxysm twisted across his exposed ribs. Alex's knees crumpled, and as he lay there he wished vaguely that he carried a pistol. He'd kill the bastard before he died. Die? Jesus Christ! he thought urgently. I'm going to die! Father will be furious. Mother will cry for months. Father was always furious when his escapades made his mother cry.

"Enough! Stop! You mad, old fool!" he cried. "I won't be much good to your precious granddaughter in my grave!"

The contempt in his tone stayed the descending arm. With torturous effort Alex rose on one elbow and somehow twisted his head around as unbearable pain burst inside his brain. A dark tide of hatred washed over him. Burning, contemptuous golden eyes met the wrath in the old chieftain's glare. "In accordance with convention," Alex spoke, breathing painfully. Hell and damnation, he silently cursed, broken ribs. Pausing briefly for a shallow breath, he continued coldly, "Allow me . . ." He stumbled a little over the wording, damning the fate that had brought him to this pass and hoping vindictively that every evil of man and God rapidly descend on this old man. "Allow me to request permission to marry your granddaughter." Then he promptly fainted.

Iskender-Khan laid his cudgel aside and lifted one hand negligently in a gesture of behest. Two men materialized from behind the curtain of a doorway. "Carry my future grandson-in-law to his chamber. He will need his rest for the wedding tomorrow."

Very late that night a visitor was ushered into the private apartments of Iskender-Khan. "Nikki!" the old chieftain exclaimed in warm greeting. "Welcome. Welcome, old friend."

"Iskender, it's a pleasure to see you again," Nikki replied cordially, and the two men embraced affectionately.

"Sit down. I'll have some brandy opened. As I remember, it's your favorite."

"Still up to your old pursuits, it appears."

"Oh, we occasionally ambush and plunder a wealthy merchant or raid a village. It gives diversion to one's existence. There hasn't been a full-scale uprising in the mountains or a foreign campaign in three years. I think this brandy is from a fat Armenian's supply. It's tolerable, I'm told, although I prefer our local Kakhetian wine."

The bottles were delivered and glasses poured while the two men talked in general terms of the events that had transpired since they had last gone campaigning together against the Turks in '78.

A small silence fell after a time. Iskender-Khan broke the stillness. "You've come from Kislovodsk?"

"Yes," Nikki replied.

"You haven't forgotten our trails, traveling at night too. Your memory is very good, and your horse must be superb to navigate our byways by moonlight."

"One from my stud. A damn fine Stryelet. Let me send you some."

Another brief silence ensued. "I presume you know your son is here," the old chieftain said softly.

"I gathered as much."

"I'm sorry. Honor demanded I discharge my duty toward my granddaughter."

Nikki understood the rigid code of ethics observed by the mountain tribesmen. "I know," he quietly replied.

"I wish it had not been your son, old friend."

"I too wish I had known the identity of your granddaughter sooner. Perhaps I could have seen justice done myself. I'm sorry, the boy is young and headstrong. He leads quite an independent life, and I was under a miscomprehension about Zena's heritage. I feel the blame deeply."

"Whose daughter is Zena?" Nikki asked, familiar with Iskender-Khan's family, since he had lived in Iskender-Khan's village on many occasions. He had first made the mountain chieftain's acquaintance when he came south as a brash young lieutenant of eighteen. The mountain warrior had been a virile, dashing knight of thirty then, reckless, foolhardy, and a superb soldier and leader. He and Nikki had become friends that summer campaigning in the mountains during Shamyl's last uprising in '59. Intermittently over the next twenty years he and Iskender-Khan had often found themselves riding together against Turkish border tribes.

"Shouanete's daughter," Iskender-Khan answered.

"Shouanete's daughter?" Nikki paused in thoughtful deliberation. "How old is Zena?"

"Eighteen years," the gray-bearded warrior replied.

Nikki swiftly calculated the years in his mind and breathed an audible sigh of relief.

Smiling benignly, Iskender-Khan calmly said, "No fear of incest in this marriage, my friend. The girl was born to Shouanete three years after you left our valley. Wolf is fine, by the way. I sent him south to harass the Turks. He's too much like you, Nikki; it's causing trouble with the husbands in camp. All the women want him, and he cares for none of them enough to marry."

"If Zaide hadn't died giving birth to Wolf," Nikki murmured pensively, "I might have stayed in the mountains with you, Iskender. It was very tempting.

"I've wanted Wolf to come to St. Petersburg anytime in these past thirty-four years."

"I know," the old man said, "but the cities corrupt, Nikki. I wanted him to look and behave as if he had grown up in the mountains. The good qualities of the soul are formed in the mountains and only cleverness in the West."

"You're right, Iskender. Do you suppose I could persuade him to return with me now? When I saw him last in '78, he was just at an age to join the knighthood. He wouldn't hear of coming north. Has he used the yearly stipend I send to him for any purpose?"

"Like his father before him, in gifts for the ladies."

Nikki grinned. "Well, it's not wasted, then. Will he be back before I leave?"

"I'll send a message tonight before I retire. He can be back in two days if he travels hard."

"Good. I'd be pleased to see Wolf again. Perhaps this time I *can* persuade him to return with me for a visit. It would give all the jealous husbands an opportunity to cool off." Nikki smiled faintly. "Need I say I'm relieved Zena isn't my child. The consequences could have been unhappy. I've always felt guilty about Shouanete," Nikki confessed. "I invariably excused myself because of the wounds, telling myself the fever brought on by the infection made me temporarily irrational. She was too beautiful a nursemaid, Iskender, damned if she wasn't."

"No need to apologize, Nikki. She was smitten by you with a young girl's fancy. Her infatuation was as youthfully transient as a butterfly's flight. You need feel no guilt. She was very happy with the white-haired Giaour she married. I wonder, though," he teased, "if you gave her a taste for white flesh. She could have had her choice from our knights when she came of age, but she spurned them all. When the white-haired Giaour came riding into our camp two summers later, the first glimpse of him determined her mind. I will have that one, she whispered to me as we watched his approach, and she did. Shouanete was my favorite daughter. I deeply grieved her death." Tears shone in Iskender-Khan's dark eyes. "I must see to her child's welfare. You understand, my friend?"

"Of course," Nikki said softly.

The old man was lost in reverie for a moment recalling the laughing, teasing, exquisitely beautiful daughter of so many years ago.

With a visible effort he returned to his guest. He exhaled gently. "The wedding takes place tomorrow."

"Tomorrow. Very well," Nikki replied.

In the morning Alex woke to find his father seated by his bed.

"You're a long way from St. Petersburg," Alex quipped.

"I'm on a commission for your *Maman*. She worries about your affairs, and I must needs chase after you to assure her of your safety."

"I can only wish *Maman* would have become alarmed for my safety a trifle sooner. I could have used you last night." Alex grinned as every bone and muscle in his body screamed it's discontent. "Better late than never, though. Can you get me out of this?"

Nikki shook his head soberly. "It doesn't look like it. You should have told me she wasn't a streetwalker," Nikki admonished quietly.

"I have a marked dislike of having my hand forced. I resented the interference and the family inquisition into my liaisons," Alex explained wearily.

"Iskender-Khan is an old and dear friend of mine. I'm afraid you'll have to marry Zena. You understand?"

"I've a couple of broken ribs to nudge my comprehension," Alex grumbled ruefully.

"You must care about her a little," Nikki maintained. "She's lasted quite some time, plus this lengthy and, shall we say, costly (Nikki raised his eyebrows) expedition in pursuit of her."

Lord, the *père* always knew everything, Alex thought. How did he do it? Of course, emptying out half his stud at Podolsk may have given him a clue.

"Prior to Zena," Nikki continued urbanely, disregarding the look of surprise that crossed his son's face, "you were moving from bed to bed pretty rapidly. The fact that you've been with the same woman for three months and are apparently not tired of her must indicate some affection."

Alex held his father's eyes briefly and then shrugged. He didn't know, he really didn't know. He enjoyed being with Zena, enjoyed her in bed (no question there), enjoyed her constant presence, but was that enough? Was that love?

"It's not that I'm opposed to the chit," Alex explained. "I'm just opposed to the notion of marriage. So damnably final," he muttered uncomfortably.

"I'm afraid you've no choice. It's your misfortune to have seduced a young girl of impeccable background.

Now, if she hadn't had a mountain heritage on her mother's side, if she had been exclusively of Russian or European aristocracy, I could have bought your way out of this, but the ethics and moral code of the mountains require satisfaction for a dishonor, and money means nothing to them. I'm sorry. The marriage may prosper, who knows; treat her kindly and take care of the child. Make the best of a difficult and awkward situation."

Alex quirked one eyebrow sardonically. "Good advice, I'm sure," he replied dryly.

9

At breakfast Zena and Bobby were seated next to their grandfather. Zena kept her eyes on her plate, embarrassed by what she had heard from the servants about the events of the preceding night. Her grandfather had just informed her she would be married that afternoon to Alex.

Nikki was introduced, and she lifted her eyes briefly to acknowledge the introduction. During breakfast Nikki and Iskender-Khan were the only ones conversing. Alex sat stonily in silence, while Zena avoided looking at anyone, merely toying with her food. Bobby was preoccupied with arranging straight paths of raisins through his rice pudding and for the moment was unusually quiet.

"We'll dispense with *kalym* ['bride money']," Iskender-Khan said to Nikki. "I understand your son has already paid quite liberally for the company of my granddaughter, and I need no money. The festivities begin this afternoon; the entire village will participate in the celebration."

At three o'clock Alex stood waiting in the festal chamber. Zena was fetched by armed warriors, as was the custom, and entered the chamber heavily veiled. Zena and Alex were separated by a thin curtain hanging from the ceiling, their little fingers linked together while the holy man asked the required questions. Will Alex care for her, will Zena obey her husband, will they succor each other in sickness and in health? The last question to Alex in the marriage ceremony was: Are you capable of being the husband of a woman? Iskender-Khan raised his eyebrows to Nikki at the superfluous query. After Alex's response of "yes," one of the old women murmured an incantation against evil spirits. This was directed against the man's enemies, because it was thought that if in the instant in which the man says "yes" somebody draws his dagger halfway from the sheath and whispers, "It is a lie, he cannot," then the bridegroom will be impotent for one year. Injury to virility was a popular form of revenge in the mountains.

Immediately after the abbreviated ceremony Zena and Alex were parted. The women took Zena away to the room next to Alex's apartment. Now custom required that Alex encounter difficulty reaching his wife and, so at every door a veiled figure awaited him and blocked his way. He was to press gold into their hands in order to continue. Having been supplied with a bag of gold by his father, Alex impatiently passed through the gauntlet. Upon reaching his bedroom, more quaint surprises greeted him; a dozen chickens and an old crone graced his rooms. He paid off the old lady, as was required, and churlishly threw the chickens out the window. After all these disturbers of the peace had been ejected, the bride entered the chamber.

"Watch your step, my dear wife," Alex growled, "I can't vouch for the cleanliness of my quarters. Evidently some misguided tradition of these savages requires a dozen chickens share my bedchambers briefly."

"What did you do with them?"

"I tossed them out the window."

The image of Alex chasing chickens around the room forced a giggle of laughter to surface.

Alex glared at Zena for the space of one cold second and then began to chuckle himself. He winced in pain; laughing was definitely *de trop* with broken ribs.

Zena noted the sharp grimaces and experienced a quiver of remorse that Alex had been beaten because of her. "I'm really sorry, Sasha, about ... about my grandfather's cruelty to you,." she said, and her voice trembled. "I'm sorry . . . about . . . ," her hands fluttered awkwardly, "well, about all this."

"*You're* sorry, oh Lord." Alex's powerful frame sagged momentarily in weary dejection, as he gloomily reflected that he had come to a fine pass indeed, and all for a taste of one virginal cunt. What a damn fool, he thought. He gazed at his new wife stonily. "Not as sorry as I am, child, let me assure you," he replied gruffly.

Zena hung back near the door, uncertain of her coerced bridegroom, for his whole aspect was forbidding. Alex saw quite plainly the fear in her eyes as he stood considering her. Good God, his wife! She was now his wife! Finally, he smiled a hard, tight smile and growled softly, "Don't stand there like a wounded dog. I won't savage you. Come here." He held out his hand.

Zena walked over and took his hand. A strange smile came over his dark features. "I go to the devil in my own way. Stay with me, and I dare say you may be damned in the bargain. Are you sure you want this?" he said.

"I'm sure." She looked at Alex in adoration.

"Has it never occurred to you that you've attached yourself to a thoroughgoing scoundrel?" pursued Alex.

"No, Sasha," she said, "but then I didn't have much choice."

Nor I, thought Alex. The strange smile still hovered about Alex's mouth. He paused, looking at her oddly, then laughed a brief, mocking laugh.

"In that case, my dear, for better, for worse." He lifted Zena's hand to his lips and pressed a light kiss on her fingertips.

"Well," he sighed, "since this is my wedding night, broken ribs or no broken ribs, I intend to make the most of it. Take your clothes off, Princess Zena Kuzan. Let me see once again what I've purchased with both considerable gold and the bruised flesh of my body."

Sasha's tone was sardonic, but he was smiling with a dancing gleam in his eye. Was he angry? His unpredictable moods were difficult to read.

Alex stood and looked at her for a few seconds. "Afraid?" he asked, speaking softly.

"No, Sasha," said Zena, standing very straight.

Alex was watching his proud, beautiful wife with a faint smile both derisive and tender. "Then, sweet pet, do remove those native clothes."

Zena began undoing the buttons. Alex lounged against the wall to watch with intent interest. After divesting herself of the silk trousers and long tunic, she stood before him in a corset of thin morocco leather. The corset was held together by strings knotted in front. The knots were of a complicated sort that required endless care.

"Take off that corset, too, dear. I'd like to see a bit more flesh."

"It's . . . that is . . . well," she stammered, "the custom of the mountains requires the bridegroom to untie the corset on his wedding night."

Alex strolled over and drew a small gold knife from his pocket.

"Custom also prohibits cutting them, Sasha," Zena explained. "It's considered a shameful thing if the groom has that little control on his wedding night. In the morning the garment is checked to see how the knots have been undone."

Alex stood there quietly during the explanation, the small gold blade open and poised for the end of Zena's narrative. Narrowing his eyes consideringly, he viewed the formidable barrier. "Among the numerous faux pas I seem to have committed against mountain ethics and custom," he sardonically drawled, "surely one more can scarcely signify."

The blade slashed up, expeditiously severing every knot of the corset. The offending garment fell to the floor. With the usual Kuzan disregard for convention Alex had cut through society's shibboleths once again.

"There now," he exhaled softly, "quite as lovely as I remembered."

His new and very pretty wife stood in the center of the room, her bare feet pressed into the luxurious kelim carpet, her exquisitely formed legs rising to the undulations of hip and waist. A womanly softness was becoming apparent on previously boyish hips. Luscious, full breasts trembled provocatively as she shivered once in the coolness of the room.

The gleam in his eyes had turned to a leaping, fitful, passionate flame. "You're cold, dear," he said huskily. "Help me undress and then into that silken cocoon of cushions. I'd disrobe myself, but these damnable ribs are touchy. I can't manage the shirt sleeves very well."

Zena aided her bruised and battered bridegroom. She gasped at the sight of the large and vivid welts and bruises on Alex's shoulders and back, visible outside the bandages that taped his ribs firmly in place.

"Oh, darling," she cried softly, "it's awful. Is there anything I can do to help? I feel terrible."

Leading her over to the cushions, Alex said lightly, "I have an idea." Lying down gingerly on his back, he held out his arms. Almost immediately he cursed and shut his eyes against the sharp pain. "Ride me tonight, wife of mine. I'm not up to my usual activity." He pulled her over his slim hips onto his eager, pulsing erection, which stood proudly stiff displaying its broad vermillion head. Within a few brief moments it was all over.

"Sorry *dushka*, it's been a while." He slowly drew her down to kiss; her soft, warm lips burned into his, her sweet tongue darted into his mouth, and he stiffened inside her. Alex murmured against Zena's passionate lips, "Greedy little wife, don't you know, now that we're married I can be quite indifferent to your charms. It isn't respectable for a husband to desire his wife."

Zena stirred deliciously on his engorged masculinity and he groaned.

"And yet respectability has never been my forte."

Bouncing delicately on the rigid shaft, Zena smiled complacently. She caressed the taut muscles of his shoulders lightly, skipping over the bandages to slide down his belly.

Alex lifted one corner of his mouth in a fleeting smile. "I perceive you feel it's your turn now."

Zena nodded languorously as she arched her back in enjoyment. Her plump, white breasts were thrust out as she sank into the bliss of pleasure. Alex gently massaged the hard nipples poised above him. Zena moaned sensuously as tremors of blazing desire tore through her body. She pressed down, grinding the shaft of love into the depths of her warmth; ripples began to move outward, the intensity of her ecstasy mounted slowly, and wave after wave of glowing, intolerable heat grew within her until the sweet urgency broke with a flowing rush. She cried out in rapture as each new flood of joy swam over her. Sinking down on Alex's chest, she lay replete, palpitating, a gentle throbbing slowly diminishing.

Alex caressed her soft, warm back, stroked the long, flowing auburn tresses, and kissed her flushed cheeks as she lay in his embrace.

After a few moments Zena lifted to rise from him, but he stayed her movement. His hands clasped her firmly at the waist and compelled her to stay. He wasn't through with her yet.

"My wedding night, sweet, and I intend to observe it fully."

He drove into her gently while she sat, confined by his firm grasp. With a mixture of passion, selfishness, and mild resentment he kept her there.

Her opulent charms were his now. Zena's exquisite body had always kindled his passion, and Kuzan selfishness was notorious, while a latent resentment incited a mild sadism. He was, after all, married now—married against his will. The hot little cunt could pay for that coercion a bit and for the bruised, aching muscles and fractured ribs. He made her stay as he came again and again, caressing her luscious body slowly to bring himself up each time. Zena was bewildered by his silent assault. Finally she could endure no more.

"Sasha, please," she pleaded, "my legs are hurting." Her thigh muscles were painfully cramped. "Please, Sasha, let me go." Silent tears flowed down her cheeks. Alex then heard the quiet cry and noticed the tears streaming from her eyes. As swiftly as the cruel assault began, it ended.

Christ, what had come over him? He never abused women—and his own wife. Perhaps that was the problem, though. *Wife*, the word, the responsibility, the permanence, an irrefutable fetter around his life from now on. No excuse for abusing the poor thing, though.

He folded Zena into his arms, gritting his teeth against the pain of the embrace. "I'm sorry, child," he whispered tenderly. "I was a beast, forgive me. It won't happen again, I promise."

If I become that vengeful again, he thought, I'd better find some gypsy whore to abuse. Or there was always Amalie; she enjoyed little perversions.

"Go to sleep, child, I promise to never be a brute like that again."

Alex fell asleep immediately and slept like a crusader on a marble tomb. As the product of a pampered and indulged existence, Alex saw no reason to question his perversions.

Zena lay awake unable to ignore all the extraordinary ramifications of their relationship and marriage. She had vaguely understood that by his cruelty Alex was making her pay for the unaccustomed bonds that had been snapped onto his freedom. But the accomplishment of this union had been totally outside her control. No one had asked for her opinion in the arrangement of her marriage.

But amid all the bewildering tumult Zena knew she loved Alex with all her heart; knew that his body next to hers warmed her both physically and emotionally; knew she cherished the unborn child as a pledge of her love for this reckless, irresponsible, unutterably charming man. She hoped with a passionate optimism that they could build a life of joy and contentment together. She would let the future clarify and reconcile all the perplexing uncertainties.

Alex's ribs wouldn't permit an exhausting ride through the mountains yet, and so the newly married couple tarried in Iskender-Khan's village for three more days. But no one saw the honeymooning pair. They never left their apartment.

On the morning of the fourth day as they prepared to depart for Podolsk, Alex and Zena joined the family at breakfast. In addition to Iskender-Khan, Nikki and Bobby (who sported a small tcherkness in imitation of his grandfather) and a tall, dark, sun-bronzed warrior with slanted, incredibly wolfish, yellow eyes had joined the company. One glance sufficed to ascertain that Kuzan blood flowed through his veins. He was remarkably like his father.

Alex nodded to everyone at the table and seated Zena. He held out his hand to the mountain knight and said, "A half brother, I presume. Welcome to the family, although God knows if you want to admit to the relationship," he grinned.

The stern-faced warrior shook his head gravely, then returned the smile. "I'm quite content with my patrimony, little brother."

Their eyes met evenly, their broad-shouldered torsos carried analogously on slim-hipped, long-legged frames.

"You leave today?" the knight inquired.

"Yes," Alex replied.

"We'll travel together, then."

"Wolf has decided finally to accept my offer of a visit to St. Petersburg," Nikki interjected.

"In that case we can become better acquainted enroute. I don't think you've met my wife, another relative of yours, no doubt," Alex drawled.

"Yes, a cousin I believe," and he politely bowed over Zena's hand with all the grace of the most polished courtier.

On the trip back to Koslovodsk, Alex and Wolf became friends. Wolf was nonpareil as a mountain warrior, and while the cavalcade progressed at the extremely slow pace of Zena's litter, Nikki, Wolf, and Alex took the opportunity to do some hunting. The camaraderie of the expeditions off the trail was an agreeable delight to all parties. Nikki was extremely proud of his two sons. Since there was no stigma attached to irregular births in the highest Russian aristocratic circles,[8] Wolf was and would be accepted as one of Nikki's heirs with all the concomitant honors and deference. The fact that he was astonishingly handsome, like all the Kuzans, was simply an added fillip. And with the aura of wild, barbarian ruggedness surrounding him, due to his rearing in the Caucasus, he was sure to titillate every female heart in St. Petersburg. Nikki was realistic about the sensation Wolf would cause in the gilded drawing rooms of the Empire's capital. He sighed resignedly to himself. The problem of escaping numerous irate husbands in the mountains would merely be exchanged for escaping a new group of husbands.

Resting only one night in Kislovodsk, the party continued by train to Moscow. Zena, Bobby, and Alex returned to Podolsk, while Nikki and Wolf went on to St. Petersburg.

Part IV

The Arranged
Marriage

1

Zena and Alex settled down to an apparent domestic tranquillity. Alex experienced a fierce masculine possessiveness toward Zena. The circumstances that made him the first man to have touched her somehow made him proprietory, as though Zena were exclusively his. He had never experienced a feeling of possessiveness in regard to a woman before. Exclusivity had hitherto been rigorously avoided. Alex had always viewed promiscuity tolerantly, asking of his women only that the bed be vacant from the previous man. He hadn't cared particularly if the bed was still warm. Fastidiousness was no requirement.

He had been content as the pet of all the married women of St. Petersburg and Moscow, dispensing his favors like a sultan with a seraglio at his command. Each night had been a game of bedroom roulette. He was still young enough that the game had never bored him.

Now he found his friends teasing him, mocking him mildly for having settled into domesticity. Alex flared and bristled at the teasing, but underneath he was satisfied, and the lure of other women held no charm.

One evening a week after returning home, Alex and Zena attended a small dinner party hosted by Yuri. Alex, after surveying the assembled guests with very perfunctory interest, had retired to the library. Zena was off in the cardroom, having been persuaded by Yuri's aunt to join her in a hand or bridge. Alex wasn't in the mood for cards, and he certainly wasn't in the mood for dancing, which was being noisily pursued by mazurka lovers in the ballroom next door. The library was restful, and Alex was drinking himself into inebriation. The prescribed inanities of conversation rolled off his tongue more smoothly when well lubricated by brandy.

Yuri found him a quarter hour later. "Come, sit down. I'll pour us both another drink."

Dropping into deep-cushioned armchairs flanking the fireplace, the two friends drank in silence for some moments.

"All of society is buzzing over your marriage," Yuri said. Alex grimaced. "Do you know what they're saying about the Archer's marrying?" grinned Yuri.

Alex lounged in his chair and looked at Yuri, absolutely unmoved. "I never speculate on such irrelevant subjects."

Yuri laughed lightly. "Shall I tell you?"

"It appears," Alex said, smiling a little, "you are bent on just that."

"They are saying 'God help his wife'," said Yuri with a comical twist of his eyebrows.

"Amen," Alex muttered inarticulately and drained his glass. Giving Yuri a keen look, Alex uttered a laugh that was not without its cynical edge. "Society's concerns are as pressingly significant as usual, I see."

"Speaking of significant concerns, allow me to congratulate you on the tender event in store. I understand, Sasha, your young wife is with child," Yuri said with a discerning look.

"Good Lord, damnable gossip travels fast. We've been back in town scarcely a week, and I didn't even know myself until a few weeks ago," Alex retorted, somewhat chagrined at his best friend's leer.

"Ah, well, the knowing eye of a woman scorned is astonishingly keen, I've always found. Sweet Amalie informed me of the news yesterday, and no doubt the entire range of acceptable Moscow society has also been titillated by the news. I give it twenty-four hours at the outside to reach the scandalmongers in St. Petersburg."

"As long as that," drawled Alex ironically.

"They'll be counting on their fingers for weeks," Yuri warned.

Alex shrugged an elegant shoulder. "There's only one way to handle it, and that's to brazen it out, as usual, while the gossips have a field day. No matter how they count, they're going to come up short. We've been married only three weeks. It's a Kuzan family tradition, these short pregnancies after marriage," Alex said with a guileless smile.

"Must say, my friend, I envy you the next few months," Yuri sighed eloquently. "My experience proves there's never a more amorous period in a woman's life than the early months of gestation."

"I wouldn't know, Yuri, since I've never endured one woman's company for more than a fortnight previously," Alex retorted dryly.

"In that case," Yuri suggestively grinned, "you are, my fine stud, in for a pleasant education."

The days swiftly passed, Alex's moods varying erratically. By and large he was content, having settled down to changes in his life that weren't altogether distasteful, but on occasion he was not altogether reconciled to his new state of matrimony. The days of absolute freedom were gone, and when he dwelt on it, it was galling. He had always ordered and ruled everything to his will and was unaccustomed to the slightest check. In the following weeks one could often see impatience on his face as he fumed at the extra strain of the inevitable maneuverings necessary in a household no longer bachelor.

But then his mood would fluctuate fitfully, and those dark thoughts would vanish. Zena's presence pleasured him, and the gentle swelling of her body gave him an inexplicable feeling of pride. His child was growing in her; the notion of fatherhood hitherto studiously ignored was a pleasant conceit to him.

Zena attempted to accommodate herself to his temperamental mood swings. He was rarely uncivil, but unnerving disinterest would appear transiently, and a chill would run through her. It seemed at those times as though he was unconscious of her presence. Generally, though, he treated her with a courteous affection, and on the rare occasions when Sasha exerted his unutterable charm, her life approached perfection.

2

One evening the prince and princess traveled into Moscow to attend an evening's entertainment. Immediately Alex walked in, he knew the Barinskys' party was the usual affair: the same people, the same card games, the same dances. Christ, Alex thought irritably, enough was enough! The pose of dutiful husband squiring his wife about was quickly wearing thin. Damn it, he was going to refuse to leave the *dacha* for at least a month. Idiotic people. With the exception of Yuri and one or two other of his friends, the rest of society could very gladly go to the devil. In that genial frame of mind he poured down another drink and strolled into the cardroom. Gambling at least offered some respite to these dull soirees.

Several hours later, considerably drunker and considerably richer for the interval, Alex leaned back in his chair and loosened his cravat. Signaling for a fresh bottle of brandy, he began shuffling the deck of cards.

A large, florid-faced man who had been losing rather steadily at a nearby table said, "Whose bit of fluff is the new *enceinte* female? She's a beauty but a little heavy for my taste."

Alex, seated at the outer table, raised his eyebrows mildly at the crude jest. Without pausing he said placidly, "The lady you speak of, Krasskov, is my wife." Despite the disinterested voice there was a faint challenge in the cool eyes.

The heavyset man swung around at the statement, astonishment writ large on his face. "You married, Archer?" he exclaimed in surprise. "And not a minute too soon, it appears," he finished with a bold, crude laugh.

Krasskov had been at odds with Alex ever since a pretty little playmate of Krasskov's had shown a decided partiality for Alex a year or so before. Alex never turned down a pleasing danseuse, but by making love to her in Krasskov's bed in Krasskov's bedroom, Alex had shown, perhaps, a careless disregard for her protector's prerogatives.

Alex hadn't looked up as the man spoke. Continuing to flick over his cards, he said carelessly to the players around his table, "*Vingt-et-un*. Forgive me, gentlemen, the devil's own luck is holding for me tonight," and his hand swept out lightly and gathered the thin gold markers into the heap of gold and paper before him. Only then did he raise his head to cast a bland glance toward the fleshy, broad-shouldered man at the opposite table. Amiably he said, "I don't permit public discussion concerning my wife, Krasskov. You've had too much to drink." Felix Krasskov, despite imbibing, did not miss the deliberate use of his surname. Alex had drunk a great deal, and his amiable tone was the result of supreme self-control.

"Don't permit . . . don't permit," the red-faced man sputtered, his brows creased in a scowl. "Why, you arrogant . . ."

Krasskov's companion noted the chill glitter in the prince's eyes and nudged Krasskov uneasily. "Back off, Felix. Shouldn't bait Archer tonight from the looks of him. When he's that deep in his cups, he's dangerous."

Three parts drunk the prince might be, but his senses were unimpaired. He lounged back in his chair, now coolly lighting a cigarette, but his hard stare challenged his antagonist. "Understand, Krasskov?" The inquiry was an insult.

"I don't answer to you, Kuzan," Krasskov growled.

"Don't you, now?" the prince said gently and sat calmly waiting.

There was a shocked, expectant pause.

"Felix!" Kiril interjected hastily as he rose from his seat beside Alex. "Apologize, for Christ's sake. It's his wife, after all."

"Damned if I will," Krasskov said angrily, the humiliation of Alex's behavior with his paramour goading him still.

"Sasha?" Kiril urged plaintively.

The prince shot him a bemused look. "Oh, Lord, Kiril, hush. Krasskov doesn't care to apologize to me. It's perfectly all right." Alex was still watching Krasskov. He drew leisurely on his blue silk cigarette, exhaled slowly, then leaned forward to grind it out. "No apology, my fine buck?" he inquired gently, eyes raised.

"No, blast you!" Krasskov shouted.

"In that case, Krasskov," the prince was smiling now with a tight-lipped smile, and his eyes glowed with a steady blaze, "name your weapons."

Baron Achieff lurched somewhat unsteadily to his feet, an incipient sense of duty impelling him to intervene. "Archer, leave off, you can see Felix's drunk."

"I as well, Vassily," Alex laughed shortly, "but I still can tell when a man casts a slur on my wife."

Vassily's faint hope of averting scandal died, and he was jerked back into an unwanted sobriety. One of the crowd around the table was heard to remark to his companion, "Archer's devilishly proprietary about his wife. Didn't think he gave a damn about females, let alone a wife."

"Have you seen his wife?" came the envious response. "I'd be possessive, too, if she were mine."

Then the prince sighed dramatically and murmured softly, "There's no accounting for some men's taste. I myself fancy a well-rounded female like my wife, in preference to the less generously endowed form of, shall we say," Alex paused delicately, "someone like Martine Ivanovna."

The insult seemed gratuitous and, of course, hit its mark, for Martine Ivanovna was, in fact, the contested paramour of a year before.

Krasskov jumped to his feet, crossed the short distance, and struck the table with a beefy fist, tumbling piles of gold markers in disarray. Leaning pugnaciously across the green baize surface, his corpulent face flushed with wrath, he roared, "Pistols, damn you!"

The lounging figure betrayed no agitation save the hard glitter in his tawny eyes. "Pistols it is. We'll settle it now." This was Alex at his most dangerous, cold and indifferent with a cutting edge to his voice that would have sheared through plate steel.

"Are you fit?" Kiril asked Alex anxiously.

Alex laughed. "Fit? Of course, Kiril, you know me better than that. Brandy doesn't affect my aim."

A servant was sent for the pistols, while the combatants advanced through the French doors and down the stairs to the second terrace out into a misty night.

They stripped off their coats, and the pistols were presented. They would stand twenty paces apart, and at the signal they had three shots. If neither was shot in three times, the matter would still be considered settled.

Alex raised a quizzical eyebrow when the rules were related. Three times indeed, he thought mirthlessly. Alex stood gently swinging his pistol as the seconds counted down. He looked alarmingly drowsy.

The word was given. The prince's hand crisply snapped up. A shot rang out almost simultaneously with an answering shot.

Alex dropped his pistol and flicked out his handkerchief to stanch the blood beginning to appear through the shirt sleeve of his right arm. Baron Krasskov plunged forward lifelessly. Alex turned away to pick up his coat and began strolling back to the palace.

"Damn rain, I'm getting soaked," he muttered as Kiril rushed to catch up with him. Alex was the only person unmoved.

"It looks like you might have killed him, Sasha," Kiril reported anxiously. There was no sign of agitation on Alex's face.

"Well, I should hope so," Alex replied blandly. "It was my intention." He sauntered back into the cardroom binding his arm clumsily with the silk handkerchief.

"You're hurt, Archer," an onlooker exclaimed.

"Only a scratch, nothing serious." He finished his rough bandage and shrugged into his coat.

Vassily came running in breathlessly. "He's alive, Sasha."

"Your gun throws left, Kiril. Damned if it don't. Would have had him dead on otherwise. Pity." Alex shrugged fatalistically as he reached into his pocket for his cigarette case.

Strolling into the ballroom he advanced slowly, moving with his own peculiar arrogance of bearing, a cigarette between his lips, a deep gleam in his eyes. The press opened to let him through, and he dropped into a sprawl next to Zena on the settee.

"You've rain in your hair, darling," Zena remarked. "Outside in a storm like this?" she inquired, puzzled.

"Only briefly, my dear. The air in the cardroom was oppressive." He sat and visited with his wife and friends for twenty minutes, refreshing himself with several glasses of champagne.

As the minutes passed, he participated less in the conversation and at last sat in silence while Zena chatted with her crowd of admirers. She was surprised he didn't ask her to dance.

Yuri pushed through the crowd and whispered agitatedly in Alex's ear, "Kiril said you were wounded."

Overhearing the exchange, Zena turned pale and cast a frantic glance at her lounging husband.

"A mere trifle, I assure you, dear," Alex replied in answer to her horrified look. But when he turned and fully looked at her, she saw how pale his face was.

Bending across her husband, Zena lifted his arm. His silk shirt sleeve was soaked with blood, and a thin, crimson stream trickled from under his cuff to his glove. Numerous drops of blood had collected on the floor.

"Sasha," her voice trembled. "You're bleeding."

"Don't look so distressed, Princess. It doesn't hurt much," he said lightly. He saw the expanding pool of blood on the parquet floor and said carelessly, "Perhaps we should bid our adieus to our hostess. If you would be so kind as to lend me your handkerchief, I think I can stanch this embarrassing flow until we get to our carriage."

Zena called a doctor immediately they reached the Kuzan apartment. Alex was deathly pale and lay down willingly.

The doctor assured Zena after he had dressed the wound that no bullet had lodged in Alex's arm, and the flesh wound, though dreadful and noisome, was not serious now that the bleeding had been stanched.

"Could have told you that myself," Alex grumbled from his sickbed. "Nothing serious, just as I said."

They returned to the *dacha* in the morning. Zena hadn't thought it wise to disturb the arm so soon, but Alex was cross and surly, intent on having his way.

When Zena questioned Alex about the duel, he replied shortly, "Krassiov, the canaille, had the impudence to discuss my wife in public. I won't allow it, and I told him so. I trust the lesson may mend his manners."

Alex's smoldering gaze lightened reflectively. "There's a certain vulgarity about Krasskov I could never abide." His voice dropped to a thoughtful, inaudible murmur. "What Martine saw in him I'll never know.

"I refuse to go to any more tedious parties for at least a month," Alex declared emphatically. "If you enjoy that sort of boredom, madame, please feel free to attend, but acquit me, my dear. I find the company intolerable."

"It makes no difference to me if I go or not. I'm perfectly content to stay in the country."

"Good, send our regrets, then, for the near future. Isn't there some social nicety, in any event, that demands *enceinte* women refrain from going out in society after a certain number of months?"

"I've never felt particularly inclined to adhere to polite social convention," Zena retorted coolly. "Are you telling me I *should* stay home?"

Alex caught the hint of chill in her tone and readily mollified his wife, relatively unconcerned with society's rules. "Don't take offense, dear. I could not care less about social custom, as you well know. I'm infinitely disinterested in what the world thinks of me. It was merely a passing thought. You have my permission to partake in society until the moment you deliver. Lord, I don't care."

"*Your permission?*" Zena enunciated icily.

"Acquiescence, assent, agreement, whatever term you prefer. I just never remember seeing patently pregnant ladies parading around at parties," he finished lamely.

"That's because you were always too busy inspecting all the voluptuous females who were casting out lures to you," Zena snapped. She wouldn't have been normal if she hadn't felt ungainly and unattractive as her pregnancy progressed. She was just being temperamental, she knew, and unjust, since Alex had been discreet since their marriage. It was difficult, however, to remain placid and tranquil and accommodating. Her independent spirit would make itself heard despite her best intention. At times it was as hard for her to assume the posture of perfect wife and mother-to-be as it was for her husband to adapt to the model of docile husband.

They were both trying, but it was as if a conscious shackle had been applied to their behavior—two temperaments so independent, high-spirited, candid. It was just a matter of time until the explosion came.

Zena could pretend she was content with the rare scraps of affection Alex offered her, but she wanted more. Alex could simulate the behavior of a contented husband, but a bold, reckless nature chafed at the sham.

3

Alex was busy the next few weeks. He immersed himself in the business of the estate. The hay harvest was being taken in, and the rye was too dry. They needed rain; then it rained for eight days. The rye began showing signs of rot, and he was busy setting up drainage in the fields. He also initiated several new building projects, overseeing the construction of a new barn and an addition to the stables and granaries. Once a week he presided as counselor for village disputes. He was trying to live a circumspect life, attempting to settle down into the routine of married life. He was tense and abrupt, mentally pacing like a caged animal but never actually admitting it to himself. Even in sleep there was a sense of contained, resolute energy, taut and unrelaxed.

Occasionally Alex would ride into the club for a bachelor party. He didn't go to many, but some couldn't be avoided if a special friend was being feted.

One evening he came home very early. Zena was still awake. "Where were you?"

"At the club. I told you I was going."

"You never take *me* anywhere." Even as she said it she knew better.

"I told you to go out all you wish. I just can't stand any parties. These evenings at the club are different—just a few of my friends I can tolerate." What did she expect, he asked himself irritably. She knew him. She knew his reputation. Did she imagine he was supposed to turn over-

261

night into some tame curate? "If it bothers you so much, I won't go so often. Satisfied?"

Alex was becoming weary of Zena's constant need for reassurance, and much as Zena tried, she couldn't overcome this compelling need.

"I'm sorry, Sasha, it's just feminine vapors." They were as distracting to Zena as they were to Alex. "I need you to say you care about me." Her voice was rising.

"Look, I'm with you. I care or I wouldn't be here," Alex said very slowly. "I've never stayed with any woman longer than two weeks before." He was patient but exasperated with her little tantrums. He'd married her, for Christ's sake, didn't that mean something, he thought with asperity. Good Lord, all women think about is love. He gave an impatient shrug, contemptuous of the emotions that constantly plagued women. *Merde*, will these troublesome scenes never cease?

"What more can I say," he patiently explained to her. "I want to be with you. I married you. Isn't that enough?" he finished harshly.

"I don't know," Zena answered sadly as tears spilled from her eyes. Zena knew that she shouldn't persist in these questing probes for love and affection. Alex never dispensed ready, glib phrases. She had subjugated her personality and will to suit him. What price was she paying to stay in her husband's good graces and in his bed?

"Come, *dushka*, don't cry. We're muddling along, aren't we now?" Alex inquired cajolingly. Reaching over, he tipped her chin up and forced her tear-filled blue eyes to meet his. Zena mutely nodded her head in response, stifling the impulse to complain that muddling along wasn't enough. "Don't expect too much from me, child," he said softly. "I can't rise to it."

An uneasy truce prevailed the next few days, each taking special care to avoid antagonizing the other. It was unnatural, and the resultant strain put pressure on both Alex and Zena.

4

Yuri's brother was leaving for a governorship in an eastern province. The festivities to wish him *bon voyage* were at the end of the week, and naturally Alex was invited.

"It's Yuri's brother; otherwise I wouldn't consider going, but we've been friends for years. I won't stay long," he explained. "I'm sorry I've accumulated so many friends. I never realized what a problem it would be," he jibed brusquely as he saw the doleful expression on Zena's face.

All he received for his effort at humor was a rather cool, disdainful glance. He waved carelessly and left.

The party followed the customary format—cases of champagne, high-stake gambling, and droves of gypsy wenches and dancers.

All evening long Alex politely but firmly refused the caresses bestowed on him by countless accommodating women. He drank and gambled instead in an effort to ignore them. Very late in the evening Alex was sprawled on a couch talking to Yuri. A beautiful gypsy dancer swayed over, deposited herself on his lap, and kissed him long and seductively.

Alex gently unwrapped her arms from around his neck. The pretty, dark-haired charmer looked at him askance because in the position in which she was seated it was very obvious the handsome gentleman was interested.

Yuri quirked one brow in amazement. "No one expects you to live like a monk just because you're wed. You'd be the only married man in town doing so. Setting a new style?" he teased.

"Well . . ." Alex threw him a heated look, "damn it Yuri!" He thought about trying to explain to Yuri, whose amused eyes rested on him sympathetically, but couldn't.

Drawing the lovely wench into an ardent embrace, he kissed her thoroughly, then freed himself from her arms saying, "Some other time, my sweet." He roared then for another bottle of champagne.

Several hours later Alex arrived home, three parts drunk and feeling the martyr. Christ, he'd turned down women all night long. It was unnatural.

Entering the bedroom with less grace than usual, he caught his spurred boots on the dressing table skirt, knocked over a chair, and bruised his shin. Cursing loudly and fluently served to assuage the pain but served as well to waken his wife.

"What time is it?" Zena murmured, still half asleep.

"Lord, how do I know. It's so damn dark in here I just about killed myself." Fumbling with a match, he lit one of the wall lamps. Electricity by choice had not reached the *dacha* at Podolsk.

"If you weren't so drunk you wouldn't fall over the furniture," Zena chastised as the heavy liquor fumes quaffed their way across the room.

"I'm not drunk. I never get drunk!" The bottles of champagne seemed to have had little effect on him. Alex was steady enough, but there was that glitter in his eyes that betrayed the extent of his drinking.

"Don't yell," Zena said.

"I'm not yelling! This isn't yelling!" he yelled.

A pungent odor of musk and roses entered Zena's nostrils as Alex drew near. "Since when did your bachelor friends take to wearing musk and attar of roses?"

"May I recommend, madame, that you refrain from upbraiding me; I can't vouch for my temper at the moment," Alex said with dangerous quiet.

"There's that tone," Zena said.

"What tone now? *What* tone?" he sneered, thinking to himself this catechism was intolerable and incredible.

"*That* one, the one that puts the little wife in her place, the condescending velvet-gloved threat. You know what you can do with your threats and your condescension and the little piece that left the reek of perfume on you." Zena stared at the lip rouge on his neck. "I hope you enjoyed your tumble with the tart," she spat. "If you'd try as hard to be pleasant with your wife as you obviously did with that female tonight, perhaps we'd get along better. In the future I'd appreciate a little more discretion with your hussies. Stay overnight in town if you must."

"Oh no, madame," he said softly as he stalked to the bed, "no more musts. *Must* marry. *Must* become a father. *Must* rusticate as a docile husband at your grandfather's pleasure." The last accusation was not wholly true, and he knew it, but the rest were true and galling. "But no one says *must* to me on how I go to the devil, least of all a wife!"

"It's quite plain you've been going to the devil with no added urging from me," Zena said sweetly.

"Please, madame," he said, each word dripping with acid, "spare me any more of your damned insolence."

"And who was it tonight?" Zena purred hatefully, despising his arrogance. "Amalie's back in St. Petersburg; perhaps some ballet dancer or pliant gypsy."

"Listen, you bitch," he exploded, "don't tell me I haven't been doing my damnedest. I turned down the sweetest beauty tonight, and all I got for my pain was god-awful teasing from my friends and abuse from my wife. I'm sorry now I turned her down; for all the appreciation, I might as well have mounted the wench and enjoyed myself."

"Yes, that's all you men think of, enjoying yourself with some woman," Zena cried.

"All you *women* think about is ensnaring some man into the marriage trap. I've seen it all a thousand times, all the debutantes languishing after my title and fortune. God! I spent years watching the parade of hussies looking for husbands, their sole concern splendor and position. All the lures, enticements, beautiful clothes, soft curls, exposed bosoms—all bait until the trap snaps shut."

Prince Alexander Kuzan had known so many artful, wanton women and evaded so many carefully baited traps over the years that his perception of sincere, true innocence was distorted.

"I hope you're satisfied. You got what *you* were after. I married you. But you aren't going to get my goddamn soul, because that's not in the contract. You've got me. Isn't that what you were pursuing from the first coy approach on the Dolgorouky stairs. Very clever of you, and I fell for all the innocence, damn fool that I was. *Merde*, you women are all the same—a soft, compliant exterior, all passiveness and softness masking a core as ruthless and determined as a striking cobra."

"You arrogant bastard! So I entrapped you! Who the hell forced me during that train ride to Moscow when I pleaded and begged you to stop. You've a convenient memory, you son of a bitch. Maybe all the other women you knew were scheming to trap you in marriage, but let me assure you, my conceited, insolent stud, that I wasn't one of them. You're insufferable. You think you can have any woman you want at the snap of a finger."

"But, madame, I can," he said simply.

Zena snorted disgust at his arrogance. "Nevertheless, *you* were the one who pursued me into the mountains, if you remember," she said crisply.

"But not, I think you know full well, with the intention of matrimony," retorted the prince ignobly.

"I didn't propose to you, if you recall."

"Nor I to you. If my memory serves me, for some fiendish Tartar had beaten me almost senseless. I believe I proposed to your grandfather," he rejoined coolly.

"That was none of my doing."

"However, you acquiesced to the plan."

"They wouldn't have listened if I had protested."

"A flimsy excuse, I'd say. Did you even try?" he demanded.

"Damn you! You don't know what it's like to be a woman in a man's world!" Zena cried indignantly.

"I *do* know what it's like to be bludgeoned bloody as a seducer, though," Alex raged.

"But you're not six months pregnant with a child now, are you?"

"No, I'm not, but if I hadn't offered to marry you I'd be dead now, madame," he spat.

"You don't care at all about me, do you?" There was no mistaking the agony in her voice.

"Frankly, my dear, not at the moment."

Across the short distance they challenged each other. Blue eyes flashed hot while the gold eyes remained cold. All the repressed discontent of the past months hung in the air patently real. All pretense and sham fell away— they were antagonists.

"I'm leaving then, damn you!"

"And where does madame propose to go this time?" inquired Alex with a studied politeness. "Good God," he growled, "don't start that again. The last time you left it cost me a fortune and the inconvenience of a couple of broken ribs. I warned you. You knew you were tying yourself to a scoundrel. Grow up, for Christ's sake. Do you think most marriages are any different from ours? Those made in heaven, my dear child, are only found in romantic fiction. The ones of this world are quite a different matter, let me assure you. You can't run away every time things don't go quite right."

"*Quite right?*" Zena laughed bitterly. "I'd say this particular instance is a shade more serious than that," she snapped. "Is there *anything* right?"

Alex threw back his head and laughed. His lip curled mockingly. "Ah, the romantic female soul forever seeking perfection." His eyes narrowed savagely. "Count your blessings, pet," he sneered. "You've a roof over your head, and console yourself that you're free from the gropings of that lecherous old slug, General Scobloff."

"I can't say I find your gropings any easier to stomach."

Fifty generations of pride stiffened Alex's spine. His eyes were cold as ice as he glared at her. "Be assured, madame," he said in a chill murmur, "you need never suffer them again."

He strode to the door, paused with one hand on the crystal handle, and said, "I'll be at the club in Moscow for a few days." Then his voice softened. "Say goodbye to Bobby for me, and tell him I'll bring him back a new toy."

Alex acknowledged with a vague awareness that all these unresolved problems of their marriage were aggravated in part by himself. While aware of this view, he totally rejected the reasonable logic.

Quietly, her head held proudly, Zena watched Alex walk away.

The door shut with a soft click, and he was gone.

5

Zena collapsed on the pillow. All her worst fears were realized. She lay there filled with terror and sick at heart. It had finally been verbalized. For months she had hoped that Alex would love her. She had dreamed that underneath the apparent indifference he really cared.

Well, that cloud castle had come tumbling down. There was no more deceiving herself. Alex intended to live a marriage of convenience, had never envisioned anything more. She'd been the stupid one, weaving preposterous fancies of undying love, of mutual need and caring. Alex had gone into this marriage with both eyes mercilessly open. She was the only fool.

What to do now? Does one accept the status of a marriage of convenience, of figurehead wife and mother? Does the future hold only endless tomorrows of being a docile puppet, a dim, placid wife of convenience who appears at her husband's side at social functions?

It may work for other people, this marriage of convenience. It may even work for most other people. She didn't care if it worked for *all* people. Her independent mind rebelled at the eviscerated image of a tractable wife in a marriage of convenience. She refused to stay as an unwanted appendage to Alex's life, a nuisance to be tolerated, perhaps even hated.

She may not be happy wherever she went, but she couldn't be any more unhappy than in Alex's life when he clearly didn't want her. If she stayed, she would have to submit to the daily torment of never being able to really touch him.

If she didn't care, it would be easy. She could take her own lovers and lead as dissipated a life as her husband. They could greet each other briefly as they passed in the halls and to and from their rendezvous. Somehow she couldn't see Sasha allowing her that freedom, though; he had such a ruthless proprietary streak. But she didn't want other lovers; she wanted only Sasha. It was her misfortune to love him. If she didn't care, she could stay and endure the cold eternity of a marriage of convenience, but unfortunately she cared passionately. She would have to leave.

The next morning Ivan took charge of the departure. Zena told him simply that she and Bobby were going on a visit to her grandfather's. Servants' gossip had already spread, for Alex's thundering voice had carried well in the early morning hours, and a groom had had to saddle a horse for the prince at five in the morning for the ride back to Moscow.

Ivan, with the circumspect behavior of a kindly steward, asked no questions and efficiently took in hand the details of packing.

A carriage was taking them into Moscow. As the anger of the previous night dissipated, a sickening dread gripped Zena. This was forever—never to see Sasha again, never to wake with her beloved, never to walk with him through the country meadows. Her head throbbed.

How was she going to live life without him? What had seemed a reasonable prospect now appeared dismal. Zena's heart ached for another chance, and a sort of desperation seized her.

Oh, Lord, Sasha. Why can't you love me, she cried silently from the wretched depths of her soul. Why can't you love me as I love you? I don't want to leave I don't!

She decided to send a note to Sasha at the club telling

him she loved him and would try to live amiably in a sensible marriage arrangement. She would set aside her pride and write.

With her mind resolved, her spirits rose optimistically. Maybe by this time tomorrow she'd be back at the *dacha*. Maybe by this time tomorrow she wouldn't be miserable and dejected, but blissfully returned to Sasha's arms.

She and Bobby were deposited at the Hotel D'Angleterre and soon settled in a sunny apartment.

If she had any pride, she told herself one last time as she sat staring at the blank sheet of paper, she would refuse to ever think of Alex again. But an image of his tall figure rose in her mind, and with a sigh she sat down and dashed off the note. It was a straightforward declaration of love and her wishes for a future together. Before her courage faltered she sent it off by messenger.

Maybe Sasha would respond immediately when he read the message. Maybe she'd see him within the hour. Her heart shivered joyfully. Alex would realize his mistake. Please come home, Zena, he'd say, please take me back. She both dreaded and longed for the answer that would decide her fate.

Late that afternoon as the sun's long shadows crept into the sitting room, Zena's optimism had faded. She was morose and melancholy, half-heartedly attempting to placate a fretful three-year-old who was tired of staying indoors. "We'll go out tomorrow morning, Bobby. It'll be dark soon. I don't want to go out now."

They ate a quiet supper in their room and retired early. Sleep eluded Zena for hours. She tossed restlessly, her mind assessing the endless reasons Alex hadn't come. Deep in her heart she excused him a million ways. Maybe he'd returned home, and the note would take a day to reach him. Maybe he'd gone out with Yuri and hadn't returned yet. The excuses multiplied and mounted, her spirit unable to cope with the frightening possibility that Sasha had read the note and didn't care enough to respond. She would give herself one more day, and if she hadn't heard from him by tomorrow evening, she and Bobby would go abroad. Her whole body trembled at the thought of the future. Much as she wanted Alex, to beg was intolerable. She'd wait, hope fading, one more day. She lay in the darkness silently crying for her husband; the tears ran over her temples and into her hair.

The note in question, the missive that contained the anguished outpourings of Zena's heart, was delivered to the club promptly by the messenger. While the messenger was inquiring of the doorman the direction of Prince Alexander's room, Baron Matsenov sauntered in, returning from his afternoon ride.

"Prince Alexander Kuzan? You looking for Archer? I'm going up to see him now. I'll take it and save you the trip." Tossing a silver ruble to the messenger, he was handed the envelope and proceeded up the stairs.

The baron knocked on Alex's door. He had still been up when Alex returned to the party in the wee hours of the morning, and they had made arrangements to go look at Alex's stud at Serpukhov. Baron Matsenov didn't recall the exact details of their plans, and he was going to check on those particulars now with Alex. Knocking once more and receiving no answer, he decided Archer was either still sleeping or entertaining one of the gypsy wenches.

In any event, his questions would wait; they were all planning on meeting at Yar's for dinner that night. He could talk to Archer then. Slipping the envelope into his jacket pocket, the baron resolved to deliver the letter later. Sliding an envelope under the door might be distracting if Archer were entertaining a female.

At this point heinous fate intervened. On the way to his own room Baron Matsenov was intercepted by his cousin with both sad and happy news. The elder Baron Matsenov, from whom the son had been estranged for several years, had but recently passed to the other side in the arms of the holy monks to whom the elder was much attached and to whom the son resentfully attributed the parental estrangement. His father's death was sorrowful news, although the old baron had lived a long and pious life. Heaven would welcome him. The happy tidings were that the scandalous young baron had providentially *not* been disowned by his father's will as so often threatened.

During the past year as the health of the elder baron had seriously deteriorated, the priests from the Monastery of the Trinity and Saint Sergius had been advising the old baron to change his will. They insinuated that the manner in which his wealth would be dissipated by a licentious son would be a sin in the eyes of God.

Peotr had been aware of the machinations and lived in the very real fear that he might be left a pauper. He breathed a sigh of relief. "Maybe the old bastard cared a little about me underneath all that zealous religious frenzy," he said to his cousin. "Let's go and give him a proper burial and kick out all those priestly spongers who have been living off his estate the past ten years."

"If we hurry we can catch the four o'clock train to Nijni Novgorod," his cousin replied.

"Do I have time to change? A hacking jacket and buckskins aren't exactly proper attire for traveling."

"No time, Peotr. Good Lord, you're so rich now you can afford to be eccentric. Travel in whatever you like."

In this convoluted fashion Zena's message traveled into the country halfway to Perm in the pocket of Baron Matsenov's hacking jacket. As the affairs of the estate were in great disorder due to ten years of priestly intrigues, Baron Matsenov was forced to extend his visit several months after the burial of his father. The elegant hacking jacket hung unused in his closet. In its pocket reposed Zena's tender, anguished avowal of love for her husband.

Alex slept the entire day away, waking at seven and dressing leisurely for dinner. He and a group of his friends were dining at Yar's tonight. Memories of the quarrel kept recurring despite his best efforts. He refused to think of his marital squabbles anymore, he decided with finality. He'd go out tonight with Yuri and head back to the *dacha* after he woke tomorrow.

It was too bad all this senseless wrangling was constantly arising, but he supposed a great deal of it was his fault. Try as he would, it was impossible to reconcile himself to marriage; he was just too young to settle down. He'd talk to Zena tomorrow, quietly and rationally, when he returned home. Maybe they could come to some amiable agreement in their relationship so that this continuous bitter repartee could be ended. He had to have more freedom, that was all. Staying home every night and playing dutiful husband wasn't his style. Perhaps after the baby was born, Zena could be induced to take a prolonged vacation at one of the German health spas. Then he'd have a few months to kick off the traces and be ready to re-embrace domesticity for a time. They'd talk it over tomorrow.

In the meantime there was tonight. If that pretty gypsy charmer could be found, the tables would be turned. He'd be the pursuer this time.

While Zena sobbed herself to sleep in the gloomy solitude of her hotel room, Alex passed the evening in an atmosphere of gay conviviality in a private second-floor dining room at Yar's. The food was superb, the restaurant cellars were above reproach, and damned if Yuri hadn't known the little puss's name. The comely dark gypsy was, at the moment, seated on the table directly in front of Alex with her legs straddling his shoulders. He was partaking of dessert.

Alex spent the night in a gypsy lair deep in the heart of the city, and the sun was almost setting again by the time he emerged from the narrow, dingy street. Christ, he was tired—too fatigued to face a serious marital discussion. He decided to sleep at the club and go home the next day.

The following morning, as Alex was leisurely riding the quiet road home in the cool serenity of a summer forenoon, a tearful young woman and a young boy were boarding the train to Warsaw. She was weary, and her heart was broken. It remained only to go away, as far away as possible from the man who had crushed her soul.

Zena had decided on Nice as a destination. It was warm in winter, suitable for her child who would be born in October. The temperate climate would be healthy for a young baby during its early months. Nice had the further advantage of being a vast distance away from Sasha. As a third consideration the Mediterranean town had a large Russian colony, for the proximity to Monte Carlo was convenient. She wouldn't feel so homesick in exile if fellow countrymen could occasionally be seen. Zena had considered going to her grandfather, but the primitive remoteness of the area caused her apprehension. This was her first travail, and if something went wrong or if the delivery was difficult, she didn't want to be a seven-day journey from a doctor.

Despite her grandfather's good intentions, his autocratic attitude, nurtured by decades of obeisance, was intimidating. Perhaps he would arbitrarily decide to have her divorce Sasha and marry one of his knights. He had suggested several suitors to her before her marriage. The possibility was terrifying. Sasha may not want her, it was quite obvious, since he had declined to respond to her note, but she loved him still. The thought of being forced to marry someone else was appalling. She was afraid of her grandfather. He had been a virtual dictator for fifty years. She didn't have the audacity to withstand his authority.

As the train progressed through the gently rolling countryside, her vacant eyes stared sightlessly at the summer landscape. Over and over again painful thoughts of her unrequited passion for Sasha wove through her mind. It felt almost as though she were physically ill. She was drowning in a maelstrom of humiliation and rejection. She had been one more in a long succession of female houseguests, one who had lasted a little longer than usual and was leaving with the added burden of the prince's unwanted child. He didn't care enough even about his child to answer her note.

At those times when her mind reflected on Sasha's lack of concern for his own child, her mood would swing suddenly to the most violent anger. She would have liked to beat him with her bare hands, hurt him with any weapon she had, scream abuse into that handsome, haughty, indifferent face that could stare so blankly right through her. If she had had it in her power at those times of bitterness, she would have made him suffer. Her love was overwhelmed by such savage hate that her breathing would quicken with the fury. She wished she could hurt him as he had so carelessly hurt her. She had been merely an amusing diversion that had suddenly ceased to be amusing, and with the most casual, bland disinterest he had let her go as effortlessly as a child lets go of a balloon string.

She hated him, hated him, her miserable heart cried vehemently. But then she'd break out in a fresh torrent of tears, for underneath she wanted him still.

Zena experienced a terrible, unspeakable grief, a helpless sense of loss and loneliness. The daunting prospect of spending the rest of her life without Sasha was almost too much to bear. Then fresh resolve would prevail. Stop crying and bemoaning your fate, she sternly commanded herself. He wasn't the only man in the world, and for the next year she was going to be very busy taking care of a new baby and Bobby. The daily tasks would push aside the melancholy musings, and thoughts of caring for her baby warmed her soul.

When her thoughts would flow in that direction, she was almost cheerful again, and she twined happy dreams of herself and Bobby and the baby living peacefully in the pleasant, warm climate of Nice. They'd survive comfortably, at least for a time. She had taken all the jewelry Sasha had given her. When it was sold in Nice it would keep her comfortably for a long while.

6

Alex arrived at the *dacha* at lunchtime. Walking into the small west parlor, he expected to find Zena and Bobby eating their midday meal. Seeing no one there, he turned to inquire their direction from a servant. With faint astonishment he discovered not a muzhik was in sight. Now this circumstance was so unusual that the condition caused him the vaguest disquiet, as the French aristocrats must have felt as their servants melted away before their eyes just preliminary to their setting torch to the châteaux. Alex's mind flashed back to his greeting from Trevor at the front entrance. Very subdued, he recalled, while prior to that the groom who had taken his horse at the door seemed unusually agitated.

"Where the hell is everyone?" the prince roared in a voice that echoed through three levels of the *dacha*.

He stood in the entrance to the parlor waiting, persuaded that his household boasted a sufficiency of servants to expect some kind of response. Ivan appeared directly from his office at the back of the house.

"Where is everyone?" Alex repeated, bewildered.

Ivan pursed his lips briefly and then plunged in. As steward he supposed it was his responsibility to shoulder Sasha's wrath.

"They're avoiding you," he said quietly.

"Why?" Alex asked suspiciously. Quickly he asked, "Is

Zena all right?" Things could go wrong during pregnancies. Jesus, was she hurt?

"I think so. I'm not sure."

"You *think* so? What do you mean?"

"She isn't here, Sasha. She left with Bobby two days ago and said she was going to her grandfather's. Vladimir drove her to the Hotel d'Angleterre."

"She's gone?" Alex exclaimed incredulously. All his benevolent intentions of a rational, warm marital agreement vanished. "The bitch," he exploded. "The impudent bitch!"

Aware that his steward was still standing there, Alex curbed his wrath. "Thanks, Ivan. You're a brave soul. Tell the rest of the servants they can come out of the woodwork now. No one's head's coming off. It's not their fault she left. Have some brandy sent up to my room"

When he entered their apartment, he carefully searched all the likely places a note may have been left. No note. It would have been decent of the little bitch to at least leave a line or two. So much for his ideas about marital agreements and harmonious living.

Well, good riddance. Her grandfather was welcome to her. Talk about two birds of a feather, both of tempestuous dispositions. Christ, that old Tartar was a throwback to medieval times, still ruling a feudal fiefdom in the last years of the nineteenth century as though five hundred years had never elapsed.

If Zena was going to be that childish and run off every time they had a violent argument, then damn her, let her go. She knew where he was. She could come back when she was ready.

A soft knock on the door signaled the delivery of the brandy.

That night the dark-haired chambermaid turned down the coverlet and again cast her provocative glances at the prince; this time they weren't cast in vain.

Alex assessed her with half-closed eyes as he sprawled in a chair by the fire. "You're new here, aren't you?" he drawled. Crooking a finger negligently, he beckoned her near. "What's your name?"

"Sophia, Your Excellency." She curtsied prettily.

"Sophia," he said mildly, "why don't you take your clothes off."

Poor Sophia had, unfortunately, only one night to demonstrate her obedience and devotion, for the prince departed the next morning for St. Petersburg.

7

Never one to mope unduly or in solitude, Alex decided a return to St. Petersburg was in order. Moscow was good for rusticating, for enjoying country living and country pleasures, but when it came to pure, unadulterated dissipation, Moscow quite simply didn't offer the variety.

Early that evening he strode into the charming drawing room hung in Chinese silk in the pink marble palace on the Neva. He dropped lazily into a chair and observed his family's surprise.

"Is the prodigal son no longer welcome?" he ventured satirically.

His mother collected herself first and hastened over to warmly embrace her eldest son. Alisa exuded the soft scent of lilies. Alex closed his eyes briefly as she pressed her cheek to his. There was security in that fragrance that always denoted his mother's presence.

"Sasha, my dear," she murmured against his cheek. "We're so pleased to see you."

"Thank you, *Maman*." He lifted his eyes to hers, and she was dismayed at the intense, bitter gleam that glittered in the depths of his tawny eyes. The questions, of course, were expected.

"Where are Zena and Bobby?" his mother inquired.

"She and Bobby went on a visit to her grandfather's," Alex replied.

"When she's six months pregnant?" Nikki remarked sceptically from a chair by the window.

"Apparently she missed him," his son retorted bluntly.

"When do you expect her back?" his sister Katelina asked. She and her two children were staying on the Neva Quay while her husband was in Europe.

By grim effort he schooled his face to its habitual indifference. "She didn't say," was the urbane reply. Everyone's eyebrows raised infinitesimally.

"Have I time to change before dinner?" Alex inquired, terminating the discussion of his wife's absence. Dinner had already been announced, but Sasha's moody look had to be taken into account.

"Of course, dear," Alisa said kindly. "We'll hold dinner. Take your time."

He left the room, and Alisa raised her hand in admonition, staying the caustic remark Nikki was about to make. "Please, Nikki, be patient with him," she said anxiously. "It isn't easy to be forced into marriage at his age."

"You should know all about that, Papa," Katelina teased, her eyes shining in amusement.

"Listen here now, Katelina." Nikki scowled in mock anger, for he doted on this beautiful eldest daughter of his who reminded him so poignantly of her mother twenty-five years ago.

Katelina wasn't frightened of Nikki's counterfeit scowl any more now than she had been as a five-year-old. She knew she could twine her dear papa around her little finger and had been doing that quite successfully for twenty-five years.

"Teasing or no," Alisa interjected, "Katelina's right, Nikki. If anyone should understand the constraints, you should. Please, dear, no chafing remarks. We'll find out soon enough what happened. You can see he's harried and tense. A tranquil supper tonight? Please, dear?"

"Of course, love. You're right." Sasha's dangerous look

had not gone unnoticed by his father, and having the advantage of a good memory, Nikki could sympathize with his son's black temper. "I'll restrain my barbed crudities. We'll talk about the weather. Observe how placidly understanding I can be."

A half hour later, just as the first course was being served, Alex stared blankly, his soup spoon poised in midair, as he heard his father blandly say, "Don't you think the weather has been extremely pleasant lately, Sasha?"

Since Nikki received no answer save the continuing vacant look, he went on in mild explanation, "I find the warm summer evenings perfect for strolling about."

Alex was saved from his bewilderment by Katelina's soft gurgle of laughter and Natalie's piping voice, which declared to no one in particular, "Well, I *like* the long summer nights 'cuz I don't have to go to bed so early. Nurse can't tell me it's late when the sun is still up at ten-thirty."

"Grandpapa, will you take us to the point again tonight?" Katelina's eldest son, a tall, serious, blond boy of eight, inquired.

"Please, please," the tiny voice of his four-year-old sister added her plea.

"All right," Grandpapa Nikki agreed readily, "but only if you promise not to throw frogs at the ladies. I can't run as fast as I used to," he grinned.

"Are Georgi and Valentin both in Paris?" Alex inquired, as he noted the absence of his brothers.

"Georgi went alone," Nikki explained. "Valentin is still slightly young to undertake the . . . er, education. Georgi is apparently enjoying some of your old amusements in Paris," Nikki continued dryly. "He made the acquaintance of Honore Constance's niece and can't be lured home at the moment. Perceivably the family is looking to repeat their financial coup," Nikki murmured cryptically.

Alex shot his father a quick glance of caution, since the circumstances of his financial settlement with Honore

Constance de la Garonne had been withheld from his mother. Alisa misunderstood the masculine practice of buying off discarded mistresses. She took offense at the callous disposal. It wasn't that she was opposed to the compensation, but only to the casualness with which males conducted their liaisons, insensitively considering money a suitable recompense for a broken heart. Such nonchalant indifference she found repugnant to her romantic soul.

"If the niece is as affable as Honore Constance, the family fortune is assured," Alex replied blandly, and then quickly turned the subject. "Where is Valentin?"

"He's at Mon Plaisir," Nikki replied, "with Yukko, learning to break horses. When I was up north a week ago, he was brown as a berry and decidedly reluctant to ever return to the boredom of city life. He's becoming quite an expert equestrian under Yukko's tutelage."

"Where's Wolf?" Alex asked abruptly as he recalled his half brother's intended visit. His glance swept the table. "I thought he was staying with you."

His mother's eyes sought Nikki's, and Katelina flushed a bright red.

Nikki cleared his throat delicately. "He too ... er ... went north to Mon Plaisir for a week or so. Hasn't had a chance to see much of the pine forests. He'll be back soon."

"When?" Alex inquired, anxious to renew his acquaintance with such an interesting brother.

"Maybe in a day or so. Depends on his luck fishing."

"Or when his temper cools down," Natalie interposed ingenuously. "Boy, was he mad when he left."

Alex's brows rose. "Mad at what?" he questioned.

Katelina was staring down at her bowl, stirring the soup aimlessly, and his mother's flustered eyes met his pleadingly.

Nikki's quiet voice drew his eyes. "Apparently he has inherited the rather hasty Kuzan temper, Wolf wanted something he couldn't have, that's all. He'll cool down and come back. We won't discuss it anymore. It upsets your *Maman*.

"And miss," he said severely to Natalie, "I'll thank you to mind your manners. Your ears are much too big for your own good."

"Yes, Papa," Natalie acquiesced obediently, momentarily subdued by her father's reprimand. Her natural curiosity wouldn't be repressed for long, though. She had the kind of bubbling, vivacious personality amenable to everyone. She was friendly with all the servants, and they adored the little hoyden. Natalie knew every scrap of gossip that flowed through the house.

The subject was closed, and so Alex proposed checking with Natalie later to have his curiosity resolved. Katelina certainly was acting oddly, he mused.

Before dessert was served, Alex rose and adjusted the width of shirt cuff showing under his evening jacket, but carelessly, as though it scarcely mattered that he was point-device. He was, as usual, elegantly if somewhat carelessly dressed. His tie was knotted loosely, his overlong raven-black hair lay in graceful disarray on the back of his collar, and his watch fob was strung through the handiest waist-coat buttonhole. But he had an air about him, and a careless unaffected distinction carried easily on his tall, powerful, lithe form. All in all, he was an arrogant, spoiled rakehell with far too much charm for his own good.

Alisa and Nikka both contemplated the splendid figure of their son in evening dress, but with somewhat different views. Alisa's eyes shone with motherly love and admiration, while Nikki's pensive gaze held more gloomy presentiments. With more realism and less parental bias he wondered if it were possible for the boy to live his life without the constant threat of public scandal hovering over. But certain deeds of a misspent youth warranted Nikki an understanding of the reckless promptings of youthful indiscretion. And after all, he had been almost ten years older when married, and he must allow Alex a bit of time to adjust to his new matrimonial state. The particular circumstances that were driving Sasha were not entirely of his own making this time. Hopefully Sasha and his young wife could reconcile their differences eventually. In the meantime, it was obvious the boy was dangerously bent on raising hell.

"I think I'll see what's going on at the Nobles Club. Don't wait up for me," Alex grinned.

Much later that night Nikki and Alisa were readying for bed. Alisa was seated at her white moiré-draped boudoir table, brushing her hair. Nikki came up behind and lightly touched the golden-red tresses as they tumbled down her back. Alisa's eyes met his in the mirror.

"What are we going to do, Nikki? Two of them out on the town at one time. Between Sasha's and Wolf's wildness the scandals will be calamitous," she wailed. "Wolf alone was a handful, and now Sasha. That boy's driven, Nikki. Did you see how tense he was? And the Krasskov scandal hardly died down. Thank God he lived, anyway."

"Don't get yourself in a pet, my love," Nikki said, stroking the shiny hair under his fingertips. "Haven't I always managed to avert disaster?" he soothed comfortingly.

"I don't know, Nikki," she lamented despairingly. "He had to marry that mountain girl, and you couldn't get him out of that."

"I told you, dear, there are some debts of honor that must be paid."

"But don't you see, Nikki, anywhere else a family could have stopped short of marriage one way or another. You said he didn't want to marry her. I agree he may have acted rather thoughtlessly, but was it really necessary he marry her, Nikki?" Alisa vacillated indecisively. But her love for her son precluded any arguments of honor or justice. To her, Alex could be careless and temperamental, reckless and negligent, and always forgiven.

"It was necessary," Nikki declared patiently, tolerant of his wife's maternal emotions. He knew she was always at heart a mother. Alisa expected the answer, of course. The question was merely rhetorical; this topic had come up for discussion numerous times before. Nikki had compassion for his wife's nerves and indulgently responded to the same voiced fears over and over.

"And now Wolf with Katelina. His amorous wooing deeply disturbed Katelina; she's always been so faithful to Stefan."

Nikki's eyes narrowed grimly at this point, for the stories of Katelina's husband's errant behavior were legion. If Katelina would but say the word, Nikki reflected ominously, that husband of hers would be dealt with as he so richly deserved.

Alisa went on, "But Wolf's evidently not familiar with refusals. I hope there's no repetition of that violent scene between them when he returns from up north. He must understand that Katelina's a married woman and not interested in his addresses. I tell you, those mountain men make me nervous. You can't reason with them like ordinary people. Wolf is very nice, don't get me wrong, but so . . . so . . ."

"Ungovernable," Nikki helpfully supplied.

"Yes, exactly. I'm worried, dear. Can you really handle the escapades of both Sasha and Wolf?"

"Absolutely. Don't you know I was once just as unmanageable as they? It's quite simple, really. I learned from my father. Apply equal parts of money and influence with an occasional slight twist of the arm for effect. It's worked for centuries. If anyone dares to offend you with some unsavory gossip lamenting my sons' wickedness at some of those dull tea parties you attend, tell them ever so sweetly that vice runs undiluted in the Kuzan blood. Rest content. I'll see that no harm comes to them or to Katelina, either."

Nikki's voice softened. "Now come to bed with me." Running his hand down the satin-covered curves of her waist he murmured, "How is it you haven't altered an inch since I met you twenty-five years ago?"

Alisa rose, threw her arms around his neck, and softly replied, "Because I starve myself five days a week to stay thin for you, lecher."

"Ah, that's what I like to see," he grinned, "a dutiful wife."

8

The day after Alex's return to St. Petersburg, the mantel in his bedroom was scattered with pastel, perfumed billets-doux reminiscent of his bachelor days. His behavior the first night home assured all interested females that Alex was back in circulation. He was completely unconscious of the stunning figure he cut in the stark black and white evening rig. Every feminine eye had followed his progress that night as the spoiled darling of the St. Petersburg set reclaimed his position.

They had all missed him dreadfully these past few months. It had hardly seemed the same without him. One matron dressed in gray bombazine and seated regally on a gilt chair, commanding a fine view of the Natazins' ball, was heard to remark to her friend, "I see Nikki's boy is up to his old tricks. From the day he left his tutors at home, he's been outrageous. No doubt he was in the nursery as well, if he's his father's son. Shocking rake drinks too much like all the Kuzans, plays high, and apparently left his *enciente* young wife in the country."

"Poor young thing, one can't help but feel sorry for her," the friend remarked. "Yet with a reputation like Sasha's one could hardly expect him to settle down and become a perfect paragon."

"With Sasha back the *on-dits* should be prodigiously more interesting," the matron in gray sighted. "Faith, in spite of his wildness, one can't help but like the engaging young rascal. To tell the truth, with all the females that have chased after him since adolescence, it's a wonder Sasha's not more impossible than he is. When that boy strolls into a room, and insolently surveys the crowd through those narrowed, yellow eyes, he turns into the living image of Nikki. Do you think he matches his father's distinction in the boudoir?" the dowager in gray quizzed dubiously.

"He's given credit for acquitting himself with admirable expertise," her friend replied. And the two matrons fell into silence as pleasant memories of their youth materialized.

That initial evening back Alex graciously accepted the invitations of six of his former lovers to renew old friendships. All the pretty society women purred around him like a group of harem houris, vying with each other for the position of favorite, and behind his cynical eyes there was a twinkle of amusement. Alex flirted with them in a way that verged on the insolent, but they seemed enchanted. He needed amusement; he was bored with domestic fidelity. If your wife walks out on you, then *que voulez-vous?* He didn't guide the hand of fate.

After a week bets were being placed in the clubs as to the exact length of time the Archer could sustain the grueling pace he was setting for himself. Such behavior could hardly pass unnoticed, and within days the whispers grew. Married only three months and already he had cast off his wife. It discredited the old saw that a reformed rake made the best husband. Tongues wagged and all St. Petersburg watched and waited to see if anyone would replace her.

One guess at the Nobles Club was heard to remark, "Could even the notorious Archer maintain such arduous amatory exercise?"

His companion replied dryly, "Oh, Archer'll manage the demands put on him by the ladies easy enough if he don't drink himself to death in the meantime."

No one dared ask what had transpired, and the young prince schooled himself to never mention his wife's name.

Wolf had returned three days ago, and the handsome half brothers were now rather systematically attempting to bestow the benefits of their very attractive persons throughout the length and breadth of St. Petersburg's boudoirs.

But there were many nights when Sasha returned home and rather than seek the solace of his bed was prone to endless pacing along the terrace outside his apartments. There was the liveliest apprehension about Sasha's moods, but most of the time he was his normal self, never making reference to his wife's prolonged absence.

His and Wolf's amatory excursions continued unfalteringly. Alisa held her breath, and Katelina cried repeatedly, while Nikki mentally kept lists of complacent and noncomplacent husbands and fathers in the event some rapid decision must be determined. It didn't hurt to keep up old ties with the royal family either. He paid visits to several grand dukes who could be counted on in the event a scandal required more pressure than the Kuzan name was able to exert.

After several weeks, when this reckless dissipation provided no calumny of horrifying proportions, Alisa began breathing more easily, and Nikki ran through his mental list only once a day. Katelina's tears were intermittent now and concealed more carefully. She had acquired a reserve and reticence wholly unlike her usual teasing vivacity, presenting a calm facade to the world. It was the usual moderately repressed scandal under which the Kuzans had lived for generations.

Alex and Yuri were desultorily playing billiards one afternoon when Wolf had slipped away to visit Katelina. They were out in the garden now with her children, where Wolf was teaching her young son Aleoysia how to distinguish the character of a track through grass.

Katelina and her daughter Elizabeth lay on the green turf and watched the lesson. When Wolf was at his charming best, he was irresistible. Since he had come back from Mon Plaisir, he had been civility itself to Katelina, never overstepping the bounds of friendship. The resultant frustration and strain on the bold mountain knight during his daytime, innocent courting of Katelina sought release at night in his reckless path through the bedrooms of the aristocracy.

"Wolf is certainly paying a lot of attention to Katelina," Yuri said. "Anything to it?"

Alex shrugged. "Her eyes are red all the time; it must be love. Natalie told me Wolf and Katelina had a terrible row weeks ago. Apparently my sister, in opposition to the general trend of acceptable social behavior, feels she should be faithful to her husband. Wolf had trouble understanding that. He went north for a while to cool off and seems to have accepted her restrictions on their friendship." Alex paused and snorted disgustingly, "More fool he. There are lots of women around."

"With a husband like Katelina's I'm surprised she feels an obligation to fidelity. The swath he cuts through the ladies is about as discreet as yours. Why does she put up with it? Your father could have a divorce for her in a few days' time."

"Katelina has some misguided notion about staying together, pardon the cliché, for the sake of the children. You can tell she doesn't have a drop of Kuzan blood in her veins. Maybe the steadfastness and attention to convention comes naturally. My mother's first husband, Katelina's father, was an old, wealthy merchant, I understand; he's long dead and forgotten now. Katelina was only five when my parents married and Papa adopted her. If you ask me, she's really acting too damn conservative about this all."

"By the way, speaking of conservative, what do you think of Miss Catherine Feodovna Riminsky? A dazzling charmer, wouldn't you say?"

"Most assuredly, but a bit too straitlaced to suit me."

"Not just straitlaced, but an impregnable citadel, my friend, beyond even your cultivated expertise."

Alex laughed. "Surely you jest. Impregnable, my ass. The sheer arrogance, my friend Yuri, of the concept makes one anxious to impregnate the wench just to discredit the foolish notion."

"Are you trying to say something, Sasha?" Yuri taunted in a cultivated drawl.

"Two days, Yuri," Alex said recklessly, "no more. I'll bring her to your place to do the dastardly deed, so there's no cause to doubt."

"Tsk, tsk, extremely ungentlemanly behavior even for you, Sasha."

"Don't read me any lectures, Yuri. Are you on, or aren't you? You should know by now I always rise to the bait when anyone says impossible. You can't cast a slur on my expertise, Yuri, and go unchallenged. Play or pay. Two thousand rubles says I can carry the citadel in two days." The prince coolly contemplated his well-kept nails.

"You're a blackguard, you know," Yuri declared.

Alex's eyes met Yuri's and he laughed, and suddenly Yuri understood how much all the highborn hussies mattered to him.

"I've been called much worse, dear friend," Alex grinned. "I'm quite immune." Lifting one black brow sardonically, Alex said, "I tell you it's useless to appeal to my feelings of decency and chivalry. At the moment I'm bereft. Used up every last shred in wooing my ungrateful wife, who has seen fit to fly the coop, as they say, without so much as one word of explanation." His eyes narrowed as he spoke, and his mouth became a grim, straight line. He seemed lost in his own musings for a brief moment.

Shrugging his shoulders as if to cast away the reflections, his eyes flickered open, and the cynical smile reappeared. "Well, on or no?" he said.

"Oh, hell. On, of course," Yuri assented cheerfully.

"Have clean sheets put on your bed, will you, Yuri? These young misses are of a fastidious bent. Comes from all the healthy hygiene they're taught nowadays in their lyceum courses."

That evening Miss Catherine Riminsky encountered the full assault of Prince Alexander Kuzan's considerable charm, which had been faultlessly schooled to perfection in every fashionable salon in St. Petersburg and Paris. She was dazzled. It quite turned her head.

The straitlaced Miss Riminsky had never been the recipient of such ingratiating, outrageously sensual flattery. Alex danced with her several times and by the end of the evening, the thoroughly fascinated young lady's body fairly tingled with exciting anticipation. A hitherto unfelt yearning to be caressed most intimately inundated the beautiful, pious virginal Miss Riminsky's mind. She hardly slept that night as enchanting visions of the lean, bronzed, muscular prince bewitched her dreams.

The next night Alex deliberately arrived quite late at the dance Miss Riminsky had mentioned she was attending. It never paid to look too anxious. A full twenty minutes after his eyes had met hers casually across the ballroom, Alex crossed the expanse of polished floor in a manner that was at once languid and yet held a very distinct hint of lean, coiled, predatory energy. As he reached her side a waltz was playing. The prince's cool, golden eyes rested thoughtfully on the pretty young Miss Riminsky. Then without asking he swung the lovely *mademoiselle* out into the crowd of dancers with a natural, fluid grace, bending to whisper softly in her ear that she was the most exquisite woman in the room.

"Dark hair and milk-white skin, Kate, a glorious combination."

As he adroitly twirled them through the moving mass of couples gliding effortlessly around the room, Alex's hand on the tiny waist slipped down her silken back. Exerting the most subtle pressure, he pressed the lovely Kate against his very rigid erection. Deep green eyes lifted to his and the prince, an experienced hunter, saw the acquiescence and smiled. Miss Riminsky melted against his broad chest as Alex maneuvered them near a small side door, where his carriage was waiting.

Fifteen minutes later a very hot and flustered young couple rushed up the stairway to Yuri's elegant *pied-à-terre*. As Alex was hurriedly undressing the tremendously agitated young woman, a rude twinge of conscience reared its unnecessary head. Alex groaned inwardly. Sweet Jesus, not now. In the carriage ride over his hand had been under Miss Riminsky's skirt, and she had a hot, wet quim just dying to get fucked. He was aching to get in her; conscience he didn't need now. Damn it, you can't be forcing a cunt as wet as that one. Any fool would know that.

As he lay next to her in Yuri's bed, young Kate was rubbing against him with tumultuous fervor, timidly touching his pulsing stiffness, and all Alex could think about was his caddishness. Guilt! he thought despairingly. Was he getting old?

Sighing deeply, he lifted her pretty chin so that she was looking directly at him. "Do you know what you're doing, Kate? It will be too late soon to turn back. Are you sure?" He needed the sop of her assent. Christ, since when did he have a conscience? He *must* be getting old.

"Oh yes, Alex," she cried feverishly.

Rolling over her, he shuddered in relief as he thrust gently at first and then surged forward to break through and bury himself in the wet, tight virginal passage.

Several hours later Miss Riminsky twined her delicious

milk-white arms around Alex's neck and said, "You'll have to come home and meet Mama and Papa."

"I've already met them, my dear, and find their daughter much more delightful. Acquit me, a married man isn't exactly their idea of a suitable parti in any event," he said with unwonted frankness.

The beautiful Miss Riminsky made a moue of distaste in response to the blunt reminder. "Pooh. I suppose you're right." She brightened visibly. "Then can I meet you here again sometime?"

"Certainly, sweet. Just send me a note. I'd be happy to arrange it."

The sweetly sated Miss Riminsky clung to the prince's arm as he escorted her back into the ballroom. Their entrance caused a mild stir, as the absence of both parties had been duly noted. The cynosure of a goodly number of eyes in the crowded room, the prince, with a careless distinction of mien, walked directly across the entire floor with his clinging partner, oblivious to the vapid, venal, and frankly curious glances that followed their progress. Alex moved across the crowded room with impeccable composure as dancing couples yielded before them. The lovely, dark-haired Kate, her coiffure and gown restored to near perfection once more, glided along beside her attractive seducer. Her limpid gaze turned upon him, still warmly content from the preceding hours' activities.

Reaching the far wall, Prince Alex bowed blandly to the aunt who was chaperoning the young miss that evening. "May I restore Miss Riminsky to your company, Baroness Katernov?" Turning to Kate he bowed deeply and kissed her hand. "My thanks, Miss Riminsky, for your pleasant company."

With these brief words he left the young miss and went to seek out Yuri. He found him in the cardroom. Sinking into a vacant chair, Alex drawled indolently, "Deal me in."

As Yuri dealt the cards he cast Alex a questioning look. "Well?" Yuri queried.

"My dear Yuri, I beg you to reflect." A pained look crossed Alex's handsome face. "Would I be so maladroit as to fail?" Alex's brows drew together in mock dismay at his friend's questioning challenge. "This is my speciality, after all—years of practical application selflessly pursued, countless hours devoted to a diligent study of seduction." Suddenly Alex grinned. "You owe me two thousand rubles," he said dryly.

But now that it was all over, although the fair beauty had been a pleasant diversion, there was the same old dissatisfaction. He laughed harshly in sheer ridicule of his own jaded appetite, recognizing the indifference of satiety. Nothing attracted him anymore. A woman was a toy to amuse his wayward mood, a physical release, instant gratification. That was all, nothing more. It was depressing.

At the same party in a secluded alcove screened by numerous potted palms and bouquets of roses, Wolf sat facing Katelina, holding her dainty hands very tenderly. His fierce, golden eyes held her violet gaze as he softly murmured, "You're driving me quite insane, *ma petite*. Won't you forget for just one brief moment all your dutiful wifely strictures?"

He leaned close to brush his mouth across her pale pink lips, and she closed her eyes for an instant as a tremor of desire tore through her body. How long could she deny her feelings? How long could she withstand the growing need for this strangely gentle mountain warrior? As her dark eyes opened, Wolf's determined glance captured them once again, and his whispered query echoed her thoughts.

"How much longer will you be able to hold me off, little one? How much longer?" Expelling a soft sight of defeat, he slid his powerful hands around her white shoulders that rose enticingly above the black lace and chiffon of her ballgown and drew her into a loving embrace. "Forgive me, *ma chére*," he whispered as his mouth touched the curls near her ear. Would she freeze in his arms, or would she surrender? Her body trembled, her breath came unevenly, then with a helpless sob, Katelina's elegantly coiffed head fell against his chest, and her small hands stole around his broad back.

An exalting triumph raced through his senses as Wolf crushed her in his arms. "Tonight, sweet darling, tonight I'll make you mine," he breathed huskily as his lips traced a path across her blushing cheek. At last she had welcomed him! His heart beat with sudden elation as he contemplated the prize he so dearly coveted.

Into this lush, intimate haven of trothed passion, the air redolent of blooming roses and love's consent an intruder transgressed. Standing just inside the arched entrance so conveniently shielded by greenery, the tall, slender aristocrat with fawn-colored hair, cold, gray eyes, and a contemptuous curve to his lips expressed the acid hope that his wife was enjoying the party.

Katelina froze at the first sound of the familiar sneering voice, and Wolf saw fear flicker in her violet eyes before his own gaze swung to the figure silhouetted against the brilliance of the ballroom chandeliers. Dropping his arms from her shoulders, Wolf instantly rose with one easy movement in an unconscious reaction of protection.

Only the inherent demands of civility propelled Katelina to her feet, and she stood trembling, pale and shaken. Katelina spoke in scarcely audible tones, "Stefan, may I make known my stepbrother, Tchorook Oglou Tougouse Kuzan; Wolf, my husband, Stefan Sergeyevitch Stepniak." Bows were exchanged. "Stepbrother?" Katelina's husband inquired sceptically, as his unpleasantly cynical eyes took the measure of his wife's friendly companion.

The Daghestani warrior stood warily alert as the antagonistic husband contemplated the details of high black boots and long, graceful red tunic, the white underdress, the Eastern cut of the loose, scarlet sleeves, the gold lace trimmings, and the jeweled dress kinjal stuck in the exquisitely tooled black leather belt.

"Yes, Monsieur Stepniak," Wolf replied in a grave, controlled voice, "a stepbrother," and he waited, wished for, *dared* the man to challenge him.

Count Stepniak spent most of his waking hours in sporting pursuits of one kind or another, and his looselimbed, finely muscled body bespoke this disposition for active amusements. He was quite an excellent shot and prided himself on his steadiness of hand as well as on his string of hungers. He noted the resentful posture of the Kuzan stepbrother and felt no fear. Count Stepniak was decidedly indifferent to the Easterner's provocative glare. Ignoring the presence of Wolf, he stood with haughty composure, a metallic gleam evident in his unwavering gaze, and coolly said to his wife, "Come home tonight."

"But, Stefan, I've been staying on the Neva Quay. The children are there." Her voice was lamentably tremorous.

The faintest hint of impatience twitched in the cold, gray eyes. "I trust," the count impassively demurred, "the children can be left to the care of their nurses for two or three days without any undue harm accruing. I'll be leaving again shortly. I wish you home while I'm in town." The faintly supercilious drawl could not have been improved upon for sheer self-centered arrogance.

Wolf looked at the dismay and distress written so plainly across Katelina's face and quietly intervened.

"You don't have to go." Wolf placed his hand on the hilt of his kinjal as he uttered the terse statement through clenched teeth.

Katelina grew alarmed as Wolf's fingers shifted to his dagger, and she quickly placed a restraining hand on his arm as he began to move forward.

"I'll stop at the Neva palace," she immediately, agitatedly replied to her husband's demand as she held tightly to Wolf's rigid arm, "give instructions to the nurses, and be back to our town house tonight."

"Very wise, madame," returned her husband dryly. Having once again asserted his authority over his wife, he immediately lost interest in her. "Your servant, sir." He tipped his head briefly in Wolf's direction and left.

Anger blazed in Wolf's eyes as he shook off Katelina's hand. "Why do you go?" he snarled, resentful of her ready acquiescence. "It's very plain you don't wish to." This gorgeous woman, so long denied him, had almost been his tonight, and wrath consumed Wolf as the inequities of their disparate positions were again imposed on him.

"I have to," Katelina replied. "He *is* my husband."

"What's wrong with you? Why do you stay with him?" Wolf raged, immune at the moment to Katelina's finer sense of responsibility to her children and her concept of wifely duty.

Katelina broke into unhappy tears and said in trembling accents that of course he was right to be angry with her. Wolf heaved an exasperated sigh and pulled her into his arms, where she sobbed damply into the gold lace of his tunic.

Katelina couldn't reveal to Wolf that it wasn't duty or responsibility that prompted her submission but rather some very ugly threats coldly uttered by her husband on the two occasions she had angrily talked of divorce.

"You'll never see your children again, rest assured, madame," he had quietly breathed. "If legal means don't suffice, I'll simply take them away. Consider the consequences, I pray, before you reach any hasty conclusions." He was smiling, but she knew that smile, and fear gripped her heart.

"I must oblige you then, it seems," she had said grittily but with dignity.

"I knew you would be reasonable," he had then replied, still smiling, but very much more pleasantly now, for he had won once again. Stefan never stayed long; he would soon be gone. She could return to her children then, and in the meantime they were safe with her parents.

Presently the tears diminished. Katelina raised her eyes to Wolf's and said sheepishly, "I dare say you're in just the mood to wash your hands of me. I've been a dreadful bother to you."

"Oh, no!" Wolff said coolly as he brushed away her tears. "You're not getting away that easily."

Katelina managed a happy smile and asked frankly, "Are you sure I'm really worth all the trouble?"

Wolf laughed softly. "I'm sure."

Katelina looked happily surprised, and a dimple appeared in her cheek as she smiled up at her dear stepbrother.

"You must go to him?" Wolf asked, frowning.

The smile vanished from her face. There was an infinitesimal pause before Katelina answered, "I must."

Wolf looked thoughtful for a moment, then apparently decided to oblige her wishes, at least for the present.

"Very well, Countess Stepniak. I'll escort you back to the Neva Quay."

"You don't mind?" she timidly queried.

"Not at all," he said politely, for the sake of his heart's desire, perjuring his soul without hesitation.

After leaving Katelina at the door to her apartments, Wolf entered his own suite and informed his valet, "Two bottles of my Kakhetian wine and my pipe."

Minutes later as Wolf lounged on a couch near the balcony door, his boots kicked off and his tunic loosely open, he drew deeply on the mouthpiece of his water pipe, then closed his eyes and leaned his dark head back against the satin pillows. Despite his show of politeness to Katelina, Wolf knew the next few days were going to be bad. His hands were tied; there was nothing he could do. Ready, vivid visions of Katelina in her husband's bed were devastatingly unpalatable. He exhaled the sweetly pungent smoke thoughtfully and reached out to splash more wine into his glass.

The languid, half-dozing figure on the satin sofa was deceptively passive. He felt enormously like striking out and hitting something. An abominable restlessness had taken possession of him, and he was rapidly getting into a very bad temper. If Wolf were suddenly to take it into his head to dispatch his rival, *if* that should happen, Katelina's problems with a cruel and autocratic husband would be solved rather sooner than she expected.

The evening following Miss Riminsky's denouement Alex chose to escort Amalie home. She was familiar, comfortable; one needn't exert oneself to charm and entertain. They had both known each other for a long and physically satisfying period. One was always expected to be reverently honored by the pledges of virginity bestowed and to devote oneself accordingly to the innocent, plucked blossom, but he wasn't up to the charade tonight. Better Amalie's restful iniquitous excesses. Alex followed Amalie into the familiar setting of her pink satin and silver-gilt boudoir; so much more convenient than clinging virgins.

"So very kind of you to see me home, Prince Alexander," Amalie flirted coyly as she entered her firelit bedroom. With a flick of her hand she dismissed the young French maid who was waiting up for her mistress.

Countess Benckendorff twirled gracefully to show herself to full advantage and accidentally intercepted a familiar wink between the departing maid and Alex.

In the course of sharing conjugal rights with Count Benckendorff during the past year, Alex had often come in contact with the pretty, dark-haired maid. At first he had ignored her languishing glances, soft touches when she greeted him, and seemingly casual brushes against him while showing him into milady's boudoir. But one evening Alex had arrived early for a rendezvous with the countess. With idle time on his hands Alex looked at the countess's maid for the first time with a certain attention, then quite amiably succumbed to the dainty advances of the comely young woman. In the ensuing months the prince had been known for a rare punctuality at the Benckendorffs'. The friendship between prince and maid had blossomed.

Damn little hussy, Amalie fumed pettishly as she took notice of the maid's attractive good looks; tomorrow the brazen slut would be reassigned to duties far from the countess's boudoir.

"*Prince* Alexander?" Alex drawled. "Really, my dear. No need to choose your words. A bit late to be so discreetly politic. I'm sure most of your domestics are quite aware that our acquaintance is of long standing. Surely such pretense is unnecessary," the prince declared bluntly as he began removing his garments in a very precipitous fashion.

Amalie bristled at the gallingly insensitive attitude of her lover, who seemed interested in disrobing as rapidly as possible. But a single glimpse of the bare, muscular torso displaced such petty misgivings. The countess began untying the satin ribbons of her evening wrap.

With swift, economical motions Alex unbuttoned his trousers as he kicked off his shoes, not sparing a glance for the beautiful Amalie, who was languorously slipping a thin strap over the smooth, soft flesh of her shoulder. All her graceful, charming, seductive artifice was quite wasted on Alex, who shot a swift look from under stern black brows at the fully clothed female and expostulated exasperatedly, "Good God! Amalie! Whatever have you been doing?" In his particular frame of mind tonight the prince was not disposed to be charmed.

Feeling rankled by this callously unromantic comment,

Amalie yielded to a temptation she had scrupulously determined to avoid in her relationship with the prince. With great restraint she had always refrained from the urge to chastise Alex's behavior in any way, since the prince's reputation for abruptly terminating his tender friendships with caustic women was well documented.

Under these trying circumstances, however, the countess forgot herself sufficiently to remark testily, "I hadn't realized you were in such a rush!"

Looking heavenward in mock appeal Alex retorted sarcastically, "You're the one who said Boris may be home any minute."

"But such haste! Do you take me for some common strumpet?"

"Now, sweet, courtesy forbids me . . ."

"Sasha!"

The prince sighed softly. "Dear Amalie," he said sweetly, "need I remind you that nothing bores me more quickly than the sensibilities of an affronted woman who knows as well as I do the reason we're both here. And as far as undue haste, my pet, I'm only trying to be accommodating," he murmured suggestively as he swept a mocking gesture downward drawing attention to an obviously rigid tumescence.

The lusty display drew a gasp of appreciation from the countess, who had sorely missed Alex's unique virility and prowess these past months.

"Come, love," Alex urged more complacently, "let's make the most of our precious time."

Adverse in his present mood to be treated to any display of Amalie's sulky temper, Alex strode across the space separating them, drew Amalie familiarly into his arms, and took his own violent measures to both preclude his boredom and put an end to any further remonstrances of the fair Amalie by savagely and emphatically kissing away her objections.

Swift, experienced fingers manipulated the feminine garments, and within seconds a taffeta evening gown, petticoats, and corset rustled down to the Beauvais carpet followed by a shower of hairpins and combs. Quite oblivious to any gallantries of wooing, the prince fell on top of the lush beauty as he pushed her down on the nearest couch. He began vigorously pursuing the quickest path to a mutual and satisfying consummation.

This indecorous urgency moved the lady to exhale the softest murmur of rebuke. "Alex!"

The prince was not disposed to respond, his mouth being at present employed nibbling on one peaked, pink nipple.

"Alex! You're like an animal," the countess began admonishing the top of the dark, wavy-haired head in a severe tone that trailed off into a low moan of rapture as the prince's fingers found employment as satisfactory as that of his mouth.

Lifting his head briefly, Alex replied in a soft undertone, "An animal? Indeed? But not so repulsive for all that, it seems," and with a triumphant smile he noted the countess appeared to be no longer listening.

For the next quarter hour the loudest sound in the pink satin boudoir was the ticking of the dainty Meissen clock on the mantel.

The prince, never the hypocrite, had abandoned himself to the selfish pursuit of pleasure with his customary profligacy. Never one to moderate his excesses, Prince Alex was assiduously devoting himself to the game of love. His soft, dark curls were damply clinging to his forehead, and his lean body moved in a powerful rhythm that drew soft sighs of ecstasy from the beautiful countess as each thrusting stroke reached home.

This sensual, cresting, feverish atmosphere was abruptly shattered by the intrusion of a light but insistent rapping on the door, followed by the quietly urgent bass voice of the footman informing the two entwined forms on the couch, "Count Benckendorff's carriage drove up!"

Amalie squealed in fear and dismay, but Alex never broke rhythm as he swore savagely under his breath.

"Sasha! Sasha! Please!" Amalie begged, attempting to rise.

Indifferent to his lover's pleas, Alex growled, "I'll kill him!"

"Sasha! Please, you mustn't!" the lady entreated, taking literally the figurative exclamation of frustrated anger that burst spontaneously from the prince.

"I'll throw him down the stairs![9] Damn him! Does he know how hellishly inconvenient his timing is?" Alex snarled menacingly.

This new threat was meant quite literally, for at this point in the throes of tempestuous passion, Alex was as heedless to danger as a baited bull.

As the beautiful countess frantically whispered pleadingly realistic reasons she hoped would indicate to Alex the dire necessity to hide immediately, he finally reached consummation and in the merest passing of a second Alex's judgment returned, transforming his reckless foolhardiness to an instant sanity.

A scene with Boris lost its significant urgency, and a considerably cooler brain swiftly reasoned that discretion was perhaps the better part of wisdom at this point.

When a justly suspicious Count Benckendorff burst into the room after having been detained by the loyal footman, he intruded on an apparently placid, serene, if decidedly unorthodox, tableaux.

Countess Benckendorff wore a frothy wrapper inadequately covering her comely form. She was drooping gracefully against the satin bolsters of her Empire couch, a damp towel pressed solicitously against her brow by Prince Alex.

Boris cast a diffident, glaring look at the prince, whose

state of dress was decidedly irregular. Although an evening jacket reposed on broad powerful shoulders, his silk shirt tucked carelessly into his trousers was open casually across his hirsute chest, while black tie was conspicuously absent.

"Oh, Boris, I'm so pleased you came home," the beautiful Amalie mendaciously wailed. "I feel simply dreadful. I was overcome by a horrid fainting spell, and if the kindly prince hadn't graciously seen me home and administered comfort, it would have been a wretched ordeal."

Looking up into the tawny eyes, Amalie cooed politely, "Thank you, Prince Alex, for your obliging succor."

The prince straightened from his solicitous pose over the prostrate beauty and replied with a facile, careless mockery, "it was my distinct pleasure, Countess Benckendorff, to be able to offer you succor," and his mouth twisted into a wicked grin.

Boris was far from a fool, and the singular disarray of the prince's clothing in addition to his wife's dishabille put the lie to the sickbed scene. But while not fool enough to be taken in by the vignette of invalid and nurse, he was also not fool enough to challenge the explanation.

In this situation Boris had two choices. He could call out the prince. Even if the *on-dits* concerning Alex's latest duel with Krasskov hadn't still been current, the prince's notorious reputation with pistols would have curtailed Boris's inclination to dispute. Quietly assessing the powerful, muscular figure of the prince, Boris didn't cavil over trifles like his wife's virtue.

Boris had long ago wearied of the prized bauble he had purchased. Amalie had been another possession that seemed worth having, since she was so much sought after. But as with all his trinkets, the having never inspired the same piquant fascination as the wanting. Being a very lazy man, Amalie's demanding sensuality at first surprised him, then exhausted him, and eventually annoyed him. Boris had withdrawn from the role of husband almost immediately, preferring to patronize his mistresses, who practiced the indulgent flattery of their profession, enabling him to leisurely lie back and await satiation.

He also knew why Amalie had married him. The day after the wedding he had incidentally informed his new wife that her father's gambling debts had been discharged, and he had continued to pay the mounting losses throughout the years. Amalie had been forced to be grateful for his indulgence of her father's inadequacies and also to be grateful for his largesse toward her. But the gracious humility hadn't come easy. She was a proud and beautiful woman. A streak of cruelty in Boris had effectively kept his beautiful wife in check, for while he overlooked her numerous affairs and conceded to all her expensive whims, he never allowed her access to his fortune. She was required to petition him for all her expenses. He quite enjoyed the role of warder.

The decision was simple. "Please accept my thanks for seeing Amalie home. Have you time for a brandy and a hand of whist before you leave, Archer?" Boris inquired tranquilly.

"My pleasure, Boris," the prince returned composedly.

Amalie exhaled a tiny sigh of relief and immediately reached up to wrench off the frightful damp towel that was ruining her curls.

Boris cast her a dark look of censurious contempt as he said, "If you'll excuse us, madame, you seem to have recovered from your ordeal."

Turning to the countess, Alex, too, bid his adieus, giving Amalie a quick wink before following Boris downstairs to his study.

Several servants saw to their comforts. Brandy and cigars were presented. A fresh pack of cards was opened. Caviar and oysters were offered and refused. The men settled back in their chairs and quite amicably agreed on the merits of the brandy and Turkish leaf.

"What stakes?" Boris inquired as he leisurely shuffled the deck of cards on the exquisite ivory inlaid table.

If Alex had cared, they could have played for Amalie, ordinarily a tantalizing prize to any red-blooded male in St. Petersburg, he thought ruefully. Unfortunately he didn't want her. No one seemed worth having since Zena.

He sighed wearily, deprived of even slight exhilaration a duel would have offered. "I don't know," Alex replied, his enervated mind searching for a wager.

There they were, two jaded gentlemen who could have anything money could buy—and did.

Alex's eyes showed a spark of interest. "Your index finger against mine? Loser cuts his off," Alex suggested affably.

Boris's eyes widened in alarm; to bestir oneself to such a degree struck him as both vulgar and unnecessary. "Damn savage! You always had a reprehensible streak of madness in you, Archer," he declared with as much vehemence as his normal lethargy permitted.

"Lord, relax, Boris," Alex laughed. "You quite alarm me when you raise your voice above its normal languid murmur. Let's say your stallion Irish Hills against my new roan mare. How's that? Conventional enough?"

Boris's soft body subsided another degree into his velvet cushioned chair and nodded in grateful assent and relief. Although he appreciated Archer's macabre sense of humor, the requisite energy and spirit necessary to consummate the wager was quite beyond the limits of his torpid indolence.

"Deal, man," Alex ordered. "I feel lucky tonight."

Yuri woke Alex the next afternoon about three. "Wake up, you sluggard. This is late even for you. You must have spent all night exhausting yourself again in some female's bed. Who was it this time to fatigue you enough to sleep all day?"

"Well, Amalie began the night, if you must know, but she wasn't what exhausted me. Sat up until morning playing whist with Boris after he unexpectedly appeared."

"Unexpectedly?" Yuri inquired. "How unexpectedly?" he asked with a grin.

"Fortunately for him not *too* unexpectedly, or he'd have been tossed down the stairs. A few brief moments of warning from that footman Amalie pays so well allowed me to satisfy my rather crude passion. By the time Boris ambled into the room, most of our clothes were back on." Alex smiled faintly a the memory. "Boris appears extremely indifferent to his wife. I've never seen them together before. Treats her with almost a cruel contempt."

"I don't think he's ever forgiven her for the deception," Yuri said with a slight twist of his mouth. "He paid a high price for her, and she wasn't a virgin."

"She wasn't a virgin?" Alex exclaimed. He narrowed his eyes consideringly. "And how do you know that, may I ask?"

Yuri shrugged evasively.

"The Golden Goddess?" Alex said in astonishment. "Never say you were the first?"

"The first," Yuri acceded quietly.

"When?" Alex inquired.

"We were both fifteen," was the pensive reply.

"Good Lord, she was a fool," Alex declared. "Amalie knew even then that she must marry for money. Her father's gambling debts were notorious throughout the empire. She must have realized when you sell yourself for that high a price, the buyer at least expects a virgin."

"You know Amalie, Alex. Do you think that kind of sensual passion could have been kept chaste until she was eighteen?" Yuri quirked one eyebrow derisively.

Alex emitted a short, hard laugh. "As you say, Yuri, I stand corrected. How did it happen?"

"Our estates ajoin, as you know. We spent that summer

together; I gave Amalie her first lessons in love, having the advantage of a two-year start on her. In our remote area of the Ukraine, although *droit du seigneur* was no longer legal and hadn't been for generations, old traditions die hard, and I, as my father's heir, was offered at a very young age the pick of our peasant girls. They had some misguided notion that sleeping with the Batiushka or the Batiushka's son enhanced their reputation. So I was well schooled by fifteen.

"It was a beautiful summer, Amalie's and mine. We explored each other's bodies with infinite joy and leisure. Unfortunately too soon, the usual consequences ensued. Amalie became pregnant. I would have married her, but my wealth didn't suffice. Damn her father's black soul. In the seclusion of the country the next spring our daughter was born. Since Amalie had still to sell herself to the highest bidder, a child was an impossible encumbrance.

"I took the baby and raised her. Betsy isn't my niece but my daughter," Yuri confessed.

"I and everyone else know that, Yuri," Alex said quietly. "The only question has ever been, Who's the mother? Besty's a darling and remarkably like her father. But now that I know who the mother is, I can say also remarkably like the mother. Does Amalie ever see the girl?"

"Quite often. They're good friends, although Amalie visits as an acquaintance of mine. I told Betsy long ago her mother died in childbirth."

"Now that Amalie's father is gone to his reward and can't amass any more debts, do you ever think of marrying Amalie?"

"God, no. We've known each other too long and too intimately. Familiarity, you know, breeds contempt. She scorns my loose ways and wild, licentious living, and I've never been able to understand how she could have sold herself to that soft slug Boris. Filial piety has its limits, it seems to me. Betsy's rather spoiled anyway; we're a very good team, my beautiful daughter and I. And marriage hasn't exactly agreed with you, my fine stud. What makes you think I'm interested in that misery?" Yuri jibed.

"Touché," Alex grunted. "Marriage and living with one woman is an unnatural state."

"I'll drink to that," Yuri laughed. Reaching for the decanter, he poured two brandies and handed Alex his. "To the natural state of bachelorhood."

They both drained their glasses.

"Well, what's on the agenda tonight? Do we check the flesh on display at Orenburg's ball or straight away to the Islands and the accommodating gypsies? What say, Alex?"

"Let's skip the simpering society masses," Alex said, wrinkling his beautiful aristocratic nose. "I'm not in the mood tonight to offer even the barest civility for a fuck. The gypsies will suit me well. With them it's a business arrangement—no distasteful emotional outbursts, no spurious tender sentiments, so much more convenient.

"Let's see if Wolf's up yet. I lost him last night almost as soon as we entered Princess Nagarin's party. She dragged him away, and neither one of them had reappeared by the time I left with Amalie. Kitty certainly didn't play the perfect hostess last night. Well, no doubt she did to one of her guests," Alex amended laughingly. "Let's go find Wolf. He'll be interested in the Islands tonight." And so the diligent quest to elude boredom continued.

A week later at a small card party lorgnettes were raised, pince-nez adjusted, brows delicately quirked, and eyes narrowed as the room's aristocratic occupants carefully scrutinized and assessed the bald temerity of the young Kuzan heir. No one had ever conceded that Alex had pretty manners; he had very little at all, and although fully noted for his reckless, impudent manner of address, he had, in this latest remark, far surpassed a hitherto notorious reputation for plain-speaking.

As Alex had been introduced to a stunning brunette visiting from Paris, a guest of the hostess, he had declared in a resonant carrying baritone, "Honore Constance, as I live and breathe, what a damnable pleasure to see you again. And how are the softest, most delectable thighs in Christendom?"

The lady in question had good-naturedly tapped his cheek lightly with her ivory and lace fan and replied sweetly, "The same old Alex, I see." Then lowering her voice to a seductive murmur, she added, "And how is the best tool of pleasure in Christendom, *mon ami?*"

Their eyes met over her fan, and Alex replied quietly with a gallic shrug and a small smile, "I'm staying in practice, madame, so as not to lose my fine edge."

Her eyes gleamed appreciatively.

"Taking pity on all the languishing, inviting St. Petersburg females, Sasha?" she queried flippantly.

"Pity?" inquired the prince delicately, his gleaming eyes half closed in amusement. "I've found, my dear," Alex drawled sardonically, "it's something quite different they're after."

Honore trilled a soft, musical peal of mirth, then directed a frank, open glance into those amused eyes. "But you're married, I hear," the gorgeous Frenchwoman said.

"That I am," Alex replied unreservedly. "A fate which befalls all of us eventually. And you too, I understand. Are you and *monsieur la comte* happy?" he asked with a comic look in his cat's eyes.

"Together you mean? Sasha, *really*, such naïveté for an abandoned reprobate like yourself," she chided. Her eyes twinkled. "But my marriage has its advantages."

"Such as?" Alex drawled.

"Monsieur is never home."

"How convenient," Alex murmured. "We seem to have similar marriages. Princess Kuzan prefers the salubrious air of the mountains to the company of her husband."

"In that case, Sasha, *mon ange*. Perhaps we can console each other in our privation," and she allowed her radiant eyes to meet his with a challenge.

The prince was not slow to take it up. "Honore, my darling," he whispered softly. "I have always admired your tenderhearted compassion. Your scheme of mutual commiseration has an intriguing appeal. How soon can you leave this dreary affair?"

Honore rippled a low laugh of satisfaction. "An hour?" she suggested with a quirk of her charming mouth.

"An hour?" Alex lamented jestingly. "Have pity, I detest bridge parties."

"Thirty minutes, then," Honore allowed charitably with a tilt of her beautiful head.

"Ten," Alex said, and his eyes met hers with unreserved ardor.

"Ten," she whispered, shaken by the candid sensuality and by memories of the prince's passion.

And so they consoled each other quite assiduously, for they were old friends.

Alex, schooled in the Kuzan tradition of private tutors and university on the Continent, had first met Honore six years before, when he had spent two years in Paris. Outside the obligations of his university tutoring in law, he thoroughly enjoyed the wildly dissipated counter-culture available in Paris during *La Belle Epoque*, conducting himself in the normal fashion of a healthy, young Russian prince. Honore Constance, the daughter of an ancient but genteelly impoverished French family, had warmed Alex's bed for the two years of his sojourn. Alex had protected Honore from malicious remarks and any would-be traducers during the years of his friendship, for no one of even the dullest intellect chose to publicly come to verbal blows with a Kuzan. On one occasion when Honore had chided her young lover on his intimidating address to a French count of her acquaintance, Alex had replied, "I am a prince, *mademoiselle*. It is my prerogative to be intimidating."

When it came time for the prince to return to Russia upon completion of his studies, he left a suitable fortune as gratitude for Honore's fidelity and passion. The magnitude of the wealth entailed on her continued to protect Honore in her lover's absence and served as well to assure her continued entree into even the most conservative homes, although it was common knowledge that Prince Alex had first ruined her and then installed her as his mistress. France was ever a nation with a shopkeeper's mentality, and gold spoke powerfully at all levels of society. No doors were closed to Honore Constance de la Garonne, and her fortune assured her a splendid array of marriage suitors.

A fortnight sped by that summer, as Honore and Alex renewed their friendship, but much as he enjoyed her company, when it was time for Honore to return to France, she left no great emptiness in his heart.

The next week he resumed his amorous attentions to the ladies of St. Petersburg, but within days the old depression returned. No matter how he devoted himself to pleasure, his discontent and boredom mounted. No matter how many times the evening ended in some woman's arms, he was never satiated. The woman he had each night wasn't the woman he wanted. He told himself he was a pleasure seeker by choice but found uneasily that the pleasure was never more than the most fleeting fulfillment.

Despite his best efforts to the contrary, he was missing Zena. Many women had been uncomfortably chagrined as the inebriated prince had on numerous occasions addressed them as Zena in ardent phrases of passion.

It was more than six weeks now since Zena had left. Every pregnant woman he saw made him wince in dismay. Strange, he had never noticed pregnant females before, and now it seemed wherever he looked his eyes espied the blooming form of an *enceinte* woman. He was tormented with memories of their idyllic retreat at the *dacha*. Visions of her laughing smile, her delicate winsome face, and her perfect form all touched him with remorse.

Then for the first time the veneer of his self-absorption seemed to crumble and he thought with new stabs of pain how she might be suffering. He began to worry, imagining her in countless discomforts of poverty. Could she take care of herself and Bobby? Was she the victim of some brute who abused her? Was she healthy? Was she happy?

Lord, he missed her. He finally admitted to himself that he missed her, and he really cared about her. This is what caring is, he thought, wanting the person near you always. Love was enjoying an intimacy that wasn't fleeting, but deep and enduring and, as he'd found out, often difficult. Was it too late for them? Did she hate him now? Had she turned lightly to another man? Had she forgotten him already? The harsh, cheerless questions were achingly un-palatable.

He checked at his bank, and no funds had been with-drawn by his wife. The news left him slightly shaken, but he cautioned himself to composure. If she had gone to her grandfather, there was no need for money. But no one was absolutely certain she had gone there. He sent a telegram south. To hand deliver it the distance to the mountain aul took some time. Six days later he had his reply. Zena was not there.

He panicked then. She was out in the world alone, or at least without him. In fewer than four days it would be September. In fewer than two months his child would be born, and he didn't even know where Zena was. His wife and child were vulnerable in the midst of a perilous, treacherous world. He was frantic to find them and make them safe. Detectives were set on the trail almost two months old. The results were negative. All inquiries came to naught. His agents had drawn a blank.

Anxiety for Zena became a very real fear. The most frightful visions tormented him. How could she live without funds? How could she support herself and Bobby without using his money? She couldn't keep a job when she was almost eight months pregnant. What if she had placed herself under some man's protection? His rage would mount furiously at the prospect.

God, what was he going to do? All avenues led to a dead end. Six detectives had been unable to find a clue to Zena's destination. She had for all intents dropped off the face of the earth.

9

Unaware of the desperate efforts to locate them, Zena and Bobby were living very quietly in a pension on a quiet street in Nice. Zena's landlady was kindly and politely tactful about questioning her new guest. The striking young widow was beautifully dressed but very frugal in her habits. She spoke French without accent, although her name, Mrs. Nazarin, was definitely Russian. The beautiful widow was a perfect tenant, however, never noisy or demanding, living a very circumspect, routine existence, taking her small son to the park both morning and afternoon, doing her own cooking and retiring early in the evening.

Zena's landlady observed the peaceful, placid habits of her guest and concluded Mrs. Nazarin was tranquilly awaiting the birth of her second child. Zena had schooled herself on the train from Moscow to present a serene face to the world. It was essential for Zena to maintain this exterior at variance with the inner reality. Outwardly she obeyed the rules of civilized behavior. But despite her best efforts, the first weeks in Nice were just a black anguish, hardly separate one from the other.

As the feeling of numbness subsided, Zena consciously hoped to eventually make the sham a reality. All it takes is time, she told herself. Time would soothe the spiritual wounds of pain and despair that tormented her. Time would cure and restore the deep hurt of her rejection.

Time would dignify the humiliation of her inglorious, un-requited love.

But the practicality and logic of sensible reason didn't easily withstand the strength of willful emotions and a temperament decidedly less than practical.

The remembrances of Sasha's gentle touch, the warmth of his boyish laugh, the infinite pleasures he could pro-voke, pushed aside all sensible emotions. Passionate mem-ories of love reacted very poorly to cold rationality. With an effort of will Zena sent away the images of Sasha that mysteriously appeared before her. In the meantime, she had lost ten pounds. So much for good intentions.

Shortly after her arrival, Zena made the acquaintance of an English gentleman who frequented the little park near her pension. He had kindly played catch with Bobby one morning when Zena had become fatigued with Bobby's in-exhaustible reserves of energy. She had caught and chased Bobby's erratic throws for quite some time before the gen-tleman had politely offered to relieve her. He had taken over as partner to Bobby's youthful enthusiasm, allowing Zena a much needed rest. When Bobby later entertained himself by tossing bread crumbs to the pigeons, the tall man sat down and introduced himself. He was Alistair Prescott, Earl of Glenagle. Zena offered a minimum of in-formation, introducing herself as Mrs. Nazarin, a widow from Moscow who had recently lost her husband.

The earl made it a habit after that first meeting to fre-quent the park at the same times Zena did, and over the ensuing weeks they had become friends. He played child-ish games with Bobby and then chatted or strolled with Zena when Bobby was preoccupied with his own activities. Oddly enough, Zena noted Bobby had never taken to call-ing the earl "Papa," as he had done immediately with Sasha.

The earl was kindness itself to them both, bringing small gifts for Bobby occasionally or presenting Zena with a dainty bouquet of violets or primroses, often leaving a book he recommended. After a fortnight of such pleasant attentions, Zena invited him for tea one afternoon, and the invitation was reciprocated several days later as Zena and Bobby took tea with the earl in his little villa two streets away. The earl, it turned out, was a childless widower, his wife of ten years having died of consumption two years before after a lengthy illness. He came to Nice in the off season, preferring the relative peacefulness to the tremendous crowds of late winter. He was gentlemanly in every way, observing the proprieties of courtesy and politeness in his association with Zena. Alistair Prescott had fair skin and light brown silky hair combed back from a fine, aristocratic forehead. Pale blue eyes looked out serenely from under straight dark brows. A refined, high-bridged nose attested to centuries of good breeding, while his straight slash of a mouth was capable of the most disarming smiles. He carried his height gracefully on a slim, muscular frame tanned from the suns of thirty-nine years. He was everything Sasha was not: placid, serene, polite, understanding, deprecatingly modest, and compassionately kind to both Zena and Bobby. Zena couldn't help but be drawn to the tender comfort he offered in her world of tumultuous memories and tortured, painful emotions. He was like a strong, steady rock of solace and consolation in a world that had in the past few months been tempestuously, violently agitated by the stormy upheavals of love and passion.

Zena's sad, poignant beauty had drawn the earl, the lure of such delicate loveliness more than his usual discretion could withstand. Quite unaccountably he had approached her as a perfect stranger, decidedly *outré* behavior for the civil, refined earl. Despite her obvious pregnancy, or perhaps because of it, the childless earl had viewed the fair, comely woman as a pensive, modern madonna. Sometimes her deep blue eyes expressed a pain so pure, so pitiful and tragic, that it left him yearning to remedy her heartache. Over the weeks he had often seen the sadness dispelled from those cobalt eyes and a warm friendliness shine out toward him. He had kissed her once briefly as he stood near her, devouring the stunning quality of her beauty, but she had trembled so in anxious fear that he had resolved to restrain himself in the future until such time as she could perhaps return his feelings.

The earl had been her compassionate friend now for more than six weeks, spending much time in amiable companionship. Zena cherished the serene comfort of Alistair's affection. She chastised herself at times for accepting his solace, when she knew she could never return his love, but she was so dreadfully alone that she selfishly allowed herself to succumb to his consolation. Being alone was so devastating after one had known the violent pleasure roused by Sasha's presence. She needed someone, no matter how different, to fill some of the terrible void. Alistair had been pressing her for two weeks to consider marrying him. She hadn't revealed that she was still married, but if she decided to accept his offer, a divorce could be obtained. Alex would never contest it. In fact, he would probably be extremely grateful if she freed him from his matrimonial bonds. So the germ of acceptance began to grow. She had had her brief fling of madness and passion. It had been a sweet glimpse of paradise, but it was over, and common sense required she set aside childishly silly, romantic dreams of eternal love and settle down to a life that could be very pleasant and serene. The jewelry she had sold since leaving Moscow had met her expenses adequately, but it wouldn't last indefinitely. With two children soon to support, perhaps she should begin to consider Alistair's kind offer. He loved her very much, he declared, and although Zena couldn't return his love, she could be kind to him. Having been a participant in a one-sided love affair, she was very aware that it could work. If Sasha had simply returned her passionate love with a kind affection, she could have survived. But his casual indifference was too bitter to bear. She vowed if she decided to accept Alistair's marriage proposal, she would never forget to show her affectionate devotion to his very great kindness in befriending her.

PART V

Paradise Regained

1

Alex existed in a vortex of clubbism and social intercourse, each day becoming more depressingly frustrating and melancholy due to the thwarted efforts to locate Zena. He was drinking more than usual and surly to a dangerous degree, but then no one could be expected to know how much alcohol it took to drown out the echo of his voice telling Zena he didn't care for her and that she need never suffer from his touch again.

Everyone concurred that apparently marriage had not agreed with young Prince Alex. He was exceeding even his previous unsurpassed wildness. If anyone had dared, he would have been called out a dozen times in the past few weeks.

Zena lived her routine life in Nice, missing Sasha with a daily remorse that showed no obvious signs of decline despite the passing weeks. As she lived unobtrusively in the warm, temperate climate of the seaside town, she began to consider the necessity of remarriage.

The second week in September Alex was out for the evening as usual. It was still early, and he and Yuri were beginning the night at the Acheevs' before moving on to more abandoned entertainment. Wolf had chosen not to join them tonight, muttering something about needing his rest. Yuri had shot a cynical look at Alex but refrained from immediate comment. Later, as they strolled down the marble steps of the Neva palace, Yuri remarked sardonically, "Into Katelina's bed, finally, it appears."

"Apparently," Alex replied. "They've had the most doleful, serious look about them lately. Can't think of any other reason Wolf would be going to bed at home at ten o'clock."

"It's about time Katelina began enjoying herself. She must be the only married beauty in St. Petersburg who has been chaste, and with a husband like hers. Ridiculous!"

"That's what I've been trying to tell her," Alex said. "But she's always said she finds promiscuity a bore." He paused for a moment. "She might have something there." He had come up to St. Petersburg weeks ago to be amused, but somehow the old pleasures had lost their piquancy and he was bored. "Been damned dull, lately. Must be getting old," he said with a grimace of disgust. At four and twenty, the prince could scarcely be deemed old; his problem was that he simply had had the world at his feet too long.

"You'd be even more damned bored celibate," Yuri snorted derisively.

"True, true," Alex grinned. "Common sense like that is not to be controverted. Well, my partner in vice, shall we try again tonight to press back the ennui. Where do we start?"

"We meet Kasimir at Acheev's. He wants a chance to recoup his losses of last night. We promised him an hour or two of baccarat. Then maybe on to Amalie's; she guarantees some new dance troupe she's picked up is worth seeing. After that I don't care—perhaps the Countesses Golgorky. Care for an orgy with the Golgorky twins? Those two nymphomaniacs always ensure an enlivening evening," Yuri said with a wide grin.

"You know the classic line, Yuri," Alex drawled impudently. "You could call the Golgorky twins nymphomaniacs if you could slow them down a little." He shrugged and grimaced ruefully. "Frankly, I don't know if I'm up to the performance tonight. It's been a heavy schedule of late. Let's see how we feel in a few hours," he said abruptly, thinking to himself that he'd run through the whole gamut of amusements St. Petersburg had to offer, and he was weary to the soul.

At the Acheevs' Yuri wandered into the cardroom while Alex followed a footman carrying a tray of champagne glasses into the ballroom. Taking one in each hand, he quickly downed them both and set the glasses on the nearest table. Catching sight of Kasimir, he strolled over to him. They casually eyed the flesh on display as silken-clad ladies adorned with sparkling jewels flitted before them.

Even in the midst of the gaiety, rustling silks, light laughter, brilliant bejeweled nobles, and merry music, Alex's thoughts were elsewhere, his eyes unfocusing, unguarded, brooding. A disreputable comment of Kasimir's, concerning the acrobatic expertise of a certain young matron dancing by, served to return Alex to the present. He forcibly cast aside his bitter musing. As they were discussing the merits of the various females, in the bantering crudeness so typically male, Kasimir's wife detached herself from a group across the floor and made her way toward the two tall men in black evening dress. Her eyes dwelt on the handsome, arrogant figure of the prince.

She cast a sidelong glance at Alex from under long, black lashes before turning to her husband, who was busy helping himself to more champagne from a passing footman.

"Kasimir, will you be in the cardroom long? The mazurkas begin soon," she pouted prettily.

"Mazurkas?" the baron harrumphed, clearing his throat. "Egad, woman, find some courtly ladies' man to dance attendance on you, my dear. You know I abhor dancing."

That was exactly the answer the lady expected, allowing her to pursue the actual dancing partner she had in mind.

Flashing Alex a seductive look, she swayed toward him just sufficiently to allow an apparently unstudied brush of her magnificent bosom against his arm. Alex glanced at her cleavage, and his eyes widened in surprise. This startled look did not go unnoticed by the Baroness Demidoff, and she preened coyly, attributing the prince's keen stare to admiration of her luscious,' white breasts.

"Do you dance the mazurka, Prince Alexander?" the baroness breathed intimately.

Alex raised his stunned eyes to the pretty but vacant face and smiled warmly to erase the lie. "Perhaps later, my dear baroness, but for the moment I've promised Kasimir and Yuri a chance for revenge after my inordinate luck at their expense last night. I'm desolate to have to refuse such a charming partner," and he bowed over her hand, acknowledging the pressure of her fingertips by a suitably grateful expression. She tittered and glided away.

Baroness Demidoff had been in hot pursuit for several weeks now, but Alex had eluded with an expert grace. She was not in his style, although God knows, he was realistic enough to expect a minimum of intellect in the society belles; Baroness Demidoff, however, was so featherheaded as to dismay the most hardened cynic. He had had the misfortune to occasionally bed her type and knew, for a fact, he quite definitely abhorred giggles in the boudoir.

The baroness would have been chagrined had she known it wasn't her expanse of pale bosom that had agitated Alex's astonished eyes. What had caught his eye, prompting his reaction of surprise, was the sight of the Falize necklace—*Zena's* necklace, one of a kind that he had purchased for her at Alexandre's—resting on the baroness's opulent breasts.

In one of the last weeks they were together, Alex had presented Zena with the emerald, diamond, and cloisonné Aexis Falize necklace, composed of Tudor rose pendants of cloisonné enamels set in gold and suspended from a sinuous chain of gold, emeralds, and diamonds. This was given in the hopes of lightening her melancholy moods that were appearing with more frequency. He had known she was unhappy at times, but he had brushed aside his misgivings and allowed himself to banish these qualms with extravagant gifts.

The necklace was a rare piece executed by Alexis Falize and his son Lucien in 1867. They had the distinction of being the first to employ the Japanese technique of cloisonné enamels in jewelry. The necklace had originally been purchased in Paris in 1867 by Henry Makin for his wife and had reappeared on the market when Alex purchased it. There wasn't another necklace like it in the world.

Zena had very little money when she left. It was to be expected the jewelry would be sold.

"Kasimir," Alex said with a nonchalance he was far from feeling, "your wife's necklace was extremely fetching. Did you buy it for her?"

"Me? God, no! What do I know about women's fripperies. Come, let's find Yuri; I want a chance to recoup my losses, you damnable devil."

Not wishing to expose himself to any embarrassing questions, yet driven to find out where the necklace was purchased, Alex allowed himself to be propelled into the cardroom. As Kasimir caught sight of their friend and proceeded across the crowded room to Yuri's table, Alex tried again. "That necklace was so unusual I'd like to buy one for my mother. Do you know where your wife bought it?"

Kasimir snorted. "Don't come on too brown with me, Alex. Your mother, indeed! Some tart or society hussy, more like! Damned if I can remember, though. Probably Nice or Monte Carlo or Biarritz, one of those places, I'm sure. Vickie insisted on dragging me to Florence last summer. Can you imagine Florence in the summer? Must have gone soft in the head to consent, but then Vickie can be persuasive." He raised an eyebrow and winked wickedly at Alex. "Poor empty-headed chit had some damnable notion about seeing some frescoes that one of those bluestocking females had told her about. I said wait until winter when it's respectable to go to Florence, my pet, but she insisted. Said the frescoes were crumbling from the damp or something and would soon be gone. Anyway, to make up for those dismal damp underground chapels with peeling frescoes I was forced to endure, I demanded we swing through the gambling spas, although in the sweltering heat of July only the natives remain.

"Nice, that's it, my boy. Nice, I remember now. Hello, Yuri, feel lucky tonight?" Kasimir cheerfully queried as he dropped his frame into a gold bamboo chair beside the table.

Nice! Zena had been in Nice! Alex didn't betray himself with so much as a flicker of an eyelid.

"Cut, man," Kasimir directed Yuri as he waved Alex into another chair. "I feel primed tonight, I warn you, Sasha. Even your phenomenal luck won't be enough the way I feel."

"What about Nice, Kasimir?" Alex persisted quietly, years of self-control keeping him urbanely cool when his heart was tripping like a giant sledgehammer.

"Nice, that's where Vickie bought the necklace. I remember distinctly. Talking about that damnable heat reminded me. Hell of a good day despite the temperature, I'll say," and he chuckled warmly to himself. "Reason I remember," he continued with a wide grin, "is that I didn't mind that Vickie spent a hundred thousand francs for that necklace, because it took her all afternoon to shop for it and gave me the opportunity to engage in one of the more memorable events of that odious trip to view fading frescoes."

"Find some good cunt, did you?" Yuri inquired casually as he dealt out the cards.

"Two cunts, as a matter of fact," Kasimir grinned, "two hot, juicy quims. Damn, I could use them now!"

"Don't keep us in suspense," Yuri drawled. "The lurid details, my friend."

"Well," Kasimir related, his smile deepening as his memories of that afternoon returned, "I had intended to nap, as it was too beastly hot to even move around. Went into my bedroom at the Negresco to lie down and what do I find but two pretty chambermaids putting clean linen on the bed. One was saucy and pert as you please, looking me over quite boldly.

" 'Not gambling, Baron?' she says as she bends over the bed to adjust the sheet, and shows me her nice, fat boobies.

" 'Too hot,' I says, 'going to take a nap,' and I begin to take off my jacket.

" 'Here, let me help,' she says, and next thing you know I don't have much on, and she's rubbing against me hot as a cat in heat. Let me tell you, it didn't take me long to have her bare and on her back in bed. I'm all set to really go at her, and I look around and damned if that other little mouse of a maid isn't standing there, gawking big as you please.

" 'What're we going to do with her?' I whisper to this hot bitch beneath me, and she says, impudent as a jade, 'Let her watch. It'll do her good. She might as well make herself useful,' and she sings out to this little thing standing there with eyes big as saucers, 'Bring a fan over here and keep us cool!'

"I wasn't in the mood for any more delays, so I lay into the cunt, and she gives me a ride that blasts my head off. When we're both finally coherent enough to breathe normally again, I feel this cool breeze on my back, and damned if that little chambermaid ain't still there. She looks delightfully fresh and innocent, and what the hell, I thought, she can't be too abashed at this all if she's still here after what she saw. So I reach my hand out and slip it up her skirt and run my fingers over the wettest little slit you ever did feel. I shoved my fingers in a little way and pulled her onto the bed. She didn't say a word, but she didn't protest either, so I undressed her while my first pert piece keeps up a running narrative of the charms I'm unveiling, and my cock is coming up to the mark quick as a wink with that quivering, tiny slit only inches away.

"To make a long story short, those two pussies took turns fanning and servicing me until I couldn't get the old boy up again no matter what they tried. Paid the sweet beauties off, and damned if it wasn't worth every franc; best afternoon nap I've ever enjoyed.

"When Vickie came back later with that ridiculously expensive necklace and another odd dragonfly pendant, too, all set to be seductively pleasing to me so that I wouldn't get angry at her, I just patted her hand fondly and pleaded a headache. Couldn't have got my cock up for Venus herself just then. So Nice it was, Sasha, my boy, although what the hell difference it makes escapes me, since you can simply have Fabergé copy Vickie's if you want a necklace like that. It's not necessary to go to Nice."

During this entire recital Alex was responding with the requisite interest and attention, giving the appearance of his normal cool insouciance, playing the game with his usual expressionless indifference, shuffling cards with apparently effortless ease when his hands could barely conceal their tremor. Icy nerves served to suppress a raw, tumultuous excitement that threatened to explode, and he lost deliberately, graciously, and rapidly so that he could get the hell out of this confining, boring, excruciating, and painfully trivial atmosphere.

He'd be on the midnight train for Warsaw.

Alex swiftly exited the cardroom, a startled Yuri trailing in his wake.

"What the hell came over you? I've never seen anyone lose so deliberately in my life."

Not pausing in his rapid stride down the hall, Alex tersely said, "Zena's necklace. Kasimir's wife had on Zena's necklace."

"The necklace Vickie bought in Nice?"

"Right. Who'd ever think the child would go abroad. I searched all over the empire; I never thought she'd leave and go to Europe."

By this time the prince's urgent pace had brought them to the entrance hall.

"Going to Nice, then?" Yuri asked.

"Leaving tonight. I'll send you a telegram if I have any luck. I hope I do,' Alex said in a worried undertone.

"Can I give you some advice?" Yuri's eyes, very steely under their fair brows, were unwaveringly upon Alex.

Alex paused at the door and gave his friend a searching glance, then quirked a rueful smile. "Sure, I've bungled this one so badly maybe I can use some advice," he said tolerantly. "Fire away."

"Zena's not like all your other women. Don't treat her like them. It's a mistake."

"Don't worry, fool that I am, I've finally realized that. I thought I could live without love, but I found it intolerably lonely. I was a damn ass. Sure you don't want to kick me for behaving like a brute to Zena?"

"Not when you've been kicking yourself so effectively," Yuri grinned. "Good luck." Yuri clasped Alex's hand.

All the lazy, moody disinterest with which Alex normally surveyed the world was stripped from his face; his eyes blazed with a wild and brilliant excitement, his mouth curved into a half-smile of elation.

"Thanks, I'll probably need it. Don't know if she'll have me back even if I do find her. That impudent miss has a temper as volatile as mine. But I'll tell you, there's no power on earth that's going to stop me from trying to talk her into taking me back." He paused. "In truth, Yuri, I'm terrified of failure. Exempting that awesome triviality," Alex continued with a wry grin, "I'm exceedingly optimistic."

"Give Zena a kiss from me," Yuri teased, attempting to lighten his friend's obvious uncertainty.

"Never, you knave," Alex retorted cheerfully and left the palace.

2

Alex set out with apprehension. Not having received Zena's note, he believed she had left him angry and uncaring. Would she, indeed, have him back? He had been trying to suppress his love for Zena by encouraging reckless diversions and trying to get tired enough to be indifferent to emotion. But tonight he was ready to make any bargain with Fate for the sight of her face, the sound of her voice, the feel of her in his arms. Nothing could divert and console him any longer. Only Zena could bring back his joy in life.

Returning home he feverishly threw a few clothes pell-mell into a valise. He paused before Katelina's door. His parents were out for the night. He should tell someone he was leaving; dare he interrupt Katelina? Was Wolf there already?

Hell! he thought, they're both family. Raising his hand, he banged impatiently on the door. When Katelina opened the door he walked in, unconcerned with her obvious agitation.

"What is it, Sasha?" She glanced nervously at her closed bedroom door.

"I think I've located Zena, and I'm off to Nice tonight. Thought I'd better tell someone before I go, as the parents are out."

"Oh, darling, I'm so pleased," she cried and flung her arms about her brother's neck and hugged him.

Clasping her warmly, Alex murmured, "I'm very pleased too."

The bedroom door crashed open and Wolf, clad only in trousers stood in the doorway glaring at the embracing couple.

"How touching, madame," he sneered.

Alex set Katelina aside and quickly said, "Wolf, back off. I don't have amorous intentions toward Katelina. She's my sister, for Christ's sake."

"And mine as well, brother," Wolf replied gently.

Alex looked from Katelina's horrified face to the menacing visage of his half brother, then laughed softly. "Can you keep such towering jealousy under control, little sister? He doesn't seem to want to share you."

Swinging to face Wolf, Alex jubilantly declared, "I only stopped by to tell Katelina my good news. Zena might be in Nice, and I'm going tonight to try to find her. Katelina was just congratulating me on the glad tidings." Alex's face sobered. "My child will be born soon, in only a few weeks. I hope I find Zena."

The scowl disappeared from Wolf's face. "Do you need help, Sasha, to bring her back? Perhaps she's no longer alone, and you could use another warrior at your side."

"Thanks, but I think I can manage. Take care of Katelina, Wolf. Bye, love." He kissed Katelina and was gone.

Zena hadn't slept well. She had hardly slept at all. Long before the town was awake, she and Bobby slowly walked the considerable distance to the Promenade des Anglais. Normally she avoided the fashionable walkway by the sea, but at this early hour of the morning one needn't fear meeting any socialites.

Yesterday Alistair had pressed her again about marriage. His insistence had been gently couched, as was typical of him, but she felt his urgency nonetheless. Last night in

Zena's restless quest for sleep all the alternatives, options, and obligations of her future swam in muddy confusion through her uneasy, sleepless mind. Could she marry Alistair? Could she live alone? Could she ever forget Sasha? Helpless longing raised havoc with careful logic, and through the long, dim hours of the night she searched for some measure of peace for her troubled spirit.

It was scarcely six o'clock as Zena strolled on the stylish promenade lined with palms, Bobby tripping yards ahead with unrestrained childish energy. The warm rays of the morning sun caught the silken waves of her auburn hair tied up loosely under a wide-brimmed, flower-strewn leghorn hat. Her jonquil yellow lawn dress floated in gentle rhythms in the sea breezes blowing softly from the south. The full sleeves fluttered in tiny ruffled movements as wisps of morning zephyrs danced over the blue Mediterranean. Zena and Bobby were quite alone on the deserted walkway.

Even the adjacent drive was nearly free of carriages at this early hour. Only one open barouche was visible on its slow journey westward. A lounging gentleman was its sole passenger. The man was oddly dressed, a foreigner from the looks of him. He wore the flowing garments of the Middle East and had a brown complexion and a neatly trimmed black beard. The figure resting back against the seat was considerably fatigued, having spent a long and exhausting night gambling in Monte Carlo. He was within sight of his hotel and soon would welcome the comforts of his bedchamber.

Zena continued her leisurely passage along the sea path, oblivious to any external phenomenon and quite preoccupied with her own disordered thoughts.

The normally vivid black eyes of the man in the passing barouche were half closed as he lazily, absently viewed the sea on his left.

Suddenly his eyelids snapped open. In one flash of

movement the lounging figure shot upright and barked a
harsh command. "Stop!"

The driver obeyed immediately, heedless of his horses'
mouths, for he was eminently familiar with the eccentric-
ities and tyrannies of the rich. Swiveling around, he discerned his intently alert passenger focusing on some object
in the direction of the water. Casting a look toward the
Mediterranean, the driver saw nothing unusual. The blue
expanse of water was empty of vessels; only a few seagulls
wheeled overhead in search of their breakfast. A woman
and a small boy were walking along the promenade; otherwise the view was devoid of interest.

The black-bearded gentleman continued to stare, his
eyes narrowed speculatively for a minute. Then he snapped
brusquely, "To the hotel quickly!"

The minute the carriage reached the hotel's entrance, the
tall, dark-skinned Turk tossed some money at the driver
and jumped out. Moving quickly through the lobby, he declined waiting for the lift and raced up the two flights of
stairs to his suite. Rushing through the doorway, he immediately uttered several sharp, curt orders.

"Ali, Kufir, Softi, get down to the promenade this instant." His bodyguards jumped to attention from their
couches where they had been sleeping. "Follow the woman
in yellow with the young child. I want to know where she
lives."

Even as their master concluded his commands, the first
man was already out the door, followed closely by his two
cohorts. Seconds later, the room now deserted, Ibrahim Bey's
young nephew Abdulhamit dropped into a chair, leaned
back comfortably, flexed his fingertips lightly, and smiled
with delight.

He had just seen Delilah.

Unaware of the newly assigned surveillance, Zena and
Bobby rested on one of the benches facing the white sand
beach. After several minutes of relaxation they journeyed

back up the hill to their apartment. The restless night and contemplative walk had been useless. Despite the hours of rumination Zena was no closer to a decision than she had been yesterday.

Why couldn't she drive memories of Sasha from her mind? Then the decision would be so simple. Just say yes to Alistair, and she would be loved and taken care of. Just say yes, she told herself.

But late in the day during teatime when Alistair renewed his suit, Zena didn't say yes. Instead she said, "Please, Alistair, forgive me, but I need more time."

Within the hour Abdul's bodyguards had reported the address, and their master promptly went to bed. After sleeping through until late afternoon, Abdul rose, bathed, dressed, and began to make his plans. One guard had been left on duty throughout the day near Zena's pension, and when he was relieved at six o'clock, Abdul was given additional information from the shopkeepers of the neighborhood.

Delilah, it seems, was a widow. Odd, in the few short months that had elapsed. Was that possible? No matter. What did matter was the fact that she apparently lived alone with the young boy. An Englishman spent much time with her, but she lived alone.

The beautiful, delectable Delilah, it appeared, would grace his harem after all, Abdul gloated. Allah was benevolent.

He must execute his mission for Ibrahim Bey first, but very soon he would have Delilah back in his seraglio. Abdul was resting transiently in Nice and gambling at Monte Carlo before continuing north to Paris as an envoy for his uncle to the French foreign minister. He would cut short his gaming now and leave directly tomorrow morning for Paris. Three days at the outside to deliver his dispatches, and then he and his new luscious traveling companion could leisurely journey back to Kurdistan.

His searching gaze had ascertained that Delilah was pregnant, quite *enceinte*, in fact, and looked soon to deliver. Within the year, though, he vowed with a libertine glint of carnal desire in his velvet eyes, she would give him a child, too. The thought of possessing her, owning her, planting his seed in her, stiffened his powerful manhood. What a beautiful creature he would have to delight and tantalize him. He had never quite resigned himself to her loss in the bidding with Prince Alexander Kuzan. To relinquish a female he desired to a barbaric Russian had always rankled.

Abdul paced restlessly as the afternoon sun cast lengthening rays into his sitting room, his stomach tightening in anticipation. He was scarcely able to contain his pent-up energy as he contemplated having the fair Delilah. As soon as it was absolutely dark, Abdul and his three guards left the hotel. All four men were dressed in black robes, and as they moved swiftly through the streets toward Zena's pension, their presence was muted, blending silently with the murky shadows of the moonless night.

Upon reaching the pension on the hill, Ali was directed toward the back door of the building. Kufir was posted outside the main entrance, while Softi and Abdul proceeded very quietly up the stairway to Zena's second-floor apartment. "Stay outside in the hallway," Abdul whispered to Softi. "When I need you I'll call. Now the door."

Softi extracted a slender, rigid wire from the folds of his burnoose and cautiously inserted it into the lock. With infinite care and a methodical patience his thin, precise fingers twisted the wire gently until he felt the sliding movement of the latch release. Turning the knob noiselessly, he raised his head and smiled at his master. Abdul slipped inside the door into the dim foyer, gesturing Softi to close the door behind him.

Stealthily, his thin-soled morocco leather slippers silent
on the polished wood, Abdul crossed the small inlaid floor
and looked down the darkened hallway. Only one room
had light shining beneath the door. Abdul's breathing
quickened as Delilah lay within his grasp.

Moving down the narrow hall, he stood outside the door
for a second. Abdul threw open the door, scanned the
lighted area with a roving glance, and swept across the
short space of carpet to clamp a rough hand over Zena's
mouth as she sat in bed, wide-eyed and panic-stricken, too
petrified with terror to scream.

Working swiftly, Abdul tied his silk handkerchief
around Zena's head as a gag. This accomplished to his satisfaction, he took a silk cord from around his waist,
twisted Zena's arms behind her back with effortless ease,
and secured them tightly. Zena's terrified eyes recoiled at
his cruel actions while some obscure memory stirred at the
sight of him. The black-haired man looked vaguely familiar. Had she met him somewhere? Where had she seen
him? At the slave traders? Her indefinite recognition was
elusive. It must have been at the desert camp. Those were
the only Turks she had seen. The brigands who had ab-
ducted her were clean-shaven. An unpleasant memory
slowly surfaced. Now she remembered the encounter.
When she had been sold by the brigands, Ibrahim Bey's
nephew was at his side. This was the nephew! She quailed
in revulsion at the memory, at the connotations of this assault, at the unholy scrutiny from those jet eyes.

Abdul was standing beside the bed, a tremendous, powerful man, staring unreservedly at his captured prize. His
beautiful, noble features fell into fascinated contemplation.
Previously his plans were to carry Delilah and the boy immediately by private carriage to Paris. But as he stood surveying the thinly clad woman, her auburn tresses
tumbling around her white shoulders, the abundant
breasts, full and swollen with pregnancy, he beheld a fas-

cinating sensual feast. The object of his sexual hunger, the sweet morsel he had almost possessed months ago, was only an arm's reach away. She was tied and trussed, warm, and nearly naked—a voluptuous earth mother, splendidly fertile, like a lush sacrifice, a sensuous allegorical vessel just waiting to serve his worshipping phallus. What a temptation to push the fragile gown from her shoulders and expose those breasts straining against the fabric. Her large nipples were thrusting in twin high peaks, stretching the diaphanous silk into symmetrical areolas of bursting ripples. What a temptation to take her immediately.

He decided quite abruptly, his penis rising at the sight, perhaps he could spare a half hour to taste and know the lush, warm feel of this exquisite goddess before the journey to Paris began. Reaching out a lean, brown hand, he mutely slipped Zena's sleeping gown down over her shoulders, taking both hands to ease the fine silk and lace when it tightened, then caught across the jutting pressure of the extravagant, satiny bosom. He used both hands to inch the fabric slowly down over the ripe, taut, distended breasts. The thin material sprang free and the full, magnificent globes were displayed in all their lush splendor. He ran his hands admiringly over the marvelous roundness like an appreciative connoisseur. Zena cringed back against the headboard at his touch.

"Delectable, Delilah. A feast for the gods," Abdul murmured. Her breasts were more beautiful than any he had ever seen, placed high and absolutely round. They seemed to point hungrily, provocatively near his mouth, thrusting upward for his kiss. He could see those delicious, luxurious breasts could very easily become an obsession. His erection expanded.

Why was he calling her Delilah? Why was this terrible, dark, savage man calling her Delilah? Zena couldn't understand the reason, and he gave no explanation. The hashish and drugs administered to her at Ibrahim Bey's command had quite effectively obliterated any recollections of her stay in his camp. Zena had no memory of the night of the feast in Ibrahim's tent.

Abdul unhooked the gold filigree and moonstone clasp at his neck, and the light wool garment fell open. He slid his arms from the loose, flowing sleeves of the desert coat. With a slow, quiet grace Abdul discarded his outer robe, and clad in a black silk tunic sat down next to Zena on the bed.

"Don't be frightened, Delilah. I won't hurt you," he softly whispered, but the soothing words did little to calm Zena's fears. She was dreadfully afraid and shrank from him.

"Such lovely, enormous breasts, my little mother," Abdul said quietly as his fingers delicately traced a circle around the enlarged nipples.

Female breasts had always held a certain fascination and attraction for him. His Svanetian mother was a concubine in a large harem of an old sultan. Since she was a favorite of the aging ruler, her whims had been indulged, one of which was to follow the universal custom of her tribe to nourish their children for as long as possible with women's milk. The Svanetians felt it was especially strengthening, and it appeared to suit them admirably, as the children flourished extraordinarily. After the third year two and sometimes three nurses were required to satisfy the appetite of the growing child. In Abdul's case, since he was her only child, his mother was allowed to suckle him until he left the harem at age seven. The swarthy Turk was, in truth, a testimonial to the diet, for he was extremely tall and long-limbed with a finely wrought muscular strength.

With gentle fingers Abdul kneaded Zena's breasts in a steady, firm rhythm. Zena sat rigidly upright against the bed, her bound arms pressing into her back, unable to move as the fine-featured, black-bearded Turk stroked and squeezed the rounded, swollen breasts, touching the hardened tips of her nipples occasionally, then resuming his sensuous rhythm.

"I'll find a wet nurse for your child, sweet Delilah," he crooned, as his fingers tightened on her swelling, firm breast, "and your flow of milk will be mine." His tongue licked one large nipple. "I'll have bosa ['mead'] sent down from my mother's tribe in the mountains for you. Drinking it daily ensures a copious supply of milk. I warn you, fair flower, my appetite for your milk will be demanding. I must see that you are rested and healthy so that you will be fit to supply my needs."

His low, deep, murmuring voice sang in her ears while those expert fingers practiced their sensitive sorcery. Zena began to glow to the pulsing in her breasts as they warmed to Abdul's deft touch. A tingle crept to the crest of her nipples as little droplets formed on the rosy tips. The minutest flow of milky fluid oozed gently forth, and Abdul bent his dark head to suck the moist gift. The feel of his lips sent unwanted waves of sensual pleasure throbbing through her body like a tide. My God, was she wanton? What was happening to her? How could this dangerous, cruel stranger force her to feel this way?

Unhampered by similar moral scruples, Abdul was quite content. He suckled each breast with gentle lips, delighting in the roused, taut nipples. He licked the hardened crests until an answering spasm tingled through Zena's breast, and several drops of fluid fell from the budding pink nipple into Abdul's mouth. Thusly he moved from one pulsating, plump mound to another until his prick throbbed violently with a craving hunger.

Laying Zena on her side he lifted the hem of her gown. She felt the silk being raised, felt her legs exposed to the air, felt him staring at her. With one hand he caressed her legs softly, slowly, feeling the smooth passage as he slid his hand between her thighs. Softly touching the cleft of plea-

sure with delicate, lightly teasing fingers, he found the
opening wet and unfolded like a sweet rose.

"Ah, little mother, you've been a widow too long. Let
me help you ease your frustration." He began to undo the
belt around his waist.

Zena lay helpless on the bed, her wrists tied so tightly
any movement pained her, powerless before this dark,
swarthy Turk who intended to carry her back to his harem.

After he untied the belt, Abdul's black silk tunic fell
open, and the evidence of his lust rose stiffly arched
against his stomach, the head dark and red. He stood very
tall and lithe, his muscles and nerves like those of a panther ready to spring. Zena's eyes widened in alarm as she
saw the enormity of his manhood.

Abdul's jet gaze was blazing with predatory hunger as
he reached down to untie the gag around Zena's head.

Zena attempted ineffectually to move away from the
touch of his hands.

"I suggest, my lovely," Abdul murmured softly, as his
impersonal finger traced the curve of her cheek from ear to
chin, "I suggest you welcome my advances, for if you insist on being recalcitrant, my luscious, I shall become annoyed. I may decide to leave that young boy in the next
room behind when I take you away. Do you understand?"
he asked coolly and pitilessly as his fiery eyes held Zena's
captive for a lingering moment.

Zena realized wretchedly she could do nothing against
his force and will. He was the ruler. He demanded submission with his ominous threat. She was defeated. Zena's
tense muscles yielded and relaxed beneath his fingers.

"There now, you *do* understand." He smiled.

The instant the handkerchief was released, he caught
fistfuls of her hair and pulled her face to his. She became
his slave. Abdul smothered her full mouth with kisses. He
forced her lips apart and savagely searched her mouth with
his warm tongue, holding her face firmly between his

hands. His hands savored every area of her body, leaving nothing untouched, bending her to suit his will, his mouth, his tongue.

A shaky tremor helplessly rose in Zena as his roving, urgent mouth plundered hers. His hands stroked her slim neck and naked shoulders, caressed the pulse in her throat as his fingers slipped into the valley between her breasts, and swept upward to lift both heavy mounds to his hungry, insatiable mouth. A sudden, unbidden surge of warmth scorched through her. It had been months since she lay with Sasha, and this dark Turk had caressed and suckled until every sensitive nerve was receptive to his touch. Every tingling sensation seemed to travel down her belly to the very core of fire that waited now to be exploded.

Stimulated, sensitized, painfully susceptible after all these months, vividly aware of a throbbing, sybaritic yearning, Zena sighed softly in erotic lethargy, no longer able to deny or resist her body's craving. Abdul could feel the sudden compliant capitulation. Responding to her surrender, he gently slipped his fingers down Zena's back and released the silken cords binding her wrists.

Zena shuddered at his touch, at her release, at the urgency of her need; every hot-blooded animalistic urge cried for that quenching repletion. Her hands stole up to embrace this dark stranger who intended to plunder her body. Abdul's lean, brown fingers skimmed lightly over her breasts and hips, fondling tenderly, sliding over her white thighs. Lazily one finger sought her damp cleft and slowly opened her rosy, full, distended vulva, stroking with catlike softness back and forth. Then his dark fingers entered. How delicately he touched, she thought, and she felt a languid dissolving feeling as the secret liquid was brought from hidden recesses to show shining wet between her legs. Zena was sinking into a bliss of sensation, divorced from sanity, immune to all coherent thought save

the single driving need to reach the peak of exquisite gratification.

Taking her docile hand, Abdul guided it to his rigid,
arched penis and as her fingers closed around the pulsing
shaft, Zena felt him catch his breath. A low, anguished
groan escaped him, and he knew he could wait no longer.

Swiftly rolling Zena over so that her back was to him,
his hands captured her hips. He slipped his erect penis between her legs, and she felt the first swelling pressure of
his probing entrance. His penis touched her lightly over
and over again at the most vulnerable tip of her pulsing
desire. Then he entered her for the first time, pushing very
delicately, advancing only half an inch at a time, resting,
then slipping in another inch or so. This gave Zena plenty
of time to feel the stirring presence, to feel the tight fit
between soft walls of flesh. His gradual entrance ignited
invisible currents inside her that warned of the coming explosion. Restless nerves lay waiting as her flesh yielded
more and more until he filled her completely, touching the
very depths of her womb.

Both hands gripped her softly rounded hips firmly, and
he pushed deeper. Zena wanted to scream in pure, sensual
bliss. Sweet honey was pouring from her as he swung in
and out, moving slowly, teasing her to the edge of excruciating pleasure. But as soon as her breathing hastened he
drew himself out, all hard and glistening. Zena trembled
at the unexpected loss.

"A lesson, sweet Delilah," Abdul breathed and caressed
her cheek lightly as she quivered in unfulfilled yearning.
"My pleasure comes first. Remember, I am master."

He withheld himself, completely disregarding the lower
half of her body, which shuddered and writhed. Instead, he
languidly filled his hands with her breasts, fondling the
two heavy globes, swinging them lightly back and forth,
caressing and stroking with a silken touch. He lazily toyed
with his magnificent baubles, noting with roguish eyes the

sensual tremors that seized Zena as the convulsive pulsing built in her soft, sweet canal.

Pleasantly roused by her enchanting sexuality, Abdul fancied a different stimulation. Releasing the soft, pliant flesh of her breasts, he swung himself up into a sitting position.

With an easy, lithe motion, Abdul moved in front of Zena. He rubbed his swollen love shaft, wet with Zena's honeyed juice, over her cheeks and mouth. Zena turned her head to escape it, raised her hands to resist the assault, but the brown-skinned Turk quietly said, "Remember the young boy; it's my whim that decides whether he goes or stays." Zena's tossing head stilled, and her repudiating hands fell back.

Abdul handled his enormous penis naturally, easily, like an indulged plaything, massaging it over Zena's now unresisting face. He slid it down her neck to sink it in the deep valley between her breasts, rested it there as his hands squeezed her breasts against it, then ran it over the twin ivory mounds, leisurely enjoying the tantalizing feel. As it wandered back up to her mouth, he held the shiny red tip near her lips and ordered in a very low voice, "Hold me and tell me you want to kiss this big, hard organ that offers so much joy to that dripping cunt of yours."

Zena's eyes opened in dismay. "No!" she cried.

"Now, sweet one, remember the boy," Abdul reminded persuasively. After the merest hesitation Zena's small hands rose to clasp the noble erection. Abdul shifted forward an inch until the swelling end touched Zena's tightly closed lips.

"Tell me you want to kiss it. Say 'Let me kiss my pleasure shaft, master'." Zena resisted, remained silent, unmoving. Abdul chuckled indulgently. "What a little, stubborn jade. Come, if you learn your lessons well, I can be a very generous master. Your hot little cunt will be

stretched again by my lance, and then the boy will not
stay behind. You can't shirk your duties to me. You must
obey. It's not so difficult. Gratify me with a pretty submission. Say it for me."

Deeply humiliated, wretchedly aware he was only
toying with her, Zena's lips parted as she began the faltering sentence. With each word her full mouth brushed
the swollen head of Abdul's penis, her lips whispered the
words softly against the sensitive, responsive organ. "Let
me . . . kiss . . . my pleasure shaft . . . master."

"Very, very good, my charming little student," Abdul
commended as he drew in a deep breath. "Open your delectable lips," he whispered huskily.

As Zena obeyed reluctantly, Abdul slowly slid in his
long, rigid penis, and her lips closed over the hardness.

"Let your fingers and tongue caress me, petite slave,"
Abdul murmured as he stroked her pale cheek.

Zena yielded; her fingers brushed the base of his penis,
moving downward to feel and touch the heavy testicles
that hung pendulously near her neck, while her tongue
and teeth licked and nibbled obediently on the
mushroom-shaped tip. Abdul's eyes shut as the erotic tide
inundated his senses.

"Ah, what a seductive little bitch," he sighed as he held
Zena's head between his hands and slid slowly back and
forth. After several minutes a few drops of salty fluid
oozed from the pulsing tip and slid down Zena's throat;
Abdul reluctantly withdrew.

"What a delightful houri you are. I can make you do
anything for me. But I must save myself to pleasure that
wet cunt of yours."

His hands glided down to lift Zena's ripe breasts.
"These engorged, heavy udders of yours, Delilah." Abdul
weighed them lightly in both his hands. "Whose property
are they now? Who will they nourish in a few short
weeks?" His fingers pinched the pulsing nipples, and sev-

eral drops of opaque liquid flowed out and glistened on the velvet nipples. Abdul's attentive eyes moved from admiration of the fertile spectacle to calm contemplation of Zena's flushed face. "Answer, my sweet, Whose property are you?"

Zena's eyes dropped before his intent gaze.

"Yours," she whispered.

"Yours, what?" he prompted softly as his fingers roved between her thighs to the full, pouting lips. Delicately stroking the slippery, rosy vulva, open and welcoming like flower petals, he slid three fingers past the entrance, forcing open the quivering interior while he waited for his answer. As he shoved those hard fingers deep within, stretching the passage, he repeated, "Yours, what?"

Zena caught her breath, trembling on the brink of ecstasy as Abdul's long, thick fingers sank in up to his palm. Her eyes blurred in a sensual haze, and in a small voice she breathed, "Yours, master."

Abdul smiled faintly.

"A very apt pupil, dear Delilah. You'll serve me well."

Feeling satisfied that the woman had been adequately subdued and tutored in the lesson ruler and slave, he swung behind her again and pressed his thoroughly roused penis into the sweet, receptive gates of paradise. Holding the head just within the warm entrance for a blissful moment, he felt the swollen lips of her vulva close around him in rapturous welcome, and then he felt the faintest hint of movement as she searched, reached for more.

"Delilah, my sweet," he whispered into the damp curls near her ear, "the long wait is over. Your reward for obedience."

With one violent push he sank to the bottom of her flaming hot cunt. Zena gasped as a shocking burst of unutterable pleasure shook her. Abdul plunged deeper, thrusting with all the powerful strength of his lower body, bracing his feet so he surged forward to touch her very quick, touching and forcing open the soft, fleshy walls again and again. His breath came heavily as his fever rose; he gored her furiously, deliciously until the feverish intensity rent their bodies like lightening in a wild, screaming torrent of carnal hysteria as his penis quivered, then exploded into her palpitating womb. Zena fell away suddenly, fainting from the violent, convulsive orgasm.

Her ravished body lay limp as Abdul rolled away from her. He was smiling, panting faintly. There was a throbbing ache between her legs, and only dimly Zena heard Abdul whisper tenderly, "I shall make you my first wife, lush flower. No one shall come before you." Her clouded brain refused to absorb the horrifying statement, and she sank deeper into unconsciousness.

Alistair made a habit of walking in the evening, and invariably he found himself passing Zena's apartment. He would chastise himself moderately for behaving like a foolish, lovesick boy, but the habit persisted despite his valid and logical admonitions. Tonight he and his man Ridgely, who often accompanied him, lifted silent eyebrows of inquiring comment at each other as they observed the black-robed Turk standing guard outside the entrance to Zena's building. Strolling by without remark, Alistair tersely whispered, "I don't like the look of that Mussilman. Let's check the back."

Moving stealthily through the small, walled gardens behind the buildings, they were alarmed to discover the back door was also posted with a black-robed figure. A worried frown appeared on the earl's fine brow. "I think we should look into this, Ridgely," he said with growing apprehension. "Do you have your knife with you?"

In a swift flash of motion Ridgely produced the double-edged Persian dagger he kept in his boot. "Aye, yer honor. At yer service." He grinned momentarily, disturbing briefly the dour, staid lines of his craggy Scot's face.

Alistair's eyes searched the roof with a rapid, fleeting glance. Then his mouth quirked in an answering grin. "Best up and over it seems, Ridgely, if we're to avoid the Turks."

"Like in Marrakech, eh, yer honor? Up it is." The pale, gray eyes of the earl's man glinted with a rare and animated excitement. Ridgely had been with the Earl of Glenagle since Alistair had been the young heir sent down to Cambridge. He had continued serving as valet after his marriage, had followed him with Kitchner in Africa and after the earl's wife died two years ago accompanied his master on a year's trek across Turkey, Persia, and Bashan to China. This past year after their return from the East had been too tame to suit Ridgely, and he smiled warmly in anticipation of some stimulating sport.

The earl, as was typical of gentlemen of his class, was a sportsman of note. His leisured life was regularized only by the calendar of sporting seasons: salmon fishing in the summer, grouse and partridge shooting in fall and early winter, fox hunting until the spring rains made the ground too muddy and treacherous, then skiing and mountain climbing in Switzerland. During the brief lull in late spring when other people enjoyed London's season, he usually went abroad. All in all the outdoor life had developed and honed the earl to a peak of faultless, physical excellence.

Executing a furtive, chary detour around the bodyguard at the back, Alistair and Ridgely entered a building two doors north of Zena's pension and took the several flights of stairs three at a time to the roof. Letting themselves out onto the small walkway flanked by the surrounding expanse of red tile, they carefully made their way across the slick surface, lowered themselves the few feet to the roof next door, and then repeated the slow, cautious procedure until they dropped quietly onto the roof of Zena's building. Ridgely pried open one of the dormer windows of the attic, and both men passed through, gaining access to the barren fourth floor of the pension. Alistair unobtrusively lifted the trapdoor to the attic and peered into the third-floor hallway. Seeing nothing in the hushed, darkened hall, he dropped lightly to his feet onto the landing below. Ridgely followed like a silent shadow.

Hugging the wall, they stole down the carpeted stairs to the second floor. Motioning Ridgely to halt, Alistair eased his head around the corner of the stair landing and searched the dimly lit hallway that passed Zena's door.

Another black-robed Turk was stationed before Zena's door! The earl's blood pounded to his temples as mad rage leaped into his normally rational mind. Zena was in danger! His first wild impulse was to sink Ridgely's dagger in the bloody dog's back, but sensible considerations overcame his disordered fury.

Softi was lounging against the wall with his back to Alistair. Using sign language, Alistair issued his instructions to Ridgely, and with an expertise acquired over many months from the North African Bedouins, the earl and his man crept silently to within striking distance of the unapprehending guard. With stunning, snakelike speed Ridgely clamped his left hand over Softi's mouth at the same time his right hand held the double-edged dagger against the jugular of the astonished Turk.

Alistair quickly secured Softi's hands with his leather belt and efficiently gagged him with his neck scarf, while Ridgely bound the guard's ankles with the silk cord of his own burnoose. In less than a minute the trussed Turk was carried down the hall and deposited inside a supply closet.

When they returned to Zena's door, Alistair hesitated. If they broke down the door, and someone was inside, Zena might be seriously harmed. Several seconds passed as the earl considered his alternatives. He had just decided there was no choice but to break the door in when lady luck intervened. The doorknob began to turn.

The earl and Ridgely leaped aside, flattening themselves against the wall on opposite sides of the door that was slowly opening.

From inside the darkened apartment Abdul stepped out to engage Softi's help in carrying the unconscious Delilah and the young boy. Alistair's temper rose irrationally, and black outrage gripped him as he saw the tall Turk emerge from Zena's apartment. Wanting to lash out and destroy this alien, he didn't wait for Ridgely to move with his dagger. The earl clasped his hands tightly together into a fist, swung his arms back to shoulder level, and drove from the height of that sweeping movement with all the force of his body, smashing his clenched fists into Abdul's Adam's apple.

Ibrahim Bey's young and handsome nephew dropped like a slaughtered sheep.

Without so much as a glance Alistair stepped over the still body and ran to Zena's bedroom. Entering the lamplit room, he perceived immediately what had happened. Alistair slammed the door shut.

Zena lay unconscious on the rumpled bed. Although her hands were free, Alistair discerned the silk cord tossed carelessly aside and saw the red welts on her wrists. Her night dress had been pulled down hastily over her thighs, but vestiges of Abdul's passion stained the silken fabric.

Alistair was seized with a sudden urge to kill the savage animal who had violated this woman who meant so much to him. A tremor of uncontrollable fury gripped him, and his hands clenched and unclenched convulsively at his sides. He whirled on his heel, intent on murdering the fallen Arab in the hallway if the cur wasn't already dead. The beast deserved no less. As his hand touched the door latch, Zena moaned weakly.

Dashing back to the bed, he gently raised the half-conscious, half-clothed woman into his arms. Zena's eyes fluttered open. The earl exhaled a sigh of relief and tightened his hold on her soft shoulders.

"Alistair," Zena whispered shakily. "Oh, Alistair." She trembled under his fingers while tears streamed down her cheeks. "Thank God you came. He . . . he . . . was taking me away."

"Hush, hush, my sweet," he soothed. "It's all over. I'll take care of you. I'll always take care of you." He tightened his grip on her. "You must marry me. You can't live alone. Say you'll marry me now. Say yes, my darling."

Zena looked up into his kind, warm eyes and shuddered at the frightful memory of what had just passed. If Alistair hadn't come to save her, she would have spent the rest of her life in a Turkish harem.

"Say you will, dear Zena," Alistair insisted gently.

Zena had never felt so dreadfully alone and helpless as in the past hour. She had always prided herself on being resolute and persevering, always able to cope with her many problems. But tonight the feeling of utter, appalling despair had been overwhelming while the thought of being spirited away to spend the rest of her life as a brood mare in some faraway seraglio had been terrifying in its imminence. The possibility of that long, dreary, endless life in such a prison had broken her proud spirit. She was at the moment truly afraid to be alone, and she suddenly needed the affection Alistair offered or maybe the security, or maybe the passion.

Zena gazed into Alistair's gentle eyes and out of weakness and fear whispered, "Yes, I will." Her future lay not with the dream of Sasha, who was lost to her forever, but with the reality of Alistair, and she wisely accepted the fact. She purposely reminded herself of the deep wound of Sasha's savage rejection, and the pain helped her face the future. Today she began a new life.

Alistair's face lit with unadultered joy at her acquiescence, which he had waited for so long. "You won't regret it, darling," he murmured. "I'll see that you're happy."

Oh, God, Zena thought, I have to tell him about Sasha, about the need for a divorce, about all the complications of my life. Not now, though, she considered wearily. Tomorrow I'll tell him, tomorrow . . . or the next day.

In the jubilation of his triumph the Earl of Glenagle was inclined to disregard his previous bloodthirsty urge to brutally kill. After tucking Zena into bed with the promise that he would stay with her until morning, Alistair instead called the police superintendent. Upon his arrival, the earl succinctly described the events that had transpired in a mild, prosaic fashion, editing the details that would prove awkward to Zena.

There was a man in the hall closet as well as the one lying in the hallway, he said, and apparently the two guards outside had discreetly disappeared as the police arrived. The earl explained in well-bred, quiet accents that he wished to avoid scandal for the lady's sake and would press no charges if he could be assured the Arabs would be out of the country by morning.

"All will be accomplished, my lord," the gravely courteous police officer had guaranteed.

With good-tempered amiability and manners the earl thanked the diplomatic police superintendent and bid him a cordial good night.

As Nice's police superintendent walked back down the stairs, he reflected pensively on the singular peculiarities and incongruities of the phlegmatic English. It was remarkable to contemplate that quiet, calm, civil earl conducting himself like the most perverse Marseilles cutthroat. That young Turkish sheikh would be lucky if he could talk at all for several months. Indeed, the Frenchman speculated pragmatically, the young scoundrel was fortunate to still be alive.

· · ·

Alex arrived in Nice two days later. It was the middle of September. Although he hadn't been there in three years, his villa was fully staffed and in readiness. Only his valet accompanied him from St. Petersburg.

Detectives were hired immediately to determine whether Zena was still in the city. During the following days as the search was in progress, Alex was feted by society. A rich, young bachelor was always welcome at any social event and a handsome, rich, young bachelor could discard more invitations than he could accept. Prince Alexander Kuzan's picture was splashed across the society pages of the local paper, his elegant figure shown at a ball, a garden party, at the races, and on his yacht.

Zena unfortunately read the paper and saw those photos. Her husband seemed to be amusing himself very well without her. She had always been aware of that, though. Tears spilled over onto her cheeks and traced silent paths downward. Why, oh, why did she have to be reminded of that fact just at a time when she had regained some control over her feelings and her future.

Sasha was as startlingly handsome as ever, his easy air of assurance and patrician cast of countenance evident in every photo: standing bronzed and poised in white flannels at the rail of his yacht; entering the enclosure at the races in Cagnes-sur-Mer; or leaning casually against a veranda support at some afternoon party. Staying home in staid seclusion while he sought Zena had never occurred to Alex. He was born and bred to participate in these society amusements; and he partook of them through force of habit and as an alternative to drinking alone.

Four days later the detectives discovered Zena's pension and reported to Alex. He left immediately to see her. His carriage drove him to the area of town in which Zena's lodgings were located. As they passed by the little park near Zena's apartment, Alex caught a glimpse of his wife.

Ordering the driver to stop, he descended from the vehicle and paused briefly.

Bobby was playing with a ball on the grass near Zena. She was seated on a bench under the shade of a lime tree, apparently weeping. A man sat intimately near her, and as her shoulders shook with sobs, the man placed his arm around Zena and drew her head onto his chest.

His wife! And in the arms of another man! Alex's temper flared dangerously. God damn it! Some other man fondling his wife! A white heat of rage ignited within seconds as his proprietory impulses surged.

I'll kill him! I'll kill him! The incendiary malediction coursed through his raging brain.

With a conscious effort he regained control of his rationality. Consider now, he reflected reasonably, you've been far from virtuous these past few months trying to forget Zena. It's a two-way street; Zena had need of companionship, too. You couldn't very well expect her to be chaste while you were sampling every erotic pleasure in St. Petersburg.

This reasonable, logical recapitulation of the common-sense motives influencing both his and Zena's behavior lasted precisely four seconds. Sensitive, moderate judiciousness had always eluded him. Touch my wife, will he?

I'll kill him! the prince repeated violently. He was smiling now, and his eyes blazed. In a white-hot fury Alex started across the busy street, oblivious to the flurry of vehicles on the congested thoroughfare. Alex dodged the first phaeton successfully and blindly avoided the second vehicle with the luck reserved for small children and angels, but even the providential good fortune of inveterate gamblers is subject to occasional reverses. The street was much too crowded with dashing conveyances, while his ferocity obscured any caution he might have had. The driver of a speeding curricle sawed back cruelly on his reins in an attempt to avoid the tall figure who had dashed out in front of his team. Despite the driver's urgent measures, his best efforts were futile. The horses veered sharply to the right, screaming wildly, convulsed by the pain as the bits tore into their tender mouths. But the desperate action was a fraction too late as the left forward wheel of the curricle crashed into the chest of the sprinting man.

All was tumultuous confusion as vehicles of every description screeched to a halt in a muddled hodgepodge of turbulent pandemonium: drivers cursing, animals squealing, panic-stricken pedestrians surging out into the center of the street to gawk at the victim who was lying unconscious. Several small pools of blood began to form under this head and legs.

Zena jumped up at the uproar and called warning to Bobby before he rushed off to view the spectacle.

"Let me go and see what happened, Zena," Alistair cautioned. "In your condition it isn't wise to subject yourself to calamitous experiences."

He returned shortly. "It seems some fellow was struck down by a carriage. Quite gruesome, my dear, not a sight for you to be exposed to. Blood everywhere and the chap is unconscious. I'll take you and Bobby back home." Gently placing Zena's arms through his, they walked slowly back to her apartment. When they arrived, Zena made her excuses.

"If you don't mind, Alistair, I think I'm going to lie down and rest this afternoon. I'll see you tomorrow."

"Very well, dear," he acceded gently. "Tomorrow."

3

Since Alex's pictures had appeared in the paper, all the careful defenses that Zena had conscientiously constructed had come tumbling down. Four days of seeing Sasha as society's darling, four days of knowing he was near enough to see had quite effectively demolished those judiciously built bastions. They had not seen each other for more than two months, and she had been losing hold of the memories of him. Now all she wanted to do was lay her head on the bronzed skin of his chest, feel the beating of his heart and the lazy caress of his hand over her hair, feel his mouth on hers. The torment had returned full force.

She cried forlornly again for her lost love and wondered how she could ever have considered marrying Alistair no matter how gracious and kindly. After putting Bobby to sleep that night, she sat morosely near the fire and felt an uncontrollable, unforgivable moment of terror. She wondered how she was going to face the future, how she was even going to be able to go through childbirth alone. What had seemed like a rational solution six days ago—marrying Alistair—now seemed the most impossible action in the world. Do you pretend he's Sasha when you lie in his arms? Do you have Sasha's child call him Papa? Do you think of the future stretching ahead twenty years from now and see yourself still content as the Countess of Glenagle.

Oh, why, she cried, had Sasha come back into her life to

uproot her dearly purchased serenity, to upset the fragile structure of her placid friendship with Alistair? How was it possible he could still hurt her so?

What was she going to do? In three weeks she was going to have a child; she would need money eventually. She could return to her grandfather, but she didn't want to. She could petition Sasha for money, but the thought was reprehensible under the circumstances. He hadn't even bothered acknowledging her note when she had poured out her love for him. Her absence hadn't affected him at all but to allow him the freedom he had always craved. No matter how she turned the problem around, no better solution appeared. Alistair was the only reasonable option.

Zena stayed in the next morning, burrowing under the covers, unable to face the melancholy of her thoughts, unable to face her usual visit with Alistair at the park. The loss she thought she had begun to overcome was raw and bleeding again. Bobby crawled up onto the bed and spent the morning playing with his toy soldiers while Zena slipped inside her grief and pushed away the world. She would not permit herself to think. The softness and warmth of the comforting bed would saturate her and soothe the cold, sick ache in her heart. When she was strengthened, she'd face it all and decide what would be best for her to do.

Alistair waited patiently on the park bench, passing the time reading the morning paper. He wasn't surprised Zena hadn't arrived. She had appeared more distraught than usual yesterday. The past few days he had noted an increased agitation, a vacillating gloom that he concluded was the result of her advanced pregnancy. It was only to be expected that a young female alone in the world should experience tremors of trepidation and anxiety as her time drew near, and the harrowing experience with the Turk had taken its toll. Alistair decided he'd drop by to visit this afternoon if she didn't come to the park. He leisurely finished reading the paper, the local news headlined by the accident that had occurred across the street yesterday. Apparently the victim of the crash was some Russian prince. The report stated the prince had regained consciousness and was resting at his villa on the sea. Those Russians were always of a volatile, wild character. Imagine, attempting to cross such a busy street in the middle of the thoroughfare.

Rising from his idle perusal of the news, the Earl of Glenagle casually pitched the paper into the waste receptacle and continued on his way home. I wonder if Zena knows this Russian, the earl mused vaguely, then cast the thought aside. Impossible! She was quite different from the general run of headstrong, hard-gambling, party-going Russian aristocrats who dwelt in Nice. She was really very subdued. He wondered if her mother could have been European. He must ask her sometime.

The earl delivered a gorgeous bouquet of white roses that afternoon when he visited Zena. She thanked him gratefully and explained she hadn't felt well enough that day to venture outside.

"Do you think you should have a doctor call?" the earl asked anxiously, concerned with the new pallor of Zena's complexion.

Zena demurred tactfully, unable to account for the actual reason.

After Zena had made tea, the earl chatted congenially about the society events he had read of in the paper. Seeing that society news was apparently not brightening her spirits, he thought perhaps she might enjoy hearing about one of her fellow countrymen.

"By the way," he said, holding his cup out to be refilled, "the chap in the accident yesterday was a Russian too. Wonder if you might have heard of him. Fellow by the name of Kuzan, a prince, I believe."

The blue and white faience teapot dropped from Zena's

grip, crashing into the plate of teacakes, spilling sweet, brown liquid across the table. Zena turned a deadly white and crumpled to the floor.

Impeded by the table between them, Alistair was unable to break her fall. Lunging from his chair, he knelt fearfully by the still, pale form, patting her hand ineffectually for a moment before running downstairs and demanding the concierge send for a doctor.

Rushing back to the apartment, he gently lifted Zena onto her bed. She was unbelievably frail despite the added weight of the baby, much too delicate, it seemed, to be able to sustain the burden of another life. Pressing a damp towel on her forehead, he saw her eyes flutter. Wiping her cheeks with the cool cloth, he was relieved to look into the dark blue eyes so familiar to him.

"How are you, dear? I've sent for a doctor. You should have had one immediately this morning. Don't talk, just rest. He'll be here soon."

"Is Sasha alive?" she whispered.

"Who?" Alistair inquired bewildered.

"The prince—is he alive?" she repeated softly.

"Oh, the accident. *That* prince. Yes, he's alive, broken bones, that's all."

Zena closed her eyes in relief.

The earl was too polite to demand an explanation of such an odd question, although curiosity consumed him. After the doctor left, Alistair insisted Zena remain in bed.

"Very well, Alistair, but I'm feeling quite well again, really. You needn't be concerned."

After a half hour of persistent placating, she finally persuaded him to leave.

Her spirits were tumultuously happy. The shock of thinking Sasha dead had convinced her that her love for him was as strong as ever. She smiled sadly to herself while she reflected what a foolish thing pride was, and all the other shams like self-pity, hatred, vengeance, which had almost robbed life of the only thing she really wanted. What nonsense was pride! She wanted to see Sasha and be with him. She wanted at least another chance to talk to him again. If he didn't want her, then she would decide what she'd do with her life. But she was a silly fool to sit here and mope without trying even once to win Sasha back.

Disregarding Alistair's admonitions, Zena threw back the covers and quickly dressed in a cerulean blue dress, one of Sasha's favorite frocks. He had teased her that she looked like a budding cornflower in it. It was soft silk, fluttering ruffles, and ribbons.

Calling for a carriage, she and Bobby set out. Apprehension and qualms of misgiving stirred within her. You're half Daghestani, she bolstered her failing courage, and they fear no one. All he could do was send her away, and she was already living apart from him.

An immaculately raked carriage drive curved up to a refined Moorish palace situated superbly on the crest of a rocky cliff. The sun was setting low over the Mediterranean, casting mauve and golden rays over the azure sea.

Descending from the carriage, she nervously commanded it to wait. Despite her unease, she would not give way to the weakness that threatened to overwhelm her. She kept her mind steadily fixed on the object she had in view—to see Sasha one more time. Taking Bobby's hand in hers, Zena walked up to the brass-studded wooden door and struck the knocker. She was admitted to the foyer, where a forbidding butler looked down at her from a great height and said haughtily, "Yes, madame?"

"I'd like to see Sasha . . . er . . . Prince Alexander."

"The prince is not home to visitors, madame."

"Perhaps if you just brought a message to him," she pleaded.

"I'm afraid that's impossible. He can't be disturbed. If you could return, madame, at some future date. . . ."

"I want to see him today," she stubbornly insisted, her temper rising at the overbearing indifference of the man.

The butler had learned long ago that the prince rarely wished to be disturbed by females of any kind, particularly—and his eyes swept Zena's protruding belly sardonically—pregnant females. As majordomo he was there to discourage just that sort of distraught individual. The prince demanded privacy in his own home.

"Madame, I'm very sorry." His chill murmur was quelling.

Tears of frustration stung Zena's eyes. Bobby tugged on her hand and piped up sweetly, "See Papa, me see Papa!" he had understood the mission they were on.

The butler was far too well trained to display emotion, but he was definitely staggered. Good God! the august butler thought. Papa! At all costs he must see them out! The prince would definitely not want to receive these visitors. Firmly taking Zena's elbow, the stately, dutiful servant began guiding her to the door.

A light footfall was heard on the stairs rising to the first floor, and a voice exclaimed, "The little prince!"

All three figures turned to see Alex's valet, Feodor, descending the marble staircase. Bobby loosened his grip on Zena's hand and bounded toward his old friend.

"It's all right, Harrison," Feodor explained. "In fact, it's perfect. This is Zena, Harrison, Princess Kuzan."

The butler was profuse in his apologies. The entire staff knew of the prince's frantic search for his wife, but gossip had failed to note the fact that she was pregnant and had another child. He was contrite and humble over his mistake.

"The Batiushka only woke from his sedative, madame," Feodor said. "Please come up."

Zena followed him up the stairs and down a long corridor to a room on the south side of the palace commanding a magnificent view of the sea. Zena stood in the open doorway with Bobby while Feodor diplomatically withdrew.

4

Alex lay in an austere mahogany bed, the entire room sparsely furnished in a very masculine, severe Chippendale Chinoiserie style. It was a thoroughly incongruous sight in the ornate and filigreed Moorish palace. He looked splendidly well despite the bandages—very bronzed against the white linen, his dark hair brushed back, his eyes closed as he rested against the bolster of pillows. Glass doors were open onto a balcony overlooking the blue Mediterranean. The lengthening beams of the late afternoon sun streamed in, lighting the room with a diffuse golden glow.

"May I come in?" Zena asked softly.

At the sound of her voice Alex's eyes snapped toward the door, and the melancholy vanished from his expression. His face lit into his old, warm, inviting smile that had always struck Zena to the soul. His beautiful golden eyes met hers, and Zena almost cried aloud. His first thought as he saw her framed in the doorway was that she was more beautiful than he had remembered. Her memory had lived in his every waking moment despite his ruthless attempt to dispel and crush that tormented memory.

"Darling!" His eyes blazed with joy; then he fell silent, uncertain for the first time in his life of his reception by a woman.

Still standing at the door, Zena began, stammering, "Sasha, if . . . if . . . you want me, well, it won't matter . . ."

"*If* I *want* you, child," Alex said somewhat unsteadily.

When she had walked into his room, it seemed his heart had stopped. "There's nothing in this world I want more. I'll stop going to the Club. I'll stay home every night. Whatever you want." He halted abruptly in the midst of his explanation, frustrated.

"Damn it!" Alex exploded. "I can't get up. Come here!"

Zena flew across the room and fell hungrily into his embrace.

Alex kissed her with the pent-up privation and need of a hundred fruitless nights of searching for her in other women's arms. Her lips were as sweet and soft as he had remembered. His eager longing deepened, and a savage need for her overwhelmed him. Zena clung to him as a drowning person clings to life. He *was* her life, and she was in his arms. Heaven could offer no more.

He folded her to his heart, and they murmured their love for each other, trying to assuage the thirst and yearning of all their days of anguish. As he hugged her to him, as Zena pressed against the shelter of his chest, a little warm body squirmed and wiggled up onto the bed and burrowed between them.

"Papa, me—me, too," Bobby squealed insistently.

Alex looked down into the imploring child's eyes, wrapped one strong arm lightly around Bobby, and hugged him close. It always amazed Zena how this large, powerful man could be so gentle when he wanted to.

"I missed you, 'me too'," Alex grinned at the beaming cherubic face framed in dark curls. "Have you been keeping your sister busy?"

"Zena not play much. I like Papa. He always play. Papa play now!" he demanded.

"In a minute, Bobby. Papa wants to talk to Zena. Go and take a look in that dresser drawer over there." Alex pointed toward the chest on the opposite wall. "I think you'll find something to amuse you." The toys had been purchased in Warsaw on the trip south. Alex had been optimistically hopeful of reconciliation. Bobby nodded his understanding, slid off the bed with energetic vigor, and was soon seated on the floor supremely satisfied with the array of toys he had pulled pell-mell out of the drawer.

Alex grinned. "I have a way with children, wouldn't you say?"

Then his eyes sobered. He ran his hand over Zena's obtrusive stomach. "So, I've done this to you." He paused. "Do you hate me for it?" Zena's eyes dropped before his keen, searching gaze.

"No, Sasha," she murmured, "not now."

"Could you ever want me back?" he asked gently.

Tears rose in Zena's eyes. "Yes, Sasha," she whispered hardly aloud, "with all my heart."

His grip tightened convulsively in thanksgiving. "After you left without a trace . . ."

"But I sent you a note."

"A note? Where?"

"To the Club."

"I never received it. Christ!" he gave a little bitter laugh. "You mean I could have avoided all the misery of the past few months?"

"You never received it?" Zena whispered.

"No, and I tried to make myself cynical again and forget all the beauty and joy you had brought into my life. I wanted to stop all the memories of you, and I did everything I could to distract myself. Then I saw your necklace."

"My necklace?"

"Yes, on Kasimir's wife. And in that instant I knew nothing had been of any use. I loved you and wanted you back.

"Damn it, I'm no good at saying the right words," he declared in a low, brutal rasp. "I've never used them before—only seductive words, the playful, make-believe, required words—never the real ones. . . ." He stumbled over the explanation, this charming rogue who had given so many women so much pleasure but never his love. When he spoke again, his voice was low. "I love you," he said very simply. "Do you still love me? Or is it too late?"

"I never stopped loving you. I tried, I really tried, but I couldn't."

"I think I tried, too. It didn't work. I found I only missed you more. No woman ever was able to replace you."

"Women?" Zena said with an undisguised pique.

Alex's eyes began to glitter ominously. "And the man in the park?" he inquired suspiciously.

"*That's* how you were run over, then," Zena exclaimed understandingly.

"*That's* how I was run over. The blind rage obscured my vision," he grinned. "Now about the man in the park," he repeated menacingly.

"Alistar is just a friend."

"Alistar?" her husband queried forbiddingly.

"He was very kind to me, Sasha."

"How kind?" He couldn't help himself. Despite his own profligacy he had this ungovernable jealousy regarding Zena. It simply didn't respond to any reasonable logic.

"Just kind," Zena answered emphatically. She went on to explain. "He's English. Two years ago he lost his wife after a long illness. I think he's lonely."

"Hell, if he's lonely, I'll send him a dozen women tomorrow to keep him company. He doesn't need my wife!" Alex declared indignantly.

"Oh, Sasha, he's not wild like you." Her eyes sparkled at the thought of a dozen women deposited on Alistair's doorstep. "He's very quiet and sedate."

"In that case, I'll send him a dozen very quiet and sedate women."

"You're not serious, are you?" Zena asked apprehensively.

"Of course not," was the light reply. Then Alex sternly said, "But he damn well better leave my wife alone."

Zena's eyes shone. "Why, Sasha, you're jealous."

"You noticed," he growled grumpily.

"Are you going to be difficult?" she teased, warmed by the thought that he cared so deeply, enchanted by his jealousy.

"I'm always difficult, if you remember, pet," and he smiled. "And while I'm being difficult, one slight demand more." Zena raised her brows provocatively. "I'm serious now," he retorted. "We must be married immediately."

"Whatever for?"

"Tribal rites may be all well and good, charming, quaint, filthy chickens and all," he grimaced at the reminiscence, "but my child must be born under a legal and binding decree. I want no problems with inheritance."

"Nonsense!" came the curt reply. "The empire has always recognized the tribal marriages."

"Through necessity, dear, only through necessity. They can't enforce one single statute a half mile off the military roads," Alex said.

"It's ridiculous, needless. Don't even talk about it," Zena firmly replied, sentimentally feeling that her parents' marriage ceremony had been tribal and blessed with happiness.

"I've been thinking," Alex went on calmly, "that if the wedding took place here quietly at the end of next week, we might run over to Algiers in my yacht for a honeymoon. Biskra is pleasant enough now."

"A honeymoon!" Zena exclaimed. "Wouldn't I look just perfect on a honeymoon!"

"Just perfect, my dear," returned Alex. "Now I'm glad you're beginning to consider the notion."

"You misunderstand!" Zena shot back tersely.

"Ah! You prefer that it should be earlier than next week. Why didn't you say so?"

"Sasha, you idiot, you're impossible."

"Well, sweet, I never said I was perfect. Now, if it's St. Petersburg you're holding out for and a large society wedding, do say so at once," continued Alex, "for with . . . well, the . . . extenuating circumstances," and he cast a mocking glance at her enormous stomach, "we'll have to make the beastly journey posthaste."

"Listen to me, damn you!" Zena cried. "Haven't I made it decidedly clear that another marriage is not necessary?"

"All I beg is that you'll not run me too fine," went on Alex imperturbably. "One can seldom get the Lady of Kazan Cathedral in St. Petersburg under two or three days' notice."

Zena stared at Alex wide-eyed at his impudence.

"Sasha!" bewailed his wife. "Why do you harass me?"

"So you'll say yes, love," he replied plainly, "and so I'll be able to sleep again at night knowing my child is secure in his patrimony."

"Does it mean that much to you?" she gravely asked.

"It does." His eyes were quite somber. He held her glance while she hesitated. He really was serious. Perhaps he was right about the inheritance; she had never given it a thought.

"Very well," she agreed.

He sighed in relief.

"Good, now that's all settled. When?" he asked. "And where?"

"I don't care, Sasha. Somewhere quiet. When you're more than eight months pregnant, a large wedding isn't *comme il faut*."

"Child," he said earnestly, "if you want a large wedding, you'll have a large wedding."

"No, no, Sasha. I didn't mean that at all," she rushed to say. He was deadly serious. His sweetness and arrogance were quite heartwarming. "There wouldn't be any time to have a dress made," she impishly continued.

"Hell, that's no problem, if that's all that's worrying you." He was still perfectly willing to oblige her.

"Really, Sasha, I was only teasing about the dress."

"Are you sure?" he searchingly replied. He understood that women had a fondness and enthusiasm for wedding niceties, and their first one had certainly not been tonish. He was content to have the most grandiose wedding the world had seen if Zena wanted one.

She returned his look with eyes brimming with love. "Yes. I'm really sure. The Russian Chapel and two witnesses would be fine."

"Is tomorrow too soon?" Alex asked anxiously. "My ribs are strapped pretty well. I think I can manage. Let's hope this will be the last time we're married. I seem to have the unfortunate habit of incurring broken bones immediately prior to my marriages. I don't know if I care to go through this a third time."

Zena said calmly, "Tomorrow's fine," and her heart sang.

5

By dint of moving heaven and earth, for the wheels of French bureaucracy moved with irksome sluggishness, they were married in the small jewel of the Russian Chapel at Nice.

Zena had written a note of apology to Alistair for any unhappiness she may have caused him. He responded with his customary sweet, tender understanding, wishing only sincere joy and good fortune in her reconciliation with Sasha.

Alex also received a note from the Earl of Glenagle but declined mentioning it to Zena.

Despite his light disclaimer to his wife apropos gifts of females, Alex *had* sent his rival a dozen women; he hoped they were all suitably quiet and sedate, although he had had the devil of a time searching his memory in order to procure that particular style of woman, since his reckless, unorthodox nature normally avoided the type.

The "gift" had been dispatched in two carriages with a note expressing his gratitude for the earl's devotion and defense of his wife. The note also expressed in a thoroughly masculine, ribald way, the whimsical hope that one or several of these women might be a modest, trifling consolation for the loss of Zena. A postscript had suggested the gift not be acknowledged, since Zena wouldn't approve.

Alistair responded nevertheless, sending Ridgely with a

personal message to the prince, in which he indicated his hearty approval of Alex's taste in women. With his usual well-bred, understated reserve, he declared that while the loss of Zena was inconsolable, it had been mitigated considerably by the very pleasant, delightful company of twelve beautiful and genial women.

Alex quirked an understanding, exceedingly satisfied smile and tossed the note into the fire.

Because of the physical limitations of both bride and groom, their second honeymoon night was quiet. Telegrams had been sent to their family and friends informing them of the reconciliation and remarriage. They were staying that night in the villa and then leaving in Alex's yacht, the *Southern Star*, for a brief cruise to Biskra, with the intention of returning to Nice in two weeks to await the birth of their child.

As they lay in each other's arms that night, Alex noted a subdued mood had descended on Zena.

"Penny for your thoughts, child," he whispered. Despite the bulk of the baby she still seemed very fragile and young to him.

"Sasha, is it ungrateful after all our tumultuous problems, is it childishly ungrateful to have the tiniest wish to occasionally be something more than a lover, wife, and mother?"

"Woman," Alex retorted with a mocking pomposity, "what was good enough for my mother is good enough for my wife."

"Don't tease, Sasha, I mean it."

Smiling warmly at her he said gently, "Ah, the bluestocking soul lives on. It's all right, dear. If you were a bubble-headed society miss, I wouldn't want you. They are quite literally available by the carriage load. Miss Bluestocking doesn't have to be locked away, dear, just because you're a wife and mother. Listen, sweetheart, if you want to be involved in the new wave of women's rights, I'll build you a women's college. Just name the site. It's yours. We'll have the most insufferably bright children in the empire. Or if you want to research those migration routes your father was interested in, do that. I'll put together whatever caravan you need. We'll spend the rest of our lives clinging to rocky mountain byways. Look, I'll go and pack right now." He grinned and began to get out of bed.

Zena pushed him back. "You're mocking me, scoffing at me."

"Christ, no, I'm being full of understanding and all those husbandly attributes. Well, one small favor, perhaps. Could you wait a week or so until our baby is born? The idea of you delivering my firstborn on some precarious mountain eagle's nest worries me somewhat."

Maybe he was teasing slightly, but at bottom, Alex meant what he said. He would give Zena whatever she wanted. Her happiness and pleasure were his delight. If it was bluestocking notions and historical surveys, she would have them.

"And I'm not mocking you, little one. Good Lord, what do I have to do, anyway? Hunting in winter, war games in August, the social season in St. Petersburg and Paris—the life of an idle aristocrat I will gladly relinquish without a qualm. All those stale amusements only serve as change of scene in the endless tedium. If you could see your way to take a break or two in your life scheme of feminine progress to give me two or three children, I and the nursery will be more than happy to spend eternity as companions to you in a continuous trek up and down the mountain trails. So come here, my little suffragette, and tell me our itinerary."

"Sasha, really? You wouldn't mind?" Her eyes sparkled. Then her face dropped, and she looked dismayed. "But a little baby. It wouldn't work."

"Like hell, it won't, *dushka*." Alex lifted Zena's chin,

and his golden eyes held her. "You don't know the power of the Kuzan fortune. I'll hire enough litter bearers to hand-carry you and Bobby and that little tyke of ours and nursemaids and nannies and governesses up and down every mountain peak and in and out of every mountain village and hamlet in the Caucasus. That's what I'm here for, to lean on, to rely on. I'll carry you myself, if need be, and do your walking for you." He took her beautiful, provocative face between his hands and said quiet simply, "I'll take you wherever you want to go whenever you want to. You're never leaving my sight again. I don't have the courage to face the awful agony of being separated from you. Promise me." He was very solemn. "Promise you'll never leave me."

An instant, unbidden joy pervaded Zena's heart. "I promise, Sasha," she softly whispered.

One powerful arm encircled her waist and, drawing her against his hard body, he covered her trembling lips with a tender, restrained kiss that spoke potently of his protective love. "I will take care of you, child," he murmured huskily.

They left for Biskra the next morning and spent ten glorious days cruising the Mediterranean, arriving back in Nice quite literally in the nick of time. Zena had gone into labor twenty miles out, and the engines were pushed to their maximum to rush back. Alex carried Zena to the waiting carriage and held her on the journey up the shore to the palace on the cliff.

The best doctors in Nice were in attendance and, after having heard the story of his birth numerous times over the years, Alex also took the precaution of assembling the best of Nice's midwives.

The crowd of assistants hovered over Zena's bed as she labored to deliver Sasha's child into the world. Alex never left her side, comforting her in his awkward distress as best he could. The sight of his beautiful, delicate wife enduring such agonies caused him the most penitent feelings of guilt. Good God, did all women go through this? Was he being too sensitive? Was this sort of pain supposed to be brushed off nonchalantly as part of living? He held her hand and watched, attempting realistic smiles of support when Zena searched his face with bleak, suffering eyes. Maybe they should consider adopting children if they wanted more, he thought. The travail was becoming unbearable for his fragile wife. Why weren't all these people doing something? he raged indignantly.

"Can't you do something!" he snapped at the illustrious assembly of prominent doctors.

"Madame is progressing extremely well, Prince Alexander," the spokesman for the black-coated array declared insensitively. "Husbands usually prefer to wait outside, my lord. Perhaps you'd like to step out . . ."

Alex shot him a withering glance, and the sentence died ignominiously. His eyes searched the faces of the four midwives, not trusting the word of the doctors. "*Is* she all right?" he asked anxiously.

"*Monsieur*, only a few minutes more, and her pain will be over," one old woman replied sympathetically.

Alex gripped Zena's limp hand fiercely and prayed the old lady was right.

Indeed, she was, and the old midwife was well rewarded for her competence. Five minutes later she presented Alex his son and heir wrapped in soft, white linen. "A fine, lusty boy, *monsieur*." Alex gratefully accepted the child, relieved Zena's ordeal was over.

She opened her eyes briefly and smiled at Alex weakly. "Is it over?" she asked.

"Over, my love, and thank you for a beautiful, strong son."

"A boy." She smiled triumphantly. "A boy like you," she murmured, shutting her eyes again. She drifted off to sleep.

Alex gently laid the wrapped child next to Zena in bed and thought ruefully, not *exactly* like me. The baby lying beside his wife had blond hair and blue eyes.

If his memory served him right and historical fact was accurate, there had never been a blond, blue-eyed Kuzan.

As a matter of fact, there had been a blond, blue-eyed Kuzan once, but if the circumstances had been known to Alex, they wouldn't have cheered him.

The tale is one of long ago and of great detail. Suffice it to say, several centuries ago, in the early years of the sixteenth century, an infusion of foreign, non-Russian blood produced a golden-haired, blue-eyed Kuzan—a Prince Kuzan, by the way, only by reason of Old Muscovy's code of jurisprudence, hereditary statutes, and the grace of a benevolent God.

The fair-haired Prince Kuzan's paternity, you see, would not have withstood close scrutiny.

On the day Alex's telegram arrived from Nice, Amalie had been visiting Yuri. They were partaking of tea and brandy in Yuri's study on a rather dull, cloudy, fall afternoon. Yuri's butler brought the wire in on a silver salver. After quickly perusing its contents, Yuri tossed it over to Amalie, who was avid with curiosity. A doleful expression slowly appeared on her beautiful face as she read the jubilant message.

"Damn!" she swore softly under her breath as she came to the end of the sheet.

Yuri lounged back in his chair, assessed the golden-haired belle through heavy-lidded eyes, and murmured commiseratively, "Slipped through your beautiful fingers, didn't he, *ma cheri?*"

Amalie looked up and cast her soulful lavender eyes in Yuri's direction. "The marriage seems very certain this time." Her pastel eyes shone as a glimmer of an idea appeared. "Do you think the remarriage is for the sake of the child?" she asked hopefully.

Yuri noted the buoyant eagerness in Amalie's expression and felt a sadness for her. "Don't be a fool, Amalie," he said gently. "Sasha wanted Zena back desperately. He had finally recognized he loved her. It's not that his child's future didn't concern him, but if that were his only apprehension, money would have solved that dilemma very nicely."

The shining eyes dulled in gloomy understanding.

"You can't have every man you want, little one," Yuri said tenderly.

"But I always have, Yuri," Amalie wailed.

"Sasha's different," he said flatly.

"I know that," she replied unhappily. "Don't I know," Amalie sighed deeply.

"I'm twenty-two years old, Yuri," she cried piteously.

"You're talking to an old friend, Amalie, not a current lover," said Yuri. "Twenty-four. But at any age," he gallantly added, "you're a prime piece."

Too deeply overcome by her own morose reflections, Amalie overlooked Yuri's inelegant interjection. "What's going to happen to me? All men like young girls. I don't want to turn into some faded beauty who has to start chasing men. It's degrading. I've always had them come to me. I'm afraid, Yuri. Oh, Yuri, my whole life is a mess." Tears welled up in the exquisite lavender eyes.

He lowered his glance, because, for the first time in his life, he saw tears in hers.

"Never say the Golden Goddess is crying," Yuri teased, hoping to distract her morbid thoughts. But the tears astonished him, for he remembered the fifteen-year-old girl whom he had loved and who had loved him, giving birth to their daughter after a long and terrible labor of three days. Even then she had never cried, not once. From an early age she had been forced to be strong, compelled to take care of a father who was weak. She knew she must endure the delivery and then put it behind her. She had not allowed herself to be weak. Her future and her father's future depended on her.

Amalie wrung her white kid gloves distraughtly as Yuri pensively recalled the past. "I have feelings too, Yuri. Oh, Lord," she moaned, "I'm so unhappy."

Yuri viewed the stately, stunning beauty before him: classic, patrician features; high cheekbones; marvelous eyes; frankly sensual mouth; heavy cornsilk hair; and magnificent body.

"Don't cry, dear. Your stunning looks are quite unimpaired. The future's not as bleak as you envision. Twenty-four isn't old, little one," he whispered.

But the vision of the gorgeous beauty in burgundy was overcome by the image of the sweet young girl of fifteen, who had flung herself into his arms in the flower-strewn summer meadow and clung to him with the deep, sweet passion of first love. The slim, willowy young girl was gone, replaced by this dazzling creation of nature and the consummate artifice of man. But underneath, he thought to himself deliberatively, there still remained at base the uncertain little girl who knew she had to be strong, who knew she must resolutely and unwaveringly persevere despite her fears and qualms.

She had carried the role indomitably for almost ten years. Now with Alex irrevocably gone the Golden Goddess had come to an impasse, the first defeat in a life crowned with successes. Her successes were attributed to the sure and positive managing of that great assest, her flawless beauty. It had brought her the much-needed rich marriage. It had brought her men fawning and fetching and dying of adoration for her. The ominous threat of perhaps other defeats in the future was terrifying and daunting.

"I'm afraid, Yuri," Amalie whimpered. "I'm afraid."

Yuri rose, crossed the small distance between them, picked up the tearful woman, and sat down again, cradling her in his arms.

Her body was warm and soft beneath his hands, and the sweet, musky scent of her hair brushed his nostrils as she lay with her head on his shoulder.

He was utterly astonished to hear himself saying in avuncular tones, "What the hell, Amalie. You know you can't stand Boris, and you can't have Alex; might as well settle for me. And since I can't have Zena, I might as well settle for you."

Amalie sat up with a start and fixed her piqued gaze on Yuri. "Zena?" she groused. "You, too?"

"She's quite a remarkable woman, dear, if you'd given yourself half a chance to know her—as courageous and tenacious as you with the most enchanting mind in addition to the obvious winsome beauty."

At first Amalie was affronted at the careless proposition, offered as almost a callous solution to their mutual deprivation. But the warm country girl still dwelt beneath the society facade, and she had never been able to completely erase the memories of that summer years ago.

"I don't know, Yuri," she said hesitantly.

"You could have married me ten years ago, you know," Yuri reminded her.

"You didn't have enough money," Amalie said.

"But Papa and his dangerous gambling fever are gone now. Right?" he drawled.

"Right," she sighed quietly.

"How about it, Rosie," he grinned, using her childhood name. "I'll have a divorce for you in a fortnight, and we can begin making more of those golden children."

"It'll ruin my figure," she pouted playfully, making a pretty moue of distaste.

"Do you really care?" Yuri inquired huskily in her ear as his embrace tightened.

"Not if you don't," she smiled sweetly.

"You'll always look good to me, Rosie, figure or no figure. We'll sit on the veranda of our home in the Ukraine and watch our crowd of children grow."

Amalie visualized the idyllic picture. She had always wanted children and deeply regretted the loss of her daughter. Necessity had decreed she give Betsy up, but she had somehow never been able to consider having children by Boris. Not only was he physically unattractive, but the cruelty and viciousness he displayed dismayed her. What if her child would inherit those qualities?

Yuri was lazily nibbling on her ear as his hands stroked and caressed each voluptuous curve. As his fingers reached up and began unbuttoning the neckline of her dress, he whispered softly, "And if you become plump, my sweet, after all our children, I'll just have more to love."

Amalie wrapped her arms around Yuri's powerful shoulders, and one hand slid up to caress the back of his neck where his long, golden hair fell in soft curls.

"Will you take me home, Yuri," Amalie breathed happily. "Can we really go back?"

"I'll take you home, my darling, and never let you go."

The next morning Alex and Zena received a telegram from Yuri.

Alex, Zena, and the children were outside on the terrace overlooking the sea. Zena was resting on a wicker chaise lounge, the baby sleeping in her lap. Bobby was riding his tricycle up and down the marble floor at breakneck speed. Alex, seated next to Zena, smiled as he read the lengthy telegram.

"Yuri and Amalie are getting married," Alex explained, "and Yuri says Amalie apologizes for all the discourteous behavior to you." Laughing softly, he raised his brows sceptically and said, "Can the Golden Goddess really sheath her claws? I wonder."

"I'm happy for her anyway, Sasha," Zena said. In the utter bliss of her own unparalleled happiness she benevolently wished the whole world well. "But what an odd match."

"Not actually," Alex declared. "Amalie and Yuri grew up together on adjoining estates in the Ukraine. Almost like brother and sister, but with the usual experimental lovemaking in adolescence."

Zena opened her eyes in astonishment.

Alex responded to the surprise. "It's really quite commonplace, my pet. You just never had any cousins or young friends around. Amalie had to marry for money. Yuri has tolerable wealth, but not unlimited funds like Boris. I don't think either one of them really realized their attachment was more than old friendship. They scrapped and bickered like family. Yuri consorted with the usual variety of women but never seemed to find anyone that mattered enough to marry."

Alex cast a rueful smile at Zena. "We both felt that way, love, felt we were too young to consider marriage. All that debauchery beckoned. I think with my leaving, Amalie and Yuri were probably thrown in each other's company more and *voila!* I'm happy for them. Yuri always used to tell me I didn't understand his Rosie, and I guess he was right. I never saw that side of her character. It was concealed too well for anyone but an old childhood friend like Yuri to see." Alex grinned boyishly. "Yuri says to expect to be a godfather in nine months. They're moving back to the country."

"I wish them happy," Zena sighed felicitously. "They'll have beautiful children."

"They already have a daughter. A very pretty little blonde girl almost ten now."

Zena looked up in amazement.

"So they had more than an old friendship to draw them together," Alex drawled.

"They must have both been very young," Zena said.

"Very young," Alex agreed. "Yuri's raised his daughter alone and has done a marvelous job of it."

Glancing at the fair-haired baby sleeping on his wife's lap, Alex remarked mockingly, "If I didn't know better, I'd say Yuri had a hand in this one, too." He was teasing, but underneath a tiny, nagging doubt wouldn't be stilled.

"Sasha, what a thing to say."

"Well, it seemed Yuri was always underfoot."

"But you were there, too."

"How do I know what happened after I passed out? I was more drunk than sober most of the time, and I've known Yuri too long to be under any illusions about his moral character."

"What about my moral character?" Zena asked, mildly affronted.

"Well, sweet, since you ask. . . ."

"Sasha!"

"Really, my dear, consider," he said crushingly. "I picked you up on the street, had my way with you in mere hours, and settled you in as my latest mistress within a day. Hardly the virtuous conduct of a paragon of womanhood I would be apt to trust with a practiced rake like Yuri."

"Do you believe me when I say you're the only man I've ever made love to?" Zena disallowed the Arab's rape, feeling that being tied, gagged, and sexually molested hardly constituted making love.

"If you say so."

"Sasha!"

"Of course, my love, I believe you," he soothed chivalrously. Whether he did or did not mattered infinitely less to him than having Zena back. And cruel suspicion aside, he was prone to believe her more than to disbelieve. But considering the prince's broad and varying experience with women, one must allow his cynical demon.

The dark, wolfish, swarthy Kuzan physical attributes had, after all, been amazingly dominant through the male line for generations, but Alex had decided on the day of the baby's birth, after the first staggering sight of the fair child, that regardless of patrimony, his or not, he'd love the boy because it was Zena's. She was more important to him than all the children in the world, and they could have other children later if he could ever repress the terrible memories of Zena's travail. Consideration of the possibility of losing her in childbirth was too agonizingly real to contemplate. The feeling of utter helplessness that had overwhelmed him as he sat impotently and watched her in labor was both unique and unnerving.

"My father had blond hair and blue eyes, and so do many of the tribesmen in my mother's aul," Zena said tranquilly.

"Of course, dear," Alex smiled reassuringly, determined to never again so much as intimate his uncertainties. "You're absolutely right." His love for Zena was the first and only strong passion he had ever known, and all else paled before its urgency.

Zena was the only woman he had ever wanted, and nothing must come between them. He couldn't take a chance of damaging their new happiness. The joy they shared was too hard won and too fragile to chance any arguments over the baby. He couldn't stand the thought of losing her again. He set his teeth, determined never to allude to his son's coloring again. The subject was closed.

Later that evening as they enjoyed a quiet supper *à deux*, Bobby in bed and the baby sleeping, two more telegrams arrived.

"Good God," Alex exclaimed as he was handed the missives. "Is there somewhere in this world we could go for some peace and quiet?"

Ripping open the first one, he swore several times as he

read through it. He silently handed it to Zena while he opened the second one.

Zena swiftly read the warning sent by Katelina. Katelina's husband upon returning once more from Europe had reacted violently to the knowledge of his wife's friendship with Wolf. He was threatening to take the children away; Wolf was threatening to take Katelina *and* the children away and gratuitously kill the husband to boot. Katelina had prevailed upon Wolf to desist at least temporarily from his savage plan and was simply relating the story to Alex in the event Wolf should come to him for help. Wolf had left in a fury, and she didn't know where he had gone.

"Interesting family," Zena smiled impishly.

"*Père* will see to everything, never fear, he always does. But it burns me to see Katelina at the mercy of that cad of a husband she has." He made a face of mild distaste. "I agree with Wolf there, a nice swift bullet would ease the world of an unnecessary burden.

"In the meantime, more family, dear." He handed her the second telegram.

"Congratulations," Nikki had written. "Your mother seems to think she should see her grandson. Be down in a week."

"Let's get the hell out of here," Alex said tersely. The thought of his parents' faces when they saw their blond blue-eyed grandson discomfited him.

"Should we, Sasha, with your parents coming? It wouldn't be very polite."

"Let's take the *Southern Star* out, just to get away from all these people for a while. I suppose we can come back in a week. They won't be here before then." He'd have to confront it eventually, might as well get it over with. No one would say a word, of course. Everyone would be too polite. But the prospect galled him nevertheless. Was this what was commonly called one of fate's little ironies? For someone who had all the illegitimate children he could wish for, all disturbingly and unquestionably Kuzans, when he finally had a legitimate heir, the child wasn't even his. A strange feeling of ruffled disquietude appeared in his heart.

Several days later as they lay under an awning on the *Southern Star*, letting the light sea breezes wash over them, Zena finished nursing the baby and rose to change into something cooler. The afternoon was becoming warm.

"Sasha, will you hold Apollo while I go below and change?"

Their child had been named Apollo not because of Alex's teasing but because Zena had found the name so startling appropriate. Alex had acquiesced to his wife's wishes on the name as he had lightly promised so many months before. To Zena the fair, bright, golden child had seemed the perfect embodiment of the name Apollo—the Sun God.

"Just put him in his basket, love. He'll be more comfortable in this heat."

Zena had become disturbingly aware as the days passed that Sasha took very little interest in his son. At first she thought perhaps it was simply normal for a first-time father. Sasha was still young, and maybe the conception of fatherhood sat ill with him. But as time passed, she noted with baffled dismay that it wasn't simply that he took little interest in the child; rather he actually studiously avoided any contact with the baby.

Zena was correct in her assumption. Alex was very scrupulously avoiding any contact with Apollo. Despite his best efforts every time he saw the light blond child, his stomach tightened in frustrated anger, and a tic would appear high on his cheekbone. If Alex had been less prone to his morbid jealousy and looked closely at the child, he would have noted, as had Zena, that Apollo's eyes slanted upward at a slight angle just like his father's. His faint, downy, dark brows winged aloft, framing those elongated oval eyes exactly like his father's. Instead Alex nursed his miserable suspicions and fell occasionally into his melancholy fits of old.

This time, Zena thought with asperity, you're not going to dismiss your child so easily. Her temperament was as capable of volatile moodiness as Alex's.

"You can hold Apollo for a minute while I go below," she insisted peevishly and placed her young son in Alex's lap.

For the first time since his birth Alex was forced to look closely at this heir of his. Glancing down at the little, chubby form making wordless soft noises as he lay looking serenely up at his father, Alex's indifferent gaze changed suddenly into a startled expression of amazement.

From under delicate, wispy brows and lacy, fine lashes sparkled golden, tawny eyes caught up in the corners like little cat's eyes, golden cat's eyes, the powerful mark of Kuzan blood through the centuries.

"Zena!" Alex screamed, arresting her descent below. "Apollo's eyes are gold!"

Zena had noticed the change beginning days ago as the blue eyes common to all babies at birth had begun lightening with gradually increasing flecks of gold. As she returned to his side at the joyful shout, Alex whispered with great emotion, "A Kuzan without question." The prince gently cradled the little golden-haired baby who was his son, and the harsh-featured face lit with an eager, proud jubilation.

Bewildered but gladdened by the sudden, elated interest in his child, Zena said teasingly, "Did you ever doubt it?"

Alex paused for a second as he looked at his beautiful precious wife, and then he grinned effervescently.

"Never, darling," he lied gallantly, "not for a minute."

EPILOGUE

In the following months, while Alex conducted himself like a devoted husband and father, Zena would occasionally chide, "I can't believe this is the same man who firmly declared just short months ago that he wasn't interested in a wife and children."

Alex would smile ironically and say, "Nor I, madame, nor I."

Their second child, a daughter named Ninia, was born two years later in a mountain aul, and the family prospered, vastly content with each other.

They raised their small family essentially outside the society of the world, endless versts from the nearest town. Alex made peace with the old Tartar, his grandfather-in-law, for they had much in common; they were both autocratic, arrogant, proud, and self-willed.

Over the years, Alex became indistinguishable from his mountain brethren. When he wore the tcherkness and sheepskin papak, rifle slung on his shoulder and kinjal thrust in his belt, a more vivid likeness of a wild mountain tribesman you couldn't conceive.

The Alexander Kuzans would spend portions of the year at the *dacha*, briefly visiting St. Petersburg and Nice. The small family much preferred the peace and tranquillity of the high mountain valley, where Alex had built for them a fortress aerie clinging to the harsh granite escarpment like a bird of prey.

Zena traveled throughout the labyrinthine mountain auls, researching and compiling a definitive study of migration routes through the transcaucasian corridors to Europe. As each volume was completed, Alex had it published, beautifully illustrated with intricate maps, magnificent aquatints by Vrubel, and countless photographs that he as amateur photographer contributed.

"Luckily," he would tease Zena lightly, "I have a tremendous ego, a notable lack of inclination to excel, prompted no doubt by the idle leisure of my upbringing, and unfathomable love and admiration for my wife. Else I could be quite quelled by the prominent reputation you are developing as historian."

He was flatteringly kind in his raillery and inexpressibly modest of his own achievements, for not only did he run five large estates efficiently and profitably but in conjunction with his father and brothers oversaw the sprawling, prosperous industrial empire of gold mines, oil wells, and refineries, which was the base and mainstay of the Kuzan fortune.

As the years passed, father and son became a familiar sight roaming the mountain trails. An incongruous pair at first glance, the son was as light and fair as the father was dark. But the slanting eyes bespoke consanguinity, and the stark cheekbones and straight noses duplicated each other, while the formidable, powerful strength of limb and muscle was already evident in the lean, strapping adolescent who rode at his father's side. Reared to respect the mountain ways, the young boy learned to ride with daring, speak the truth, and never show fear.

Ibin Iskandar As-saqr As-saghir the lithe, tall, blond stripling was called. Alexander's Boy, The Young Falcon.

The rumblings of discontent, the growing flames of revolutionary fervor, the violent, chaotic disruptions of society, fed by the winds of peasant despair, were heard but from

a great distance. The majestic mountain ranges protected
the prince's family from these turbulent discontents. Alex
was aware that the floodgates would soon break, and he
had made the necessary emergency plans for his family's
future. Gold had been sent abroad, and the *Southern Star*
had been moved from Nice to Poti. But he was hopeful
that the mountains would continue to protect his family as
they had the countless mountain tribes dwelling two thousand years apart from the mainstream of history. Perhaps
they could remain in their mountain aerie, aloof from the
smoldering disintegration of the thousand-year-old empire
that was being torn asunder because of disparate, discor-
dant political schisms and an inept, blundering, intractable tsar.

Alex hoped to remain apart from the fractious dissent,
preferring to nurture his family in peaceful solitude. But if
that wasn't possible, an escape route had been readied. His
prudent caution was wasted on his son, though. The
Young Falcon had different ideas, ideas fostered in years of
mountain rearing, where the warrior's life becomes all.

Despite his father's wariness and worldly counsel, the
young boy already had quite different ideas. He had chosen with all the idealism of youth; bold, sure, and certain
of his reasons. When the conflagration came, he rode off
against his parents' wishes to fight for his heritage.

NOTES

1 The practice of using diminutives for formal names is extremely popular in Russia. Family names were always tender derivations of the baptismal names, and the Russians were very inventive in their endearments. The custom of applying English diminutives for Russian names was a deep-seated affectation prevalent from the early years of the nineteenth century. With the rise of the Pan-Slav movement in the '70s and '80s, there was a slight return to the use of old Russian names, but within the elegant, aristocratic circles, the pet Anglophile names still prevailed. It was an amusing, clubby sort of exclusivity, at the same time *au naturel* and mannered. Tolstoy's characters have names like Dolly and Kitty even in an old, traditional Moscow family residing in the ancient capital of the empire, which was considerably less European in its tastes than St. Petersburg. Since Catherine and Elizabeth are very popular Russian names, Kittys and Betsys were very general. Many Alexanders were familiarly called Sandy, while Paul became Bobby. Hence the apparently un-Russian name for Zena's brother. (page 10)

2 The Russian name *Vauxhall* for their railway stations evolved in a convoluted and curious way. The first railway opened for passenger service was the Liverpool and Manchester in 1830. Five years later Nicholas I determined to have his own railroad and ordered a line to be constructed

between St. Petersburg and Tsarskoe Selo, where the impe-
rial family retreat was located, a distance of 14 miles. The
railway was opened in 1837. Since there were no interme-
diate stations and only the royal family and a few courtiers
used the line, it was not a commercial success. Then someone had the notion to build an amusement park along the
style of the Vauxhall Gardens in South London, which was
enormously popular at the time. The Tsarskoe line was extended two miles to Pavlosk, and fifty acres of land was
donated to the railway company. The Pavlosk Vauxhall was
constructed, surpassing its London prototype in attrac-
tions, and immediately became extremely popular with the
residents of St. Petersburg. The trains were crowded with
passengers, and the railway came out of the red. Since the
Tsarskoe station was the only railway station then in existence in St. Petersburg, the populace got into the habit of
directing their coachmen or cabdrivers simply to go to
Vauxhall. So the name came gradually to be applied to the
actual station building in St. Petersburg. When the Nicholas railway to Moscow was completed, the station became
known as the Moscow Vauxhall. Eventually it spread until
every railway station in the empire from the Baltic to the
Pacific derived its name from the original pleasure garden
in South London. (page 17)

3 The Russian aristocracy were never as discreet as their
European counterparts. The absolutism of government and
the extraordinary legal privileges of the upper classes, no
doubt, contributed to their disregard of accepted behavior.
Two examples are cited that are symptomatic of this pre-
disposition to neglect the finer strictures of society.

Alexander II took his mistress, Princess Catherine
Dolgorouky, whenever he traveled abroad, and once when
he passed through Berlin on his way to Ems, they stopped
overnight at the Russian Embassy. The old Kaiser and the
Empress Augusta of Germany were horrified at the tsar's

boldness. Empress Augusta immediately took to bed so that she wouldn't have to receive her nephew the tsar. This same Tsar Alexander II also brought Catherine to the winter palace to live when nihilist attempts on his life made it difficult for him to walk freely about. He installed her and their three children in rooms situated immediately above those occupied by his wife, the empress, who was forced to listen to the patter of little feet, the little feet of her rival and her husband's children. The empress eventually succumbed to tuberculosis but lingered as an invalid for almost twenty years, perhaps out of spite, for immediately upon her death the tsar married his mistress.

A grand duke of a different generation typifies this continuing pattern of self-indulgence and indiscretion. Grand Duke Michael was the brother of Nicholas II, the last tsar. The grand duke was a captain in the Regiment of Yellow Cuirassiers stationed at Gatschina. Among the officers of the corps was a certain Captain Wulffert who was married to a very beautiful and extremely intelligent divorcée. She was most attractive and hospitable, and their house was a meeting place for all her husband's comrades, who always found a warm welcome and an excellent dinner. Before long everyone in St. Petersburg was aware of Michael's romance with pretty Madame Wulffert. The clever woman had set her sights on royalty and had been successful. Captain Wulffert showed himself an astute man, and he furnished his wife with all the necessary reasons to enable her to obtain a divorce. When the divorce was accomplished, the lady returned to St. Petersburg and settled there quite openly in a magnificent apartment paid for by the grand duke. (page 179)

4 The Caucasus range served as both a protection and a barricade against the progress of events. Ancient patterns of life survived there long after they had succumbed in the outside world, and very little is known of their source. The

origins of many of the Caucasian tribes is a mystery. Of the dozen languages that have been investigated, only a few resemble the other languages of man. The rest are isolated; not every race or language has a name. Many of them have no word designating *our people* or *our language*. There are some 80,000 people in one district of Daghestan who speak a uniform language and have no name. They are arbitrarily named Avars by scholars, although they had nothing in common with the old Avars. Thousands of years ago perhaps they were conquered and annihilated by new immigrants, all except the small residue that were forced back into the mountains and survived. Or maybe they were just a fragment of an earlier migration that had remained deep in the mountain valleys. The larger mountain tribes—the word *large* is used in a very limited sense—possess a very modest literature. They all live according to their complicated mountain law, the adat, which differs with each race and is known by heart by the elders. For most Caucasians the word *nation* is incomprehensible. Families and circles of friends take the place of nations, and they are together styled *societies*. The members of a society or a family are answerable for one another and bound to afford each other every protection. Degrees of relationship are meaningless, and the greater the number of members of the family or society, the greater is its importance in the mountains. Even in the tribes still resolutely feudal in character, a prince without family connections is a man without power and respect. But with a family of many warriors and wealth (not in terms of gold, but in horses, sheep, cattle, crops) a mountain chieftain commands the respect of all lesser societies. Wealth, as in every culture, is required for power. Even the great Shamyl, Russia's most formidable foe in the Caucasus, who waged a holy war against the empire for twenty years, couldn't exact the obedience, strength, or loyalty of the Daghestani warriors. The fiercely independent Daghestanis wouldn't fight for a

Moslem holy man from a poor and undistinguished family.
(page 166)

5 Much as the Greeks called everyone who wasn't Greek
by the all-encompassing term *barbarian*, and the Russians
designated all foreigners as Germans, so too the mountain
people denoted all Russians or Muscovites by the appella-
tion *Giaour*. The word comes from the Turkish *Gyáwur*
and signifies in a general, disparaging way an alien in race
and an infidel in religion. (page 189)

6 Zena's tracks in the blue–gray shale mud were startlingly significant to Alex and Ivan. Tracks have an indi-
viduality of their own. No two men or animals leave the
same record on the ground. The size and shape of the footprints, the distance between them, the outward turn of
the feet, the space between the toes or claws, the drag of
the hind legs, are all combined in any track in a manner
that is never repeated a second time. For a tracker each
combination is a thing as truly individual and as little to
be confounded with anything else as a face or a picture.
When he has examined it and fixes it in his memory, he
is able to recognize it again under all its changes of appearance. He will be able to identify the tracks of a full-
grown horse as those of an animal whose tracks he had
taken notice of when it was one year old, and this with as
little difficulty as an ordinary person experiences in recognizing a man he has known as a boy.

Marks are significant and tell something about the person or animal to which they belong and the circumstances
under which they were made. Everyone can tell a man's
footprint from a cow's or a dog's from a horse's, and with
such ease and certainty that we never think how to do it.
A trained tracker draws inferences much less obvious, but
with the same certainty and unconsciousness in a process
so instantaneous and so habitual as to resemble intuition.

He knows, for instance, men leave different marks from women and children, a young person from an old, a runner from a walker. The footprints of a man are coarser and larger than those of a woman, and the stride is longer. A child's track is sometimes like a woman's, except the foot is not so well formed and is narrow in front. A woman's foot is small, thin, the instep more elegant, her stride short. A woman with child has a still shorter stride and is heavier on her heels. This particular feature of Zena's footprints was obvious to Ivan and Alex. In an instant they both knew she was pregnant.

Track reading in tribal societies is a body of knowledge acquired during ages in a school where every theory is sifted, and mistakes come home to those who make them in the form of suffering and loss. A knowledge of tracks is the general lore of these tribes and common heritage of all its members. The following story of a European observer relates this expertise.

There were five flocks of sheep and goats, averaging perhaps ninety to one hundred fifty head each, watering at a well at the same time. When they went away in different directions and the European had started filling his water tank, a Maaza Bedouin woman returned. He asked her what she wanted, and she said that three of her goats had gone off with some of the other flocks. She identified the tracks of all of them and found to which flock her goats had attached themselves, then went to get them though the flocks had by this time gone out of sight. Subsequently she returned with her goats, thinking nothing of what she had done. (page 194)

7 Although the Moslem religion was diffused throughout the Caucasus in 1899, it was embraced with varying degrees of acceptance. Islam was professed by all, but its duties and observances were only slightly cultivated. The old pagan rituals and superstitions still clung to many parts of

the Caucasus. Separate deities were offered sacrifices and looked to for blessing. Divination was ceremoniously observed, and soothsaying prevailed. Autumnal sacrifices were rendered to Seoséres, and Merissa was propitiated for her honey. The religious groves, or kodosh, were still objects of veneration far more real than the mosques, and the festivals still solemnized in them drew greater multitudes. Islamism was respected, but paganism from its associations with its customs, habits, and feelings was still very popular. In other areas of the mountains remnants of Christianity remained in curious, metamorphosed ways: one tribe still wore the cross of St. George on their tunics, descendents, some scholars surmise, of crusaders who found refuge in the mountains.

Although the Koran forbids alcoholic beverages, this observance was not generally followed. Local wines as well as a potent sort of mead called *bosa* were commonly drunk. Turkish sheikhs such as Ibrahim Bey observed a long tradition of ignoring the dutiful precepts of the Koran when it came to the appreciation of strong drink. The list of sultans who died early deaths due to drinking would be long, and from the ruler down, despite the reproving, teetotaling injunctions of the Koran, drinking wine was general among the wealthy. (page 201)

8 Illegitimacy was not frowned on as long as one was wealthy and well bred. There are countless instances in Russian history. Two examples of the phenomenon follow:

Count Michael Voronzov, a brilliant, handsome man who became the Viceroy of the Caucasus, married the Countess Elizabeth Branizky. She was, if not exactly beautiful, blessed with grace, charm, and *joie de vivre* and considered the most seductive woman of her day. Born towards the end of the 18th century, she was the child of Prince Potemkin (Catherine the Great's most adored lover) by his favorite niece, Alexandra Englehardt (all of his four nieces had been his mistresses and accompanied their lusty uncle on his travels). Alexandra married the Polish Count Xavier Branizky, an extremely wealthy man, who accepted the baby Eliza as his own. Upon his death, Potemkin bequeathed most of his vast fortune to Alexandra, and when her daughter, Elizabeth Branizky, married Voronzov, her dowry was computed at 30 million rubles, the historic Potemkin diamonds, 200,000 serfs, innumerable salt mines, and a number of almost limitless estates scattered throughout Russia. Illegitimacy had not ruined Eliza's life, as you can see.

Alexander Herzen, one of the early dissidents, was also born of an irregular union. His father was from the ancient, wealthy Yakovlev family of Moscow. At a very young age he resigned his commission in the Guards to spend the remainder of his long life in self-indulgent idleness. On a trip to Germany he carried back with him Henrietta-Wilhelmina-Luisa Haag, a sixteen-year-old daughter of a respectable civil servant of Stuttgart. She became his mistress, and though he never married her, she was recognized as the head of his household. Alexander Herzen was the eldest child of this union. He received the imaginary surname Herzen, which was also conferred on a son born to Yakovlev many years before by a serf-woman. Alexander grew up as his father's favorite child; Herzen never suffered reproach or found his career impeded on the score of his origin. He received the normal education of a young Russian artistocrat and then entered Moscow University. When his father died in 1846 and left his fortune to his favorite son, Alexander Herzen became a very wealthy man. (page 246)

9 This statement is not without historical precedent.

"La Belle Comtesse Beauharnais," beautiful, fascinating, and irresistible, was the wife of the Duke of Leuchtenberg, who was a member of the Russian royal family. Zenaïda, or

Zina as she was called, was one of the most admired and envied women of her day, not only because of her charm and brilliant marriage but also because she possessed a royal indifference to gossip and tittle-tattle. She was intoxicating and arrogant. One of her assiduous admirers was the Grand Duke Alexis Alexandrovich, and the story is related that one night her husband, the Duke of Leuchtenberg, returned home late from the club, where he loved his game of cards, and found his wife's bedroom locked against him. He proceeded to knock and shout, insisting he be let in, all in all creating quite a disturbance. Presently the door was opened, and the herculean Alexis came out (formidable height was hereditary in the royal family; many of its grand dukes and tsars were well over 6'5"). Alexis thoroughly thrashed the noisy intruder and then kicked the injured husband down the stairs, where he was obliged to spend the rest of the night sleeping on the sofa in his study. The next day the outraged husband went straight to Tsar Alexander III and complained of his treatment. The tsar quietly told him that if he was incapable of managing his wife, he couldn't expect other people to help him. The tsar also stated that he would not tolerate any sensational divorce. So the Duke of Leuchtenberg prudently spent his nights in his study henceforth. Over the years this *ménage à trois* must have come to some amiable understanding, because the trio was very frequently seen in all the smart restaurants and places of amusement both in Russia and abroad, especially in Paris. (page 306)

ABOUT THE AUTHOR

Susan Johnson, award-winning author of nationally bestselling novels, lives in the country near North Branch, Minnesota. A former art historian, she considers the life of a writer the best of all possible worlds.

Researching her novels takes her to past and distant places, and bringing characters to life allows her imagination full rein, while the creative process offers occasional fascinating glimpses into complicated machinery of the mind.

But perhaps most important . . . writing stories is fun.

Bestselling Historical Women's Fiction

⸸ AMANDA QUICK ⸸

____28354-5 SEDUCTION . . .$6.50/$8.99 Canada

____28932-2 SCANDAL . . . .$6.50/$8.99

____28594-7 SURRENDER . . . .$6.50/$8.99

____29325-7 RENDEZVOUS . . . .$6.50/$8.99

____29315-X RECKLESS . . . .$6.50/$8.99

____29316-8 RAVISHED . . . .$6.50/$8.99

____29317-6 DANGEROUS . . . .$6.50/$8.99

____56506-0 DECEPTION . . . .$6.50/$8.99

____56153-7 DESIRE . . . .$6.50/$8.99

____56940-6 MISTRESS . . . .$6.50/$8.99

____57159-1 MYSTIQUE . . . .$6.50/$7.99

____09355-X MISCHIEF . . . .$22.95/$25.95

⸸ IRIS JOHANSEN ⸸

____29871-2 LAST BRIDGE HOME . . .$4.50/$5.50

____29604-3 THE GOLDEN

  BARBARIAN . . . .$4.99/$5.99

____29244-7 REAP THE WIND . . . . . .$5.99/$7.50

____29032-0 STORM WINDS . . . .$4.99/$5.99

Ask for these books at your local bookstore or use this page to order.

Please send me the books I have checked above. I am enclosing $____ (add $2.50 to cover postage and handling). Send check or money order, no cash or C.O.D.'s, please.

Name _____

Address _____

City/State/Zip _____

Send order to: Bantam Books, Dept. FN 16, 2451 S. Wolf Rd., Des Plaines, IL 60018
Allow four to six weeks for delivery.
Prices and availability subject to change without notice.   FN 16 2/97

Bestselling Historical Women's Fiction

❊ IRIS JOHANSEN ❊

____28855-5 THE WIND DANCER   . . .$5.99/$6.99

____29968-9 THE TIGER PRINCE   . . .$5.99/$6.99

____29944-1 THE MAGNIFICENT

ROGUE . . . .$5.99/$6.99

____29945-X BELOVED SCOUNDREL .$5.99/$6.99

____29946-8 MIDNIGHT WARRIOR . .$5.99/$6.99

____29947-6 DARK RIDER . . . .$5.99/$7.99

____56990-2 LION'S BRIDE . . . .$5.99/$7.99

____56991-0 THE UGLY

DUCKLING . . . .$5.99/$7.99

❊ TERESA MEDEIROS ❊

____29407-5 HEATHER AND VELVET .$5.99/$7.50

____29409-1 ONCE AN ANGEL . . . . .$5.99/$6.50

____29408-3 A WHISPER OF ROSES .$5.50/$6.50

____56332-7 THIEF OF HEARTS . . . .$5.50/$6.99

____56333-5 FAIREST OF THEM ALL .$5.99/$7.50

____56334-3 BREATH OF MAGIC . . .$5.99/$7.99

____57623-2 SHADOWS AND LACE . .$5.99/$7.99

THE VERY BEST IN CONTEMPORARY
WOMEN'S FICTION

SANDRA BROWN

___28951-9 Texas! Lucky $6.50/$8.99 in Canada

___28990-X Texas! Chase $6.50/$8.99

___29500-4 Texas! Sage $6.50/$8.99

___29085-1 22 Indigo Place $5.99/$6.99

___29783-X A Whole New Light $5.99/$6.99

___56768-3 Adam's Fall $5.50/$7.50

___56045-X Temperatures Rising $5.99/$6.99

___56274-6 Fanta C $5.99/$7.99

___56278-9 Long Time Coming $5.50/$7.50

___57157-5 Heaven's Price $5.50/$6.99

TAMI HOAG

___29534-9 Lucky's Lady $5.99/$7.50

___29053-3 Magic $5.99/$7.50

___56050-6 Sarah's Sin $5.50/$7.50

___56451-x Night Sins $5.99/$7.99

___29272-2 Still Waters $5.99/$7.50

___56160-X Cry Wolf $5.99/$7.99

___56161-8 Dark Paradise $5.99/$7.50

___09959-0 Guilty As Sin $21.95/$26.95

NORA ROBERTS

___29078-9 Genuine Lies $5.99/$6.99

___28578-5 Public Secrets $5.99/$6.99

___26461-3 Hot Ice $5.99/$6.99

___26574-1 Sacred Sins $6.50/$8.99

___10514-0 Sweet Revenge $16.95/$23.95

___27283-7 Brazen Virtue $5.99/$6.99

___29597-7 Carnal Innocence $5.99/$6.99

___29490-3 Divine Evil $5.99/$6.99

DEBORAH SMITH

___29107-6 Miracle $5.50/$6.50

___29092-4 Follow the Sun $4.99/$5.99

___29690-6 Blue Willow $5.99/$7.99

___29689-2 Silk and Stone $5.99/$6.99

___28759-1 The Beloved Woman $4.50/$5.50

- -

Ask for these books at your local bookstore or use this page to order.

Please send me the books I have checked above. I am enclosing $____(add $2.50 to cover postage and handling). Send check or money order, no cash or C.O.D.'s, please.

Name _____

Address _____

City/State/Zip _____

Send order to: Bantam Books, Dept. FN 24, 2451 S. Wolf Rd., Des Plaines, IL 60018

Allow four to six weeks for delivery.

Prices and availability subject to change without notice.

FN 24 10/96